# The Disciples of Cthulhu

## Second Revised Edition

# Chaosium Cycle Books

*Tales That Define the Cthulhu Mythos*

CALL OF CTHULHU® FICTION

# The Disciples of Cthulhu

## SECOND REVISED EDITION

by

A. A. Attanasio

Eddy C. Bertin

Ramsey Campbell

Walter C. DeBill, Jr.

Fritz Leiber

Brian Lumley

Robert M. Price

Bob van Laerhoven

James Wade

Selected and edited by Edward P. Berglund
Chapter decorations by Earl Geier

**A Chaosium Book**

**1996**

# CONTENTS

# Preface to the Revised Edition

It pleases me that, after almost two decades, Chaosium has decided to bring this anthology back into print. In 1976 this anthology probably would not have seen print if it had not been for the late Donald A. Wollheim (1914-1990), publisher of DAW Books, Inc., who himself was a fan of the work of H. P. Lovecraft. Don took a chance and thus was born the first professional, all-original, Cthulhu Mythos anthology. Even August Derleth, in *Tales of the Cthulhu Mythos*, published by Arkham House in 1969, used mostly reprints. Ramsey Campbell's all-original anthology, *New Tales of the Cthulhu Mythos*, would not see print by Arkham House until 1980. And there would be no others until the 1990's.

Writers involved with this anthology who are no longer with us are Robert Bloch (1917-1994), James Wade (1930-1983), Joseph Payne Brennan (1918-1990), Lin Carter (1930-1988), and Fritz Leiber (1910-1992). It is sad to know that they were unable to see the resurgence of interest in Lovecraft's creation through anthologies from Chaosium, Fedogan & Bremer, and other publishers.

One noteworthy story, "The Tugging" by Ramsey Campbell, was even nominated for a Science Fiction Writers of America Nebula Award. Unfortunately, it didn't make the final ballot. But this is the *only* Cthulhu Mythos story (to the best of my knowledge) that has received such recognition.

As to this being a revised edition, let me say that the Ramsey Campbell and Brian Lumley stories have been slightly revised. "Zoth-Ommog" by Lin Carter, in the original edition, has been dropped, as Robert M. Price is putting together a collection of Lin's stories for publication by Chaosium. In its place, we present an original story by the estimable Price, which is dedicated to Lin Carter and Robert E. Howard, as it utilizes Carter's Dr. Anton Zarnak and Howard's Steve Harrison. Its style brings back memories of the weird mysteries which Howard was noted for.

I have also had to drop "The Feaster from Afar" by Joseph Payne Brennan. As far as I have been able to ascertain, sad to say, there is no literary agent for the Brennan estate. And nobody seemed to know who represented his estate *in toto*. In its place, I have reprinted the story by A. A. Attanasio included herein. Technically speaking, Al's story was the very first story I received and accepted for this anthology, but Jerry Page already had his contract from Arkham House, and thus it led off Jerry's anthology *Nameless Places*.

For those readers who have read the original anthology, renew old thrills once again (and one new one). For those readers new to this anthology, read and enjoy.

*Edward P. Berglund*
Jacksonville, North Carolina
December 26, 1995

# Preface to the Original Edition

In 1974, while compiling a bibliography of the Cthulhu Mythos, created by Howard Phillips Lovecraft and added to by numerous other writers, I noticed that there were enough professional writers interested in the Cthulhu Mythos that it would be possible to compile an original anthology of such stories. The result you now hold in your hands—*The Disciples of Cthulhu.*

At that time I also noticed that there were groupings of writers, depending on a nondefinite cycle of interest in the works of Lovecraft. When Lovecraft was still living, and afterward, his correspondents and other writers who admired his work contributed stories to what became known as the Cthulhu Mythos. I have called these writers the first generation of disciples of Cthulhu. Technically, there is no representation from this generation in this volume (with the exception of Robert Bloch, who wrote the guest introduction), though James Wade's first Cthulhu Mythos story, "Those Who Wait" (published in the second issue of the fanzine *The Dark Brotherhood Journal* in 1972), was actually written in the forties, and Fritz Leiber's contribution to this volume is a collaboration between Fritz Leiber in 1937 and Fritz Leiber in 1975.

The early sixties produced the second generation of disciples, which lasted until around 1965. Those authors represented in this collection and their first stories are Joseph Payne Brennan ("The Seventh Incantation" in *Scream at Midnight* by Joseph Payne Brennan, Macabre House, 1963); (J.) Ramsey Campbell ("The Church in High Street" in *Dark Mind, Dark Heart* edited by August Derleth, Arkham House, 1962); and Fritz Leiber ("To Arkham and the Stars" in *The Dark Brotherhood and Other Pieces* by H. P. Lovecraft and Divers Hands, Arkham House, 1966).

The third generation of disciples was ushered in with their contributions in 1969. They and their first stories are represented by Eddy C. Bertin ("Darkness, My Name Is" in this volume); Lin Carter ("The Doom of Yakthoob" in *The Arkham Collector* for Summer 1971); Walter C. DeBill, Jr. ("Homecoming" in the fanzine *Nyctalops* for February 1972); Brian Lumley ("The Cyprus Shell" in *The Arkham Collector* for Summer 1968); Bob Van Laerhoven ("All-Eye" in this volume); and James Wade (see above).

Whether or not there is a market for the Cthulhu Mythos stories, established and amateur writers will continue to write them for their own and their friends' amusement and enjoyment. It is inevitable that one or more readers of this volume will be influenced into trying his hand at writing within the Cthulhu Mythos genre.

Read and enjoy. And thanks to those who had the faith in me to contribute to an original anthology on speculation.

*Edward P. Berglund*
Jacksonville, North Carolina
October 13, 1975

# Introduction

## by Robert Bloch

We start with history.

1929 was not generally regarded as a vintage year in the annals of literature. No book attained best-seller status with sales of a million or more copies within that period. The closest contenders were Earl Derr Biggers' *Behind That Curtain* and Vina Delmar's *Bad Girl*, followed by Ernest Dimnet's *The Art of Thinking*. The most successful offerings of the Book-of-the-Month Club were Thornton Wilder's *The Bridge of San Luis Rey* and André Maurois' biography, *Disraeli*.

Presumably, mystery fans discussed Mr. Biggers' novel, housewives gossiped happily about the "spicy" passages of *Bad Girl*, and the intelligentsia extolled the efforts of Wilder, Maurois, and Dimnet. These works were widely and thoroughly reviewed, both in the popular press and the literary periodicals of the day.

During that same period, in its February issue, a magazine called *Weird Tales* published "The Call of Cthulhu", by H. P. Lovecraft—and to the best of my knowledge, it received no reviews at all.

This in itself is not surprising. *Weird Tales* was only one of the hundreds of pulp-paper magazines which inundated the newsstands of the twenties, ignored by the *literati* and equally disdained by the smugly superior readers of the "slicks." It wasn't even a commercial success; despite its exorbitant price of twenty-five cents per issue, average sales scarcely covered the costs of production. And its subject matter, supernatural horror and forays into science fiction, had little appeal to the self-styled sophisticates of the Jazz Age.

As for H. P. Lovecraft—an obscure New England resident living in genteel poverty on a minute family income meagerly augmented by ghost-writing, revisions of the work of other nonentities, and the infrequent sales of his own short stories—his name meant nothing to the general reader or the particular critic. He wasn't even the most popular contributor to *Weird Tales* and had never attained the minor distinction of having one of his works selected for cover illustration.

Certainly "The Call of Cthulhu" merited no such treatment; it did not deal with a half-naked heroine held captive by an inhuman or nonhuman fiend nor her rescue by a brawny, machismo-motivated hero or a mercurial detective. The title of the story itself was enough to put people off—who or what was *Cthulhu* and how in hell did you pronounce it?

And who cared, anyway?

The answer has been many years in coming.

A little group of *Weird Tales* readers cared. A hard-core coterie of Lovecraft aficionados gradually emerged, much in the manner that the strange monster-god Cthulhu surfaced in the story from his lair at the bottom of the sea. Unlike Cthulhu, these followers of Lovecraft's fantasies did not sink back again; they began to make waves. Though these waves were scarcely more than ripples in the then small and almost stagnant pool of fantasy, they bore Lovecraft's career and kept it afloat in a fashion which encouraged him to continue his efforts. He had previously written a few stories dealing with kindred subject matter and subsequently he wrote more, consciously elaborating upon his earlier concepts.

Lovecraft's tales of encounters with Cthulhu, Yog-Sothoth, Azathoth, and other Great Old Ones, or their forces and surviving worshipers, constitute what today has become known as the Cthulhu Mythos.

The small band of Lovecraft devotees included writers as well as readers. Not a few of the former had been aided in their own work by his generous advice and criticism. Influenced by his style and subject matter, a number of these writers, members of the so-called "Lovecraft Circle", contributed stories which were also based on the Mythos. Since Lovecraft had invented a legendary book, the *Necronomicon*, supposedly a source of ancient secrets, his followers in turn supplemented their own tales with references to other, equally fearsome volumes of lost lore pertaining to the Great Old Ones and their magic. They also created additional gods for the pseudo-pantheon and utilized Lovecraft's fictitious locales used in the Mythos stories: the decadent New England villages of Arkham and Innsmouth, and the ivied (or perhaps more properly, fungous) halls of Miskatonic University.

Like Great Cthulhu himself, the Mythos expanded, took form, and extended tentacles. And, again like Cthulhu, the Mythos began to disturb the dreams of writers and artists, influencing their output.

But the influence was slow and gradual, and of little benefit to the man who inspired it. At the time of H. P. Lovecraft's death in 1937, at the tragically early age of forty-six, no collection of his work had yet attained book publication; a number of his stories had not reached print in magazines.

To remedy this situation, two of his friends and literary *protégés*—August Derleth and Donald Wandrei—set up a small mail-order publishing firm, Arkham House, for the express purpose of bringing out Lovecraft's tales in hard covers. The first of these volumes, *The Outsider and Others*, was hardly a candidate for 1939's best-seller lists; at the time of its publication only one hundred and fifty advance sales had been realized against a modest total printing of less than thirteen hundred copies. But thanks to the efforts of its founders, Arkham House survived and four years later issued a second Lovecraft omnibus, *Beyond the Wall of Sleep*—again in an edition of under thirteen hundred copies.

During the forties further collections of Lovecraftiana came from Arkham House along with books by various members of the "Lovecraft Circle." During World War II other Lovecraft collections were finally made available in paperback, including one Armed Services Edition which enjoyed a respectable circulation; gradually his hitherto unpublished stories appeared in magazines. His poetry and essays also saw print, and now Lovecraft's writings began to be widely anthologized here and abroad.

Aside from a few dismissals and disparagements, the critical establishment continued to ignore the impact of Lovecraft's work, though devotees of the tales started to publish essays and commentaries in amateur journals. But it was not until the sixties that the Cthulhu Mythos attained stature. The steadily increasing sales of his stories in both hardcover and paperback reprints, together with the enthusiastic reception accorded them in foreign editions, finally led to a sometimes grudging acknowledgement of his popularity. It also led to the nagging realization that literary critics in other lands were perhaps more perceptive in hailing Lovecraft as the modern inheritor of the mantle of Poe.

Imitation is the sincerest form of flattery. August Derleth had written a number of "posthumous collaborations"—more properly, pastiches—which utilized elements of the Cthulhu Mythos. And now the younger writers, newcomers to the fantasy field, began to model short stories and novels on Lovecraft's style and themes. By the early seventies these and dissertations appeared from the university presses and courses were conducted which dealt seriously and searchingly with Lovecraft's work and its influence. Mirroring the growing success of the conventions sponsored by science-fiction fandom, a First World Fantasy Convention was scheduled in Providence in 1975, honoring Lovecraft in the place of his birth.

Now, almost a half-century since the 1929 publication of an obscure story by an obscure writer in an obscure magazine, H. P. Lovecraft emerges as a recognized literary figure. Biographies and full-length studies of his work are presently appearing and receiving serious attention.

There are still those who profess to disdain the quality of his writing, just as they disdain the efforts of A. Conan Doyle, Edgar Rice Burroughs, and L. Frank Baum. But in point of fact, no objective literary school can ignore the lasting influence of Sherlock Holmes, Tarzan, and the Wizard of Oz upon contemporary culture. At the moment it appears that the unpronounceable Cthulhu may well be fated eventually to join their ranks.

Few of today's younger readers can identify Earl Derr Biggers, long since overshadowed by his own creation, Charlie Chan. Fewer still would recognize Vina Delmar. Ironically, Thornton Wilder is more apt to be remembered for his association with the pop musical *Hello, Dolly* than for his metaphysical engineering feats on *The Bridge of San Luis Rey*. Maurois may still be found on the dusty shelves of secondhand bookstores, along with Disraeli's own works; both are respectable but equally dead in terms of present-day interest. As for *The Art of Thinking*, one has merely to take a cursory glance at the contemporary scene to realize what little influence it has had upon the world.

But—

> *That is not dead which can eternal lie,*
> *And with strange aeons, even death may die.*

So saith the *Necronomicon*, in a cryptic couplet referring to the immortality of Great Cthulhu.

And behold, the prophecy seems fulfilled, for Cthulhu lives on, in the continued and growing recognition of Lovecraft's work, and in the creation of a new generation of writers inspired by the Cthulhu Mythos.

Edward P. Berglund, himself a qualified Cthulhuean, has herein assembled a pristine anthology of Mythos tales by some of these talents whom he refers to as *The Disciples of Cthulhu*. Behold a wide variety of talent—from Fritz Leiber, a Lovecraft contemporary and correspondent, to Bob Van Laerhoven, who was not born until sixteen years after Lovecraft's death. The other contributors—Ramsey Campbell, Lin Carter, James Wade, Brian Lumley, Eddy C. Bertin, Joseph Payne Brennan, and Walter C. DeBill, Jr.—have elsewhere established their literary credentials as full-fledged *Disciples*. Their offerings herein handsomely attest their right to such a designation.

Parenthetically, I myself have some minor accreditation for inclusion in their ranks. As a fifteen-year-old boy I wrote my first fan letter to Lovecraft in Rhode Island, and thanks to his suggestion and encouragement I began my own professional writing at the age of seventeen. It might truly be said, therefore, that I owe my career to an act of Providence.

*Providence. Disciples.* There's a religious ring to these words, and perhaps an appropriate one.

In seeking the sources of continuing interest in the Cthulhu Mythos we cannot ignore the metaphysic behind the myth. No need to belabor the point—Lovecraft has actually created an imaginary religion, complete with ancient gods, the *Necronomicon* as a bible, and a cult of reader-writer followers.

Has he, as the late Carl Jung might affirm, unwittingly evoked a chord which resonates in racial memories? Or has he merely embodied a universally common paranoiac belief that we are all the victims of dark forces beyond our ken or control? In either case I feel that the real appeal of the Cthulhu Mythos lies in a strange, subconscious recognition that behind fantasy and parable lurks a possibility of truth.

Indeed, somewhere in my own files there reposes a series of notes for a novel about a future in which Cthulhu and the other Great Old Ones have actually become the central figures in a new religion which has taken over our decadent society, and in which Lovecraft is venerated as a prophet. I tend to think that Lovecraft, himself a strict materialist, would have found the notion amusing. As for me, I'm not so sure.

But I *am* sure that on the level of sheer fantasy you will be entertained by the present efforts of *The Disciples of Cthulhu*. Read, and enjoy.

And who knows? Perhaps you may become a convert yourself!

*Robert Bloch*
1975

# The Fairground Horror

## by Brian Lumley

The funfair was as yet an abject failure. Drizzling rain dulled the chrome of the dodgem-cars and stratojets; the neons had not even nearly achieved the garishness they display by night; the so-called 'crowd' was hardly worth mentioning as such. But it was only 2:00 p.m. and things could yet improve.

Had the weather been better—even for October it was bad—and had Bathley been a town instead of a mere village, then perhaps the scene were that much brighter. Come evening, when the neons and other bright naked bulbs would glow in all the painful intensity of their own natural (unnatural?) life, when the drab gypsyish dollies behind the penny-catching stalls would undergo their subtle, nightly metamorphosis into avariciously enticing Loreleis—then it *would* be brighter, but not yet.

This was the fourth day of the five when the funfair was 'in town.' It was an annual—event? The nomads of Hodgson's Funfair had known better times, better conditions and worse ones, but it was all the same to them and they were resigned to it. There was, though, amid all the noisy, muddy, smelly paraphernalia of the fairground, a tone of incongruity. It had been there since Anderson Tharpe, in the curious absence of his brother, Hamilton, had taken down the old freak-house frontage to repaint the boards and canvas with the new and forbidding legend: TOMB OF THE GREAT OLD ONES.

Looking up at the painted gouts of 'blood' that formed the garish legend arching over a yawning, scaly, dragon-jawed entranceway, Hiram Henley frowned behind his tiny spectacles in more than casual curiosity, in something perhaps approaching concern. His lips silently formed the ominous words of that legend as if he spoke them to himself in awe, and then he thrust his black-gloved hands deeper into the pockets of his fine, expensively tailored overcoat and tucked his neck down more firmly into its collar.

Hiram Henley had recognized something in the name of the place—something which might ring subconscious warning bells in even the most mundane minds—and the recognition caused an involuntary shudder to hurry up his back. 'The Great Old Ones!' he said to himself yet again, and his whisper held a note of terrible fascination.

Research into just such cycles of myth and aeon-lost legend, while ostensibly he had been studying Hittite antiquities in the Middle East and Turkey, had cost Henley his position as Professor of Archaeology and Ethnology at Meldham University. 'Cthulhu, Yibb-Tstll, Yog-Sothoth, Summanus—the Great Old Ones!' Again an expression of awe flitted across his bespectacled face. To be confronted with a … a *monument* such as this, and in such a place …

And yet the ex-professor was not too surprised; he had been alerted to the contents of Anderson Tharpe's queer establishment, and therefore the fact that the owner had named it thus was hardly a matter of any lasting astonishment. Nevertheless Henley knew that there were people who would have considered the naming of the fairground erection, to say nothing of the presence of its afore-hinted *contents,* blasphemous. Fortunately such persons were few and far between—the Cult of Cthulhu was still known only to a minority of serious authorities, to a few obscure occult investigators, and a scattered handful of esoteric groups—but Hiram Henley looked back to certain days of yore when he had blatantly used the university's money to go in search of just such items of awesome antiquity as now allegedly hid behind the demon-adorned ramparts of the edifice before him.

The fact of the matter was that Henley had heard how this Tomb of the Great Old Ones held within its monster-daubed board-and-canvas walls relics of an age already many millions of years dead and gone when Babylon was but a sketch in the mind's eye of Architect Thathnis III. Figures and fragments, hieroglyphed tablets and strangely scrawled papyri, weird greenstone sculptings and rotting, worm-eaten tomes: Henley had reason to believe that many of these things, if not all of them, existed behind the facade of Anderson Tharpe's horror house.

There would also be, of course, the usual nonconformities peculiar to such establishments—the two-headed foetus in its bottle of preservative, the five-legged puppy similarly suspended, the fake mummy in its red- and green-daubed wrappings, the great fruit ('vampire') bats, hanging shutter-eyed and motionless in their warm wire cages beyond the reach of giggly, shuddering women and morbidly fascinated men and boys—but Hiram Henley was not interested in any of these. Nevertheless, he sent his gloved right hand awkwardly groping into the corner of his overcoat pocket for the silver coin which alone might open for him the door to Tharpe's house of horror.

Hiram Henley was a slight, middle-aged man. His thin figure, draped smotheringly in the heavy overcoat, his balding head and tiny specs through which his watery eyes constantly peered; his gloved hands almost lost in huge pockets, his trousers seeming to hang from beneath the hem of his overcoat and partly, not wholly, covering the black patent leather shoes upon his feet; all made of him a picture which was conspicuously odd. And yet Hiram Henley's intelligence was patent; the stamp of a 'higher mind' was written in erudite lines upon his brow. His were obviously eyes which had studied strange mysteries, and his feet had gone along strange ways; so that despite any other emotion or consideration which his appearance might ill-advisedly call to mind, still his shrunken frame commanded more than a little respect among his fellow men.

Anderson Tharpe, on the other hand, crouching now upon his tiny seat in the ticket-booth, was a tall man, well over six feet in height but almost as thin and emaciated as the fallen professor. His hair was prematurely grey and purposely grown long in an old-fash-ioned scholarly style, so that he might simulate to the crowd's satisfaction a necessary erudition; just such an erudition as was manifest in the face above the slight figure which even now pressed upon his tiny window, sixpence clutched in gloved fingers. Tharpe's beady eyes beneath blackly hypnotic brows studied Hiram Henley briefly, speculatively, but then he smiled a very genuine welcome as he passed the small man a ticket, waving away the sixpence with an expansive hand.

'Not *you*, sir, indeed no! From a gent so obviously and sincerely interested in the mysteries within—from a man of your high standing'—again the expansive gesture—'why, I couldn't accept money from you, sir. It's an honour to have you visit us!'

'Thank you,' Henley dryly answered, passing myopically into the great tent beyond the ticket booth. Tharpe's smile slowly faded, was replaced by a look of cunning. Quickly the tall man pocketed his few shillings in takings, then followed the slight figure of the ex-professor into the smelly sawdust-floored 'museum' beyond the canvas flap.

In all, a dozen people waited within the big tent's main division.
A pitifully small 'crowd.' But in any case, though he kept his
interest cleverly veiled, Tharpe's plans involved only the ex-professor. The tall man's flattery at the ticket booth had not all been
flannel; he had spotted Henley immediately as the very species of
highly educated fly for which his flypaper—in the form of the new
and enigmatic legend across the visage of the one-time freak-
house—had been erected above Bathley Moor.

There had been, Tharpe reflected, men of outwardly similar
intelligence before at the Tomb of the Great Old Ones; and more
than one of them had told him that certain of his *artifacts*—those
items which he kept, as his brother had kept them before him, in a
separately enclosed part of the tent—were of an unbelievable antiquity. Indeed, one man had been so affected by the very sight of such
ancientness that he had run from Tharpe's collection in stark terror,
and he had never returned. That had been in May, and though
almost six months had passed since that time, still Tharpe had come
no closer to an understanding of the mysterious objects which his
brother Hamilton had brought back with him from certain dark
corners of the world; objects which, early in 1961, had caused him
to kill Hamilton in self-defence.

Anderson had panicked then—he realized that now—for he
might easily have come out of the affair blameless had he only
reported Hamilton's death to the police. For a long time the folk of
Hodgson's Funfair had known that there was something drastically
wrong with Hamilton Tharpe; his very sanity had been questioned,
albeit guardedly. Certainly Anderson would have been declared
innocent of his brother's murder—the case would have gone to court
only as a matter of formality—but he had panicked. And of course
there had been ... complications.

With Hamilton's body secretly buried deep beneath the freak-
house, the folk of the fairground had been perfectly happy to believe
Anderson's tale of his brother's abrupt departure on yet another of
his world-spanning expeditions, the like of which had brought
about all the trouble in the first place.

Now Anderson thought back on it all ...

He and his brother had grown up together in the fairground, but
then it had been their father's property, and 'Tharpe's Funfair' had
been known throughout all England for its fair play and prices.
Wherever the elder Tharpe had taken his stalls and sideshows—of
which the freak-house had ever been his personal favourite—his

employees had been sure of good crowds. It was only after old Tharpe died that the slump started.

It had had much to do with young Hamilton's joy in old books and fancifully dubious legends; his lust for travel, adventure, and *outré* knowledge. His first money-wasting venture had been a 'treasure-hunting' trip to the islands of the Pacific, undertaken solely on the strength of a vague and obviously fake map. In his absence—he had gone off with an adventurous and plausible rogue from the shooting gallery—Anderson looked after the fair. Things went badly, and all the Tharpes got out of Hamilton's venture were a number of repulsively carved stone tablets and one or two patently aboriginal sculptings, not the least of which was a hideous, curiously winged octopoid idol. Hamilton placed the latter obscenity in the back of their caravan home as being simply too fantastic for display to an increasingly mundane and sceptical public.

The idol, however, had a most unsettling effect upon the younger brother. He was wont to go in to see the thing in the dead of night, when Anderson was in bed and apparently asleep. But often Anderson was awake, and during these nocturnal visits he had heard Hamilton *talking* to the idol. More disturbingly, he had once or twice dimly imagined that he heard something talking back! Too, before he went off again on his wanderings in unspoken areas of the great deserts of Arabia, the sensitive, mystery-loving traveller had started to suffer from especially bad nightmares.

Again, in Hamilton's absence, things went badly. Soon Anderson was obliged to sell out to Bella Hodgson, retaining only the freak-house as his own and his prodigal brother's property. A year passed, and another before Hamilton once more returned to the fairground, demanding his living as before but making little or no attempt to work for his needs. There was no arguing, however, for the formerly sensitive younger brother was a changed, indeed a saturnine, man now, so that soon Anderson came to be a little afraid of him.

And quite apart from the less obvious alterations in Hamilton, other changes were much more apparent; changes in habit, even in appearance. The most striking was the fact that now the younger Tharpe constantly wore a shaggy black toupée, as if to disguise his partial premature baldness, which all of the funfair's residents knew about anyway and which had never caused him the least embarrassment before. Also, he had become so reticent as to be almost reclusive; keeping to himself, only rarely and reluctantly allowing himself to be drawn into even the most trivial conversations.

More than this: there had been a time prior to his second long absence when Hamilton had seemed somewhat enamored of the young, single, dark-eyed fortune-teller, 'Madame Zala'—a Gypsy girl of genuine Romany ancestry—but since his return he had been especially cool towards her, and for her own part she had been seen to cross herself with a pagan sign when he had happened to be passing by. Once he had seen her make this sign, and then he had gone white with fury, hurrying off to the freak-house and remaining there for the rest of that day. Madame Zala had packed up her things and left one night in her horse-drawn caravan without a word of explanation to anyone. It was generally believed that Hamilton had threatened her in some way, though no one ever took him to task over the affair. For his own part, he simply averred that Zala had been 'a charlatan of the worst sort, without the ability to conjure a puff of wind!'

All in all the members of the funfair fraternity had been quick to find Hamilton a very changed man, and towards the end there had been the aforementioned hints of a brewing madness ...

On top of all this, Hamilton had again taken up his nocturnal visits to the octopoid idol, but now such visits seemed less frequent than of old. Less frequent, perhaps, but they nevertheless heralded much darker events; for soon Hamilton had installed the idol within a curtained and spacious corner of the tent, in the freak-house itself, and he no longer paid his visits alone ...

Anderson Tharpe had seen, from his darkened caravan window, a veritable procession of strangers—all of them previous visitors to the freak-house, and always the more intelligent types—accompanying his brother to the tent's nighted interior. But he had never seen a one come out! Eventually, as his younger brother became yet more saturnine, reticent, and secretive, Anderson took to spying on him in earnest—and later almost wished that he had not.

In the months between, however, Hamilton had made certain alterations to the interior of the freak-house, partitioning fully a third of its area to enclose the collection of rare and obscure curiosities garnered upon his travels. At that time Anderson had been puzzled to distraction by his brother's firm refusal to let his treasures be viewed by any but a chosen few of the freak-house's patrons: those doubtfully privileged persons who later accompanied him into the private museum never again to leave.

Of course, Anderson finally reasoned, the answer was a simple as it was fantastic: somewhere upon his travels Hamilton had learned the arts of murder and thievery, arts he was now practicing in the freak-house. The bodies? These he obviously buried, to leave behind safely lodged in the dark earth when the fair moved on. But the money ... what of the money? For money—or rather its lack—patently formed the younger brother's motive. Could he be storing his booty away, against the day when he would go off on yet another of his foolish trips to foreign places? Beside himself that he had not been 'cut in' on the profits of Hamilton's dark machinations, Anderson determined to have it out with him; to catch him, as it were, red-handed.

And yet it was not until early in the spring of 1961 that Anderson finally managed to 'overhear' a conversation between his brother and an obviously well-to-do visitor to the freak-house. Hamilton had singled out this patently intelligent gentleman for attention, inviting him back to the caravan during a break in business. Anderson, knowing most of the modus operandi by now and aware of the turn events must take, positioned himself outside the caravan where he could eavesdrop.

He did not catch the complete conversation, and yet sufficient to make him aware at last of Hamilton's expert and apparently unique knowledge in esoteric mysteries. For the first time he heard uttered the mad words Cthulhu and Yibb-Tstll, Tsathoggua and Yog-Sothoth, Shudde-M'ell and Nyarlathotep, discovering that these were names of monstrous 'gods' from the dawn of time. He heard mention of Leng and Lh'yib; Mnar, Ib and Sarnath; R'lyeh and 'red-litten' Yoth; and knew now that these were cities and lands ancient even in antiquity. He heard descriptions and names given to manuscripts, books, and tablets—and here he started in recognition, for he knew that some of these aeon-old writings existed amid Hamilton's treasures in the freak-house— and among others he heard the strangely chilling titles of such works as the *Necronomicon*, the *Cthaat Aquadingen*, the *Pnakotic Manuscripts* and the *R'lyehan Texts*. This then formed the substance of Hamilton's magnetism: his amazing erudition in matters of myth and time-lost lore.

When he perceived that the two were about to make an exit from the caravan, Anderson quickly hid himself away behind a nearby stall to continue his observations. He saw the flushed face of Hamilton's new confidante, his excited gestures; and, at a whispered suggestion from the pale-faced brother, he finally saw that gentleman nodding eagerly, wide-eyed in awed agreement. And after the visitor had gone, Anderson saw the look that flitted briefly across his brother's features: a look that hinted of awful triumph, nameless emotion—and, yes, purest evil!

But it was something about the face of the departed visitor—that rounded gentleman of obvious substance but doubtful future—which caused Anderson the greatest concern. He had finally recognized that face from elsewhere, and at his first opportunity he sneaked a glance through some of the archaeological and anthropological journals which his brother now spent so much time reading. It was as he had thought: Hamilton's prey was none other than an eminent explorer and archaeologist; one whose name, Stainton Gamber, might even be higher in the lists of famous adventurers and discoverers but for a passion for wild-goose expeditions and safaris. Then he grew even more worried, for plainly his brother could not go on forever depleting the countryside of eminent persons without being discovered.

That afternoon passed slowly for Anderson Tharpe, and when night came he went early to his bed in the caravan. He was up again, however, as soon as he heard his brother stirring and the hushed whispers that led off in the direction of the freak-house. It was as he had known it would be, when for a moment pale moonlight showed him a glimpse of Hamilton with Stainton Gamber.

Quickly he followed the two to the looming canvas tent, and in through the dragon-jawed entranceway, but he paused at the door-flap to the partitioned area to listen and observe. There came the scratch of a match and its bright, sudden flare, and then a candle flickered into life. At this point the whispering recommenced, and Anderson drew back a pace as the candle began to move about the interior of Hamilton's museum. He could hear the hushed conversations quite clearly, could feel the tremulous excitement in the voice of the florid explorer:

'But these are—*fantastic!* I've believed for years now that such relics must exist. Indeed, I've often brought my reputation close to ruin for such beliefs, and now ... young man, you'll be world famous. Do you realize what you have here? Proof positive that the Cult of Cthulhu did exist! What monstrous worship—what hideous rites! Where, *where* did you find these things? I must know! And this idol—which you say is believed to invoke the spirit of the living Cthulhu himself! Who holds such beliefs? I know of course that Wendy-Smith—'

'*Hah!*' Hamilton's rasping voice cut in. 'You can keep all your Wendy-Smiths and Gordon Walmsleys. They only scraped the surface. I've gone inside—*and outside!* Explorers, dreamers, mystics—mere dabblers. Why, they'd *die,* all of them, if they saw what I've seen, if they went where I've been. And none of them have ever dreamed what I *know!*'

'But why keep it hidden? Why don't you open this place up, show the world what you've got here, what you've achieved? Publish, man, publish! Why, together—'

'Together?' Hamilton's voice was darker, trembling as he suddenly snuffed the candle out. 'Together? Proof that the Cult of Cthulhu *did* exist? Show it to the world? Publish?' His chuckle was obscene in the dark, and Anderson heard the visitor's sharp intake of breath. 'The world's not ready, Gamber, and the stars are not right! What you would like to do, like many before you, is alert the world to *Their* one-time presence, the days of *Their* sovereignty— which might in turn lead to the discovery that *They are here even now!* Indeed Wendy-Smith was right, too right, and where is Wendy-Smith now? No, no—*They* aren't interested in mere dabblers, except that such are dangerous to *Them* and must be removed! *Iä, R'lyeh!* You are no true dreamer, Gamber, no believer. You're not worthy of membership in the Great Priesthood. You're ... dangerous! Proof? I'll give you proof. Listen, and *watch*—'

Hearing his brother's injunction, the secret listener would have paid dearly to see what next occurred. A short while earlier, just before Hamilton had snuffed out the candle, Anderson had managed to find a hole in the canvas large enough to facilitate a fair view of the partitioned area. He had seen a semicircle of carved stone tablets, with the octopoid idol presiding atop or seated upon a throne-like pedestal. Now, in the dark, his view-hole was useless.

He could still listen, however, and now Hamilton's voice came— strange and vibrant, though still controlled in volume—in a chant or invocation of terrible cadence and rhythmic disorder. These were not words the younger Tharpe uttered but unintelligible *sounds,* a morbidly insane agglutination of verbal improbabilities which ought never to have issued from a human throat at all! And as the invocation ceased, to an incredulous gasping from the doomed explorer, Anderson had to draw back from his hole lest he become visible in the glow of a green radiance springing up abruptly in the centre of Hamilton's encircling relics.

The green glow grew brighter, filling the hidden museum and spilling emerald beams from several small holes in the canvas. This was no normal light, for the beams were quite alien to anything Anderson had ever seen before; the very light seemed to writhe and contort in a slow and loathsomely languid dance. Now Anderson found himself again a witness, for the shadows of Hamilton and his intended victim were thrown blackly against the wall of canvas. There was no requirement now to 'spy' properly upon the pair; his view of the eerie drama could not have been clearer. The centre of the radiance seemed to expand and shrink alternatively, pulsing like an alien heart of light. Hamilton stood to one side, his arms flung wide in terrible triumph; Stainton Gamber cowered, his hands up before his face as if to shield it from some unbearable heat—or as if to ward off the unknown and inexplicable!

Anderson's shadow-view of the terrified explorer was profile, and he was suddenly astonished to note that while the man appeared to be screaming horribly he could hear nothing of the screams! It was as if Anderson had been stricken deaf. Hamilton, too, was now plainly vociferous; his throat moved in crazed cachinnations and his thrown-back head and heaving shoulders plainly announced unholy glee—but all in stark silence! Anderson knew now that the mad green light had somehow worked against normal order, annulling all sound utterly and thereby hiding in its emerald pulsings the final act in this monstrous shadow-play. As the core pulsated even faster and brighter, Hamilton moved quickly after the silently shrieking explorer, catching him by the collar of his jacket and swinging him sprawling into the core itself!

Instantly the core shrank, sucking in upon itself and dwindling in a moment to a ball of intense brightness. But where was the explorer? Horrified, Anderson saw that now *only one shadow remained faintly outlined upon the canvas—that of his brother!*

Quickly, weirdly, paling as they went, the beams of green light withdrew. Sound instantly returned, and Anderson heard his own harsh breathing. He stilled the sound, moving back to his spy-hole to see what was happening. A faint green glow with a single bright speck of a core remained within the semicircle; and now Hamilton bowed to this dimming light and his voice came again, low and tremulous with emotion:

*Iä, naflhgn Cthulhu R'lyeh mglw'nafh,*
*Eha'ungl wglw hflghglui ngah'glw,*
*Engl Eha gh'eehf gnhugl,*
*Nhflgng uh'eha wgah'nagl hfglufh—*
*U'ng Eha'ghglui Aeeh ehn'hflgh …*
That is not dead which can eternal lie,
And with strange aeons even death may die.

No sooner had Hamilton ceased these utterly alien mouthings and the paradoxical couplet that completed them, and while yet the green glow continued to dim and fade, than he spoke again, this time all in recognizable English. Such was his murmured modulation and deliberate spacing of the spoken sequences that his hidden brother immediately recognized the following as a translation of what had gone before:

Oh, Great Cthulhu, dreaming in R'lyeh,
Thy priest offers up this sacrifice,
That thy coming be soon
And that of thy kindred dreamers.
I am thy priest and adore thee …

It was only then that the full horror of what he had seen—the cold-blooded, premeditated murder of a man by either some monstrous occult device or a foreign science beyond his knowledge—finally went home to Anderson Tharpe, and barely managing to stifle the hysterical babble he felt welling in his throat, he took an involuntary step backwards … to collide loudly with a cage of great bats.

Three things happened then in rapid succession before Anderson could gather his wits to flee. All trace of the green glow vanished in an instant, throwing the tent once more into complete darkness; then in contrast, confusing the elder brother, the bright interior lights blinked on; finally, as he sought to recover from his confusion, Hamilton appeared through the partition's canvas door, his eyes blazing in a face contorted in fury!

'You!' Hamilton spat, striding to Anderson's side and catching him fiercely by the collar of his dressing gown. 'How much have you seen?'

Anderson twisted free and backed away. 'I … I saw it all, but I had guessed as much some time ago. Murder—and you my brother!'

'Save your sanctimony,' Hamilton sneered. 'If you've known so much for so long, then you're as much a murderer as I am! And anyway'—his eyes seemed visibly to glaze and take on a faraway look—'it wasn't murder, not as you understand it.'

'Of course not.' Now it was Anderson's turn to sneer. 'It was a—a "sacrifice"—to this so-called "god" of yours, Great Cthulhu! And were the others all sacrifices, too?'

'All of them,' Hamilton answered with a nod, automatically, as in a trance.

'Oh? And where's the money?'

'Money?' The faraway look went out of the younger Tharpe's eyes immediately. 'What money?'

Anderson saw that this was no bluff; his brother's motive had not been personal gain, at least not in a monetary sense. Which in turn meant—

Had those rumours and unfriendly whispers heard about the stalls and sideshows—those hints of a looming madness in his brother—had they been more than mere guesswork, then? Surely he would have known. As if in answer to his unspoken question, Hamilton spoke again—and listening to him Anderson believed he had his answer:

'You're the same as all the others, Anderson—you can't see beyond the length of your greedy nose. Money? Pah! You think that *They* are interested in wealth? *They* are not; neither am I. *They* have a wealth of aeons behind *Them*; the future is *Theirs* ....' Again his eyes seemed to glaze over.

'Them? Who do you mean?' Anderson asked, frowning and backing farther away.

'Cthulhu and the others. Cthulhu and the Deep Ones, and *Their* brothers and kin forever dreaming in the vast vaults beneath. *Iä, R'lyeh, Cthulhu fhtagn!*'

'You're quite—mad!'

'You think so?' Hamilton quickly followed after him, pushing his face uncomfortably close. 'I'm mad, am I? Well, perhaps, but I'll tell you something: when you and the others like you are reduced to mere cattle, before the Earth is cleared off of life as you know it, a trusted handful of priests will guard the herds for *Them*—and I shall be a priest among priests, appointed to the service of Great Cthulhu Himself!' His eyes burned feverishly.

Now Anderson was certain of his brother's madness, but even so he could see a way to profit from it. 'Hamilton,' he said after a moment's thought, 'worship whatever gods you like and aspire to whatever priesthood—but don't you see we have to live? There could be good money in this for both of us. If only—'

'No!' Hamilton hissed. 'To worship Cthulhu is enough. Indeed, it is *all!* That, in there'—he jerked his head, indicating the enclosed area behind him—'is His temple. To offer up sacrifices while yet thinking of oneself would be blasphemous, and when He comes I shall not be found wanting!' His eyes went wide and he trembled.

'You don't know Him, Anderson. He is awful, awesome, a monster, a god! He is sunken now, drowned and dead in deep R'lyeh, but His death is a sleeping death and He will awaken. When the stars are right we chosen ones will answer the Call of Cthulhu, and R'lyeh will rise up again to astound a reeling universe. Why, even the Gorgons were His priestesses in the old world! And you talk to me of money.' Again he sneered, but now his madness had a firm grip on him and the sneer soon turned to a crafty smile.

'And you're helpless to do anything, Anderson, for if you breathe a word I'll swear you were in on it—that you helped me from the start! And as for bodies, why, there are none. They are gone to dreaming Cthulhu, through the light He sends me when I cry out to Him in my darkness. So you see, nothing could ever be proved ...'

'Perhaps not, but I don't think it would take much to have you, well, *put away!*' Anderson quietly answered.

The barb went straight home. A look of terror crossed Hamilton's face and, plainly aware of his own mental infirmity, he visibly paled.

'Put me away? But you wouldn't. If you did, I wouldn't be able to worship, to sacrifice, and—'

'But there's no need to worry about it,' Anderson cut him off. 'I won't have you put away. Just see things my way, show me how you dissolve them in that green light of yours—I mean, in, er, dreaming Cthulhu's light—and then we'll carry on as before, except that there'll be money—'

'No, Anderson,' the other refused almost gently, 'it can't work like that. You could never believe—not even if I showed you proof of my priesthood, which hides beneath this false head of hair that I'm obliged to wear, the very Mark of Cthulhu—and I can't worship as you suggest. I'm sorry.' There was an insane sadness in his face as he drew out a long knife from its sheath inside his jacket. 'I use this when they're stronger than me,' he explained, 'and when they're liable to fight. Cthulhu doesn't care for it much because he likes them alive initially and whole, but—' His knife hand flashed up and down.

Only Anderson's speed saved him, for he turned quickly to one side as the blade flashed down toward his breast. Then their wrists were locked and they staggered to and fro, Hamilton frothing at the mouth and trying to bite, while Anderson grimly struggled for dear life. The madman seemed to have the strength of three normal men, and soon they fell to the ground, a thrashing heap that rolled blindly in through the flap of the canvas door to Hamilton's 'temple.'

There it was that finally the younger brother's toupée came away from his head in the silent struggle—and in a burst of strength engendered of sheer loathing Anderson managed to turn the knife inward and drive it to the madman's heart. He was quick then to be on his feet and away from the thing that now lay twitching out its life upon the sawdust floor—the thing that had been his brother—which now, where the top of Hamilton's head had been, *wore a cap of writhing white worms of finger thickness, like some monstrous sea-anemone sucking vampirishly at the still-living brain!*

Later, when morning came, even had there been someone in whom he might safely confide, Anderson Tharpe could never have related a detailed or coherent account of the preceding hours of darkness. He recalled only the general thread of what had passed; frantic snatches of the fearful activity that followed upon the hideous death of his brother. But first there had been that half hour or so of waiting—of knowing that at any moment, attracted perhaps by strange lights or sounds, someone might just enter the tent and find him with Hamilton's body—but he had been *obliged* to wait for he could not bring himself to touch the corpse. Not while the stubby white tentacles of its head continued to writhe! Hamilton died almost immediately, but his monstrous crown had taken much longer ...

Then, when the loathsome—parasite?—had shuddered into lifeless rigidity, he had gathered together his shattered nerves to dig a deep grave in the soft earth beneath the sawdust. That had been a gruesome task with the lights turned down and Cthulhu's stone effigy casting a tentacled shadow over the fearful digger. Anderson later remembered how soft the ground had been—and wet when it ought to have been dry in the weatherproof tent—and he recalled a powerful smell of deep ocean, of aeons-old slime and rotting seaweeds; an odour he had known on occasion before, and always after one of Hamilton's 'sacrifices.' The connection had not impressed itself upon his mind as anything more than mere coincidence before, but now he knew that the smell came with the green light, as did that strange state of soundlessness.

In order to clear what remained of the fetor quickly—having tamped down the earth, generally 'tidied up' and removed all traces of his digging—he opened and tied back the canvas doors of the tent to allow the night air a healthy circulation. But even then, having done everything possible to hide the night's horror, he was unable to relax properly as daylight had crept up and the folk of the funfair began to wake and move about.

When finally Hodgson's Funfair had opened at noon, Anderson had something of a shaky grip on himself, but even so he had found himself drenched in cold sweat at the end of each oratorical session with the crowds at the freak-house. His only moments of relaxation came between shows. The worst time had been when a leather-jacketed teenager peered through the canvas inner door to the partitioned section of the tent; and Anderson had nearly knocked the youth down in his anxiety to steer him away from the place, though no trace remained of what had transpired there.

On reflection, it amazed Anderson that his fight with his brother had not attracted someone's attention, and yet it had not. Even the fairground's usually vociferous watchdogs had remained silent. And yet those same dogs, since Hamilton's return from his travels abroad, had seemed even more nervous, more given to snapping and snarling than ever before. Anderson could only tell himself that the weird 'silent state' which had accompanied the green light must have spread out over the entire fairground to dissipate slowly, thus disarming the dogs. Or perhaps they had sensed something else, remaining silent out of fear ...? Indeed, it appeared his second guess was correct, for he discovered later that many of the dogs had whimpered the whole night away huddled beneath the caravans of their masters ...

Two days later the funfair packed up and moved on, leaving Hamilton Tharpe's body safely buried in an otherwise empty field. At last the worst of Anderson's apprehensions left him and his nerves began to settle down. To be sure his jumpiness had been marked by the folk of the funfair, who had all correctly (though for the wrong reasons) diagnosed it as a symptom of anxiety about his crazy, bad-lot brother. So it was that as soon as Hamilton's absence was remarked upon, Anderson was able simply to shrug his shoulders and answer: 'Who knows? Tibet, Egypt, Australia—he's just gone off again—said nothing to me about it—could be anywhere!' And while such inquiries were always politely compassionate, he knew that in fact the inquirers were greatly relieved that his brother had 'just gone off again.'

Another six weeks went by, with regular halts at various villages and small towns, and during that time Anderson managed to will himself to forget all about his brother's death and his own involvement—all, that is, except the nature of that parasitic horror which had made itself manifest upon Hamilton's head. That was something he would never forget, the way that awful anemone had wriggled and writhed long after its host was dead. Hamilton had called the thing a symbol of his priesthood—in his own words: 'The Mark of Cthulhu'—but in truth it could only have been some loathsomely malignant and rare form of cancer, or perhaps a kind of worm or fluke like the tapeworm. Anderson always shuddered when he recalled it, for it had looked horribly *sentient* there atop Hamilton's head; and when one thought about the *depth* at which it might have been rooted ...

No, the insidious gropings of that horror within Hamilton's brain simply did not bear thinking about, for that had obviously been the source of his insanity. Anderson in no way considered himself weak to shudder when thoughts as terrible as these came to threaten his now calm and controlled state of mind, and when the bad dreams started he at once lay the blame at the feet of the same horror.

At first the nightmares were vague shadowy things, with misty vistas of rolling plains and yawning, empty coastlines. There were distant islands with strange pinnacles and oddly angled towers, but so far away that the unknown creatures moving about in those island cities were mere insects to Anderson's dreaming eyes. And for this he was glad. Their shapes seemed in a constant state of flux and were not—pleasant. They were primal shapes, from which the dreamer deduced that he was in a primal land of aeons lost to mankind. He always woke from such visions uneasy in mind and deflated in spirit.

But with the passing of the months into summer the dreams changed, becoming visually sharper, clearer in their insinuations, and actually frightening as opposed to merely disturbing. Their scenes were set (Anderson somehow knew) deep in the dimly lighted bowels of one of the island cities, in a room or vault of fantastic proportions and awe-inspiring angles. Always he kneeled before a vast octopoid idol ... except that on occasion it was *not* an idol but a living, hideously intelligent Being!

These dreams were ever the worst, when a strange voice spoke to him in words that he was quite unable to understand. He would tremble before the towering horror on its throne-like pedestal—a thing one hundred times greater in size than the stone morbidity in the freak-house—and, aware that he only dreamed, he would know that it, too, was asleep and dreaming. But its tentacles would twine and twist and its claws would scrabble at the front of the throne, and then the voice would come ...

Waking from nightmares such as these he would know that they were engendered of hellish memory—of the night of the green glow, the deep-ocean smell, and the writhing thing in his brother's head—for he would always recall in his first waking moments that the awful alien voice had used sounds similar to those Hamilton had mouthed before the green light came and after it had taken the florid explorer away. The dreams were particularly bad and growing worse as the year drew to a close, and on a number of occasions the dreamer had been sure that slumbering Cthulhu was about to stir and wake up!

And then, himself waking up, all the horror would come back to Anderson, to be viewed once more in his mind's eye in vivid clarity; and knowing as he did that his brother too had been plagued by just such dreams prior to his second long absence from the fairground, Anderson Tharpe was a troubled man indeed. Yes, they *had* been the same sort of nightmares, those dreams of Hamilton's; hadn't he admitted that 'Cthulhu comes to me in dreams?' And had the dreams themselves not heralded the greater horrors?

And yet, in less gloomy mood, Anderson found himself more and more often dwelling upon Hamilton's weird murder weapon, the pulsating green light. He was by no means an ignorant man, and he had read something of the recent progress in laser technology. Soon he had convinced himself that his brother had used an unknown form of foreign science to offer up his mad 'sacrifices to Cthulhu.' If only he could discover how Hamilton had done it ...

But surely science such as that would require complex machinery? It was while pondering this very problem that Anderson hit upon what he believed must be the answer: whatever tools or engines Hamilton had used, they must be hidden in the octopoid idol, or perhaps built into those ugly stone tablets which had formed a semicircle about the idol. And perhaps, like the electric-eye beams which operated the moving floors and blasts of cool air in the fairground's Noah's Ark, Hamilton's chanted 'summons' had been nothing more than a resonant trigger to set the hidden lasers or whatever to working. The smell of deep ocean and residual dampness must be the natural aftermath of such processes, in the same way that carbon monoxide and dead oil are the waste from petrol engines and the smell of ozone is attendant to electrical discharges.

The tablets, the idol too, still stood where they had stood in the time before the horror—the only change was that now the canvas partition was down and Hamilton's ancient artifacts were on display with the other paraphernalia of the freak-house—but just suppose Anderson were to arrange them *exactly* as they had been before, and suppose further that he could discover how to use that chanted formula. What then? Would he be able to summon the green light? If so, would he be able to use it as he had tried to convince Hamilton it should be used? Perhaps the answer lay in his dead brother's books ...

Certainly that collection of ancient tomes, now slowly disintegrating in a cupboard in the caravan, were full of hints of just such things. It was out of curiosity at first that Anderson began to read those books, or at least what he *could* read of them! Many were not in English but in Latin or archaic German, and at least one other was in ciphers the like of which Anderson had only ever seen on the stone tablets in the freak-house.

There were among the volumes such titles as Feery's *Notes on the* Cthaat Aquadingen, and a well thumbed copy of the same author's *Notes on the* Necronomicon; while yet another book, handwritten in a shaky script, purported to be the *Necronomicon* itself, or a translation thereof, but Anderson could not read it for its characters were formed of an unbelievably antiquated German. Then there was a large envelope full of yellowed loose leaves, and Hamilton had written on the envelope that this was 'Ibn Shoddathua's Translation of the Mum-Nath Papyri.' Among the more complete and recognizable works were such titles as *The Golden Bough* and Miss Margaret Murray's *The Witch-Cult in Western Europe*, but by comparison these were light reading.

During December and to the end of January, all of Anderson's free time was taken up in studying these works, until finally he became in a limited way something of an authority on the dread Cthulhu Cycle of Myth. He learned of the Elder Gods, benign forces or deities that existed 'in peace and glory' near Betelgeuse in the constellation Orion; and of the powers of evil, the Great Old Ones! He read of Azathoth, bubbling and blaspheming at the center of infinity—of Yog-Sothoth, the 'all-in-one and one-in-all', a god-creature coexistent in all time and conterminous with all space—of Nyarlathotep, the messenger of the Great Old Ones—of Hastur the Unspeakable, hell-thing and 'Lord of the Interstellar Spaces'—of fertile Shub-Niggurath, 'the black goat of the woods with a thousand young'—and, finally, of Great Cthulhu himself, an inconceivable evil that seeped down from the stars like cosmic pus when Earth was young and inchoate.

There were, too, lesser gods and beings more or less obscure or distant from the central theme of the Mythos. Among these Anderson read of Dagon and the Deep Ones; of Yibb-Tstll and the Gaunts of Night; of the Tcho-Tcho people and the Mi-Go; of Yig, Chaugnar Faugn, Nyogtha, and Tsathoggua; of Atlach-Nacha, Lloigor, Zhar, and Ithaqua; of burrowing Shudde-M'ell, flaming Cthugha, and the loathsome Hounds of Tindalos.

He learned how—for practicing abhorrent rites—the Great Old Ones were banished to prisoning environs where, ever ready to take possession of the Earth again, they live on eternally. Cthulhu, of course, having featured prominently in his brother's madness—now supposedly lying locked in sunken R'lyeh beneath the waves, waiting for the stars to 'come right' and for his minions, human and otherwise, to perform those rites which would once more return him as ruler of his former surface dominions—held the greatest interest for Anderson.

And the more he read, the more he became aware of the fantastic *depth* of his subject—but even so he could hardly bring himself to admit that there was anything of more than passing interest in such 'mumbo-jumbo.' Nevertheless, on the night of the second of February, 1962, he received what should have been a warning: a nightmare of such potency that it did in fact trouble him for weeks afterwards, and particularly when he saw the connection in the *date* of this visitation. It had been Candlemas, of course, which would have had immediate and special meaning to anyone with even the remotest schooling in the occult. Candlemas, and Anderson Tharpe had dreamed of basaltic submarine towers of titanic proportions and nightmare angles; and within those basalt walls and sepulchers, he had known that loathly Lord Cthulhu dreamed his own dreams of damnable dominion ...

This had not been all. He had drifted in his dreams *through* those walls to visit once more the inner chambers and kneel before the sleeping god. But it had been an unquiet sleep the Old One slept, in which his demon claws scrabbled fitfully and his folded wings twitched and jerked as if fighting to spread and lift him up through the pressured deeps to the unsuspecting world above! Then, as before, the voice had come to Anderson Tharpe—but this time it had spoken in English!

'*Do you seek,*' the voice had asked in awesome tones, '*to worship Cthulhu? Do you presume to His priesthood? I can see that YOU DO NOT, and yet you meddle and seek to discover His secrets! Be warned: it is a great sin against Cthulhu to destroy one of His chosen priests, and yet I see that you have done so. It is a sin, too, to scorn Him; but you have done this also. And it is a GREAT sin in His eyes to seek to use His secrets in any way other than in His service—AND THIS, TOO, YOU WOULD DO! Be warned, and live. Live and pray to your weak god that you are destroyed, in the first shock of the Great Rising. It were not well for you that you live to reap Cthulhu's wrath!*'

The voice had finally receded, but its sepulchral mind-echoes had barely faded away when it seemed to the paralyzed dreamer that the face tentacles of slumbering Cthulhu reached out, groping malignantly in his direction where he knelt in slime at the base of the massive throne!

At that a distant howling sprang up, growing rapidly louder and closer; and as the face tentacles of the sleeping god had been about to touch him, so Tharpe came screaming awake in his sweat-drenched bed to discover that the fairground was in an uproar. All the watchdogs, big and small, chained and roaming free alike, were howling in unison in the middle of that cold night. They seemed to howl at the blindly impassive stars, and their cries were faintly answered from a thousand similarly agitated canine throats in the nearby town!

The next morning speculation was rife among the showmen as to what had caused the trouble with the dogs, and eventually, on the evidence of certain scraps of fur, they put it down to a stray cat that must have got itself trapped under one of the caravans to be pulled to pieces by a Great Dane. Nevertheless, Anderson wondered at the keen senses and interpretation of the dogs in the local town that they had so readily taken up the unnatural baying and howling ...

During the next fortnight or so Anderson's slumbers were mercifully free of nightmares, so that he was early prompted to continue his researches into the Cthulhu Cycle of Myth. This further probing was born partly of curiosity and partly (as Anderson saw it) of necessity; he yet hoped to be able to employ gainfully his brother's mysterious green light, and his determination was bolstered by the fact that takings of late had been dismal. So he once more closed off the previously partitioned area of the tent, and his spare-time studies now became equally divided between Hamilton's books of occult lore and a patient examination of the hideous idol and carved tablets. He discovered no evidence of hidden mechanical devices in the queer relics, but nevertheless it was not long before he found his first real clue towards implementing his ambition.

It was as simple as this: he had earlier noted upon the carved tops of the stone tablets a series of curiously intermingled cuneiform and dot-group hieroglyphs, two distinct sets to each stone. This could not be considered odd in itself, but finally Anderson had recognized the pattern of these characters and knew that they were duplicated in the handwritten *Necronomicon*; and more, there were translations of that work into at least two other languages, one of them being the antiquated German in which the bulk of the book was written.

Anderson's knowledge of German, even in its modern form, was less than rudimentary, and thus he enlisted the aid of old Hans Möller from the hoopla stall. The old German's eyesight was no longer reliable, however, and his task was made no easier by the outmoded form in which the work was written; but at last, and not without Anderson's insistent urging, Möller was able to translate one of the sequences first into more modern German (in which it read: *Gestorben ist nicht, was für ewig ruht, und mit unbekannten Äonen mag sogar der Tod noch sterben*), and then into the following rather poor English: 'It is not dead that lies still forever; Death itself dies with the passing of strange years.'

When he heard the old German speak these words in his heavy accent, Anderson had to stifle the gasp of recognition which welled within him. This was nothing less than a variation of that paradoxical couplet with which his brother had once terminated his fiendish 'sacrifice to Cthulhu!'

As for the other set of symbols from the tablets, frustration was soon to follow. Certainly the figures were duplicated in the centuried book, appearing in what Anderson at first took to be a code of some sort, but they had not been reproduced in German. Möller— while having not the slightest inkling of Anderson's purpose with this smelly, evil old book—finally suggested to him that perhaps the letters were not in code at all, that they might simply be the symbols of an obscure foreign language. Anderson had to agree that Möller could well be right; in the yellowed left-hand margin of the relevant page, directly opposite the frustrating cryptogram, his brother had long ago written: 'Yes, but what of the *pronunciation?*'

Hamilton had done more than this: he had obligingly dated his patently self-addressed query, and the surviving Tharpe brother saw that the jotting had been made prior to the fatal second period of travel in foreign lands. Who could say what Hamilton might or might not have discovered upon that journey? Without a doubt he had been in strange places. And he had seen and done strange things to bring back with him that hellish cancer growth sprouting in his brain.

Finally Anderson decided that this jumbled gathering of harsh and unpronounceable letters—be it a scientific process or, more fancifully, a magical evocation—must indeed be the formula with which a clever man might call forth the green light in his dead brother's 'Temple of Cthulhu.' He thanked old Hans and sent him away, then sat in his caravan poring over the ancient book, puzzling and frowning long into the evening; until, as darkness fell, his eyes lit with dawning inspiration ...

And so over the period of the next few days the freak-house suffered its transition into the Tomb of the Great Old Ones. During the same week Anderson visited a printer in the local town and had new admission tickets printed. These tickets, as well as bearing the new name of the show and revised price of admission, now carried upon the reverse the following cryptic instruction:

> Any adult person desiring to speak with the proprietor of the *Tomb of the Great Old Ones* on matters of genuine occult phenomena or similar manifestations, or on subjects relating to the Great Old Ones, R'lyeh, or the Cthulhu Cycle of Myth, is welcome to request a private meeting.
>
> Anderson Tharpe: Prop.

The other members of the fairground fraternity were not aware of this offer of Anderson's—nor of his authority, real or assumed, in such subjects to be able to make such an offer—until after the funfair moved into its next location, and by that time they too had discovered his advance advertising in the local press. Of course, Bella Hodgson had always looked after advance publicity in the past, but she could hardly be offended by Anderson's personal efforts toward this end. Any good publicity he devised and paid for himself could only go towards attracting better crowds to the benefit of the funfair in general.

And within a very short time Anderson's plan started to bear fruit, when at last his desire for a higher percentage of rather more erudite persons among his show's clientele began to be realized. His sole purpose, of course, had been to attract just such persons in the hope that perhaps one of them might provide the baffling pronunciation he required, an *acoustical* translation of the key to call up the terrible green glow.

Such authorities must surely exist; his own brother had become one in a comparatively short time, and others had spent whole lifetimes in the concentrated study of these secrets of elder lore. Surely, sooner or later, he would find a man to provide the answer, and then the secrets of the perfect murder weapon would be his. When this happened, then Anderson would test his weapon on the poor unfortunate who handed him the key, and in this way he would be sure that the secret was his alone. From then on ... oh, there were many possibilities ...

Through early and mid-April Anderson received a number of inquisitive callers at his caravan: some of them cranks, but at least a handful of genuinely interested and knowledgeable types. Always he pumped them for what they knew of the elder mysteries in connection with the Cthulhu Cycle, especially their knowledge in ancient tongues and obscure languages, and twice over he was frustrated just when he thought himself on the right track. On one occasion, after seeing the tablets and idol, an impressed visitor presented him with a copy of Walmsley's *Notes on Deciphering Codes, Cryptograms, and Ancient Inscriptions*; but to no avail, the work itself was too deep for him.

Then, towards the end of April, in response to Anderson's continuous probing, a visitor to his establishment grudgingly gave him the address of a so-called 'occult investigator', one Titus Crow, who just might be interested in his problem. Before he left the fairground this same gentleman, the weird artist Chandler Davies, strongly advised Tharpe that the whole thing were best forgotten, that no good could ever come of dabbling in such matters—be it serious study or merely idle curiosity—and with that warning he had taken his leave.

Ignoring the artist's positive dread of his line of research, that same afternoon Anderson wrote to Titus Crow at his London address, enclosing with his letter a copy of the symbols and a request for information concerning them; possibly a translation or, even better, a workable pronunciation. Impatiently then, he watched the

post for an answer, and early in May was disappointed to receive a
brief note from Crow advising him, as had Davies, to give up his
interest in these matters and let such dangerous subjects alone.
There was no explanation, no invitation regarding further corre-
spondence; Crow had not even bothered to return the cryptic
paragraph so painstakingly copied from the *Necronomicon.*

That night, as if to substantiate the double warning, Anderson
once more dreamed of sunken R'lyeh, and again he kneeled before
slumbering Cthulhu's throne to hear the alien voice echoing
awesomely in his mind. The horror on the throne seemed more
mobile in its sleep than ever before, and the voice in the dream was
more insistent, more menacing:

*'You have been warned, AND YET YOU MEDDLE! While the Great
Rising draws ever closer and Cthulhu's shadow looms, still you choose to
search out His secrets for your own use! This night there will be a sign;
ignore it at your peril, lest Cthulhu bestir Himself up to visit you personally
in dreams, as He has aforetime visited others!'*

The following morning Anderson rose haggard and pale to learn
of yet more trouble with the fairground's dogs, duplicating in detail
that Candlemas frenzy of three months earlier. The coincidence was
such as to cause him more than a moment's concern, and especially
after reading the morning's newspapers.

What was it that the voice in his dream had said of 'a sign?'—a
warning which he should only ignore at his peril? Well, there had
been a sign, many of them, for the night had been filled with a
veritable plethora of weird and inexplicable occurrences—strange
stirrings among the more dangerous inmates of lunatic asylums all
over the country, macabre suicides by previously normal people—a
magma of madness climaxed, so far as Anderson Tharpe was concerned, by second-page headlines in two of the national newspapers
to the effect that Chandler Davies had been 'put away' in Wood-
holme Sanatorium. The columns went on to tell how Davies had
painted a monstrous *G'harne Landscape*, which his outraged and
terrified mistress had at once set fire to, thus bringing about in him
an insane rage from which he had not recovered. More: a few days
later came the news via the same papers that Davies was dead!

If Anderson Tharpe had been in any way a sensitive person, and
his evil ambition less of an obsession—had his *perceptions* not been
dulled by a lifetime of living close to the anomalies of the erstwhile
freak-house—then perhaps he might have recognized the presence
of a horror such as few men have ever known. Unlike his brother,

however, Anderson was coarse-grained and not especially imaginative. All the portents and evidences, the hints and symptoms, and accumulating warnings were cast aside within a few short days of his nightmare and its accompanying manifestations, when yet again he turned to his studies in the hope that soon the secret of the green light would be his.

From then on the months passed slowly, while the crowds at the Tomb of the Great Old Ones became smaller still despite all Anderson's efforts to the contrary. His frustration grew in direct proportion to his dwindling assets, and while his continued advance advertising and the invitation on the reverse of his admission tickets still drew the occasional crank occultist or curious devotee of the macabre to his caravan, not one of them was able to further his knowledge of the Cthulhu Cycle or satisfy his growing obsession with regard to that enigmatic and cryptical 'key' from the hand-written *Necronomicon*.

Twice as the seasons waxed and waned he approached old Hans about further translations from the ancient book, even offering to pay for the old German's services in this respect, but Hans simply was not interested. He was too old to become a *Dolmetscher,* he said, and his eyes were giving him trouble; he already had enough money for his simple needs, and anyway, he did not like the *look* of the book. What the old man did not say was that he had seen things in those yellowed pages, on that one occasion when already he had looked into the rotting volume, which simply did not bear translation! And so again Anderson's plans met with frustration.

In mid-October the now thoroughly disgruntled and morose proprietor of the Tomb of the Great Old Ones looked to a different approach. Patently, no matter how hard he personally studied Hamilton's books, he was not himself qualified to puzzle out and piece together the required information. There were those, however, who had spent a lifetime in such studies, and if he could not attract such as these to the fairground—why, then he must simply send the problem to them. True, he had tried this before, with Titus Crow; but now, as opposed to cultists, occultists, and the like, he would approach only recognized authorities. He spent the following day or two tracking down the address of Professor Gordon Walmsley of Goole, a world-renowned expert in the science of ciphers, whose book, *Notes on Deciphering Codes, Cryptograms, and Ancient Inscriptions*, had now been in his possession for almost seven months. That book was still far too deep and complicated for Anderson's fathoming, but the author of such a work should certainly find little difficulty with the piece from the *Necronomicon*.

He quickly composed a letter to the professor, and as October grew into its third week he posted it off. He was not to know it, but at that time Walmsley was engaged in the services of the Buenos Aires Museum of Antiquities, busily translating the hieroglyphs on certain freshly discovered ruins in the mountains of the Aconcaguan Range near San Juan. Anderson's letter did eventually reach him, posted on from Walmsley's Yorkshire address, but the professor was so interested in his own work that he gave it only a cursory glance. Later he found that he had misplaced it, and thus, fortunately, the scrap of paper with its deadly invocation passed into obscurity and became lost forever.

Anderson meanwhile impatiently waited for a reply, and along with the folk of the fairground prepared for the Halloween opening at Bathley, a town on the northeast border. It was then, on the night of the twenty-seventh of the month, that he received his third and final warning. The day had been chill and damp, with a bitter wind blowing off the North Sea, bringing a dankly salt taste and smell that conjured up horrible memories for the surviving Tharpe brother.

On the morning of the twenty-eighth, rising up gratefully from a sweat-soaked bed and a nightmare the like of which he had never known before and fervently prayed never to know again, Anderson Tharpe blamed the horrors of the night on yesterday's sea wind with its salty smells of ocean; but even explained away like this the dream had been a monstrous thing.

Again he had visited sunken R'lyeh—but this time there had been a vivid *reality* to the nightmare lacking in previous dreams. He had known the terrible, bone-crushing pressures of that drowned realm, had felt the frozen chill of its black waters. He had tried to scream as the pressure forced his eyes from their sockets, and then the sea had rushed into his mouth, tearing his throat and lungs and stomach as it filled him in one smashing column as solid as steel. And though the horror had lasted only a second, still he had known that there in the ponderous depths his *disintegration* had taken place before the throne of the Lord of R'lyeh, the Great Old One who seeped down from the stars at the dawn of time. He had been a sacrifice to Cthulhu ...

\*   \*   \*

That had been four days ago, but still Tharpe shuddered when he thought of it. He put it out of his mind now as he ushered the crowd out of the tent and turned to face the sole remaining member of that departing audience. Tharpe's oratory had been automatic; during its delivery he had allowed his mind to run free in its exploration of all that had passed since his brother's hideous death, but now he came back to earth. Hiram Henley stared back at him in what he took to be scornful disappointment. The ex-professor spoke:

'"The Tomb of the Great Old Ones", indeed! Sir, you're a charlatan!' he said. 'I could find more fearsome things in *Grimms' Fairy Tales*, more items of genuine antiquarian interest in my aunt's attic. I had hoped your—*show*—might prove interesting. It seems I was mistaken.' His eyes glinted sarcastically behind his tiny spectacles.

For a moment Tharpe's heart beat a little faster, then he steadied himself. Perhaps this time ...? Certainly the little man was worth a try. 'You do me an injustice, sir—you wound me!' He waxed theatrical, an ability with which he was fluent through his years of showmanship. 'Do you really believe that I would openly *display* the archaeological treasures for which this establishment was named?—I should put them out for the common herd to ogle, when not one in ten thousand could even recognize them, let alone appreciate them? Wait!'

He ducked through the canvas doorflap into the enclosed area containing Hamilton's relics, returning a few seconds later with a bronze miniature the size of his hand and wrist. The thing looked vaguely like an elongated, eyeless squid. It also looked—despite the absence of anything even remotely mundane in its appearance—utterly evil! Anderson handed the object reverently to the ex-professor, saying: 'What do you make of that?' Having chosen the thing at random from the anomalies in his dead brother's collection, he hoped it really was of 'genuine antiquarian interest.'

His choice had been a wise one. Henley peered at the miniature, and slowly his expression changed. He examined the thing minutely, then said, 'It is the burrower beneath, Shudde-M'ell, or one of his brood. A very good likeness, and ancient beyond words. Made of bronze, yet quite obviously it predates the Bronze Age!' His voice was suddenly soft. 'Where did you get it?'

'You *are* interested, then?' Tharpe smiled, incapable of either admitting or denying the statements of the other.

'Of course I'm interested.' Henley eagerly nodded, a bit too eagerly, Tharpe thought. 'I ... I did indeed do you a great injustice. This thing is *very* interesting! Do you have ... more?'

'All in good time.' Tharpe held up his hands, holding himself in check, waiting until the time was ripe to frame his own all-important question. 'First, who are you? You understand that my—*possessions*—are not for idle scrutiny, that—'

'Yes, yes, I understand,' the little man cut him off. 'My name is Hiram Henley. I am—at least I was—Professor of Archaeology and Ethnology at Meldham University. I have recently given up my position there in order to carry out private research. I came here out of curiosity, I admit; a friend gave me one of your tickets with its peculiar invitation. I wasn't really expecting much, but—'

'But now you've seen something that you would never have believed possible in a place like this. Is that it?'

'Indeed it is. And you? Who are you?'

'Tharpe is my name, Anderson Tharpe, proprietor of this'—he waved his hand deprecatingly—'establishment.'

'Very well, Mr. Tharpe,' Henley said. 'It's my own good fortune to meet a man whose intelligence in my own chosen field patently must match my own—whose possessions include items such as this.' He held up the heavy bronze piece and peered at it again for a moment. 'Now, will you show me—the rest?'

'A glimpse, only a glimpse,' Tharpe told him, aware now that Henley was hooked. 'Then perhaps we can trade?'

'I have nothing with which to trade. In what way do you mean?'

'Nothing to trade? Perhaps not,' Tharpe answered, holding the canvas door open so that his visitor might step into the enclosed space beyond, 'but then again ... how are you on ancient tongues and languages?'

'Languages were always my—' The ex-professor started to answer, stepping into the private place. Then he paused, his eyes widening as he gazed about at the contents of the place. 'Were always my—' Again he paused, reaching out his hands before him and moving forward, touching the ugly idol unbelievingly, moving quickly to the carved tablets, staring as if hypnotized at the smaller figurines and totems. Finally he turned a flushed face to Tharpe. His look was hard to define; partly awed, partly—accusing?

'I didn't steal them, I assure you,' Tharpe quickly said.

'No, of course not,' Henley answered, 'but ... you have the treasures of the aeons here!'

Now the tall showman could hold himself no longer. 'Languages,' he pressed. 'You say you have an understanding of tongues? Can you translate from the ancient to the modern?'

'Yes, most things, providing—'

'How would you like to *own* all you see here?' Tharpe cut him off again.

Henley reached out suddenly palsied hands to take Tharpe by the forearms. 'You're ... joking?'

'No.' Tharpe shook his head, lying convincingly. 'I'm not joking. There is something of the utmost importance to my own line of—research. I need a translation of a fragment of ancient writing. Rather, I need the *original* pronunciation. If you can solve this one problem for me, all this can be yours. You can be ... part of it.'

'What is this fragment?' the little man cried. '*Where* is it?'

'Come with me.'

'But—' Henley turned away from Tharpe, his gloved hands again reaching for those morbid items out of the aeons.

'No, no.' Tharpe took his arm. 'Later—you'll have all the time you need. Now there is this problem of mine. But later, tonight, we'll come back in here, and all this can be yours ...'

The ex-professor voluntarily followed Tharpe out of the tent to his caravan, and there he was shown the handwritten *Necronomicon* with its cryptic 'key.'

'Well,' Tharpe demanded, barely concealing his agitation, 'can you read it as it was written? Can you *pronounce* it in its original form?'

'I'll need a little time,' the balding man mused, 'and privacy; but I think ... I'll take a copy of this with me, and as soon as I have the answer—'

'When? How long?'

'Tonight.'

'Good. I'll wait for you. It should be quiet here by then. It's Halloween and the fairground is open until late, but they'll all be that much more tired ...' Tharpe suddenly realized that he was thinking out loud and quickly glanced at his visitor. The little man peered at him strangely through his tiny specs; *very* strangely, Tharpe thought.

'The people here are—superstitious,' he explained. 'It wouldn't be wise to advertise our interest in these ancient matters. They're ignorant and I've had trouble with them before. They don't like some of the things I've got.'

'I understand,' Henley answered. 'I'll go now and work through the evening. With luck it won't take too long. Tonight—shall we say after midnight?—I'll be back.' He quickly made a copy of the characters in the old book, then stood up. Tharpe saw him out of the caravan with an assumed, gravely thoughtful air, thanking him before watching him walk off in the direction of the exit; but then he laughed out loud and slapped his thigh, quickly seeking out one of the odd-job boys from the stratojet thrill ride.

An hour later—to the amazement of his fellow showmen, for the crowd was thickening rapidly as the afternoon went by—Anderson Tharpe closed the Tomb of the Great Old Ones and retired to his caravan. He wanted to practice himself in the operation of the tape recorder which he had paid the odd-jobber to buy for him in Bathley.

This final phase of his plan was simple; necessarily so, for of course he in no way intended to honour his bargain with Henley. He *did* intend to have the little man read out his pronunciation of the 'key', and to record that pronunciation in perfect fidelity—but from then on ...

If the pronunciation were imperfect, then of course the 'bargain' would be unfulfilled and the ex-professor would escape with his life and nothing more; but if the invocation worked ...? Why, then the professor simply could not be allowed to walk away and talk about what he had seen. No, it would be necessary for him to disappear into the green light. Hamilton would have called it a 'sacrifice to Cthulhu.'

And yet there had been something about the little man that disturbed Anderson; something about his peering eyes, and his eagerness to fall in with the plans of the gaunt showman. Tharpe thought of his dream of a few days past, then of those other nightmares he had known, and shuddered; and again he pondered the possibility that there had been more than met the eye in his mad brother's assertions. But what odds? Science or sorcery, it made no difference, the end result would be the same. He rubbed his hands in anticipation. Things were at last looking up for Anderson Tharpe ...

At midnight the crowd began to thin out. Watching the people move off into the chill night, Anderson was glad it had started to rain again, for their festive Halloween mood might have kept them in the fairground longer, and the bright lights would have glared and the music played late into the night. Only an hour later all was quiet, with only the sporadic patter of rain on machines and tents

and painted roofs to disturb the night. The last wetly gleaming
light had blinked out and the weary folk of the fairground were in
their beds. That was when Anderson heard the furtive rapping at his
caravan door, and he was agreeably surprised that the ever-watchful
dogs had not heralded his night-visitor's arrival. Possibly it was too
early for them yet to distinguish between comers and goers.

As soon as he was inside Henley saw the question written on
Tharpe's face. He nodded in answer: 'Yes, yes, I have it. It appears
to be a summons of some sort, a cry to vast and immeasurably
ancient powers. Wait, I'll read it for you—'

'No, no—not here!' Tharpe silenced him before he could com-
mence. 'I have a tape recorder in the tent.'

Without a word the little man followed Tharpe through the dark
and into the private enclosure containing those centuried relics which
so plainly fascinated him. There Tharpe illumined the inner tent
with a single dim light bulb; then, switching on his tape recorder,
he told the ex-professor that he was now ready to hear the invocation.
And yet now Henley paused, turning to face Tharpe and gravely
peering at him from where he stood by the horrible octopoid idol.

'Are you—sure?' the little man asked. 'Are you sure you want me
to do this?' His voice was dry, calm.

'Eh?' Anderson questioned nervously, terrible suspicions suddenly forming in his mind. 'Of course I'm sure—and what do you
mean, "do this?" Do what?'

Henley shook his head sadly. 'Your brother was foolish not to see
that you would cause trouble sooner or later!'

Tharpe's eyes opened wide and his jaw fell slack. 'Police!' he
finally croaked. 'You're from the police!'

'No such thing,' the little man calmly answered. 'I am what I told
you I was—and something more than that—and to prove it ...'

The sounds Henley uttered then formed an exact and fluent
duplication of those Tharpe had heard once before, and shocked as
he was that this frail outsider knew far too much about his affairs,
still Tharpe thrilled as the inhuman echoes died and there formed
in the semicircle of grim tablets an expanding, glowing greenness
that sent out writhing beams of ghostly luminescence. Quickly the
tall man gathered his wits. Policeman or none, Hiram Henley had
to be done away with. This had been the plan in any case, once the
little man—whoever he was—had done his work and was no longer
required. And he had done his work well. The invocation was
recorded; Anderson could call up the destroying green light any

time he so desired. Perhaps Henley had been a former colleague of Hamilton's, and somehow he had come to learn of the younger Tharpe's demise? Or was he only guessing! Still, it made no difference now.

Henley had turned his back on Anderson, lifting up his arms to the hideous idol greenly illumined in the light of the pulsating witchfire. But as the showman slipped his brother's knife from his pocket, so the little man turned again to face him, smiling strangely and showing no discernible fear at the sight of the knife. Then his smile faded and again he sadly shook his head. His lips formed the words, 'No, no, my friend,' but Anderson Tharpe heard nothing; once more, as it had done before, the green light had cancelled all sound within its radius.

Suddenly Tharpe was very much afraid, but still he knew what he must do. Despite the fact that the inner tent was far more chill even than the time of the year warranted, sweat glistened greenly on Anderson's brow as he moved forward in a threatening crouch, the knife raised and reflecting emerald shafts of evilly writhing light. He lifted the knife higher still as he closed with the motionless figure of the little man—*and then Hiram Henley moved!*

Anderson saw what the ex-professor had done and his lips drew back in a silent, involuntary animal snarl of the utmost horror and fear. He almost dropped the knife, frozen now in midstroke, as Henley's black gloves fell to the floor and the thick white worms twined and twisted hypnotically where his fingers ought to have been!

Then—more out of nightmare dread and loathing than any sort of rational purpose, for Anderson knew now that the ex-professor was nothing less than a Priest of Cthulhu—he carried on with his interrupted stroke and his knife flashed down. Henley tried to deflect the blow with a monstrously altered hand, his face contorting and a shriek forming silently on his lips as one of the wormish appendages was severed and fell twitching to the sawdust. He flailed his injured hand and white ichor splashed Tharpe's face and eyes.

Blindly the frantic showman struck again and again, gibbering mindlessly and noiselessly as he clawed at his face with his free hand, trying to wipe away the filthy white juice of Henley's injured hybrid member. But the blows were wild and Hiram Henley had stepped to one side.

More frantically yet, insanely, Tharpe slashed at the greenly pulsating air all about him, stumbling closer to the core of the radiance. Then his knife struck something that gave like rotting flesh beneath the blow, and finally, in a short-lived revival of confidence, he opened stinging eyes to see what he had hit.

Something coiled out of the green core, something long and tapering, greyly mottled and slimy! It was a tentacle—a *face*-tentacle, Tharpe knew—twitching spasmodically, even as the hand of a disturbed dreamer might twitch.

Tharpe struck again, a reflex action, and watched his blade bite through the tentacle unhindered, as if through mud—*and then saw that trembling member solidifying again where the blade had sliced!* His knife fell from palsied hands then, and Tharpe screamed a last, desperate, silent scream as the tentacle moved more purposefully!

The now completely sentient member wrapped its tip about Tharpe's throat, constricting and jerking him forwards effortlessly into the green core. And as he went the last things he saw were the eyes in the vast face; the hellish eyes that opened briefly, saw and recognized him for what he was—a sacrifice to Cthulhu!

Quickly then, as the green light began its withdrawal and sound slowly returned to the tent, Hiram Henley put on his gloves. Ignoring as best he could the pain his injury gave him, he spoke these words:

> Oh, Great Cthulhu, dreaming in R'lyeh,
> Thy priest offers up this sacrifice,
> That Thy coming be soon,
> And that of Thy kindred dreamers.
> I am Thy priest and adore Thee ...

And as the core grew smaller yet, he toppled the evil idol into its green center, following this act by throwing in the tablets and all those other items of fabled antiquity until the inner tent was quite empty. He would have kept all these things if he dared, but his orders—those orders he received in dreams from R'lyeh—would not allow it. When a priest had been found to replace Hamilton Tharpe, then Great Cthulhu would find a way to return those rudimentary pillars of His temple!

Finally, Henley switched off the single dim light and watched the green core as it shrank to a tiny point of intense brightness before winking out. Only the smell of deep ocean remained, and a damp circle in the dark where the sawdust floor was queerly marked and slimy ....

Some little time later the folk of the fairground were awakened by the clamour of a fire engine as it sped to the blaze on the border of the circling tents, sideshows and caravans. Both Tharpe's caravan and The Tomb of the Great Old Ones were burning fiercely.

Nothing was saved, and in their frantic toiling to help the firemen the nomads of the funfair failed to note that their dogs again crouched timid and whimpering beneath the nighted caravans. They found it strange later, though, when they heard how the police had failed to discover anything of Anderson Tharpe's remains.

The gap that the destruction of the one-time freak-house had left was soon filled, for 'Madame Zala', as if summoned back by the grim work of the mysterious fire, returned with her horse and caravan within the week. She is still with Hodgson's Funfair, but known to anyone with even the remotest schooling in the occult, she is sometimes seen crossing herself with an obscure and pagan sign ...

# The Silence of Erika Zann

## by James Wade

I still stroll over to Ashford Street sometimes and look at the vacant lot where The Purple Blob used to stand. In its heyday it had been one of the earliest and best of the psychedelic light-show clubs, and even had a mention once in *Time* magazine. But the rock-music scene changes fast, and the San Francisco skyline even faster. Last time I was over there, I was startled to see that the foundations of a new building have been started on that lot. It seemed to me that those power scoops were burying some part of my life for good—a part that was still alive and screaming wordlessly down there.

Everybody but me seems to have forgotten The Purple Blob ever existed. But I'll never forget the old place, with its glaring ricocheting lights and its mind-blowing music—for it was there that I experienced the most tragic and bewildering event of my life, the silence of Erika Zann.

I'm not really into rock music and the hallucinogenic kick all that much, and I never was. I grooved on some of the zany, far-out groups, and there for a while I swallowed or smoked about anything anybody handed me—and that's quite a variety, in San Francisco— just to see what it was like. But I'm enough over thirty, and sort of an instinctive Mr. Straight when you come right down to it, that I didn't try to keep up with the kids who were real swingers. I didn't even feel comfortable with the new lingo. "Groovy" and "right on" had quotation marks around them in my mouth, and I think I'll stop using that jargon here for easy atmosphere. (If I'm going to write this right, I'll have to dig, that's for sure, but not in the current slang sense of the word.)

What I actually used to do, after tending to my boring nine-to-five job, was sit around as a bemused spectator of all those new sights

and sounds the Bay Area was turning on to in those days—just a
few years back, actually, though now it seems ages ago. The kids
needed an audience more than they needed more freaks and exhibi-
tionists. As a relative newcomer from the Midwestern hinterlands,
I suppose I was lonely enough that a mostly passive part seemed to
me better than no role at all in the big excitement.

That was how I started going to the Purple Blob, and how I met
the lead vocalist of their star rock band, which was called, with the
usual elephantine whimsy, The Electric Commode.

I had heard of Erika Zann before I met her. She'd made a few
obscure records, farther-out stuff than the early material she used
with the Commode. There was one disk devoted entirely to a
Satanist mass, I remember, and Erika was involved in that, along with
a really astonishing range of sound effects, plus human ululations
of ecstasy, fright, and less identifiable feelings. (Later she told me
she'd broken with the black-magic bunch, but she didn't say just
why, though I think she hinted that money trouble was involved.)

Since Satanism was never my bag, that didn't especially impress
me; but just to have any recording artist in a place like The Blob
in those early days was a sort of status symbol, so Erika got star
billing, even though she didn't start out winning any popularity
polls. In fact, for that kind of spot, her performance at first seemed
remarkably subdued and downbeat, though it didn't stay that way
for long.

I remember ambling in one evening, nodding to the club manager, Pete Muzio, and picking up a beer at the bar. The place had
been a tavern before, and still kept its liquor license, though the
hippies from the Hashbury were already bringing their own kicks
with them in their pill boxes and grass bags.

A lot of those oddly dressed types in beards were sitting around
at tables, more or less stoned—you don't need me to describe the
counterculture specimens at this late date—while a guitarist and
bongo player up on stage noodled imitation ragas picked up secondhand on Beatles records. Not much was happening, except
maybe inside the skulls of those already launched into acid orbit.

Manager Muzio sidled over to me at the bar. If I'd been him
and had all those broken teeth, I wouldn't have grinned so wide all
the time.

"Got a new group on deck since I saw you here last," he muttered.
For the manager of a high-decibel joint, he certainly talked soft,
which was often a strain on communication.

"Who are they?" I asked, to be polite. Pete Muzio was the one fixture I didn't especially fancy about The Purple Blob.

"Name's The Electric Commode. Nothing special up to now, but they've got a new vocalist who's cut a few grooves. Haven't had time yet to get her posters up, but the name's Zann, Erika Zann. German chick, I understand."

After a while the group came on and Erika sang a few loud but forgettable numbers. The acid-rock arrangements were in that year, and if you'd kept up to date you could tell just where The Electric Commode was snitching its charts. The Blob was between lighting specialists just then, and Pete ran the strobes himself, which didn't add much to the total effect.

After the set, he brought Erika over to the bar and mumbled an introduction. Since I had a straight job and money to spend, unlike many of his regulars, Pete tried to be nice to me.

I bought her a beer and handed her a few formal compliments. She shot back, "We're doing pretty tame stuff now, but Tommy— that's our lead guitar—just hired a new arranger. He's working up some fantastic new things—really far out, with a lot more electronic effects. Wait'll you hear 'em."

I sized up Erika Zann. Standard sequined gown, nice figure but too thin. A wide forehead accentuated by a bushy flare of ash-blond hairdo. Big, deep purple eyes, her only claim to beauty; she admitted the color came from contacts. Tiny pointed chin beneath a mouth that seemed too small for the voice that came out of it. Definitely nervous, maybe a twitch, like many performers on the scene.

To make conversation, I remarked, "Pete says you're German."

She laughed mechanically. "Not really. I was born in Europe right after the war. My folks were refugees and got to the States a few years later. I don't even remember."

"Musicians?"

"My dad's dead now, but he was a violinist. So was my grandfather, but he's been gone a long time. Funny thing."

"What is?"

"Grandpa Erich Zann left his family in the 1920's and settled in Paris. He played in a pit band, though Dad said he used to be good. He was a mute—not deaf, of course, but he couldn't utter a sound. Here I'm named after a dummy, and I make my living yelling my head off."

What else we talked about wasn't memorable, and I certainly didn't fall for that wiry, uptight blond at first sight.

In fact, I didn't come back to The Blob for a week or two after that, and when I did it was simply out of curiosity about the new sounds I'd heard were erupting over there.

Things were different, all right. Pete was packing them in, and his craggy smile was wider than ever as he surveyed the crazy-quilt crowd surging under dim overheads, and counted the take from the gate charge he'd slapped on as soon as he thought he could get away with it. Erika's posters were all over the place. When you walked in the reek of marijuana made your eyes smart; the tangled, ropy coils of smoke were thick enough to dim the lights even more. Pete Muzio must have used part of his profits to pay off the neighborhood fuzz, since the place was never busted that I know of.

He'd used part of the take, too, in hiring a good light man, and replacing the guitar duo with a Hammond organ virtuoso. Just now they were doing things to a Bach fugue with jazz percussion added that Disney and Stokowski never dreamed of.

If you thought that was wild, all you had to do was wait for the main event. The Electric Commode had certainly snagged a new arranger, though no one ever found out his name. (Once, when he was especially high, the lanky lead guitarist everyone called just Tommy was heard to claim that their cleffer was "a black man—not a Negro, just a black man." I wondered what he meant by that.)

The first thing about their new sound, it was loud, so loud that if you'd already blown your mind, this music might blast it back in again. Second, it was electric. There were half a dozen new instruments to back up the guitars and sax and trumpet and drums that no one had ever seen, or heard, anything like before, except maybe in Dr. Frankenstein's lab on the Late Show.

Third, there was Erika. Whether she'd always had it in her or the new gimmicks added something, wailing was no word for it. At the climaxes of those long sets, which left her drained and shaking, she'd take off into wordless stratospheric flights that reminded you of Yma Sumac, the freak Peruvian soprano of a while back.

The total effect, while not exactly rock—or not entirely rock—was, in any event, searing. Some of the regular customers had convulsions, literally, but since they kept coming back, I guess that's what they were there for.

Every once in a while would come what seemed to be an offstage stereo effect, a sort of wide-range, omnidirectional growl that built and built, like someone was sprawled full length along the keyboard of a great cathedral organ. Nobody could guess what it was, and only one thing was sure: The sound didn't come from that hyped-up little Hammond on stage. At those times the colored lights in the room would start to skitter and skim like reflections from the heart of hell, and Erika outdid herself to rise above the racket. I could almost swear the look of mingled fear and exultation on her face wasn't a put-on.

The audience ate it up, and The Blob became an "in" spot, naturally attracting reporters, tourists, and slummers, in that order. Pete Muzio bought out the espresso coffee shop next door and knocked down the intervening wall to get more floor space.

I was hooked too, and kept coming back week after week, even though I realized at last that it wasn't the music which attracted me—that began to seem vaguely disquieting, if not odious—but Erika herself.

I'd gotten to know her a bit better by the simple expedient of buying the band drinks between sets, or passing around the grass. She was a strange, evasive kid, but I felt more and more certain she was at times scared blue, and so I suppose my feeling for her was deepened by a sort of pity or protective instinct.

One night we were drinking alone at a side table and she finally started to level with me. I'd made some sort of inane remark about how she seemed nervous, which was simply my way of trying to break down her standoffishness—she always seemed nervous, actually, no more so one time than another.

"Nervous? I suppose I am." She took a drag on her cigarette, an ordinary one this time. "It goes with the business. Only, I used to be able to unwind with some grass, or a few fingers of gin. Now nothing seems to help."

"What's the trouble?"

"Oh, lots of little things." She drew in a deep breath and let it out slowly. "That creepy manager isn't leveling with us on our slice of the bread. And the drummer's putting the make on me, or on Tommy, or maybe on both of us ... who knows?

"Tommy's changed, too. He won't tell the rest of us where he's getting the arrangements or those crazy instruments. Did you know that the new side men and the light man don't even talk about the jobs they've played before?"

"Does that scare you?"

"Maybe it should. I was in pretty deep with the devil-worships gang I told you about. That wasn't all they were up to, either. Some of them have it in for me but good, and I thought I recognized the new man on vibes as one of that bunch, but he won't talk, just like the rest, and I can't be sure. The vibes man is pretty thick with Pete Muzio, and they seem to have a lot of private business together. But the worst thing is the music."

"The music?" I exclaimed. "That's what made you a star."

"I know, but it still scares me. When I'm on stage I can't tell where half the sound is coming from. It's not from those crazy boxes with grids and neon tubes on them; they're mostly dummies, or just far-out decorations on ordinary electronic instruments. That roaring, moaning noise from offstage is what really gets me. I swear to God I've searched every square inch back there—there's not that much space. Unless somebody took the trouble to build a set of speakers into a solid brick wall, and conceal the outlet some way, there's just no source for such sounds. And why should anyone do that? It doesn't even make sense as a publicity stunt, since Tommy won't let anybody even talk about it."

I thought of what one hi-fi nut in the audience told me: He'd tried to tape the show with a hidden transistor set, but could never pick up the offstage sounds.

Erika finished off a martini on the rocks that was mostly water by now, and went on, "I'll tell you something I've never told anyone before. After Dad died I found a box of letters from his father, Erich Zann, addressed to my grandmother and dated Paris, mostly 1924 and 1925. I can read a little German because we used to speak it around the house.

"The letters tell about experiences the old man had playing his violin all alone at night in an old loft where he lived. He seems to be hinting that something was after him, and only the sound of his playing kept it away.

"There's one letter that mentions the guilt he felt about 'prying into things better left alone.' It doesn't sound so corny in German. And one paragraph that I translated with a dictionary talks about him looking out the window at midnight and seeing 'shadowy satyrs and bacchanals dancing and whirling insanely through seething abysses of clouds and smoke and lightning.'

"Crazy, huh? He must have been really strung out. But I found another letter in the box, a report from the Paris police saying that Erich Zann had disappeared and could not be located. It must have been an answer to a missing-persons inquiry Grandma Zann sent from Stuttgart."

Pete Muzio materialized behind her through clouds of pot smoke, like some stage devil making his big entrance. "All set, Erika? Time for the last set." His wolfish grin seemed mocking, though I don't see how he could have heard anything.

As I sat waiting for the music to start, it occurred to me that although it was hard to tell at this remove whether old Erich Zann had been crazy or not, the parallels hinted at by his freaky grand-daughter were wild enough to get her committed, if she talked to many people this way. But at the same time I could see how these apparent parallels might push someone, who was nervy and uptight to begin with, all the way over the edge.

I started trying to figure out ways for Erika to get away from The Purple Blob, maybe on the excuse of a vacation, and then later for good. But it was a dilemma: Here was where the group's success was building, and Pete Muzio, bless his pointed fangs, had them trapped in an airtight contract. For some reason the leader, Tommy, refused to cut records or say why not, though he'd turned down offers that could have led to the real big time.

Tommy, with his Jesus hairdo and half-blind, inward-peering eyes, seemed to be stoned all the time now, and if he was too far around the bend to look after his own best interests, how could anyone expect him to worry about Erika's?

Things went on but didn't get any better. Erika seemed thinner and tenser all the time, and the sets the combo played behind her got wilder and wilder, as she wailed and coloraturaed above the slam-ming beat and the ugly toneless roaring that seemed to press in on the stage from everywhere and nowhere.

The novelty was wearing off, and business—though fairly good—was largely down to the hard-core fans, or addicts, for whom an evening with Erika's symbolic struggle on the stage seemed the equivalent of some sort of emotionally cathartic trip. The reporters and the record company A&R scouts had drifted away, looking for other kinky groups that would cooperate in being exploited.

On that final evening, though, there was a standing-room crowd, because it was Friday (not the thirteenth, but a Black Friday nevertheless). I had drifted in rather late, and glimpsed Erika down front just before the last set was due to start. As I shoved my way through the crowd and approached her, I was shocked at the ravaged look on her face, and the unfocused glare of those purple eyes above a tight pucker of mouth.

I thought for a moment that she must have flipped, but she seemed to recognize me, and while the organist was winding up his polytonal calypso, I took her arm and led her off to the side.

"Erika, you look sick," I blurted, too disturbed to be polite. "Beg off and let's get out of here. You must have saved enough to buy out of your contract, with Tommy or Pete or both. You shouldn't be doing this; it's killing you by inches. I'll help—you know I like you," I added, the only declaration of my feelings toward her I ever made.

She twitched me a grateful smile, the only response to them she ever made, but her voice was a hoarse croak: the fumes of gin rode with it. "I'm afraid, not sick. It's getting louder and louder, and I can't sing over it. It's coming after me, nearer all the time. I think I know what it wants, and I'm afraid!"

"Then come away!"

"After tonight, maybe. My voice is giving out, that's no lie, but I've got to do it right, get a doctor's opinion. That way no trouble, not like last time ..."

The organist wound up with a splatter of scales trapped inside pinwheeling discords, as the strobes flared with machine-gun rapidity, turning the world into stop-motion photographs. Erika pulled away from me and walked stiffly, jerkily to the stage, a parody of some surreal silent-movie sequence.

The curtain went up on The Electric Commode, and the lights all over the room exploded in mad random patterns, like a night bombing raid in World War II. The brain-blasting strangle-scream of the combo cut in, a shriek of nerve-frazzling terror, and I knew the set would be no ordinary one, even for this group.

Erika was off and running with an up-tempo scat-vocal skimming lightly over spiky chords that sounded like Kenton's borrowings from Stravinsky in the forties. Almost immediately the deep, almost subaural roar pressed in from outside, louder than I had ever heard it before—soulless, ravening, implacable.

A hippie with fright-wig hair, the acid glow bright in his eyes, was standing beside me shouting something unintelligible. I leaned toward him and caught a few fragmentary phrases: "Blackness ... blackness of space illimitable! ... Unimagined space alive with motion and music ... no semblance of anything on Earth ..."

Erika was struggling to ride the tide, to crest the waves of sound. Faster and faster, higher and higher her voice mounted, but the

surge of noise swept past her, curled into breakers ahead of her, piled
in swift suspended combers on either side of her. The lights dimmed
to a kind of crepitating underwater green, lanced by livid streaks
of scarlet, magenta, and violet.

No one could stand such strain, I knew. I pushed my way back
to the bar where Pete Muzio skulked in a dark corner with his
knife-like smile. Grabbing his shoulder, I pressed my face close to
his and shouted amid the din: "Shut off that noise! That hyped-up
speaker set or whatever you've stashed back there—you must have
an amp control up front here somewhere. Shut it off! It'll kill her!"

Pete wasn't smiling now; he was sweating and scared, and for
once in his life, he was yelling to be heard.

"There's no tape, no speakers. I swear to God I don't know what
it is! I thought at first the band was doing it, and they thought I
was. Then the new guy warned me to mind my business if I wanted
to keep any—"

I shoved him aside and wheeled toward the stage. The sonic
outrage had mounted to an ear-splitting shriek; the players in the
combo dropped their instruments in consternation. Even the lighting display flickered out aghast, leaving a single baby spot playing
over Erika, reflecting from the metallic sequins of her gown,
glinting from the huge, hunted eyes.

She stood feet apart and braced, arms outstretched, head tilted
back, alien bellow of sound writhing about her like a visible nimbus.
She drew in a breath, contorted her lips, and bore down, squeezing
for the last tortured top note of her hysterical cadenza.

Nothing.

Not a sound, not a squeak, not even a groan came from the
stretched square of mouth. The voice, her protection from the
unknown stalker, had broken at last.

Exultantly, the all-pervading roar seemed to pounce on her and
she staggered back, stumbling over Tommy's discarded guitar,
blundering from there into the big super-amp that charged all the
electrified instruments and speakers.

There was an eruption of sparks, and I saw her hand go out to
arrest her fall, grasping at one of the strange new instruments that
stood like a sinister robot chorus surveying the scene.

Instantly the entire charge of current grounded itself, sizzling
lethally through the metal sequins of her gown. The burning and
ozone cut through the reek of marijuana.

The stage curtains bloomed into flame as the band members fled—except for Tommy, who never made it—and the audience floundered in drugged bewilderment toward the exits. The cheap streamers and psychedelic decorations of crepe paper and cheese-cloth channeled fire into every corner of The Purple Blob, lighting up the nightmare riot garishly when the fuses abruptly blew.

I was near the exit, and though I knew that Erika never had a chance, I tried to force my way toward the stage against the pressure of the crowd. The gesture was as pointless as it was futile—I was carried by the surge of the mob toward a safety I neither coveted nor valued.

It wasn't too spectacular as far as fires in crowded places of entertainment go. Besides Erika and Tommy, whose bodies were badly burned, only Pete Muzio died that night. He wasn't found till next day, crouched behind the bar near the entrance. Not a mark was on him, and it was assumed he had had a heart attack. They say his face still held the habitual broken-toothed grimace he had always mistaken for a smile.

No one was badly hurt in that stampede of zonked-out hippies, which shows that—as the squares say—God takes care of fools and children. The interior of The Purple Blob was completely gutted, but firemen had little trouble controlling the flames. Later, though, it was judged that the structure was unsound, and the shell of the building was pulled down.

I'm glad it's gone, though I can never forget it; nor will I forget the things that happened there, or the people they happened to. Least of all will I forget—though I have a notion that as time goes on, I shall more and more wish I could forget—the silence of Erika Zann.

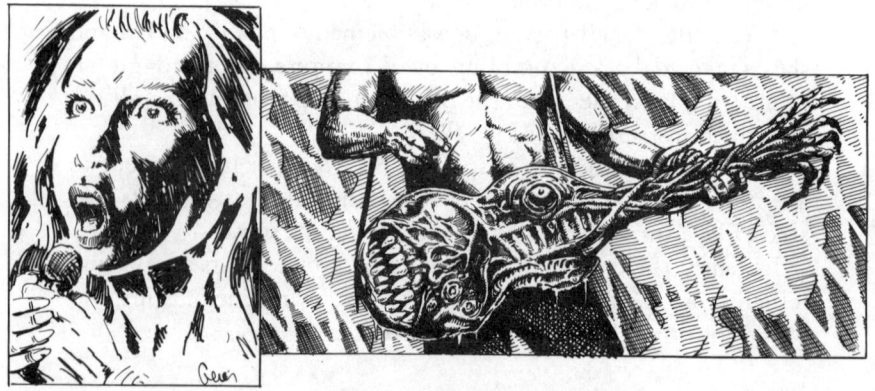

# All-Eye

## by Bob van Laerhoven

The trees glittered like bronze and rust-eaten iron in the flames of my campfire. Ten meters on my left the lead-colored river was babbling. The sky was high and dark blue with fiery pinpricks of starlight. The moon was a hazy sickle, a carved crack in the velvet night.

My mind was wandering pleasurably along the splendid lines of thought I had created and my hands were fluttering impatiently and aimlessly, like guinea pigs, to and fro.

The peace of the endless forest lay on me densely and pleasantly. I felt immensely alone and free, glad it had to be that way. I pricked up my ears and unconsciously my nose went upward when the wind suddenly changed direction and brought me the scent of half-frozen moss, bast, and something else. I shivered, but at the same time I was delighted.

A few heartbeats later I heard the yelling and my hands stopped their movement and hung stock-still in the air. Afterward the action: I got up and threw a few frosty logs on the fire. It hissed a moment, but then it revived like a flower. Silence.

The feeble whispering of the wind echoed and accented the immense kilometers of the forest.

And then I heard the yelling again and I cursed under my breath. It sounded close and was high and thin with agony. Of course.

The veils of the fog lifted a little more and the stars reflected like chains of vague cat eyes in the big roaring river. The nocturnal haze still clung along the banks, but in the middle of the river the water was glittering coldly, deadly, threatening.

I stopped and grabbed the rifle in the tent. In the distance I heard the thin cracking of breaking twigs and *pumf-pumf-pumf-DRUFF-DRUFF!* There was nearly no underwood on the trees. A man wouldn't break any branches or twigs, but ...

I fired a few shots in the air. Then I heard a buzzing noise that seemed to fill kilometers of forest and I tensed. I knew *he* was angry now and rage and despair filled my heart. The crash was heavy and for one moment I thought I would lose because *he* was so young and wild, but *he* was far from the *Power*, and *he* gave up.

A high, howling scream climbed above the high fir trees, bordered by the silver-colored spruce firs, and whistled around the decreasing buzzing. A high scream it was, but not a scream of death, no scream of death.

I wanted to laugh, but it was too early.

The buzzing vanished, but I still heard slight noises. I pointed my rifle upward and fired a few more shots. Branches on the fire, the reviving flower, meters high now, fast, fast.

There was a sudden movement between the trees farther up the river and I stared.

A man dashed into the light thrown by my fire. For a moment his parka glittered like snow, next to the blazing fire, and I quickly averted my eyes.

The charm of the virginal snow ...

One moment it seemed as if he wanted to run on, as if he were frightened of me, as if my eyes were red and my teeth long, distorted by the firelight, but then he stood before me and he pulled wildly at my fur coat.

"Hinnngoo-oo ...," he gasped, his voice whining strangely. "Hinngoooo!" He started to cry softly, and his fingers clawed in the fur of my coat. He stood there like a child with crooked knees and his crying sounded now like the click-clacking of the antlers of the caribou when they were fighting for a female.

"Steady," I said and I led him to the fire. "Just sit down by the fire. Steady now, you're completely safe here."

"Hinnn ... nn ... goo," he said softly, lamenting like a child and shaking his head up and down.

I understood he wouldn't say anything coherent that night and I pointed at the dark opening of the tent.

"I'm Dr. Egmers," I said. "You'll come to no harm here. You're safe. Look, I've got a rifle and I'll keep watch. You look tired. Go to sleep, tomorrow you'll be better." I was talking to him as if to a little child and the movements of his head became slower.

"Danco is dead," he said with a hardly audible voice. "Throw more wood on the fire. Much more wood on the fire!"

Obediently I threw a few logs on the fire. It threw a pale shadow on his face and made his eyes seem darker. Smears of amber and faded gold colored his face again. He stared over the quiet water and I knew he was listening intensely for something. He was listening for the dreadful buzzing, but I knew he wouldn't hear it again this night.

"There's nothing around here," I said soothingly. "Why did you scream like that? Have you seen a wild elk?"

He looked at me with black-and-gold-edged eyes and a muscular spasm moved across his cheeks and let them relax again.

"An—elk?" he said. "An elk? No, no, no ... no elk. Not at all." He pronounced the words mechanically and stiffly and he tiredly wobbled with his upper body. "Danco ...," he said. "Danco." And then slowly he fell sideways.

I picked him up carefully and laid him on a bed of moss in the tent and threw a few blankets over him. He didn't even move when I picked him up. Then I went and sat by the fire and began to think.

"I'm Defgas," he said with his hands clamping the burning hot cup of tea. "I was born in Quebec and I've always lived there."

"So you're not a man of the wilderness," I said. "What brought you here, then?" He looked over his cup of tea into which he had been staring unceasingly and our eyes met. He was still scared to death, but he was also a little ashamed. Well. I smiled.

"If you don't want to tell me, it's OK, you know. Men of the wilderness aren't usually so curious. But you came here without a weapon or equipment and you were so frightened."

"It ..." He stammered and suddenly the words began to stream out of his mouth. "I'm studying at the University of Quebec. I've always been interested in history and so on. Especially legends about strange places and about old, nearly unknown people. I was fascinated by their cultures. My studies at university enabled me to examine rare books, and that was my favorite pastime. I was studying anthropology, but every free moment I had I spent in the library.

"One day I read a very rare volume: the journal of a Frenchman who made an expedition through the immense forests of Canada, about a century ago, in 1826 I believe. A few Hurons, one of the dominating Indian tribes then, accompanied him and after the journey he spent a few more years with them. The writer's name was Echard and in that weather-beaten manuscript he was always talking about 'the gods of the endless forests' and 'descendants of the very old gods out of the dark holes in space' and so on. But often he mentioned a splendid, very ancient little statuette that archaeologically must have been worth millions. He described the hiding place of the sculpture very precisely, but wrote vaguely that for one or another reason, he didn't dig it up himself. It was called All-Eye by the Indians, who said it was the image of a terrible sea god 'with many arms.' And that intrigued me because they lived deep in the forests so it would, anthropologically speaking, be natural for them to imagine forest gods. Immediately I thought about old legends that I had read in other manuscripts. They too had spoken about a god-octopus, Cthulhu, and I wondered if there was a relationship between some of those legends and the statements of Echard. Of course, it could also be that Echard was a little crazy, yet the manuscript made a big impression on me because of its details. Ten months later, because of a very successful thesis, I won a traveling scholarship from the university and I decided to sail down the River Maguse together with a guide I hired in Eskimo Point until ..." He broke off his agitated sentences and hid his face in his hands.

The sun stood high in the nearly wintry sky like a hazy, milk-colored globe and the tops of the firs around us glittered like silver or dark steel. The air was cold and prickling and a violent wind was blowing. In the east, dull gray clouds were pressing together. The trees around us were lightly swaying, making their typical noises.

"The old gods do exist," Defgas stammered tonelessly. "I ... we ... I've seen them, one of them. Danco, my guide, first advised me not to enter this district of Hudson Bay, but he agreed later for the money I offered him. In the university library I spent hours and hours to put the position of the 'All-Eye' on a map, and I was quite sure of myself. The statuette would stand in a cave on the bank of the River Maguse. Of course, I didn't *really* expect to find anything, but it was a destination as good as any other, don't you understand? I was studying the pattern of the trappers and the hunters of Canada, but that secret hiding place gave my trip a romantic touch. Civilization seems to stand still here. Anyway, the hiding place is about three kilometers from here. We saw the cave Echard had also described and I started to tremble; it was as if the atmosphere suddenly changed. We were sitting in our canoe and there wasn't much wind. There was, like always, some fog hanging above the water. Everything appeared to be normal, but there was that *silence.* Not a normal silence, because the trees were rustling and the water was babbling against our boat, but it was more a *mental* silence. I had a very strange feeling, Egmers, just like a child who's afraid of the dark. The banks were too rocky to bring my canoe ashore and we had to land about a kilometer farther on. When we started to make our camp, the wind suddenly doubled its force. It seemed as if those damned trees on that bank were talking to each other!

"It soon was dark and I decided to wait until the following morning to head for the cave. We pitched out tents and ate our supper. The fire didn't burn well; although we used dry wood it gave off a lot of smoke. It was getting rather cold and Danco wasn't doing anything about it. He sniffed the air like a dog. I could smell only the sharp smoke of our campfire, but his sniffing around made me frightened. I began to feel awfully alone and then there was that dreadful silence I have already mentioned. It was the silence of something that was *preparing* itself! One moment I thought I could hear something: a kind of buzzing that at the same time sounded like laughing, and it came from the river. Then I saw something big moving in the fog above the water as if it were *floating* in those fog-banks. It gave the mist a strange glitter. But then I laughed when I understood it was only the rising moon and that because of it the low-hanging fog would make strange shadows and color effects. Yet there was something wrong, and Danco felt it even more than I. His ancestors were Indians and maybe he still had their delicate sense organs. It was that *loneliness,* I think. To know that maybe there were no other men around for a hundred kilometers. Of course, we didn't know that you were camping here, but that's a lucky coincidence. Otherwise, what is a hundred kilometers in these forests? Nothing, just a footstep, not more! Where is the protecting coat of civilization around here? Once upon a time, in former days, when man was still one with nature, he must've had contact with beings, beings which still exist."

Exhausted, he stopped talking and guzzled his strong tea. I looked at him closely. He was a dark, lean man with a long face and a thin beard. He didn't wear glasses, but his eyes were glittering myopically. He had long, thin hands with proportionally broad wrists. His boots were of a striking small size for someone of his height. His eyes were hazy light gray, like the scales of a muddy fish, and his hair was lank and very closely shaved at the temples.

"And what happened then?" I asked.

"At last we went to bed," he said tonelessly. "And believe me, Egmers, my body was constantly prickling as if it were reacting more instinctively than my mind. I began this journey to gain contact with nature and study the Eskimos, to understand a little how prehistoric man must have felt, without giving too much credence to Echard's manuscript. I already told you that the position of the All-Eye, together with the legends, gave my journey a romantic touch. I didn't really expect to find that so-called hiding place, but it was there! And that had to make me think. Anyway, I slept very badly. I dozed off and woke up again. I was looking at Danco's dark back, but all the time I imagined that something heavy was pressing on the canvas of the tent, something that made it come down slowly until it would suddenly fall upon us with a horrible scream: a fierce mass of teeth, claws or ... something worse.

"And then I imagined I could hear footsteps crunching outside. There was snow on the slopes of the terrain and against the trunks of the trees, just like here. I heard the snow crunch; then for a while I couldn't hear anything anymore, and then it started again as if someone were approaching our tent slowly from snowbank to snowbank. I was shivering and then I really was scared *because there was an agitated, gasping breathing in the tent.* My first impulse was to jump up and run away. But then I pressed myself deeper into my bed of moss and started to sob audibly. I couldn't get away, the gasping was much too close. It would be faster than I was! I could only ... and then I realized it was Danco who was gasping, that he was not asleep. I saw his back going up and down violently and it was *as if his back had become larger.* And then I heard something outside. A kind of buzzing ... or a yell. I don't know, but it sounded like distorted laughter or a kind of funny hiccuping. At the same time a violent gust of wind shook the tent, and for a moment I saw an enormous shadow on the canvas. I was scared to death and I shook Danco's back. It felt ice cold, and suddenly I felt an overwhelming fear of him. I was afraid he would turn around, that he would show his face and *his eyes.* The back bent a little as if he wanted to turn around, and then I couldn't stand it any longer. I jumped up yelling ... and saw a glimpse of his face when he turned around. I ran ... I lost my mind, Egmers, but those eyes! I swear that ..." He broke off, and hid his head in his hands.

"Defgas," I said softly and soothingly, "it'll be better to give you a sedative. You know I'm a doctor. I visit the lonely hunters and trappers and wood merchants who sail down the river this time of year. I've seen some of them who were in a worse way than you are, Defgas. The forest had overwhelmed them, the snow filled their brains, and sometimes they imagined the strangest things. Things of which your story ..."

He shook his head slowly but definitely and I stopped.

"No, Egmers," he said, softly gasping. "I'm sure I ... but let me
go on with my story, Doctor, so that you know too what I know, so
that I'm no longer alone with my knowledge, even if you don't
believe me."

"OK," I said, "go on, then. And ... I believe those things have
happened, Defgas. *But in your mind.* But don't think I'm laughing
at you."

"Perhaps," he said slowly. "Anyway, somehow I got out of the
tent and dashed into the forest. Behind me I heard that buzzing
sound and there was something grating too. And then I heard
footsteps. But they were not human footsteps! It sounded as if an
enormous caribou were chasing me. But I'm sure that you as well
as I can tell the difference between the sound of a running *four*-
footed beast and a *two*-footed one. Well, this noise belonged to a
running *two*-footed thing that weighed at least three hundred
kilograms. Besides the lead-heavy thumping I also heard something
splashing, as if my pursuer were wet. I ran and my heart was beating
like mad, Egmers. I felt that *hatred* was pursuing me, *hatred* mixed
with *mockery.* The trees were just blurs and my feet were burning
bullets of speed. Its buzzing, that buzzing filled the atmosphere,
climbed above the trees, and covered the entire area with a dome of
evil. I ran and yelled because I knew *it* was close by. But then, as if a
heavy load fell off my back, the buzzing sound abated. The thumping footsteps vanished suddenly, but I ran on until I heard your rifle
shots. I still don't know why it suddenly stopped, but I do know
my feet still want to run to get farther and farther away from it."

He looked at me wildly, with wide-open pupils. His face looked
like gelatin, with its sagging, relaxed muscles.

"Does it seem likely to you that Danco's looking for you?" I
said calmly.

"What?"

"Do you think Danco's looking for you?" I asked patiently.
"You've never been in these forests before this journey, have you?"

He shook his head with a jerky movement.

"Well, does it seem likely that it was a wild elk pursuing you?
Or that you imagined everything?" I said. "Do you know how much
experience you need before you can differentiate between the run of
a two-footed thing and that of a four-footed one? And why should
Danco—who was very nervous at the time, because all Indians are
superstitious as hell—pursue you? And *if* it was Danco pursuing
you, why did he suddenly stop?"

"*That wasn't Danco anymore,*" he said with clenched teeth and pulled-back lips as if he wanted to attack me. "It was ... it only took possession of Danco to play with me. You should've seen his eyes, Egmers."

"Who was it, then?" I asked as calmly as possible.

He clenched his fists and for a moment I had the impression he would run away. His feet made peculiar shuffling movements, as if they yearned to run.

"Hingoo," he said, suddenly hardly audible. "Echard called him the Hingoo. Hingoo, one of the descendants of the gods from space, and god of the wind and the wilderness."

"Because Echard knew about a cave along the River Maguse, that doesn't prove anything," I said soothingly. "Anybody can write there's a cave here and there and there's an ancient sculpture lying in it."

He stared at the hissing water of the river. It babbled softly and whispered against the irregular sandy banks. The violent wind rustled fitfully. Like always, the wind had a complete symphony of voices to use. It whispered between the trees, whistled over the waves, licked the mud and snow of the riverbanks. The wind ...

"Maybe Echard became mad," he said slowly, "from what he had seen! Maybe 'Hingoo' is just another name for 'the Wendigo, the Being that Walks on the Wind!' All those legends throughout the world are related to each other! There must be some truth in them! I don't know anymore ... I only know I must get away from here ..."

"The Wendigo is only the personification of the wind," I said calmly. "You should know that if you study anthropology, Defgas. All those legend-creatures are nothing but animated nature-elements. You'd better think of Danco. Are you going to leave him behind?"

He looked at me with wild, dark eyes. "Danco?" he asked in a weak voice. "He's dead, don't you understand? He's only a wrapping now, a balloon of skin. It almost seized me too. It must've emptied him just when I dozed off, you see. And because it is malicious by nature, it wanted to tease me. It wished to devour my fear before taking me completely."

"And yet I think we've got to go and take a look," I said. "I'm sure you've had an hallucination. Did you know that in this season trees spread a resin that, combined with the smoke of a campfire, can cause hallucinations? You told me yourself the fire gave off a lot of smoke in that spot. And of course your mind was already in a mood conducive to hallucination because you were so close to your 'mysterious' destination. You know, I treat people here more for their minds than for their bodies. Usually they are perfectly healthy because of the salubrious climate and the hard physical work. But these woods influence the mind; perhaps they drag prehistoric memories out of us. For example, you told me that buzzing noise filled the whole area: *But I didn't hear anything, Defgas!* And I was fully awake. How can you explain that?"

He examined me carefully and a strange light came into his eyes.

"Haven't you ever heard that noise?" he asked slowly.

"Defgas," I answered. "I've treated people who traveled for months and months through the forests without eating anything other than roots and leaves, hunting one or another fallacy. These immense stretches of forest can influence the mind of modern man. Civilization is standing here before an awesome unity, a silent greatness, and city people especially feel the enormity and pressure of that greatness. I wander from settlement to settlement, otherwise I couldn't stand it any longer than they do. But these men need help. No, I haven't heard that noise and if it had been there I would've. I heard only your yelling and the cracking of small branches. I supposed that someone was in distress and that's why I fired my rifle. Now tell me: Can you explain why your pursuer gave up suddenly, without a reason? If he was as terrible as you told me I couldn't have frightened him. Look, if we go and take a look now it'll be broad daylight when we reach your camp. It won't even be midday and you know midday is a very safe time, too prosaic for 'supernatural beings.' I think you owe it to your guide. In the wilderness you must be a man. And you won't be alone, I'm going with you. What can happen then?"

He shook his head slowly now, but his eyes were calmer.

"I don't know," he muttered, "what you said sounds good, but ..."

"It has been a terrible experience," I went on. "An experience your mind has staged for you. I'll tell you something: Once I had an hallucination and it seemed as if the river were shouting something to me with a thousand voices. You've heard that senseless babbling of the water, haven't you? Well, I believed it was a message and when my mental intoxication was over, I burst out laughing. Such an intoxication can overpower you without a warning, but it usually never comes back again. Cheer up, fellow! We'll eat a bit first and then you can make up your mind."

I saw that he was nearly reassured now. Because I had confessed to him that I also had had an hallucination, he was enormously soothed. Like all people, he felt better as soon as he knew he wasn't the only one with such an experience.

"I'll think about it," he said slowly.

While we were eating, the wind had heightened in power and the big undulating river had become a swirling, roiling mass. In half an hour the faint sun had disappeared and had made room for high gray clouds that heralded snow. It wasn't completely freezing yet, but it was cold enough. There was a thin scraping sound over the water now: the sound of pebbles grating and rattling over the bottom of the river pushed by the current of the water.

During the silent meal I saw that Defgas was having a violent inner conflict. He was absently chewing his food, but his eyes were roaming around. When I felt he was looking at me, I smiled and he quickly averted his eyes. But he was no longer agitated. He moved more steadily now and his eyes had lost that look of a caged animal.

"It's eleven o'clock now," I said when we had finished. "Don't you think we should look for your friend now? He must be very worried about you and it will be impossible for him to find your tracks. Later on he'll go to a settlement and report your disappearance. ... In any case I'm going. Are you coming with me?"

He blushed slightly and looked down at his hands.

"Yes. I think we'd best go and take a look," he said, stammering. "I ... well, maybe you're right. It could have been my nerves, or that resin, or something like that ... but it seemed so real ..."

"If you knew what those 'voices of the river' told me," I said airily, "you'd be surprised."

He smiled slightly and he suddenly stood up decisively.

"Let's go and take a look *now*," he said.

I guided him through the trees where the wind was rushing past and he followed me with hesitating steps, but faithfully.

It started to snow slightly and the wind began to shake the branches of the trees fiercely.

I took care not to lose sight of the river. The water bubbled and hissed, roared and giggled. At first the snow fell with soft specks, but it soon grew heavier. Our footsteps crunched softly in the deepening snow.

"These woods are without peer in the whole world," I said. "But in spite of all, civilization is inflicting itself. The paper industry is taking a lot of these trees away and yet there are areas of forest greater than England and France together. It seems as if the forest is keeping itself alive, but it'll have to give way in the long run. Give it another hundred years and it'll be gone, if nothing happens. What a prosaic end for a land with 'supernatural powers', don't you think so, Defgas? Understand me well: I'm not laughing at you, I'm only trying to make you understand, in spite of the mysteries that still surround these marvelous trees, how ordinary and colorless it all is."

"Yes," he answered, hesitating. "I think you're right."

But the sound was a mockery of his words.

It came from the bank about ten meters on our left and it quickly filled the forest. It was angry and it was terrible.

Swiftly I looked at Defgas and in that moment his face had become a naked mask of fear and horror, incredible horror.

It was a contemptible mask and I hated it.

"You've got me," he rattled. "God, you've got me!"

Something cramped screaming in his throat and his eyes rolled wildly to and fro.

The buzzing dominated the whole river. A terrifying, possessed sound, but I laughed, laughed, laughed.

*And my voice dominated the plains of the forest and the winds!*

I turned around and grabbed Defgas's arm. He howled when my cold, cold hands touched him.

"Fool," I shouted with a flame in my eyes. "Hingoo, Hingoo, a victim, a *man* for you, Hingoo, mighty Hingoo!"

I couldn't deal with him any longer because Hingoo, my young rival, friend-enemy and younger brother, approached—and in spite of his melodramatic manner he had more power than I had then, while he drained the *Power* out of All-Eye.

A lumpy shape appeared between the veils of snow and the last thing I saw of the miserable Defgas were his eyes following me dazedly and fixing a reduced, monstrous picture of my *real* shape in their pupils.

As a parting gift I threw the empty wrapping of Dr. Egmers to him. Then I flew to the cave in the bank and I shouted triumphantly with my voice of the wind, when I heard cracking and a monstrous shriek behind me. The impetuous Hingoo was tempted, just as I had hoped.

I flew into the cave and my night eyes saw the hazy glittering shape of Haigh-Ohgi, or Cthulhu, the All-Being. My leather wings touched the stone and the *Power* flowed into me quickly. My eyes became forest fires and my wing-clapping thundered with the powers of all the winds of Earth! There came into me an untameable, lonely, grandiose freedom and I rejoiced! But I listened also—something that Hingoo never could do!

The message of Cthulhu, who dreamed in his lonely realm, flowed into me and I knew what had to be done.

A mighty sound at the opening of the cave made me turn around. My red eyes reflected darkness because Hingoo stood in front of me and he was dripping human blood.

But he was beaten and he knew it.

"Now the *Power* is in me, Hingoo," whispered my mouth, full of the liquid fire of enormous forest lightnings. "Now it's again *My Power,* younger brother."

"How could you do it?" he roared, and the river drew a whirling pattern of roiling water before the opening of the cave. "How *could* you do it?"

"Hingoo," I hissed, with the voice of a thousand rattlesnakes. "playing games is over. The statuette gave you my *Power,* but you wouldn't listen to the message of our master. We can't regard human beings as lower animals any longer. We've slept too long and we've got to combine power with guile now, just as I've done now for the first time. I've waited patiently for a long time, Hingoo, and I ignored the call of the wind. I possessed the figure of a stupid, clumsy human shape, a victim I killed. I *knew* that one day human beings would come into your realm again and I *hoped* you would play with one of them, so that he would fall into my hands. That happened and I gained his confidence and brought him back here. You couldn't resist your passion and you fell upon him, and so you couldn't prevent me from taking *the* Power *that was rightfully mine.* What have you done with it? You ignored the callings of our god, you fooled around, gargled in the river, screamed in the ice, shouted in the wind, jumped with fierce paws over the glaciers, but nothing else. From over the world we must come together again and combat man. We've got to use the *Power* better, Hingoo! Above all, you hate humans, but I hate them too, I hate them too ... and I'll use the *Power* otherwise and better. ... Soon, Cthulhu will awake ..."

# The Tugging

## by Ramsey Campbell

### I

When Ingels awoke he knew at once he'd been dreaming again. There was an image, a memory clamoring faintly but urgently at the edge of his mind; he snatched at it, but it was gone. He swung himself off the crumpled bed. Hilary must have gone to do her research in the library hours ago, leaving him a cold breakfast. Outside hung a chill glazed blue sky, and frost was fading from the window pane.

The dream continued to nag at his mind. He let it pluck at him, hoping that the nagging would turn by itself into a memory. He slowed himself down, dressing slowly, eating slowly, to allow the memory to catch up. But there was only the insistence, like a distant recollection of a plucked tooth. Through the wall he could hear a radio announcer's voice in the next flat, a blurred cadence rising as if to leap a barrier that obscured its words completely. It buzzed at his mind, bumbling. He washed up quickly, irritably, and hurried out.

And found that he couldn't look up at the sky.

The feeling seized his neck like a violent cramp, forcing his head down. Around him women were wheeling prams in which babies and groceries fought for space, dogs were playing together in the alleys, buses quaked at bus stops, farting. But on Ingels, pressing down from a clear rather watery blue expanse to which he couldn't even raise his eyes, weighed a sense of intolerable stress, as if the calm sky were stretched to splitting: as if it were about to split and to let his unformed fear through at him.

A bus braked, a long tortured scraping squeal. When Ingels recovered from his heart-clutching start he'd jolted off the fear. He ran for the bus as the last of the queue shuffled on. *Scared of the sky indeed*, he thought. *I've got to get more sleep. Pill myself to sleep if I have to.* His eyes felt as if floating in quicklime.

He sat among the coughing shoppers. Across the aisle a man shook his head at the tobacco smoke, snorting like a horse. A woman threw herself and three carrier bags onto a seat, patting them reassuringly, and slammed her predecessor's open window. Ingels rummaged in his briefcase. He'd left one notebook at his own flat, he discovered, muttering. He flicked through the notes for his column, holding them flat on his briefcase. *Wonder if the fellow whose knee I'm fighting recognizes my style. World's champion egotist*, he rebuked himself, hiding the notes with his forearm. *Don't worry, he won't steal the copyright*, he scoffed, pulling his arm back. He put the notes away. They looked as bleary as he felt.

He gazed around the bus, at the flat stagnant smoke, at the ranks of heads like wig blocks, and settled on headlines over the shoulder in front of him:

### IS THE SOLAR SYSTEM ON TOW?

Six months ago an amateur astronomer wrote to us, warning that a planet might pass dangerously close to Earth.

### THE ASTRONOMER ROYAL'S COMMENT:

#### 'UTTER TWADDLE.'

*Now the world's leading astronomers have agreed to let us have the facts.*

### TODAY WE TELL ALL.

In an exclusive interview

But he'd turned over, to the smaller print of the story. Ingels sat back again, remembering how the *Herald* had received a copy of that letter six months ago. They hadn't published it, and the letters editor had gazed at Ingels pityingly when he'd suggested they might at least follow it up. 'I suppose you arts people need imagination,' he'd said. Ingels grimaced wryly, wondering how they would handle the story in tonight's edition. He leaned forward, but the man had reached the editorial comment: 'Even if his aim was to prevent panic, are we paying the Astronomer Royal to tell us what too many people are now suggesting was a lie?'

Ingels glanced out of the window. Offices flashed past, glazed displays of figures at desks, the abrupt flight of perspective down alleys with a shock like a fall in a dream, more displays. The offices thinned out and aged as the bus gathered speed towards the edge of Brichester. *Nearly there*, Ingels thought, then realized with a leap from his seat that he'd passed the *Herald* building three stops back. For a second he knew where he'd been heading. *So what?* he thought savagely, the rims of his eyes rusty and burning, as he clattered downstairs. But once he was on the street he wished that he'd thought to remember: now he couldn't imagine where he could have been going in that direction.

BRICHESTER HERALD: BRICHESTER'S EVENING VOICE. The iron poem (two-thirds of a haiku, he'd thought until he grew used to it) clung to the bricks above him. The foyer was quiet. He wondered how long it would be before the presses began to thump heartily, disproving the soundproofing. Not long, and he had to write his column.

His mind felt flat and empty as the elevator. He drifted numbly through the hundred-yard open-plan office, past the glancing heads behind glass personalized in plastic. Some looked away quickly, some stared, some smiled. *My God, I don't even know his name*, Ingels thought of several. 'Hello, Moira,' he said. 'How's it going, Bert?' Telephones shrilled, were answered, their calls leapt prankishly across the floor. Reporters sidestepped through the aisles. Smells of deodorant and sweat, tang of ink, brandished paper, scurrying typewriters, hasty agitated conferences.

Bert had been following him to his desk. 'Don't wait for your personal bulletin,' Bert said, throwing a telex sheet on the desk. 'The latest on your wandering planet.'

'Don't tell me I've convinced you at last.'

'No chance,' Bert said, retreating. 'Just so you don't start turning the place upside down for it.'

Ingels read the sheet, thinking: *I could have told them this six months ago.* The Americans had admitted that an unmanned probe was well on its way to photograph the wanderer. He rested his elbow on the desk and covered his eyes. Against the restless patches of light he almost glimpsed what he'd dreamed. He started, bewildered; the noise of the newspaper poured into him. *Enough*, he thought, sorting out his notes.

He typed the television review—a good play from Birmingham, when are we going to see a studio in Brichester—and passed it to Bert. Then he pawed desultorily at the day's accumulation on his desk. *Must go and see my folks this week. Might drain my tension a little.* He turned over a brown envelope. A press ticket, elaborately pretty lettering: exhibition of associational painting—the new primitivism and surrealism. *Ugh*, he thought, and whatever you say to surrealists. Private view this afternoon. Which means now. 'You can have a local arts review tomorrow,' he said, showing the ticket to Bert, and went out.

Once out of the building his mind teetered like a dislocated compass. Again the sky seemed brittle glass, ready to crack, and when he moved to shake off the obsession he found himself urged towards the edge of Brichester. A woman flinched from him as he snarled himself to a halt. 'Sorry,' he called after her. *Whatever's in that direction, it isn't the show I've been invited to. But there must be something there. Maybe I went there when I was young. Have a look when I can. Before I sleepwalk there.*

Although he could have taken a bus into Lower Brichester, where the exhibition was, he walked. *Clear my head, perhaps, if I don't get high on petrol first.* The sky was thin and blue; nothing more, now. He swung his briefcase. *Haven't heard of these artists before. Who knows, they could be good.*

He hadn't been through Lower Brichester for months, and was taken aback by its dereliction. Dogs scrabbled clattering in gouged shop-fronts, an uprooted street lamp lay across a road, humped earth was scattered with disembowelled mattresses, their entrails fluttering feebly. He passed houses where one window was blinded with brick, the next still open and filmy with a drooping curtain. He examined his ticket. *Believe it or not, I'm on the right track.*

Soon whole streets were derelict. There was nothing but Ingels, the gaping houses and uneven pavements, the discreet sky, his footsteps alone; the rush of the city was subdued, quiescent. The houses went by, shoulder to shoulder, ribs open to the sky, red-brick fronts revealing their jumble of shattered walls and staircases. Ingels felt a lurking sympathy for the area in its abandonment, its indifference to time. He slowed down, strolling. *Let myself go a bit. The private view's open for hours yet. Relax.* He did, and felt an irrational impulse pleading with him.

*And why not*, he thought. He glanced about: nobody. Then he began to lope through the deserted streets, arms hanging, fingers almost touching the road. *Unga bunga*, he thought. *One way to prepare myself for primitives, I suppose.*

He found his behavior touched a memory; perhaps the memory was its source. A figure running crouched through ruins, somewhere nearby. A kind of proof of virility. *But they hadn't been deserted city streets*, he thought, loping. Just flat blocks of black rock in which square windows gaped. Abandoned long before but hardly affected by time. A figure running along a narrow path through the stone, not looking at the windows.

Clouds were creeping into the sky; darkness was suffusing the streets around him. Ingels ran, not looking at the houses, allowing them to merge with the memory they touched. It was coming clearer. You had to run all the way along one of the stone paths. Any path at all, for there were no intersections, just a straight unbroken run. You had to run fast, before something within the windows became aware of you, rather as a carnivorous plant becomes aware of a fly. The last part of the run was the worst, because you knew that at any moment something would appear in all the windows at once: things that, although they had mouths, were not faces—

Ingels stumbled wildly as he halted, glaring up at the empty windows of the houses. *What on earth was that?* he thought distractedly. *Like one of those dreams I used to have, the ones that were so vivid. Of course, that's what it must have been. These streets reminded me of one of them.* Though the memory felt much older, somehow. *From the womb, no doubt*, he shouted angrily at his pounding heart.

When he reached the exhibition he walked straight past it. Returning, he peered at the address on the ticket. My God, this is it. Two of a street of dingy but tenanted terraced houses had been run together; on the front of one, in lettering he'd taken for graffiti, were the words LOWER BRICHESTER ARTS LAB. He recalled how, when it had opened last year, the invitations to the opening had arrived two days later. The project he'd described after a hurried telephone interview hadn't looked at all like this. *Oh well*, he thought, and went in.

In the hall, by the reception desk, two clowns were crawling about with children on their backs. One of the children ran behind the desk and gazed up at Ingels. 'Do you know where the exhibition is?' he said. 'Up your arse,' she said, giggling. 'First floor up,' said one of the clowns, who Ingels now realized was a made-up local poet, and chased the children into a playroom full of inflatables.

The first floor was a maze of plywood partitions in metal frames. On the partitions hung paintings and sketches. As Ingels entered, half a dozen people converged on him, all the artists save one, who was trying to relight a refractory cone of incense. Feeling outnumbered, Ingels wished he'd made it to the maze. 'You've just missed the guy from Radio Brichester,' one said. 'Are you going to talk to all of us, like him?' another asked. 'Do you like modern art?' 'Do you want coffee?'

'Now leave him be,' said Annabel Pringle, as Ingels recognized her from her picture on the cover of the catalogue. 'They're new to exhibiting, you see, you can't blame them. I mean, this whole show is my idea but their enthusiasm. Now, I can explain the principles as you go round if you like, or you can read them in the catalogue.'

'The latter, thanks.' Ingels hurried into the maze, opening the typed catalogue. A baby with an ear-trumpet, which was 2: Untitled. 3 was a man throwing his nose into a wastebasket, and Untitled. 4: Untitled. 5, 6, 7—Well, their paintings are certainly better than their prose, Ingels thought. The incense unravelled ahead of him. A child playing half-submerged in a lake. A blackened green-tinged city shouldering up from the sea. A winged top hat gliding over a jungle. Suddenly Ingels stopped short and turned back to the previous painting. He was sure he had seen it before.

22: Atlantis. But it wasn't like any Atlantis he'd seen pictured. The technique was crude and rather banal, obviously one of the primitives, yet Ingels found that it touched images buried somewhere in him. Its leaning slabs of rock felt vast, the sea poured from its surfaces as if it had just exploded triumphantly into sight. Drawn closer, Ingels peered into the darkness within a slab of rock, beyond what might be an open doorway. *If there were the outline of a pale face staring featurelessly up from within the rock, its owner must be immense. If there were*, Ingels thought, withdrawing: but why should he feel there ought to be?

When he'd hurried around the rest of the exhibition he tried to ask about the painting, but Annabel Pringle headed him off. 'You understand what we mean by associational painting?' she demanded. 'Let me tell you. We select an initial idea by aleatory means.'

'Eh?' Ingels said, scribbling.

'Based on chance. We use the I Ching, like John Cage. The American composer, he originated it. Once we have the idea we silently associate from it until each of us has an idea they feel they must communicate. This exhibition is based on six initial ideas. You can see the diversity.'

'Indeed,' Ingels said. 'When I said "eh" I was being an average reader of our paper, you understand. Listen, the one that particularly interested me was number 22. I'd like to know how that came about.'

'That's mine,' one young man said, leaping up as if it were House.

'The point of our method,' Annabel Pringle said, gazing at the painter, 'is to erase all the associational steps from your mind, leaving only the image you paint. Of course Clive here wouldn't remember what led up to that painting.'

'No, of course,' Ingels said numbly. 'It doesn't matter. Thank you. Thanks all very much.' He hurried downstairs, past a sodden clown, and into the street. In fact it didn't matter. A memory had torn its way through his insomnia. For the second time that day he realized why something had looked familiar, but this time more disturbingly. Decades ago he had himself dreamed the city in the painting.

## II

Ingels switched off the television. As the point of light dwindled into darkness it touched off the image in him of a gleam shooting away into space. Then he saw that the light hadn't sunk into darkness but into Hilary's reflection, leaning forward from the cane rocking chair next to him, about to speak. 'Give me fifteen minutes,' he said, scribbling notes for his review.

The programme had shown the perturbations which the wandering planet had caused in the orbits of Pluto, Neptune, and Uranus, and had begun and ended by pointing out that the planet was now swinging away from the solar system; its effect on Earth's orbit would be negligible. Photographs from the space probe were promised within days. Despite its cold scientific clarity (Ingels wrote) and perhaps without meaning to, the programme managed to communicate a sense of foreboding, of the intrusion into and interference with our familiar skies. 'Not to me it didn't,' Hilary said, reading over his shoulder.

'That's sad,' he said. 'I was going to tell you about my dreams.'

'Don't if I wouldn't understand them either. Aren't I allowed to criticize now?'

'Sorry. Let's start again. Just let me tell you a few of the things that have happened to me. I was thinking of them all today. Some of them even you'll have to admit are strange. Make some coffee and I'll tell you about them.'

When she'd brought the coffee he waited until she sat forward, ready to be engrossed, long soft black hooks of hair angling for her jawbone. 'I used to dream a lot when I was young,' he said. 'Not your average childhood dream, if there is such a thing. There was one I remember, about these enormous clouds of matter floating in outer space, forming very slowly into something. I mean *very* slowly …. I woke up long before they got there, yet while I was dreaming I knew whatever it was would have a face, and that made me very anxious to wake up. Then there was another where I was being carried through a kind of network of light, on and on across intersections for what felt like days, until I ended up on the edge of this gigantic web of paths of light. And I was fighting to stop myself going in, because I knew that hiding behind the light there was something old and dark and shapeless, something dried up and evil that I couldn't make out. I could hear it rustling like an old dry spider. You know what I suddenly realized that web was? My brain, I'd been chasing along my nervous system to my brain. Well, leave that one to the psychologists. But there were odd things about these dreams—I mean, apart from all that. They always used to begin the same way, and always about the same time of the month.'

'The night of the full moon?' Hilary said, slurping coffee.

'Funnily enough, yes. Don't worry, I didn't sprout midnight shadow or anything. But some people are sensitive to the full moon, that's well enough documented. And I always used to begin by dreaming I could see the full moon over the sea, way out in the middle of the ocean. I could see the reflection resting on the water, and after a while I'd always find myself thinking it wasn't the moon at all but a great pale face peering up out of the ocean, and I'd panic. Then I wouldn't be able to move and I'd know that the full moon was pulling at something deep in the ocean, waking it up. I'd feel my panic swelling up in me, and all of a sudden it would burst and I'd be in the next dream. That's how it happened, every time.'

'Didn't your parents know? Didn't they try to find out what was wrong?'

'I don't know what you mean by wrong. But yes, they knew eventually, when I told them. That was after I had the idea my father might be able to explain. I was eleven then and I'd had strange feelings sometimes, intuitions and premonitions and so forth, and sometimes I'd discovered they'd been my father's feelings too.'

'I know all about your father's feelings,' Hilary said. 'More than he knows about mine.'

Soon after they'd met, Ingels had taken her to see his parents. She'd felt his father had been too stiffly polite to her, and when she'd cross-examined Ingels he'd eventually admitted that his father had felt she was wrong for him, unsympathetic to him. 'You were going

to let me tell you about my dreams,' he said. 'I told my father about
the sea dream and I could see there was something he wasn't saying.
My mother had to make him tell me. Her attitude to the whole
thing was rather what yours would have been, but she told him to
get it over with, he'd have to tell me sometime. So he told me he'd
sometimes shared his father's dreams without either of them ever
knowing why. And he'd had several of my dreams when he'd been
young, until one night in the mid-twenties—early 1925, I think
he said. Then he'd dreamed a city had risen out of the sea. After that
he'd never dreamed again. Well, maybe hearing that was some kind
of release for me, because the next time I dreamed of the city too.'

'You dreamed of a city,' Hilary said.

'The same one. I told him about it next morning, details of it he
hadn't told me, that were the same in both our dreams. I was
watching the sea, the same place as always. Don't ask me how I knew
it was always the same. I knew. One moment I was watching the
moon on the water, then I saw it was trembling. The next moment
an island rose out of the ocean with a roaring like a waterfall, louder
than that, louder than anything I've ever heard while awake; I
could actually feel my ears bursting. There was a city on the island,
all huge greenish blocks with sea and seaweed pouring off them.
And the mud was boiling with stranded creatures, panting and
bursting. Right in front of me and above me and below me there
was a door. Mud was trickling down from it, and I knew that the
great pale face I was terrified of was behind the door, getting ready
to come out, opening its eyes in the dark. I woke up then, and that
was the end of the dreams. Say they were only dreams if you like.
You might find it easiest to believe my father and I were sharing
them by telepathy.'

'You know perfectly well,' Hilary said, 'that I'd find nothing of
the sort.'

'No? Then try this,' he said sharply. 'At the exhibition I visited
today there was a painting of our dream. And not by either of us.'

'So what does that mean?' she cried. 'What on earth is that
supposed to mean?'

'Well, a dream I can recall so vividly after all this time is worth
a thought. And that painting suggests it's a good deal more
objectively real.'

'So your father read about the island in a story,' she said. 'So did
you, so did the painter. What else can you possibly be suggesting?'

'Nothing,' he said at last.

'So what were the other strange things you were going to tell me?'

'That's all,' he said. 'Just the painting. Nothing else. Really.' She was looking miserable, a little ashamed. 'Don't you believe me?' he said. 'Come here.'

As the sheepskin rug joined their caresses she said, 'I don't really need to be psychic for you, do I?'

'No,' he said, probing her ear with his tongue, triggering her ready. Switching off the goosenecked steel lamps as she went, she led him through the flat as if wheeling a basket behind her; they began laughing as a car's beam shone up from Mercy Hill and seized for a moment on her hand, his handle. They reached the crisp bed and suddenly, urgently, couldn't prolong their play. She was all around him, working to draw him deeper and out, he was lapped softly, thrusting roughly at her grip on him to urge it to return redoubled. They were rising above everything but each other, gasping. He felt himself rushing to a height, and closed his eyes.

And was falling into a maelstrom of flesh, in a vast almost lightless cave whose roof seemed as far above him as the sky. He had a long way still to fall, and beneath him he could make out the movements of huge bubbles and ropes of flesh, of eyes swelling and splitting the flesh, of gigantic dark green masses climbing sluggishly over one another. 'No, Christ no,' he cried, gripped helpless.

He slumped on Hilary. 'Oh God,' she said. 'What is it now?'

He lay beside her. Above them the ceiling shivered with reflected light. It looked as he felt. He closed his eyes and found dark calm, but couldn't bear to keep them closed for long. 'All right,' he said. 'There's more I haven't told you. I know you've been worried about how I've looked lately. I told you it was lack of sleep, and so it is, but it's because I've begun dreaming again. It started about nine months ago, just before I met you, and it's becoming more frequent, once or twice a week now. Only this time I can never remember what it is, perhaps because I haven't dreamed for so long. I think it has something to do with the sky, maybe this planet we've been hearing about. The last time was this morning, after you went to the library. For some reason I don't have them when I'm with you.'

'Of course if you want to go back to your place, go ahead,' Hilary said, gazing at the ceiling.

'In one way I don't,' he said. 'That's the trouble. Whenever I try to dream I find I don't want to sleep, as if I'm fighting the dream. But today I'm tired enough just to drift off and have it anyway. I've been getting hallucinations all day that I think are coming from the dream. And it feels more urgent, somehow. I've got to have it. I knew it was important before, but that painting's made me sure it's more than a dream. I wish you could understand this. It's not easy for me.'

'Suppose I did believe you?' she said. 'What on earth would you do then? Stand on the street warning people? Or would you try to sell it to your paper? I don't want to believe you, how can you think they would?'

'That's exactly the sort of thing I don't need to hear,' Ingels said. 'I want to talk to my father about it. I think he may be able to help. Maybe you wouldn't mind not coming with me.'

'I wouldn't want to,' she said. 'You go and have your dream and your chat with your father if you want. But as far as I'm concerned that means you don't want me.'

Ingels walked to his flat, further up Mercy Hill. Newspapers clung to bushes, flapping; cars hissed through nearby streets, luminous waves. Only the houses stood between him and the sky, their walls seeming low and thin. Even in the pools of lamplight he felt the night gaping overhead.

The building where he lived was silent. The stereo that usually thumped like an electronic heart was quiet. Ingels climbed to the third floor, his footsteps dropping wooden blocks into the silence, nudging him awake. He fumbled in his entrance hall for the coat hook on the back of the door, which wasn't where Hilary kept hers. Beneath the window in the main room he saw her desk spread with her syndicated cartoon strip—except that when he switched on the light it was his own desk, scattered with television schedules. He peered blearily at the rumpled bed. Around him the room felt and moved like muddy water. He sagged on the bed and was asleep at once.

The darkness drew him out, coaxing him forward, swimming softly through his eyes. A great silent darkness surrounded him. He sailed through it, sleeping yet aware. He sensed energy flowering far out in the darkness, vast soundless explosions that cooled and congealed. He sensed immense weights slowly rolling at the edge of his blindness.

Then he could see, though the darkness persisted almost un- changed. Across its furthest distances a few points of light shone like tiny flaws. He began to sail towards them, faster. They parted and fled to the edge of his vision as he approached. He was rushing between them, towards others that now swooped minutely out of

the boundless night, carrying cooler grains of congealed dust around
them. They were multiplying, his vision was filling with sprinkled
light and its attendant parasites. He was turning, imprinting each
silently blazing vista on his mind. His mind felt enormous. He felt
it take each pattern of light and store it easily as it returned alert
for the next.

It was so long before he came to rest he had no conscious memory
of starting out. Somehow the path he'd followed had brought him
back to his point of origin. Now he sailed in equilibrium with the
entire system of light and dust that surrounded him, boundless. His
mind locked on everything he'd seen.

He found that part of his mind had fastened telescopically on
details of the worlds he'd passed: cities of globes acrawl with black
winged insects; mountains carved or otherwise formed into heads
within whose hollow sockets worshippers squirmed; a sea from
whose depths rose a jointed arm, reaching miles inland with a filmy
web of skin to net itself food. One tiny world in particular seemed
to teem with life that was aware of him.

Deep in one of its seas a city slept, and he shared the dreams of
its sleepers: of an infancy spent in a vast almost lightless cave, tended
by a thin rustling shape so tall its head was lost to sight; of flight
to this minute but fecund planet; of dancing hugely and clumsily
beneath the light of a fragment they'd torn free of this world and
flung into space; of dormancy in the submarine basalt tombs.
Dormant, they waited and shared the lives of other similar beings
active on the surface; for a moment he was the inhabitant of a black
city deserted by its builders, coming alert and groping lazily forth
as a pale grub fled along a path between the buildings.

Later, as the active ones on the surface had to hide from the
multiplying grubs, those in the submarine city stilled, waiting.
Ingels felt their thoughts searching sleepily, ranging the surface,
touching and sampling the minds of the grubs, vastly patient and
purposeful. He felt the womb of the sea lapping his cell. His huge
flesh quivered, anticipating rebirth.

Without warning he was in a room, gazing through a telescope
at the sky. He seemed to have been gazing for hours; his eyes burned.
He was referring to a chart, adjusting the mounting of the telescope.
A pool of light from an oil lamp roved, snatching at books in cases
against the walls, spilling over the charts at his feet. Then he was
outside the room, hurrying through a darkened theatre; cowls of
darkness peered down from the boxes. Outside the theatre he

glanced up towards the speckled sky, towards the roof, where he knew one slate hid the upturned telescope. He hurried away through the gas-lit streets, out of Ingels' dream.

He awoke and knew at once where the theatre was: at the edge of Brichester, where his mind had been tugging him all day.

### III

He rose at dawn, feeling purged and refreshed. He washed, shaved, dressed, made himself breakfast. In his lightened state the preamble of his dream seemed not to matter: he had had his inclination towards the edge of Brichester explained, the rest seemed external to him, perhaps elaborately symbolic. He knew Hilary regarded his dreams as symptoms of disturbance, and perhaps she was right. *Maybe,* he thought, *they all meant the theatre was trying to get up through my mind. A lot of fuss, but that's what dreams are like. Especially when they're having to fight their way, no doubt. Can't wait to see what the theatre means to me.*

When he went out the dawn clutched him as if he hadn't shaken off his dreams. The dull leaden light settled about him, ambiguous shapes hurried by. The air felt suffocated by imminence, not keen as the cold should make it. *That'll teach me to get up at cock-crow*, he thought. *Feels like insomnia. Can't imagine what they find to crow about.* The queues of commuters moved forward like the tickings of doom.

Someone had left a sheet from the telex on his desk. Photographs from the space probe were expected any hour. He wrote his reviews hurriedly, glancing up to dispel a sense that the floor was alive with pale grubs, teeming through the aisles. *Must have needed more sleep than I thought. Maybe catch a nap later.*

Although his dream had reverted the streets, replacing the electric lamps with gas, he knew exactly where the theatre should be. He hurried along the edge of Lower Brichester, past champing steam-shovels, roaring skeletons of burning houses. He strode straight to the heart of his dream.

One side was razed, a jagged strip of brown earth extending cracks into the pavement and into the fields beyond. But the theatre was on the other side. Ingels hurried past the red-brick houses, past the wind-whipped gardens and broken flowers, towards the patched gouge in the road where he knew a gas lamp had used to guard the theatre. He stood arrested on it, cars sweeping past, and stared at the houses before him, safe from his glare in their sameness. The theatre was not there.

Only the shout of an overtaking car roused him. He wandered along, feeling sheepish and absurd. He remembered vaguely having walked this way with his parents once, on the way to a picnic. The gas lamp had been standing then; he'd gazed at it and at the theatre, which by then was possessed by a cinema, until they'd coaxed him away. Which explained the dream, the insomnia, everything. *And I never used to be convinced by* Citizen Kane. *Rosebud to me too, with knobs on.* In fact he'd even mistaken the location of the lamp; there it was, a hundred yards ahead of him. Suddenly he began to run. Already he could see the theatre, now renamed as a furniture warehouse.

He was almost through the double doors and into the first aisle of suites when he realized that he didn't know what he was going to say. *Excuse me, I'd like to look under your rafters. Sorry to bother you, but I believe you have a secret room here. For God's sake*, he thought, blushing, hurrying down the steps as a salesman came forward to open the doors for him. *I know what the dream was now. I've made sure I won't have it again. Forget the rest.*

He threw himself down at his desk. *Now sit there and behave. What a piddling reason for falling out with Hilary. At least I can admit that to her. Call her now.* He was reaching for the telephone when Bert tramped up, waving Ingels' review of the astronomical television programme. 'I know you'd like to rewrite this,' he said.

'Sorry about that.'

'We'll call off the men in white this time. Thought you'd gone the same way as this fellow,' Bert said, throwing a cutting on the desk.

'Just lack of sleep,' Ingels said, not looking. 'As our Methuselah, tell me something. When the warehouse on Fieldview was a theatre, what was it called?'

'The Variety, you mean?' Bert said, dashing for his phone. 'Remind me to tell you about the time I saw Beaumont and Fletcher performing there. Great double act.'

Ingels turned the cutting over, smiling half at Bert, half at himself for the way he had still not let go of his dream. *Go on, look through the files in your lunch hour*, he told himself satirically. *Bet the Variety never made a headline in its life.*

LSD CAUSES ATTEMPTED SUICIDE, said the cutting. American student claims that in LSD 'vision' he was told that the planet now passing through our solar system heralded the rising of

Atlantis. Threw himself from second-storey window. Insists that
the rising of Atlantis means the end of humanity. Says the Atlan-
teans are ready to awaken. Ingels gazed at the cutting; the sounds
of the newspaper surged against his ears like blood. Suddenly he
thrust back his chair and ran upstairs, to the morgue of the *Herald*.

Beneath the ceiling pressed low by the roof, a fluorescent tube
fluttered and buzzed. Ingels hugged the bound newspapers to his
chest, each volume an armful, and hefted them to a table, where
they puffed out dust. 1900 was the first that came to hand. The
streets would have been gas-lit then. Dust trickled into his nostrils
and frowned over him, the phone next to Hilary was mute, his
television review plucked at his mind, anxious to be rewritten.
Scanning and blinking, he tried to shake them off with his doubts.

But it didn't take him long, though his gaze was tired of ranging
up and down, up and down, by the time he saw the headline:

### ATTEMPTED THEFT AT 'THE VARIETY.'
### TRADESMEN IN THE DOCK.

Francis Wareing, a draper pursuing his trade in Brichester, Donald Norden, a butcher [and so on, Ingels snarled, sweeping past im-
patiently] were charged before the Brichester stipendiary
magistrates with forcibly entering 'The Variety' theatre, on Fieldview, in attempted commission of robbery. Mr. Radcliffe, the owner
and manager of this establishment

It looked good, Ingels thought wearily, abandoning the report, tearing
onward. But two issues later the sequel's headline stopped him short:

### ACCUSATION AND COUNTER-ACCUSATION IN COURT.
### A BLASPHEMOUS CULT REVEALED.

And there it was, halfway down the column:

Examined by Mr. Kirby for the prosecution, Mr. Radcliffe affirmed
that he had been busily engaged in preparing his accounts when,
overhearing sounds of stealth outside his office, he summoned his
courage and ventured forth. In the auditorium he beheld several men

*Get on with it*, Ingels urged, and saw that there had been impatience in
the court too:

Mr. Radcliffe's narrative was rudely interrupted by Wareing, who accused him of having let a room in his theatre to the accused four. This privilege having been summarily withdrawn, Wareing alleged, the four had entered the building in a bid to reclaim such possessions as were rightfully theirs. He pursued:

'Mr. Radcliffe is aware of this. He has been one of our number for years, and still would be, if he had the courage.'

Mr. Radcliffe replied: 'That is a wicked untruth. However, I am not surprised by the depths of your iniquity. I have evidence of it here.'

So saying, he produced for the Court's inspection a notebook containing, as he said, matter of a blasphemous and sacrilegious nature. This which he had found beneath a seat in his theatre, he indicated to be the prize sought by the unsuccessful robbers. The book, which Mr. Radcliffe described as 'the journal of a cult dedicated to preparing themselves for a blasphemous travesty of the Second Coming', was handed to Mr. Poole, the magistrate, who swiftly pronounced it to conform to this description.

Mr. Kirby adduced as evidence of the corruption which this cult wrought, its bringing of four respectable tradesmen to the state of common robbers. Had they not felt the shame of the beliefs they professed, he continued, they had but to petition Mr. Radcliffe for the return of their mislaid property.

*But what beliefs?* Ingels demanded. He riffled onward, crumbling yellow fragments from the pages. The tube buzzed like a bright trapped insect. He almost missed the page.

### FOILED ROBBERS AT 'THE VARIETY.'
### FIFTH MAN YIELDS HIMSELF TO JUSTICE.

*What fifth man?* Ingels searched:

Mr. Poole condemned the cult of which the accused were adherents as conclusive proof of the iniquity of those religions which presume to rival Christianity. He described the cult as 'unworthy of the lowest breed of mulatto.'

At this juncture a commotion ensued, as a man entered precipitately and begged leave to address the Court. Some few minutes later Mr. Radcliffe also entered, wearing a resolute expression. When he saw the latecomer, however, he appeared to relinquish his purpose, and took a place in the gallery. The man, meanwhile, sought to throw himself on the Court's mercy, declaring himself to be the fifth of the robbers. He had been prompted to confess, he affirmed, by a

sense of his injustice in allowing his friends to take full blame. His
name, he said, was Joseph Ingels

Who had received a lighter sentence in acknowledgement of his
gesture, Ingels saw in a blur at the foot of the column. He hardly
noticed. He was still staring at his grandfather's name.

'Nice of you to come,' his father said ambiguously. They'd finished
decorating, Ingels saw; the flowers on the hall wallpaper had grown
and turned bright orange. But the light was still dim, and the walls
settled about his eyes like night around a feeble lamp. Next to the
coat rack he saw the mirror in which he'd made sure of himself
before teenage dates, the crack in one corner where he'd driven his
fist, caged by fury and by their incomprehension of his adolescent
restlessness. An ugly socket of plaster gaped through the wallpaper
next to the supporting nail's less treacherous home. 'I could have
hung the mirror for you,' Ingels said, not meaning to disparage his
father, who frowned and said, 'No need.'

They went into the dining room, where his mother was setting
out the best tablecloth and cutlery. 'Wash hands,' she said. 'Tea's
nearly ready.'

They ate and talked. Ingels watched the conversation as if it were
a pocket maze into which he had to slip a ball when the opening
tilted towards him. 'How's your girlfriend?' his mother said.

*Don't you know her name?* Ingels didn't say. 'Fine,' he said. They
didn't mention Hilary again.

His mother produced infant photographs of him they'd discovered in the sideboard drawer. 'You were a lovely little boy,' she said.

'Speaking of memories,' Ingels said, 'do you remember the old
Variety theatre?'

His father was moving his shirt along the fireguard to give
himself a glimpse of the fire, his back to Ingels. 'The old Variety,'
his mother said. 'We wanted to take you to a pantomime there once.
But,' she glanced at her husband's back, 'when your father got there
all the tickets were sold. Then there was the Gaiety,' and she
produced a list of theatres and anecdotes.

Ingels sat opposite his father, whose pipe smoke was pouring up
the chimney. 'I was looking through our old newspapers,' he said.
'I came across a case that involved the Variety.'

'Don't you ever work at that paper?' his father said.

'This was research. It seems there was a robbery at the theatre. Before you were born, it was, but I wonder if you remember hearing about it.'

'Now, we aren't all as clever as you,' his mother said. 'We don't remember what we heard in our cradle.'

Ingels laughed, tightening inside; the opening was turning away from him. 'You might have heard about it when you were older,' he told his father. 'Your father was involved.'

'No,' his father said. 'He was not.'

'He was in the paper.'

'His name was,' his father said, facing Ingels with a blank stare in his eyes. 'It was another man. Your grandfather took years to live that down. The newspapers wouldn't publish an apology or say it wasn't him. And you wonder why we didn't want you to work for a paper. You wouldn't be a decent shopkeeper, you let our shop go out of the family, and now here you are, raking up old dirt and lies. That's what you chose for yourself.'

'I didn't mean to be offensive,' Ingels said, holding himself down. 'But it was an interesting case, that's all. I'm going to follow it up tomorrow, at the theatre.'

'If you go there you'll be rubbing our name in the dirt. Don't bother coming here again.'

'Now hold on,' Ingels said. 'If your father wasn't involved you can't very well mean that. My God,' he cried, flooded with a memory, 'you do know something! You told me about it once, when I was a child! I'd just started dreaming and you told it to me so I wouldn't be frightened, to show me you had these dreams too. You were in a room with a telescope, waiting to see something. You told me because I'd dreamed it too! That's the second time I've had that dream! It's the room at the Variety, it has to be!'

'I don't know what you mean,' his father said. 'I never dreamed that.'

'You told me you had.'

'I must have told you that to calm you down. Go on, say I shouldn't have lied to you. It must have been for your own good.'

He'd blanked out his eyes with an unblinking stare. Ingels gazed at him and knew at once there was more behind the blank than the lie about his childhood. 'You've been dreaming again,' he said. 'You've been having the dream I had last night, I know you have. And I think you know what it means.'

The stare shifted almost imperceptibly, then returned strengthened. 'What do you know?' his father said. 'You live in the same town as us and visit us once a week, if that. Yet you know I've been dreaming? Sometimes we wonder if you even know we're here!'

'I know. I'm sorry.' Ingels said. 'But these dreams—you used to have them. The ones we used to share, remember?'

'We shared everything when you were a little boy. But that's over,' his father said. 'Dreams and all.'

'That's nothing to do with it!' Ingels shouted. 'You still have the ability! I know you must have been having these dreams! It's been in your eyes for months!' He trailed off, trying to remember whether that was true. He turned to his mother, pleading. 'Hasn't he been dreaming?'

'What do I know about it?' she said. 'It's nothing to do with me.' She was clearing the table in the dim rationed light beyond the fire, not looking at either of them. Suddenly Ingels saw her as he never had before: bewildered by her husband's dreams and intuitions, further excluded from the disturbingly incomprehensible bond between him and her son. All at once Ingels knew why he'd always felt she had been happy to see him leave home: it was only then that she'd been able to start reclaiming her husband. He took his coat from the hall and looked into the dining room. They hadn't moved: his father was still staring at the fire, his mother at the table. 'I'll see you,' he said, but the only sound was the crinkling of the fire as it crumbled, breaking open pinkish embers.

## IV

He watched television. Movement of light and colours, forming shapes. Outside the window the sky drew his gaze, stretched taut, heavily imminent as thunder. He wrote words.

Later, he was sailing through enormous darkness; glinting globes turned slowly around him, one wearing an attenuated band of light; ahead, the darkness was scattered with dust and chunks of rock. A piece of metal was circling him like a timid needle, poking towards him, now spitting flame and swinging away. He felt a contempt so profound it was simply vast indifference. He closed his eyes as he might have blinked away a speck of dust.

In the morning he wrote his review at the flat. He knew he
wouldn't be able to bear the teeming aisles for long. Blindly
shouldering his way across the floor, he found Bert. He had to gaze
at him for a minute or so; he couldn't remember immediately what
he should look like. 'That rewrite you did on the TV review wasn't
your best,' Bert said.

'Ah well,' Ingels said, snatching a copy of last night's *Herald*
automatically from his desk, and hurried for the door.

He'd nearly reached it when he heard the news editor shouting
into the telephone. 'But it can't affect Saturn and Jupiter! I mean,
it can't change its mass, can it? ... I'm sorry, sir. Obviously I didn't
mean to imply I knew more about your field than you. But is it
possible for its mass to change? ... What, trajectory as well?' Ingels
grinned at the crowd around the editor's desk, at their rapt expres-
sions. They'd be more rapt when he returned. He strode out.

Through the writhing crowds, up the steps, into a vista of beds
and dressing tables like a street of cramped bedrooms whose walls
had been tricked away. 'Can I speak to the manager, please,' he said
to the man who stepped forward. *'Brichester Herald.'*

The manager was a young man in a pale streamlined suit, longish
clipped hair, a smile which he held forward as if for inspection. 'I'm
following a story,' Ingels said, displaying his press card. 'It seems
that when your warehouse was a theatre a room was leased to an
astronomical group. We think their records are still here, and if they
can be found they're of enormous historical interest.'

'That's interesting,' the manager said. 'Where are they supposed
to be?'

'In a room at the top of the building somewhere.'

'I'd like to help, of course.' Four men passed, carrying pieces of a
dismembered bed to a van. 'There were some offices at the top of
the building once, I believe. But we don't use them now, they're
boarded up. It would be a good deal of trouble to open them now.
If you'd phoned I might have been able to free some men.'

'I've been out of town,' Ingels said, improvising hastily now his
plans were going awry. 'Found this story on my desk when I got
back. I tried to phone earlier but couldn't get through. Must be a
tribute to the business you're doing.' An old man, one of the loaders,
was sitting on a chair nearby, listening; Ingels wished he would
move, he couldn't bear an audience as well. 'These records really
would be important,' he said wildly. 'Great historical value.'

'In any case I can't think they'd still be here. If they were in one
of the top rooms they would have been cleared out long ago.'

'I think you're a bit wrong there,' the old man said from his chair.

'Have you nothing to do?' the manager demanded.

'We've done loading,' the man said. 'Driver's not here yet.
Mother's sick. It's not for me to say you're wrong, but I remember
when they were mending the roof after the war. Men who were
doing it said they could see a room full of books, they looked like,
all covered up. But we couldn't find it from down here and nobody
wanted to break their necks trying to get in from the roof. Must
still be there, though.'

'That has to be the one,' Ingels said. 'Whereabouts was it?'

'Round about there,' the old man said, pointing above a Scandi-
navian four-poster. 'Behind one of the offices, we used to reckon.'

'Could you help find it?' Ingels said. 'Maybe your workmates
could give you a hand while they're waiting. That's of course if this
gentleman doesn't mind. We'd make a point of your cooperation,'
he told the manager. 'Might even be able to give you a special
advertising rate, if you wanted to run an ad on that day.'

The five of them climbed a rusty spiral staircase, tastefully
screened by a partition, to the first floor. The manager, still frowning, had left one loader watching for the driver. 'Call us as soon as
he comes,' he said. 'Whatever the reason, time lost loses money.'
Across the first floor, which was a maze of crated and cartoned
furniture, Ingels glimpsed reminiscences of his dream: the outline
of theatre boxes in the walls, almost erased by bricks; a hook that
had supported a chandelier. They seemed to protrude from the
mundane, beckoning him on.

The staircase continued upward, more rustily. 'I'll go first,' the
manager said, taking the flashlight one of the loaders had brought.
'We don't want accidents,' and his legs drew up like a tail through
a trapdoor. They heard him stamping about, challenging the floor.
'All right,' he called, and Ingels thrust his face through drifting
dust into a bare plank corridor.

'Here, you said?' the manager asked the old man, pointing to
some of the boards that formed a wall. 'That's it,' the old man said,
already ripping out nails with his hammer, aided by his workmates.
A door peeked dully through. Ingels felt a smile wrenching at his
face. He controlled himself. *Wait until they've gone.*

As soon as they'd prised open the office door he ran forward. A
glum green room, a ruined desk in whose splintered innards squat-

ted a dust-furred typewriter. 'I'm afraid it's as I thought,' the manager said. 'There's no way through. You can't expect us to knock down a wall, obviously. Not without a good deal of consultation.'

'But there must have been an entrance,' Ingels said. 'Beyond this other wall. It must have been sealed up before you got the building. Surely we can look for it.'

'You won't have to,' the old man said. He was kicking at the wall nearest the supposed location of the room. Plaster crumbled along a crack, then they heard the shifting of brick. 'Thought as much,' he said. 'The war did this, shook the building. The boards are all right but the mortar's done for.' He kicked again and whipped back his foot. He'd dislodged two bricks, and at once part of the wall collapsed, leaving an opening four feet high.

'That'll be enough!' the manager said. Ingels was stooping, peering through the dust-curtained gap. Bare boards, rafters and slates above, what must be bookcases draped with cloth around the walls, something in the centre of the room wholly covered by a frame hung with heavy material, perhaps velvet. Dust crawled on his hot face, prickling like fever. 'If the wall would have collapsed anyway it's a good job you were here when it did,' he told the manager. 'Now it's done and I'm sure you won't object if I have a look around. If I'm injured I promise not to claim. I'll sign a waiver if you like.'

'I think you'd better,' the manager said, and waited while Ingels struggled with his briefcase, last night's *Herald,* a pen and a sheet from his notebook, brushing at his eyebrows where dust and sweat had become a trickle of mud, rubbing his trembling fingers together to clean them. The men had clambered over the heap of bricks and were lifting the velvety frame. Beneath it was a reflector telescope almost a foot long, mounted on a high sturdy stand. One of the men bent to the eyepiece, touching the focus.

'Don't!' Ingels screamed. 'The setting may be extremely important,' he explained, trying to laugh.

The manager was peering at him. 'What did you say you do at the *Herald?*' he said.

'Astronomy correspondent,' Ingels said, immediately dreading that the man might read the paper regularly. 'I don't get too much work,' he blundered on. 'This is a scoop. If I could I'd like to spend a few hours looking at the books.'

He heard them descending the spiral staircase. *Squirm away*, he thought. He lifted the covers from the bookcases gingerly, anxious to keep dust away from the telescope, as the velvety cover had for decades. Suddenly he hurried back to the corridor. Its walls bobbed about him as the flashlight swung. He selected a plank and hefting it over the bricks, poked it at the rafters above the telescope, shielding the latter with his arm. After a minute the slate above slid away, and a moment later he heard a distant crash.

He squatted down to look through the eyepiece. No doubt a chair had been provided once. All he could see was a blurred twilit sky. *Soon be night*, he thought, and turned the flashlight on the books. He remembered the light from the oil lamp lapping at his feet in the dream.

Much of the material was devoted to astronomy. As many of the books and charts were astrological, he found, some in Oriental script. But there were others, on shelves in the corner furthest from the sealed-off door: *The Story of Atlantis and the Lost Lemuria, Image du Monde, Liber Investigationis, Revelations of Glaaki.* There were nine volumes of the last. He pulled them out, curious, and dust rose about his face like clouds of sleep.

Voices trickled tinnily up the staircase, selling beds. In the close room dimmed by the dust that crowded at the hole in the roof, towards which the telescope patiently gazed, Ingels felt as if he were sinking back into his dream. Cracked fragments of the pages clung beneath his nails. He read; the words flowed on like an incantation, like voices muttering in sleep, melting into another style, jerking clumsily into another. Sketches and paintings were tipped into the books, some childishly crude, some startlingly detailed: M'nagalah, a tentacled mass of what looked like bloated raw entrails and eyes; Glaaki, a half-submerged spongy face peering stalk-eyed from a lake; R'lyeh, an island city towering triumphant above the sea, a vast door ajar. This he recognized, calmly accepting the information. He felt now as if he could never have had reason to doubt his dream.

The early winter night had blocked up the hole in the roof. Ingels stooped to the eyepiece again. Now there was only darkness through the telescope. It felt blurred by distance; he felt the distance drawing him vertiginously down the tube of darkness, out into a boundless emptiness no amount of matter could fill. *Not yet*, he thought, withdrawing swiftly. *Soon.*

Someone was staring at him. A girl. She was frowning up at the hole in the roof. A saleswoman. 'We're closing soon,' she said.

'All right,' Ingels said, returning to the book, lying face upward in the splayed light. It had settled into a more comfortable position, revealing a new page to him, and an underlined phrase: 'when the stars are right.' He stared at it, trying to connect. It should mean something. The dim books hemmed him in. He shook his head and turned the pages swiftly, searching for underlining. Here it was repeated in the next volume, no, augmented: 'when the stars are right again.' He glanced sharply at the insistent gap of night above him. *In a minute*, he snarled. Here was a whole passage underlined:

'Though the universe may feign the semblance of fickleness, its soul has always known its masters. The sleep of its masters is but the largest cycle of all life, for as the defiance and forgetfulness of winter is rendered vain by summer, so the defiance and forgetfulness of man, and of those others who have assumed stewardship, shall be cast aside by the reawakened masters. When these hibernal times are over, and the time for reawakening is near, the universe itself shall send forth the Harbinger and Maker, Ghroth. Who shall urge the stars and worlds to rightness. Who shall raise the sleeping masters from their burrows and drowned tombs; who shall raise the tombs themselves. Who shall be attentive to those worlds where worshippers presume themselves stewards. Who shall bring those worlds under sway, until all acknowledge their presumption, and bow down.'

*Ghroth*, Ingels thought, gazing up at the gap in the roof. *They even had a name for it then, despite the superstitious language. Not that that was so surprising*, he thought. *Man used to look upon comets that way, this is the same sort of thing. An omen that becomes almost a god.*

*But an omen of what?* he thought suddenly. *What exactly was supposed to happen when the stars were right again?* He knelt in the dust and flurried through the books. No more underlining. He rushed back to the telescope. His thighs twinged as he squatted. Something had entered the field of view.

It was the outer edge of the wandering planet, creeping into the telescope's field. As it came it blurred, occasionally sharpening almost into focus for a moment. Ingels felt as if the void were making sudden feeble snatches at him. Now the planet was only a spreading reddish smudge. He reached for the focus, altering it minutely. 'We're closing now,' said the manager behind him.

'I won't be long,' Ingels said, feeling the focus sharpen, sharpen—

'We're waiting to close the doors,' the manager said. 'And I'm afraid I'm in a hurry.'

'Not long!' Ingels screamed, tearing his gaze from the eyepiece to glare.

When the man had gone Ingels switched off the flashlight. Now he could see nothing but the tiny dim gap in the roof. He let the room settle on his eyes. At last he made out the immobile uplifted telescope. He groped towards it and squatted down.

As soon as he touched the eyepiece the night rushed through the telescope and clutched him. He was sailing through the void, yet he was motionless; everything moved with him. Through the vast silence he heard the ring of a lifted telephone, a voice saying 'Give me the chief editor of the *Herald*, please,' back there across the void. He could hear the pale grubs squeaking tinnily, back all that way. He remembered the way they moved, soft, uncarapaced. Before him, suspended in the dark and facing him, was Ghroth.

It was red as rust, featureless except for bulbous protrusions like hills. Except that of course they weren't hills if he could see them at that distance; they must be immense. A rusty globe covered with lumps, then. That was all, but that couldn't explain why he felt as if the whole of him were magnetized to it through his eyes. It seemed to hang ponderously, communicating a thunderous sense of imminence, of power. *But that was just its unfamiliarity*, Ingels thought, struggling against the suction of boundless space; *just the sense of its intrusion. It's only a planet, after all.* Pain was blazing along his thighs. *Just a red warty globe.*

Then it moved.

Ingels was trying to remember how to move his body to get his face away from the eyepiece; he was throwing his weight against the telescope mounting to sweep away what he could see. It was blurring, that was it, although it was a cold windless day air movements must be causing the image to blur, the surface of a planet doesn't move, it's only a planet, the surface of a planet doesn't crack, it doesn't roll back like that, it doesn't peel back for thousands of miles so you can see what's underneath, pale and glistening. When he tried to scream air whooped into his lungs as if space had exploded a vacuum within him.

He'd tripped over the bricks, fallen agonizingly down the stairs, smashed the manager out of the way with his shoulder and was at the *Herald* building before he knew that was where he intended to go. He couldn't speak, only make the whooping sound as he sucked in air; he threw his briefcase and last night's paper on his desk and sat there clutching himself, shaking. The floor seemed to have been in turmoil before he arrived, but they were crowding around him, asking him impatiently what was wrong.

But he was staring at the headline in his last night's newspaper: SURFACE ACTIVITY ON WANDERER 'MORE APPARENT THAN REAL' SAY SCIENTISTS. Photographs of the planet from the space probe; one showing an area like a great round pale glistening sea, the next circuit recording only mountains and rock plains. 'Don't you see?' Ingels shouted at Bert among the packed faces. 'It closed its eye when it saw us coming!'

Hilary came at once when they telephoned her, and took Ingels back to her flat. But he wouldn't sleep, laughed at the doctor and tranquilizers, though he swallowed the tablets indifferently enough. Hilary unplugged the television, went out as little as possible, bought no newspapers, threw away her contributor's copies unopened, talked to him while she worked, stroked him soothingly, slept with him. Neither of them felt the earth begin to shift.

# Where Yidhra Walks

## by Walter C. DeBill, Jr.

A hundred April winds disperse her fragrance,
A thousand wet Octobers scour her footprints,
The ruthless years assail the ancient memory of her presence, yet
Where Yidhra walks the hills do not forget.

— Jean Paul LeChat

## I

The river was swollen to a mad torrent, the water brown and opaque. I watched a jagged clump of brush sweep by with terrifying speed, three moccasins twined in its sodden branches. The rain had grown heavier for three days while the wind mounted steadily and, though the eye of the hurricane was expected to pass a hundred miles east and the violence of the storm decrease as it moved farther inland, I knew it would be a week before the river could be crossed here even if the decrepit trestle bridge survived. It was shuddering periodically from the strain of the current and the broken remnants of two of the trestles dangled uselessly.

As I stood on the bank a muddy pickup truck pulled up and two men in ponchos and cowboy hats began blocking the entrance to the bridge with sawhorses. One saw me eyeing the bridge and called out, "Good thing you didn't try it, mister, we already had three people drown today when a bridge washed out over by Iverston."

"Is there another bridge across this river that might still be safe? I hate to go all the way around through Barrett. That's a hundred miles out of my way."

He flashed an unsympathetic smirk, plainly intending to say no, then paused. "Well, there's an old bridge upstream five miles, where the river's not so wide. It's on the old road through Milando." He said it in a tense, subdued voice.

His companion stopped tinkering around the truck and stepped over beside him. "If you go that way I'd recommend you keep movin'. Those folks up around Milando never did like outsiders much, and what this hurricane's doin' to their orchards ain't gonna improve their hospitality." They both chuckled.

I remembered seeing Milando on the map and didn't ask for directions. I glanced in the rearview mirror as I drove off and saw them both watching me curiously from under their dripping hat brims.

I don't know why I was so anxious to avoid a detour and keep driving doggedly through the storm. My cousin in Brownsville wasn't expecting me by any fixed date and even losing a week crossing Texas wouldn't have inconvenienced me particularly. Yet the monotonous downpour lulled me into a mental torpor where thoughtless stubbornness pushed me on, and something about the mysterious raging river demanded that I cross it. And of course the peculiar attitude of the men at the bridge had aroused my curiosity about Milando. So I wound my way five miles north on a pitted blacktop road roughly paralleling the river and clattered across the plank floor of an ancient truss bridge. Less than a mile beyond the river a culvert spanning a tributary creek was under a few inches of water, but my little station wagon had a high road clearance for a small car and I decided to risk it. The wheels kept losing traction, letting the car slip sideways in sickening lurches, but I made it. I heard a groaning sound and a huge crash behind me and turned to see the culvert tube bounding jerkily downstream. I could no longer go back.

The road was tortuous and narrow as it wormed upward into the labyrinth of limestone hills, alternating gloomy tunnel-like passages overhung by gnarled live oaks with barren stretches below steep cliffs. The striking appearance of the stunted mesquite trees writhing along the clifftops continually caught my eye in spite of the hazardous driving conditions or I would never have seen the hooded figure against the darkening sky. Somehow I knew that it was a woman, though the hooded rain cape concealed both face and figure. A large dog sat at her feet. I barely had time to wonder what she was doing out there in such abominable weather before I rounded a sudden curve and had my first sight of Milando.

# II

Through a lull in the rain I saw the town spread out below me in a wedge-shaped cleft in the hills. The road snaked down a steep hillside and passed along the mouth of the cleft, where the town was perhaps a mile wide. Almost all of the town lay to the left of the road where the streets wandered aimlessly upward to the point of the wedge, nearly level with the surrounding cliffs.

As I entered the town I slowed to a crawl and began searching for a place to get something to eat. It was darkening rapidly and the slope above me was dotted with lighted windows, but every window and doorway along the main street seemed black and deserted. I almost missed the one business still open because the glow at the windows was so dim. The painted sign said SALOON-GROCERY-MEAT MARKET, so I parked and mounted the concrete porch, catching a stream of rainwater in my collar from the edge of the overhanging roof. Behind the display windows, which featured pyramids of dusty canned goods and an array of cheap pocket knives, a chest-high partition blocked most of the light and the dingy glass filtered the rest to a sickly yellow. But once I rattled my way through the heavy door it was evident that I had found the center of Milando's night life.

To my left several groups of men sat around heavy circular tables playing dominoes. Through an archway at the rear I could see more tables and dominoes. The bar ran along the right-hand side and behind it the wall was lined with rows of canned and packaged foods rising almost to the ceiling. There was no one behind the bar, but as I moved over to it an uncomfortable lull spread through the room and a bald, burly specimen detached himself from one of the games and stepped around to the beer taps in front of me.

"What do you want?" No amenities, no smile.

"Just passing through. Any place in town where I can get a meal?"

"Nope. I'll sell you some of this stuff." His long apelike arm gestured toward the shelves, apparently indicating some grimy boxes of shotgun shells, while his eyes kept me fixed.

"I guess that will have to do."

"Say, which way did you come from?"

"East. The main bridge was about gone and I didn't want to go around through Barrett."

"Well, you're gonna have to go back that way. The low-water crossing west of town's under six feet of water."

"But a culvert washed out behind me not far this side of the river. You mean I'm stuck here for the night?"

The room was silent now. "More than that. Several days, I'd say." Under the bushy brows the eyes had taken on a suspicious cast.

"Plan to check out any old Injun stories?" jeered a beery voice from one of the tables. It seemed to emanate from a set of crooked yellow teeth just below the sharp shadow of a tin lampshade.

The bartender shot a murderous glare in that direction before explaining, "Don't pay no attention to Maynard's warped sense o' humor. He's talking about a fellow name o' Harrison from Barrett, from the university, that came up here lookin' for Indian relics and traces of folklore. Seems this used to be some kind o' medicine place, somethin' to do with a cult called 'Yidhra', but people around here don't know anything about that. The dam' fool got himself lost up in the hills, never was found. This country's full of caves, deep pools, heavy brush. ... Well, I got potato chips and stuff like that, sardines—but I don't know where you're gonna stay till the water goes down. No motel or anything here ..."

A tall man sitting alone at the end on the bar stood up and turned stiffly toward me. "You can stay with us. You're welcome to have dinner. My name's Wilhelm Kramer." The bartender was not pleased and I heard Maynard chuckle nervously.

"Thanks," I said, "that would sure beat sardines and a cold night in my car." Besides, I sensed that the antagonism between him and the others might make him a good source of information about the town. He picked up a heavy rubber raincoat and a canvas fisherman's hat from the jumble of rain gear hung on a set of mounted deer antlers and we left.

In the car he didn't speak except to give terse directions to a rather small unpainted house about halfway up the slope. Crossing the screened-in front porch we entered a neat and cozy living room, warmed by a large radiant heater and the subdued, almost amber light from beneath an opaque cardboard lampshade. From a door at the left emerged a small pale woman who gave me a startled look.

"How do you do. I'm Peter Kovacs," I said, remembering that I hadn't introduced myself to Kramer at the store.

"Mr. Kovacs is staying with us until the creeks go down. The Moreno Creek culvert's washed out and the low-water crossing's under six feet."

Her colorless eyes looked even more startled and after telling us that supper would be ready in a few minutes she disappeared into the kitchen. We hung our coats on hooks by the door and Kramer settled into a threadbare but comfortable-looking armchair while I sat on the overstuffed couch.

"You seem to be the only one in Milando that cares much for strangers, Mr. Kramer," I said, hoping to draw him out about the town. He smiled.

"Yes, the others are pretty hostile to any kind of outsider." He was about forty, with rugged features just beginning to soften around the sharp lines. "Actually they still think of me as an outsider, though I've been here eighteen years. I'm originally from Iverston ... met Georgia, that's my wife, at the junior college in Mesquite City and came here to take over her father's business when his health went bad. I sell oil and gas to farmers on credit. They never did like me." He gave the impression of a normally taciturn man become garrulous under the influence of beer and fresh companionship.

I saw the little goblin faces of three small children peep through the door to a darkened rear hall, then fade away. They seemed to take after the mother.

"Are all the small towns around here this inhospitable?"

"They're all pretty clannish and ingrown, mainly because there's nothing to attract new blood, and tend to peg outsiders as 'city slickers' or beatniks, but Milando's the only one that's downright hostile to *anybody* that wasn't born and raised here. Always was. It was settled right after the Civil War by a bunch that came out together from Georgia. Never did hit it off with the other settlers around here. And then their dealings with the Indians—"

His wife appeared in the doorway, looking more alarmed than ever, and announced that the food was ready. We ate in the brightly lit kitchen. The food was as solid and simple as the furniture and there was little conversation. In the light Mrs. Kramer was faintly attractive in a pallid, wistful way, in spite of a prominent nose and weak chin which made her eyes appear to be slightly to the side of her head. I had noticed the same trait in the bartender and guessed that they were related. The children, a girl of about thirteen whom they called Georgie and two younger boys, had inherited it, along with their mother's wispy blond hair and flat, colorless eyes. They were very quiet. Toward the end of the meal Kramer and his wife had a tense exchange concerning a visit the following day from Kramer's mother-in-law. I guessed that she must live somewhere in the hills near town since having the main roads washed out didn't cancel the visit. He evidently disliked her intensely and the atmosphere became so strained that I was not surprised when Mrs. Kramer failed to join us in the living room afterward.

Kramer brought beer from the refrigerator and I had no trouble getting him back on the history of the town.

"The settlers had a hard time at first, most of the land's too rocky to farm, but once they made peace with the Comanche and started raising sheep and fruit trees, apples and peaches, it got to be the most prosperous town in the hills. Probably would've become a big trading center and county seat like Iverston if the other settlers hadn't been so leery of this bunch. Still don't get any business except from right around the town, the old families that came from Georgia."

"Comanche? I didn't know they raided this far east," I said.

"Oh, yes. They were mainly up in the Panhandle, in the flat open country, but they roamed over most of the state when they felt like it. And this area was a medicine place—the center of a special cult of a goddess called Yidhra. Not all the Comanche belonged, just certain bands. The Tonkawas that lived in the area used to allow 'em free passage to here at certain times in the spring and fall to hold their ceremonies. When the settlers came they cut 'em off, at first anyway, so the Comanche tried to drive 'em out, but after a while they made some kind of agreement with the old chief they called Snake Eyes to let the Indians come twice a year. I guess they were just tired of fighting; the settlement was pretty poor then and probably not worth fighting about. That caused a lot of bad feelings with the other settlements. The Comanche had a pretty fearsome reputation, killin' whites and other Indians was their idea of light recreation, and when they came riding through the hills with their horned buffalo-scalp headdresses and lances and such I guess it was hard to tell a religious pilgrimage from a war party. Anyway, the place became completely isolated. There were even rumors that some of the people here had gone over to the Indian religion. But about that time the place started to prosper and the people didn't care what the neighbors thought." He was slowing down now, his voice getting lower, and I thought he would fall asleep soon.

"Milando's an odd name—sounds Spanish, but I've never heard it before."

"Not Spanish, Indian. Some kind of word they got from the Comanche. They changed the town's name to that in 1887, when some of the original families pulled up and went to California. The town was originally called Kimbrough, after my wife's great-grandfather who led the original move out from Georgia. But when old Kimbrough left with the others in '87 they changed it. Some say they left because they were the only ones who wouldn't go over to the Indian cult. I won't believe that, but it's true that these people know a lot more about that Indian business than they'll ever tell anybody, even me."

I made a few more attempts to get him to say more about the town's strange history, but he had gone as far as he was willing to for the time being and seemed more and more inclined to brood and let the conversation lapse. I felt uncomfortable in the silence and was too restless to sleep at that early hour so I said I was going back to the store for cigarettes. Before leaving I brought in my overnight bag and was shown into the small rear bedroom, from which Georgie had apparently been evicted for the night, where I would sleep.

I didn't really want to go back to the dingy store with its hostile proprietor and clientele, but once in the car I realized that there was nowhere else to go. The rain had become very heavy as the evening progressed and the dirt streets of Milando were in bad enough shape to make driving too risky even if I had been able to see anything. So I crawled down the hill in second gear and parked in front of the gloomy "Saloon-Grocery-Meat Market."

This time the domino players ignored my entry. Only the bartender appeared to take notice, giving me a cold smile. "Well, did ol' Willie tell you all about Milando?"

"Just a little," I said. "Interesting place, so isolated and independent. I'd like to know more—." I was concentrating so intently on sounding banal that I didn't notice the sound of the door until I saw the bartender's eyes staring past me and heard the dead silence at the tables. I hesitated a moment before turning, not knowing whether to expect the Frankenstein monster or something worse. When I did turn I faced the most attractive woman I have ever seen.

I didn't know then what fascinated me about her and I don't know now. She was tall, very slender, even angular but graceful, and from the hooded cape I was certain she was the one I had seen just before entering the town. The long oval face with its short straight nose and almost solemn mouth was pretty, but she was beautiful far beyond any sum of physical attributes. At the time I thought it might be her eyes, they were a luminous gray and very large below a trace of eyeshadow which was the only discernible makeup, but since then I have come to believe that some women have a force of soul which casts an irresistible glamor over whatever features they possess.

She gave me a leisurely examination, then addressed the bartender. "I didn't know there was an outsider in town, Ed."

"He just came in tonight, ma'am. The road's washed out, and he's staying with Willie Kramer." His voice sounded as though he were standing at attention.

"Well, I hope you enjoy your stay, Mr. ...?"

"Kovacs, Peter Kovacs." Her high clear voice affected me hypnotically. "It's an interesting town, I'd like to find out about its history, the Indian cult ..." I was blurting it out thoughtlessly, my mind unfocused.

She had a silvery little laugh. "You'll find that the people in Milando don't have much to tell. But perhaps you'll learn enough to satisfy your curiosity. 'Where Yidhra walks, the hills do not forget.'" Memory stirred and I placed the enigmatic line from Jean Paul LeChat, the brilliant young New Orleans poet who disappeared in Chad in 1957.

"That's from LeChat, isn't it? I remember wondering what it meant when I read it. I'd never heard of the cult of Yidhra before I came here today."

"I doubt if Mr. LeChat knew much about it either," she said, brushing back the hood from her straight blond hair. "He wrote about more things than he understood."

"And Harrison? Did he understand?"

Her eyes widened and her smile became hard, even cruel. "No, not really. He was intelligent in the purely bookish sense, but not really sensitive. Not equipped to understand the real mysteries of life."

I thought she was eyeing me with increasing interest, but she turned abruptly to the bartender and said, "Ed, could I speak to you for a moment, in private?"

After a gruff "Yes, ma'am" they moved toward the archway in the rear. Her walk was fluid, utterly feminine, but not exaggerated, and I noticed that her high shiny boots were clean, though Milando was a quagmire outside and I hadn't heard a car pull up. Her dismissal of me had been rather imperious and I felt a bit sheepish, the more so because I was left standing there with no one to wait on me. I didn't really need the cigarettes so I left.

Back at the house Kramer sat alone staring into space while a backwoods preacher ranted through the static on an ancient console radio with an illuminated dial. He gave a faint grunt of acknowledgment when I said good night, not even turning his head. As soon as I lay down fatigue swept over me like an ocean wave and my mind began to dissolve into fragments of dream. I was vaguely aware of the hissing whispers of the children in the next room—they seemed to have some sort of speech impediment which made it impossible to understand what they said; I remember hearing Kramer's voice over that of the radio preacher, berating his wife about his mother-in-law; last of all before sleep came, I remember picturing with abnormal clarity every line and shadow of the woman's face, the woman in the hood.


# III


I slept late in the morning and by the time I awoke Kramer had left the house. His wife fixed breakfast for me in spite of my demurrals and apologies, seeming even more flustered and inarticulate in her husband's absence. In the awkward silence I observed her more closely than the night before. There was an almost reptilian suggestion in her features, accented by her slouching, round-shouldered carriage and shuffling walk. I wondered how much of her washed-out appearance was due to heredity and how much to a lifetime of small-town boredom and narrowness. With more spirit and a little makeup she might have been quite pretty. I thought of the woman in the hood; small-town life certainly hadn't stifled *her*. I mentioned the incident to Mrs. Kramer and asked if she knew the woman, but it turned out to be the wrong thing to do. She looked terrified and mumbled something about "Miss Yolanda." I asked if she were an outsider and she said no, she had always lived there, but beyond that she claimed to know nothing about her, which was obviously untrue.

Outside, the rain had thinned to drizzle and sunlight was starting to break through in patches. I guessed that the center of the storm had passed during the night. I decided to drive out to the low-water crossing to see if the water had begun to go down, though I was really too curious about Milando to want to leave yet. The road to the west led around a perpendicular bluff into a long narrow valley. Both sides of the road were lined with groves of apple and peach trees. I saw some fruit on the ground, but the storm had apparently done little damage. Farther from the road I caught glimpses of flocks of sheep on the lower slopes of the hills rising to the north and south. Ahead of me the road descended into churning brown water, reemerging fifty yards away. Halfway across the creek protruded the top of a concrete post. The painted line marked "4 1/2 FT" was just visible above the eddying surface. The rain had stopped and the sun was shining through a hole in the clouds, so I got out of the car and walked down to the water's edge. I stood for a while, watching and listening to the rushing stream. When I turned she was there.

She was beside the road at the top of the slope where the trees began, standing in the shade. She was wearing the rain cape with the hood back, the same calf-high boots and short skirt. I resolved not to get rattled this time; the night before I had been tired and off-balance because of the repressed menace of the xenophobic saloon crowd. By daylight she would probably be an intelligent small-town girl, perhaps moderately attractive but not exceptional. I started up the hill.

Neither of us spoke until I reached her. By then I felt the same powerful, unexplainable fascination I had in the gloom of the saloon.

"Hello, Mr. Kovacs. It looks as though you'll be with us for a while. There will be more rain." Her voice had an odd, distant quality I hadn't noticed before.

"Yes, I'd guess two days at least. Maybe I'll get a chance to find out something about this Yidhra thing, though I get the impression I might be better off digging around in the university library in Barrett than trying to get anything out of the people here. Do you know much about it, Miss ...?"

"Call me Yolanda. I guess I know as much about Yidhra as anyone around here. She's old—the Indians didn't bring the worship of Yidhra with them, they found it here. And the cult existed in the Old World. The men of Sumer knew her. But you wouldn't find out much in any university library. There have been books that told about Yidhra and other hidden things, but man has a habit of avoiding things that make him uncomfortable. In the past books like the *Chronicles of Thrang*, the *Cthonic Revelations* of Thanang Phram, the *Black Sutra* of U Pao, have been denounced, suppressed, burned. In modern times they're disposed of even more simply—the professional scholars merely declare them not authentic. Or just ignore them altogether. Perhaps it's for the best—there are elder things much less benign than Yidhra."

I thought these were rather remarkable statements, though there have been a number of fairly plausible theories about pre-Columbian contact between the Old and New Worlds. But I was more interested in hearing what she had to say than in debating with her and didn't challenge them.

"And is the cult really still carried on in Milando?"

"Yes, indeed." She turned and we began ambling side by side down the shady treeline. "Almost all of them are in it now. Kramer's not, of course. He's an outsider. They take in outsiders from time to time—Yidhra needs them—but Kramer just wasn't right for it."

I smiled. "I suppose the cult couldn't spread very far if it never took in any new members."

"No, but then Yidhra doesn't much care about spreading the cult. She's part of life and death and the earth itself; domination means nothing to her. She takes only what she needs. She was born with life itself on this planet and as life grew she grew, as life changed so she changed. And like all life she must change to live. Milando is small and inbred; to limit the cult, or this branch of it, to these people and their descendants would be stasis, a kind of death."

"You really believe in her, don't you?" I said.

Her smile was politely restrained but her gray eyes, deep set in spite of their size, were laughing at me. "Yidhra isn't a matter of faith, Peter. She's real. She does things. You saw the orchards on your way here; we had fifty-mile-an-hour winds night before last. And the sheep; thousands of sheep will take sick and die from this weather, but none around Milando. Her followers even see her, after a fashion, though the ancient books say that what they see is largely illusion, a protective glamour cast over a far more terrifying reality; only the real *participants* in the cult, the inner circle, those born of Yidhra and those chosen to mingle their blood and seed with her to renew her and bring forth new life, only those see her true form."

The sun was hot where it flickered through the leaves and the sultry soporific smell of wet vegetation became oppressive. I moved into the sunlight onto a high flat rock overlooking the water and she followed.

"I wonder if Jean Paul LeChat saw her," I said as we looked down at the stream.

"Perhaps, in Chad. He was seeking her there—all he had found in New Orleans were old books and third-hand accounts from degenerate pseudo-occultists." As she turned toward me her eyes seemed enormous. "You'll see her I think, Peter."

The spell was broken by a spatter of raindrops in advance of a ragged cloudbank. "I'll have to go now," she said.

"Can I give you a ride?"

"No, thank you, I live in the hills near here. There's a trail." She turned and slipped into an imperceptible opening in the brush. I caught sight of her willowy figure through the trees several times as she flitted up the hillside; then the sky turned gray and I had to run for the car to keep from getting drenched.

# IV

When I pulled up in front of the Kramer house and got out of the car I could hear Kramer barking at his wife about the impending visit of his mother-in-law. He had been drinking again and was apparently too engrossed in the squabble to hear me drive up so I overheard some of his taunts before I stepped up on the porch and knocked at the door. At the time I interpreted it as a standard in-law feud—she was a bad influence on the children, she was alienating them from their father, his wife's grandfather should have left with old Kimbrough instead of staying on and becoming "the worst of the lot." I regretted coming back to the house and by the time he opened the door I had made up my mind to get back out as soon as possible, even if it meant driving around aimlessly through the mud or resorting to the saloon.

His wife left the room as I entered and I told Kramer about checking the low-water crossing. When I mentioned running into the young woman I had met in the saloon he looked puzzled and asked her name.

"I didn't get her last name—her first name's Yolanda," I said.

He turned white; it was a while before he spoke. "Look here, Mr. Kovacs—it must be obvious to you by now that there's something pretty strange about this town. You might as well know that the old Indian cult is still very much alive here. They've never let me in on it, but you can't live in a town like this for eighteen years without getting a pretty good idea what's going on. And I think she's at the head of it."

"She seemed harmless enough to me," I said, "imaginative, full of wild ideas, but basically a decent girl."

"Girl, Mr. Kovacs?" He chucked wryly. "When I first saw her, about the time they started to take me for granted and quit worrying about my suspicions, she looked exactly as she does now. That was fifteen years ago."

This disturbed me more than it should have; I had found her age peculiarly hard to judge in the saloon, placing it somewhere between eighteen and twenty-eight, and after talking with her in daylight had inclined toward the lower figure. But then there had been the bartender's rigid deference toward her and the occasional hints of condescension in her attitude to warn me; why should it be so upsetting to think of her as in her mid-thirties?

"I think you'd be wise to stay away from her," he went on. "You heard about that student that came here last year—they never found him. There were others before him. She seems to be interested in you. That's a bad sign, Mr. Kovacs. These people are dangerous."

I made some vague promises to be careful and left. The rain was light but steady and I decided to risk a drive around the town. Except for the stretch of road along the foot of the hill Milando consisted of unpaved streets, now soft, slippery, and gullied, but somehow I managed to avoid getting stuck. The houses were uniformly low and wooden, with haphazard additions that gave them a rambling look in spite of their generally small size. Considering the alleged prosperity of the town, a surprising proportion were shabby and dilapidated, with ragged screens, broken wooden steps, and missing windowpanes replaced with cardboard. I wondered if this was an outward sign of the inhabitants' spiritual and mental degeneracy, of their regression into barbarous superstition. Almost none of the houses were painted, though in the few well kept specimens like Kramer's the unpainted wood gave an impression of dignity rather than squalor. I found the overall effect depressing, and the furtive sullen looks the occupants gave me before pulling down yellowed windowshades made me uneasy, so I soon headed down the hill to the saloon. I think I was hoping to run into Yolanda again in spite of Kramer's warning.

Ed, the bartender, greeted me with a nasty smile. "Still with us? I figured you would be, unless you felt like swimming out."

"You were right, looks like two or three more days before I can cross that low-water bridge. You sell beer this time of day?"

"Any time; the state liquor people don't get up here much and the county law don't care." He handed me a bottle of a popular local brand without offering a choice.

"And I suppose you're the chief of police?"

"Naw, that's Maynard. You still interested in the old Indian doings here?"

"Yes, very much."

"Well, I got Harrison's notes here, the student that disappeared. We found 'em in the brush, after Maynard called off the search and the Ranger left. Didn't seem worthwhile to send 'em on."

If the investigator sent by the state had left the search to the local people anything could have happened, anything could have been concealed. Kramer had said these people were dangerous and somehow the bartender's new congeniality was not at all reassuring.

The notes consisted of loose sheets in a cheap accordion folder. I carried them and the beer over to one of the round tables and sat down to examine them. The sheets had been dated and numbered and many pages were missing. The first few pages consisted of accounts, apparently copied from the state archives in Barrett, from early Texas settlers who had spoken to other Indian groups about the devotees of Yidhra, whom they called by many variant names such as Yee-Tho-Rah. The cult had originated somewhere east of the West Texas Plains, among unknown tribes described as tall, hairy, and very primitive, and had spread among the Comanche only a few generations before the Europeans appeared. The bands which had adopted the cult had been abhorred by the other Comanche, who seemed to consider them physically repellent as well as dangerous. They occasionally kidnaped members of other bands for some purpose, possibly ritual sacrifice, though there were rumors that some of the captives had been found or rescued alive. The Indians were curiously reluctant to speak of these captives, but the settlers concluded from various hints that they had been killed by their rescuers because of some physical deformity associated with conversion to the cult. At this point there was a break in the notes where some pages were missing.

The next section was a series of quotes from standard reference works on anthropology and folklore, interspersed with Harrison's own remarks. He seemed to have concluded that Yidhra was a version of the universal figure of the earth-mother or goddess of the underworld connected with primitive concepts of prosperity, fertility, and death, but that the cult was not directly related to any mentioned in standard sources. Toward the end of this section there were indications that he had unearthed some obscure sources, possibly in a private library, which he thought might contain information on Yidhra and planned to investigate them next. There were a number of parenthetical questions and notes such as "Related to Mlandoth cycle?", "Try the *Chronicles* on this point", and "Cf. Könnenberg's *U.S.*" Then came a large gap in the page number sequence.

The notes began again during Harrison's investigations in Milando and were plainly fragmentary and incomplete with many individual pages removed. From what remained I gathered that he had never stayed overnight in Milando, but had made numerous trips from Barrett over a period of about a month. He commented on the reticence of most of the inhabitants, but managed to contact Kramer and two others who told him essentially what Kramer had told me. There was no mention of Yolanda, though one page following a deletion began with the suggestive phrase, "... she doesn't consider me suitable." There were a few hints that he was correlating the information obtained in Milando with the obscure sources mentioned just before the big gap in the page numbers, but there was no explicit or elaborate correlation about survival of the cult into the present, but toward the end missing pages became more frequent and any references to definite discovery of cult practices must have been systematically removed. On the last page Harrison expressed frustration with the reticence of the townspeople and resolved to go exploring on foot in the hills.

Altogether the notes were less interesting than the fact that they had been shown to me. Last night Ed had been openly offensive and had tried to discourage any interest in Milando; today he affected courtesy, if not friendliness, and deliberately whetted my curiosity. A decision must have been made, undoubtedly by Yolanda, as to how I would be dealt with and he was no longer worried about me. I was to be led on, but not told too much just yet. As I sat smoking a cigarette and sipping the last of my second beer I drew two conclusions, one right and one wrong. The first was that, unlike Harrison, I was "suitable"; I had been chosen to join the cult of Yidhra. The second was that I was therefore in no danger and could proceed boldly to find out what lay in the hills behind Milando.

V

A combination of reason and intuition told me that what I wanted to know lay over the hill at the top of the cleft. Logically there was the fact that while presumably there were several hundred people involved in the cult I could see no place suitable for a large gathering, no large buildings, and nothing resembling a town square. To the north beyond the main road there was a steep rise to sheer cliffs; I had traveled the roads east and west as far as a man could conveniently walk and had seen nothing that looked like a gathering place and nothing striking enough to inspire an Indian medicine place; thus my attention was naturally drawn to the point of the wedge to the south. I had noticed that there was a break in the cliff line there where a shallow brush-choked saddle passed over the crest, but until now the weather and a vague sense of danger had cut off any thought of investigation on foot. But now it was clear that I could learn little more from random conversation and I had, I thought, a kind of immunity from the consequences of prying. I could, of course, wait for them to initiate me into the cult, but that struck me as a very dangerous course. There had been in Harrison's notes several disquieting suggestions of physical deformity connected with conversion; possibly their rites involved some form of mutilation or worse. I decided to pretend to go along with them, find out as much as possible on my own, and get out of Milando as soon as the water went down.

It was almost four o'clock when I got back to the Kramer house and I wanted to start my hike with as much daylight left as possible. The rain was light, hardly more than a mist, and I was also anxious to take advantage of this. But Kramer insisted that his wife fix a ridiculously early supper because I had missed lunch, so I was unable to get away until four-thirty. It was a dismal meal, Kramer and I sitting alone at the table with neither of us at all hungry, while his wife dutifully rattled pots and pans without speaking to us and the children hissed and whispered in the next room. He made an effort to dissuade me from going out on foot, though I hadn't told him of my plan to go over the hill, but he was too preoccupied with some worry of his own to object strenuously. His wife's presence seemed to inhibit him from referring openly to the danger he had mentioned earlier. Only at the door as I prepared to leave did he give a low-voiced warning.

"Don't underestimate these people, Mr. Kovacs. I've been seeing things for years and tried to ignore them, tried not to believe, but I know now that there's something foul going on here. There are things here that have no right to exist in a decent world."

I wore a rain hat, thinking an umbrella would be of no use in heavy brush, and changed to high-topped hiking boots even though I hoped the mud would be less of a problem on higher ground than it was in town. I took a flashlight and extra batteries in case I couldn't get back before dark. There wasn't much chance of slipping out of town unobserved, but there were few phone lines in Milando and I hoped the wet weather would delay any organized effort to stop me.

At the top of the cleft a short dirt street, populated only by two apparently deserted shacks, ran parallel to a wall of dense vegetation. I quickly found the narrow, well worn path leading into the brush and through the saddle between the cliffs. At first the trees and bushes were too high to see much, but I could tell that the path ran steeply downward. Soon I passed through several rocky spots where the brush thinned and through the light rain I saw the broad green valley into which I was descending, lush and beautiful under the gray overcast. Along the bottom ran an irregular band of darker green which must mark some narrow creek, sunk below the surrounding land by erosion. I passed rapidly down the trail and within a half hour found myself on the edge of a canyon, at least sixty feet deep and perhaps a hundred yards wide. Along the boulder-strewn bottom a racing stream wound among huge oaks and pecan trees. The path turned to the right and followed the canyon rim upstream.

When I saw the pool I knew it was the right place, the center of the cult. Aeons past an underground river had flowed there, swirling in a whirlpool two hundred yards wide until the cavern roof collapsed leaving a perfectly circular pool. Around the edges slabs of fallen limestone protruded above the surface at crazy angles. Now a waterfall ran over the lip of the crater-like depression and the circle of stone was open on one side where the creek flowed out of the pool into the canyon. The sheer walls were undercut to form a wide, sheltered ledge around the water and to the left of the cascade the black mouth of a great cavern, undoubtedly the channel of the ancient underground river, opened onto the ledge. I watched for a while to be sure the place was deserted before searching for a way down to the pool and soon found the steps cut into the rock face. The rain-slick steps had been worn smooth and hollowed almost to a ramp in the center. At the bottom a path led up to the ledge and I followed it around, intending to reach the large cavern. But behind the waterfall I found the mouth of a smaller cave, now sealed with a wooden wall. The heavy door in the center of the wall did not appear to be locked and I stepped quietly up to it. I could hear no sound within and it was fastened from the outside with a simple wooden slide latch. When I slid it back the door swung noiselessly inward. Stepping inside I switched on my flashlight and saw a narrow room extending about thirty feet back into the rock. I closed the door behind me and began to investigate its contents.

The left-hand wall was lined with a row of old-fashioned chests with bowed lids. I tried the first one and found it unlocked. On top were several robes elaborately embroidered with strange designs, but I didn't take them out and examine them closely for fear of leaving signs of my search. On the right were several ceremonial objects of exquisite workmanship, a brazier on a tripod, a four-foot candelabrum, and a peculiar thing shaped oddly. This last object was of smooth bronze and mounted on a pedestal. The others were of some alloy resembling gold, but lighter in weight and color and chased with intricate designs in which the shape of the bronze object figured prominently. Apparently it was an important symbol in the cult. The remainder of the designs bore no resemblance to the art of the plains Indian, though there were vague suggestions of South and Central American patterns. I saw a table against the rear wall of the room with some papers on it and went to see if I could find some blank paper which I could safely take to copy a sample of the designs. The papers proved to be the missing portions of Harrison's notes, the portions someone had deliberately removed to prevent my learning too much about the cult of Yidhra. There was a chair and a modern propane lamp; I lit the lamp and sat down to read what someone had sought to conceal from me.

One bundle evidently consisted of quotes from the obscure sources Harrison had turned to when the standard reference works failed. The first was headed, "Graf von Könnenberg, *Uralte Schrecken*, nineteenth-century treatise on ancient religious cults", and continued, "It is clear that the most ancient gods, the prototypes of all the gods of men, were known and worshiped before men existed; and it is further clear that the most ancient gods all proceed from the one source. That source is Mlandoth, and all gods are but varied manifestations and extensions of the One. But whether Mlandoth is a place, or a conscious entity, or an inconceivable maelstrom of unknown forces and properties outside the perceptible cosmos is not known.

"Certainly Ngyr-Khorath, the mad and monstrous thing which haunted this region of space before the solar system was formed and haunts it still, is but a local eddy of the vastness that is Mlandoth. And is not fabled 'Ymnar, the dark stalker and seducer of all Earthly intelligence', merely the arm of Ngyr-Khorath, an organ created in the image of Earthly life and consciousness to corrupt that life and lead it to its own destruction?

"And does not even great Yidhra, who was born of and with the life of Earth and who through the aeons intertwines endlessly with all Earthly life-forms, teach reverence for Mlandoth?"

The next quote was from the *Black Sutra* of U Pao, which I recognized with a thrill as one of the books Yolanda had mentioned:

"Before death was born, *She* was born; and for untold ages there was life without death, life without birth, life unchanging. But at last death came; birth came; life became mortal and mutable, and thereafter fathers died, sons were born, and never was the son exactly as the father; and the slime became the worm and the worm the serpent, and the serpent became the yeti of the mountain forests and the yeti became man. Of all living things only *She* escaped death, escaped birth. But *She* could not escape change, for all living things must change as the trees of the north must shed their leaves to live in winter and put them on to live in spring. And therefore *She* learned to devour the mortal and mutable creatures, and from their seed to change *Herself,* and to be as all mortal things as *She* willed, and to live forever without birth, without death."

There followed a note not enclosed in quotation marks which I assumed to be Harrison's own comment:

*U Pao was early Burmese sage—incredibly advanced speculation on evolutionary principles—is it possible that a protean macroorganism could have developed and survived from before the advent of reproduction and individual death? How could it have survived in competition with organisms capable of evolution? References to change in Y. very puzzling.*

The next fragment was from the *Chronicles of Thrang*:

"Yidhra devoured the octopus and learned to put forth a tentacle; she devoured the bear and learned to clothe herself in fur against the creeping ice of the north; indeed can Yidhra take any shape known to living things. Yet no shape can she take which is truly fair, for she partakes of all foul creatures as well as fair. To her followers she appears in many fair and comely forms, but this is because they see not her true form, but only such visions as she wills them to see. For as the adepts can send their thoughts and visions to one another over great distances so can Yidhra send her thoughts to men and cause them to see only what she wills. Indeed it is by sending her thoughts that Yidhra remains one in soul, for in body she is many, hidden in the jungles of the south, the icy wastes of the north, and the deserts beyond the western sea. Thus it is that though her temples are many, she waits by all, combining bodily with her diverse followers, yet her consciousness is a vast unity."

In the comment following this, Harrison's line of thought became chillingly clear:

*One of the later additions to the* Chronicles, *probably from pre-Sumerian Ngarathoe just after the last ice age. Fragmented organism linked by telepathy would explain ability to manifest herself at cult centers throughout the world—von Könnenberg and Crowley mentioned centers in Laos, New Mexico, Chad, West Texas. Telepathically induced visions could explain appearances in animal and human form. Need for evolutionary adaptation satisfied by absorbing genetic material (nucleic acids?) from organisms that reproduce—could also develop intellectual capabilities in this way.* I didn't know enough biology to judge the plausibility of this, but it was obvious that Harrison had rationalized a possible basis for the physical reality of Yidhra.

The last quotation was difficult and obscure. Harrison apparently saw it in manuscript and was unsure of its origin, though he thought it might be: *a portion of the manuscript Prjevalski found in Kashgar and attributed to the legendary "mad lama of Prithom-Yang"—Braithwaite's translation?* In spite of the obscurity of the language and exotic literary form I began to see a hideous application to the facts and hints I had concerning Milando:

> Yidhra, the Lonely One, craving the life of all things;
>   Lonely One, needing the life of the Earth.
> Yidhra, the Goddess, ruling her avatar races;
>   Goddess, of vulturine Y'hath of the sky,
>   Goddess, of Xothra who sleeps in the Earth
>     and wakes to devour;
>   Goddess, of men in strange places who worship her.
> Yidhra, the Hierophant, teaching her followers mysteries;
>   Hierophant, teaching strange tongues of the elder world.
> Yidhra, the Bountiful, making the hills and the meadows
>       green;
>   Bountiful, showing the way to the desert springs,
>   Bountiful, guarding the flocks and the harvest.
> Yidhra, the Lover, needing the seed of her followers;
>   Lover, who must have the seed of all things,
>   Lover, who must have the seed of change or die,
>   Lover, whose consorts are changed,
>     infused with the seed of the past and changed
>     to forms not of past nor of present.
> Yidhra, the Mother, bringing forth spawn of the past;
>   Mother, of all things that were,
>   Mother, of children of past and of present,
>   Mother, whose children remember all things
>     of their fathers long dead.
> Yidhra, the Life-Giver, bringing long life to her followers;
>   Life-Giver, giving the centuries endlessly
>     to her children and lovers and worshipers.
> Yidhra, the Restless One, needing the sons of new fathers;
>   Restless one, sending her followers forth
>     to seek new blood for her endless change,
>   Restless One, craving new lovers outside the blood
>     of her worshipers

lest she and her spawn and her followers
    shrivel and wither in living death.
Yidhra, the Dream-Witch, clouding the minds of her
    followers;
    Dream-Witch, hiding her shape in illusion,
    Dream-Witch, cloaking her shape in strange beauty.
Yidhra, the Shrouder, wreathing the faithless in shadow;
    Shrouder, devouring the errant and hostile ones,
    Shrouder, who hides men forever. ...

The other stack of papers proved to be the missing notes on
Harrison's activities in Milando. In one way his experience had been
the reverse of mine; the bartender had initially been cautiously
encouraging, dropping cryptic hints without giving any definite
information, but after Harrison's first encounter with Yolanda, Ed
and most of the other people in town had tried to shut him out.
Even Kramer had been afraid to speak openly of the cult, though
Harrison had become convinced that it was active and that Yolanda
was the head of it.

I came out of my rapt concentration with the feeling I had heard
something come through the rush of the waterfall, some barely
audible and unidentifiable sound that breathed terror; perhaps it
was only my imagination, stimulated by the dark hints I had been
reading, but I turned out the lamp and stepped quietly to the door.
I opened it a crack and peered into the cavern mouth to the right.
It was darkening rapidly, but I could detect movement in the
shadow. There was a large animal like a hound alternately scamper-
ing to the entrance and scuttling back into the cave in a cringing
attitude. Then a dark figure seemed to rise up from the floor of the
cavern as though emerging from a sunken stairway. I knew I did
not want to meet either of those figures and if I waited very long I
would have to find my way back in total darkness. The ledge along
which I had to return was in shadow and most of the way I would
be shielded from view by the waterfall and the fallen slabs of rock
along the water's edge. I decided to take the chance.

I ran wherever I was well screened, counting on the waterfall to
cover the sound, and made it to the foot of the stair up the cliff
without being noticed. On the stairs I was badly exposed, though
the trunks and foliage of some of the tallest trees gave some scattered
cover, but looking back from the top I could make out the hound
and its shadowy master on the ledge and they didn't seem to be in

pursuit. I was catching my breath at the top when I heard voices on the trail ahead and ducked into the brush.

Two men I hadn't seen before appeared and posted themselves near the head of the stair. I gathered from the scraps of conversation I could understand that they were part of a search party sent to find me. Their mission was to head me off if I tried to descend to the pool. They held the pool in awe and seemed to assume that if I had already gone down I would be "taken care of."

I began to make my way as quietly as possible though the rain-soaked brush, moving parallel to the path. The rain was growing heavy as darkness fell and the occasional flashes of lightning did as much to show the way as the dwindling daylight. It was slow going and progress would have been impossible without the frequent outcrops of rock to thin the vegetation. I was able to see the trail and hear voices on it much of the time and soon found that the searchers had spread out over the slope. They were all around me now, passing on both sides.

At one point two men stopped and sat down on a boulder by the trail near me so that I could overhear them clearly.

"... She says he didn't come down there. Must have gone off the trail."

"Don't know why she wants him so bad. He don't seem much different from the other one."

"They say it's somethin' about his mind. The other one wasn't as good—that's why he didn't help much an' she needs fresh blood again so soon. Or we'll all start to shrivel up like the bunch in West Texas. Did Maynard ever tell you about that? He went out there an' saw 'em. Said it was like livin' death."

"Naw, I mostly stay away from Maynard. An' Ed too. I know we're all bound to her, we've all taken the Communion and accepted the eternal life, but I think some of the big shots has had s'much to do with her they're hardly human anymore. Anyway, they give me the creeps. An' what she did to that Harrison boy! She needed him, but she hated him fer not bein' good enough. 'Course that was the full *Fusion*, not just the Communion. But ain't it about the same thing? She gets a little more like us and we get a little more like her?"

It was a relief when they stopped talking and sat in silence; the horrors of Milando were crowding too close and I had heard enough. I continued up the hill. I had not gone very far when I heard them speak again. I couldn't understand them this time, but the tone was one of respect and the answering voice was Yolanda's. I stood close to a big tree trunk to camouflage my outline and waited for her to pass on the trail. It was not completely dark yet and a moment later I could see her slender silhouette stalking up the trail. The hound was following at her heels, dashing from one side of the trail to the other. Then it gave a sort of snorting moan and ran into the brush below me. I could hear it snuffling and crashing through the bushes as it zigzagged toward me. I stood very still. Suddenly it was charging straight at me. I could make out a long muzzle, more like a crocodile than a dog, and it seemed to have a short, heavy tail. Just as it rose up and ran on two legs she called to it and it turned aside. I was trembling and it took a while for the phrase she used to sink in. She had said, "Come, Mr. Harrison."

# VI

I stood for a while under the dripping tree, trying not to think. There was a cult here, certainly, a dangerous one, but the rest was fantasy. The people of Milando had not seen a primeval abomination that dwelt in these hills; they were victims of mass hallucination or the impostures of cult leaders. And Yolanda, with a whimsical touch of black humor, had named her dog after a troublesome intruder who had caused a local sensation by disappearing. Or being murdered. The hints of *fusion* and resulting physical degeneracy were ignorant superstition; a man could not exchange genetic material with an aeons-old creature and thus become a beast. It was an ordinary hound. A hound that went sometimes on four legs and sometimes on two.

It was pitch-black now and I risked walking on the trail. Once I glimpsed a flashlight beam ahead, but I hid in the brush and the searchers passed without spotting me. After I crossed the top of the slope and entered Milando I had to avoid passing near the many lighted windows as well as worrying about exposure in the frequent lightning flashes. Half the town seemed to be out tramping through the rain and several times I passed within thirty yards of people, but they either didn't see me or assumed I was one of them. By the time I approached the Kramer house I was wondering whether the search for me could account for all the activity.

I had followed the darkest route rather than the shortest and wound up approaching the house from the east side. I could see light in the kitchen windows and hear Kramer raving in an hysterical rage. I had slipped up next to an old shed on the property next door when I heard someone walk heavily up to the other side of the shed.

"Has he been here?" said a low voice.

"No. Didn't they catch him over the hill?"

"No luck. Don't know whether he got lost in the brush or slipped back into town. How long you been watching the house?"

"About twenty minutes. Got the place surrounded. Old Kramer's really out of his mind, threatenin' to kill Miz Kimbrough an' go out an' tell everybody about Milando and everything else. We'll have to take care of him this time. We're just waitin' on *her*."

"Where is she?"

"Down at the saloon with Ed. Maynard went to get her; she should be here pretty soon."

I had blundered into a ring of watchers staked out around the house. By luck I hadn't been seen, but in getting away I might not be so lucky. The lightning flashes were coming more often now and, though I was hidden from their light by the corner of the shed, I would have to pass some long open spaces if I retreated. And I felt I had to warn Kramer that he was in danger, even though the mother-in-law's visit had triggered an explosion I had to face. But I did not have to make that decision, for a moment later the tension erupted in violence: the gutty boom of a shotgun blast, then a woman's scream silenced by another blast. Then a third and I heard small feet running across the porch. Two of the children ran into the circle of window light in front of the house, two more shots and their still forms lay in the rain. While I stood and watched in stunned incomprehension the lights went out all over Milando.

My only thought then was to get away. My car was in front of the house near the corner. With the lights out in the house I might be able to get to it and drive away before anyone could stop me. I moved as quietly as possible to the side of the house. I got there before the next lightning flash. The lightning was from the northwest, to the left and front of the house, so that the kitchen side was left in blackness. I moved to the front corner, took off my hat and stood with one eye past the corner until the next flash. Kramer was standing not fifteen feet from the car, holding the shotgun. And stealthy footsteps from behind me told me the watchers were moving in next to the house itself. Without thinking I opened the kitchen door next to me and entered the house. The click of the night latch behind me seemed terribly loud.

I stood there only a minute, with my heart pounding and the water running off my raincoat onto the floor, before I heard Yolanda's voice outside. "Kramer," she said. "Kramer, you have slain the children of Yidhra." I went to look out the small window over the sink. "You are doomed, Kramer," she said. The lightning was flashing; I could see her hooded silhouette and Kramer fumbling with the gun. He seemed to be trying to raise it and hesitating. "You cannot defy me, Kramer." Then in an extended burst of lightning I saw the hound-thing leap at him, and the gun roared. Whatever spell she held over him was broken; he raised the gun high and fired. As the lightning flickered and died away I saw her writhing on the ground, appearing grotesquely shapeless under the sprawling cloak; then she lay still.

I stood petrified. I heard Kramer's heavy tread on the porch, followed by an incongruous sound I could not at first identify. With quiet horror I realized that he was sitting in the rocking chair on the porch, rocking gently, back and forth. He must have been quite mad.

In the long minutes before I began to think again, the darkness magnified the sound horribly. The rocking chair creaked. The rain drummed on the roof, it dribbled from the eaves, it spattered into the puddles on the ground, and the rocking chair creaked. I had to get a grip on myself and think of a plan. If I could get to the car perhaps I could get out of town and hide until it was safe to swim across. I tried quietly to open the kitchen door and my stomach knotted in panic; the night latch was of an ancient type that needed a key to be opened from the inside.

The kitchen door was locked and getting past Kramer would be impossible. I could open a window, but Kramer would surely hear and come before I could climb out. And, besides, I was pretty sure someone was out there now. I remembered a back door by the room where I had slept. I would try for that. I began to feel my way toward the door to the living room, moving in slow motion to avoid hitting anything that might make a sound. The lightning through the small window wasn't much help, the light falling mainly on the side of the room away from the door. I was near the door, slowly lowering my foot, when it touched something soft. Instinct told me what it was before reason could operate and I almost lost my balance as my foot jerked back. I tried to find a way around the corpse and touched it again. I couldn't face the possibility of touching it another time; I would have to risk the flashlight. Kramer was facing

the other way and I waited for the lightning before flicking the
flashlight for the briefest instant.

The lightning must have been very near, for the thunder followed
it closely enough to cover the involuntary sound I made when I saw
the thing and knew why Kramer had gone mad and slaughtered his
wife and children. It was the mother-in-law, the daughter of old
Kimbrough's son who had been "the worst of the lot", the mother
of Kramer's wife, the grandmother of those who lay still in the rain.
Wearing ample clothing and the wig that lay beside her I suppose
she could have passed as fully human, though incredibly ugly and
deformed, but now there could be no doubt of the alien taint. No
fully human being has such wide cheekbones, or such bulging
lidless eyes set so far to the side. The ears were vestigial and there
was no hair; the back of the head and neck were scaled. The tongue
protruded and was perceptibly forked.

I forced myself to step over the thing in the dark. I remember
being obsessed with the thought that I might step on the tongue.
I was also terrified of bumping into another corpse in the hall between
the living room and the rear of the house and moved even more
slowly than before. I kept looking back and seeing Kramer silhouetted by the lightning against a window that opened onto the porch.

I hadn't gone far into the hall when I felt a presence, a numbing
sensation both calming and weirdly evil. It reminded me of the
enchantment I had felt in Yolanda's presence, but it was different,
less warm and human, more savage, more powerful. I realized the
rocking chair had stopped. Every nerve was alert as I turned to watch
the open door and window. The lightning flickered and in a hideous
stop-motion effect I saw the monstrous caped figure move toward
Kramer as he whimpered and clicked two firing pins on empty
chambers. He shrieked twice as the thing spread its arms wide and
shrouded him in the vast folds of its cloak; then he was silent.

I knew I should try to get away, but I was incapable of motion as
the thing crept slowly across the porch and through the door toward
me. It drew itself up six feet in front of me and said, "Hello, Peter,"
in a voice hauntingly, damnably like Yolanda's, but deeper, hol-
lower, indistinct, with an alien intonation like the children's hissing
whispers. I shone the flashlight on the face a full seven feet above
the floor—it was her, but larger, with hollow cheeks and sunken,
burning eyes and teeth grinning in a rigid travesty of a smile.
Kramer's shotgun had shattered the fragment of protean Yidhra that
projected the beauty of Yolanda, and in its place Yidhra had sent

another multiform fragment of herself creeping over the hill, a fragment that had not yet perfected the illusion.

The realization weakened the spell and I fought for control of my consciousness. For an instant her outline wavered, the face blurred, and in mortal fear of what I might see I turned and ran down the hall and into the first bedroom, slamming the door behind me. I found a window in the dark, threw it up and fumbled with the screen latch, and in a second was over the sill.

I heard someone running toward me along the side of the house, but jumped aside and felt him rush past. Then I ran for the car. I hit the fender running full speed, knocking the wind out of myself, but managed to feel my way to the keyhole, find the key, and get in even before I caught my breath. I backed onto the road, slammed the car into first, and started swerving down the muddy hill. A group of men tried to block the road, but when I bore down on them they jumped out of the way. I think I hit one of them. At the bottom of the hill I tried to turn right and slid off into the ditch on the left. It wasn't deep enough to flood the engine, but I thought surely I was stuck. I kept spinning the wheels and sliding till the wheels found something solid and pulled me up onto the road. I came out heading to the left and continued that way out of town.

The side roads were fewer in that direction and I kept letting them go by, wanting to get farther from town. Before I knew it I was over the hill at the flooded creek. I hit the brakes and nothing happened—they must have got soaked in the ditch. The car plowed into the water with a tremendous splash, the engine died, and I felt the car being pulled sideways by the current. I felt the car lose contact with the bottom and start floating downstream. Water was leaking in slowly but steadily and when the car rolled over on its side I knew it would soon turn upside down and I would be trapped. I got out of my boots and coat, opened the door above me, and climbed out.

There was no question of swimming purposefully in that torrent; I could only struggle to stay afloat and grasp at anything solid I bumped into. Eventually I grabbed something that held me against the current. It was a tree trunk sticking out of a brush jam and I was able to pull myself slowly and painfully to the bank. As I lay panting face down with my feet still in the water I felt the current running from my right to my left. I was on the far side. I had escaped from Milando.

# VII

When I walked into Edmondsville at dawn I was suffering from shock, exhaustion, and pneumonia, and promptly collapsed. I was more or less delirious for a week and said enough to alarm the doctor, who informed the local sheriff, who called in a state lawman. I had been completely incoherent, but they gathered that a family named Kramer and someone named Yolanda had died by violence in Milando during the storm.

When I came to my senses they showed me a newspaper article about the tragic death by fire of the Kramer family of Milando, including Mrs. Kramer's mother, Mrs. Elizabeth Kimbrough. After that I pretended to be unable to remember what had happened. I had stayed with a family named Kramer in Milando, but could remember nothing else. I knew the truth would be utterly incredible to them and was afraid to concoct some plausibly false version to stimulate an investigation. The people in Milando would refute it somehow and deceive the outside investigators as they had done before. And I would be left in grave danger.

But the authorities would not leave it at that. Though I absolutely refused to go there myself, they went to Milando as soon as the roads were open. I don't know exactly what they were told, but I understand that what finally settled the matter and convinced them I had been hallucinating was an interview with a well established citizen of Milando, alive and uninjured, a charming young woman named Yolanda Prentiss.

# Glimpses

## by A.A. Attanasio

The mysterious and indecipherable books from the forgotten people before the Ramessids period that the early myths want to tell us so much about were probably not books at all. Who can say what stone artifact discovered at Coptos is not itself some ancient body of knowledge to which we have long ago lost the key?

[Birch *Zeitschrift* 1871 pp. 61-2]

You tell me you understand no word of the first tongue spoken by the deities, no word good or bad. There is, as it were, a wall about it that none may climb. For it is a language that remembers no past and awaits no future. It is a tongue that murders the air.

[trans. by Maspero and Lang in *The World's Desire* from Papyrus Anastasi, I pl. 1. i. pl. X 1. iv.]

## The Pierced Stone

The day was smoldering at the end of the street when Gene Mirandola stepped down from the tram. The gas lamps were already lighted. And though it was April the wind that groped among the tangle of streets and alleys was cold. All day Gene had been experiencing an unreasonable tension, as if he were under surveillance. Try as he had, there was no way to alleviate the anxiety.

He stood for a moment at the corner to look about him. From a rooftop a boy was throwing crumbs into the air, fishing the sky. Around him, flocks of pigeons massed like a black fountain, blowing down and swirling up again.

Gene looked behind him and then crossed the street to buy the *Times* from the crone who perpetually waited there in front of the Little Rose Cafe. After he purchased the paper, she squinted long at the pence in her hand despising it, sucking her lips a little further into her mousehole.

With cigar in his teeth and nose to the wind, Gene walked toward the twilight, feeling even more intensely now the eyes of some unseen observer. That old woman, Ocarina, mother of murderers and madmen, Ocarina, whose neck was a chicken leg, she was there every night, rain or stars, squatting on the orange crate--she never intimidated him before. Why now were her eyes so terrible? Why were her crab's hands, her small bulk on the crate, so ominous tonight?

Momentarily overwhelmed by his imagination, Gene made his way down the street conscious of the curtains in the dust-stained storefront windows being drawn aside and the movements behind them. As he passed through the black iron gate and down the musky alley that led to the courtyard where his flat was, he struggled in his apprehension to remind himself that such unwarranted fear was incommensurable with his experience: after all, he found himself thinking as he groped for his latch key, a man of thirty-two with the responsible but not at all consequential job of chief clerk at a small publishing firm has no reason for paranoia.

Gene shut the door firmly behind him and climbed the stairs two at a step to the top floor. Already in the warmth of the building, the invisible menace diminished. It was unnatural for it to be so cold in April. And now, as the door swung open into his awkward, cherished rooms containing his familiar shelves, he was perfectly willing to believe that the weather had been responsible for his anxiety.

After a change of clothes and with a snifter of brandy in his hand, Gene's stubborn fear seemed small, and he looked out his window at the children in the alley setting fires in ash-barrels and the old men with their pushcarts loaded with fruit and vegetables and empty crates clanking away on iron wheels over cobblestones.

He settled comfortably in his large overstuffed chair, staring into the night. It was the dark of the moon. Sleep was opening in him like a blossom, and he was drifting toward it. But his drowsiness gave way gradually to a discomfort in his throat. It felt numb, and his tongue was twisting in his mouth, moving on its own. Gene was alarmed and sat bold upright as his tongue forced itself between his lips and wagged nervously in the air, curling and flapping. Leaping to his feet, he cried out loud. His tongue relaxed, but he was

shaking. He downed the rest of his brandy and after a few minutes
went to bed and tried to pray. After calming down, he felt his mouth
open and his tongue move. He couldn't control his breathing, and
the whisper that forced itself through his teeth was not his own—
*Gene, listen to me. I am a voice that has been too high for your ears for a
long time. Where do you suppose I have been since you last saw me?*

*O Christ!* Gene thought. His breath returned to him in short
gasps. *O Christ! I know that voice. It's my uncle. But, how long has it
been since he died?*

Gene Mirandola was travelling south. It was night, and from the
train window only his own round, fleshy face stared back. He had
been in the middle of a long and tiring conversation with his
traveling companion, an unknown businessman that circumstance
had put in the same compartment. Somehow, Gene's mind had
wandered to what he couldn't even now recall, and he had lost grasp
of the dialogue. As he returned his gaze to his fellow passenger, he
was not at all surprised to see that the man looked perplexed. But
just as he was about to apologize, the stranger said, "You know,
that's a very curious caricature, there." The man indicated the paper
on which Gene had been absent-mindedly doodling.

"O, I wasn't paying any attention. I—" Gene cut himself short
when he looked down at the writing tablet in his lap. There, staring
back at him from among an intricate weave of figure eights, circles,
and mandalas, was a remarkably deft drawing of his Uncle Armand
Saadi. A wall of blackness that had until then obscured whole regions
of thought suddenly gave way, and Gene remembered vividly that
night several months previous when he had felt possessed by this
very uncle. Since then he had learned, through other relatives, a few
facts about his uncle (that, indeed, he was still alive and living not
far from where Gene, on his business trip, was heading), but he had,
until now, dismissed his previous experience completely.

Gene sat numb for a long moment, unable to remove his eyes
from the seemingly too-familiar face that peered through his doo-
dles. At last he looked up at his companion, who by now had lost
interest and was leisurely engaged in his local trades-weekly. The
stranger's nonchalance about the incident grated against Gene's
excitement. The compartment that they occupied seemed foolishly
small and trivial to be housing all of the implications that a few
minutes of idle sketching had produced. Gene's life was changed

utterly—altering even as he thought about it. Chance could not explain it. Coincidence was no longer enough.

He tried to remember everything he could about his uncle. He knew that Armand had been an historian of science for a while, and that he had a passionate interest in the paintings of Manet—but these were trifles. What was it that consumed him about his uncle—that strange man he barely knew, that rare figure in his life with whom he shared not even blood?

Even after a week of business in Caernarvon, Gene Mirandola was still experiencing the peculiar attraction to his uncle. It had become only too clear to him that the matter would not resolve itself, and he made plans to take the time to pay a personal visit to Armand Saadi.

Following his relatives' best recollections and the uncertain knowledge of the local post service, Gene found himself on an overnight journey by horseback into the mountainous country of Radnor Forest. The season was agreeable to the trek, and the ride turned into a pleasant aside for what had been a week of exacting and tedious labor. The countryside was rustic, even wild, despite the fact that he was able to make most of his way on the well defined northwest highway that runs in that area from Llandudno to Carmarthon. It amazed him that he should know so little about an uncle that had apparently influenced him deeply or that he would be willing to travel at such inconvenience to visit this man he knew only by acquaintance.

Mirandola stayed overnight at the turnpike house in Maroc, and early the next morning left the highway for the short but unmapped ride to his uncle's house. The forest here was particularly thick, and shortly after the turnoff, Gene regretted not leaving his horse at the inn. The trees were uncommonly swollen and overgrown with moss and mushroom. Overhead the branches had grown so dense as to cut off most light and to filter green what little shone through. Underfoot was a tangle of thick roots and growths, and Gene found himself leading his steed most of the nine miles north to his destination.

It was well after noon when the first landmark of his uncle's estate greeted him. It was an old stone well, obviously just recovered from some terribly long period of disrepair. Gene stopped to rest there momentarily and, more for idle pleasure than necessity, prepared to draw some water. He pulled up on the new rope that was slung through the rusted iron pulley and continued to pull for a considerable time before he gave up in exasperation. The rope was endless, he thought as he watched the yards of it that he had withdrawn fly back into the darkness. Curiously, he dropped a large stone down the well, but the water gave out no bottom for as long as he cared to wait. Besides, just over the knoll was his uncle's place, and certainly there would be interesting enough things to do there than to wait on a bottomless well.

Gene led his horse over the knoll and then stopped, dismissing the strange well, forgetting the tiring walk. A stone tower, not a full three stories, stood among the thick forest. It leaned heavily to one side, its walls obviously just remortared to salvage the structure from ruin. It was such an unexpected sight, that queer little building huddled on a mountain slope, that Gene would have stood staring at it indefinitely had not a figure emerged from the door. It waved him closer, and, of course, it was his Uncle Armand. But not as he remembered him. No, not even as he had so deftly but unconsciously portrayed him a week earlier on the train from London. His uncle was more wan, more haggard and sallow than he had expected.

"Ah, at last. At last," his uncle greeted after Gene secured the horse. Armand clasped a heavy and amiable arm about his nephew. "I thought you were never coming."

"You knew?" Gene muttered, certainly not taken fully aback that his uncle had shared his unusually persistent attraction.

"Yes, of course I knew. I've been calling you," Armand claimed, ushering the young man into his house.

Inside, it was even more obvious what great labor his uncle had undertaken in restoring the timeless tower. On the floor was an intricately woven Minoan prayer rug. A large round table of oak with several cumbersome chairs, suitably antiquated, occupied most of the ground floor. Over half of the circular wall had been converted to bookshelves and held, what at first glance seemed, a disproportionate number of worn Arabic texts. The remainder of the wall space was taken up with several paintings (one remarkable balcony scene by Manet showing an old woman with a face as vapid as the long moon in the background) and unusual stuffed animals: a shark's mouth displaying several rows of teeth, the skin of a large, white cat, and the head of a fierce-looking ram. At the center of the table a dozen or so stone rubrics were arranged around a decanter of whiskey.

Armand seated his nephew, but he remained standing, aloof. After a brief period of exchanging cordialities, he left the room and returned momentarily with a square black stone the size of a liter cube. When Gene moved to touch it, Armand stopped him with a sharp command. "You must be very careful about everything you do here," the uncle told his nephew. "Fancy your coming two days out of your way to see me. You don't know me except maybe by reputation. But I know who you are. I know your deepest secret fears. How could I know such things unless I were a sorcerer? And if indeed you are in a sorcerer's house, it would be wise to be very careful about everything you do."

Gene sat back in his chair and seemed to think this over, but he was quite certain in his mind that the man opposite him was no ordinary man. He began to wish that he had not been so impulsive about coming here.

"Yes, it is too bad you are the one that had to come," Armand said. "Believe me, it would not have been a good thing for whomever providence chose—but I had no idea it would be you."

Gene felt his anxiety like a cold finger between his shoulders. He knew that it would be impossible to escape now, and that knowledge gave him a queasy feeling in his stomach.

"Ah, but you're right," his uncle continued. "All this chatter is making you uncomfortable, so I shall address the purpose of your visit directly.

"I am an old man who has undergone a long agony, and I am very impatient for my death. But before I indulge in that last and most somber denial, I must dispatch an old and pressing promise. Really, I am no different from you, except that the years and my fate have set me apart. So I can understand how what I must ask you to do for me will sound strange. I cannot possibly make my purpose fully clear to you, but I shall try to help you to understand as much as your destiny in this matter will allow."

Gene felt sick at heart because it was now apparent that the old man had not called him here to teach him but merely to have him do a favor.

Armand Saadi sensed even this and said, "What little I have to tell you is more than you can learn living another thousand years in your current fashion. Don't be distracted by thoughts of personal gain, for I repeat, you have been chosen for a distressing fate. Perhaps what little I can tell you now will be of some condolence later."

The nephew tried to control his alarm, understanding that there was no escape as long as his uncle stood between him and the door, and whatever salvation there might be would only reveal itself to a cool-headed mind.

"Yes, try to remain calm, and look closely at this," Armand said, pointing to the cube. "This is what the Arabs would say embodies *kiblah*, direction, for it shows the way to true knowledge. When I first uncovered it at a bazaar in Khartoum that is what the merchant told me it was. He also said that it had been found in the desert years ago and was considered a token of ill luck, as any such object that probably was discarded by a caravan would be. So, I was able to purchase it cheaply. It wasn't until some years later that a good friend of mine, who is an archaeologist in America, was able to tell me more about it by translating this old Arabic inscription."

Gene scrutinized the Arabic scrawl.

"*Fee mihrabeh bejanib el-bahr tantazir ahlam al-maiet Cthulhu,*" his uncle read. "It literally translates: *In his temple by the sea, dead Cthulhu's dream waits.* My American friend assumed from the use of the barbarous name Cthulhu that this relatively recent black stone which is maybe two thousand years old, houses an older artifact related to a much more ancient cult. Following his lead, I learned this secret."

Armand gently separated the black cube into two parts revealing a round stone with a hole in it, rather like a donut. On either side of this stone were inscriptions impressed in a style like cuneiform. Gene ran his fingers over them and noticed that on the periphery of the stone a snake was raised, encircling the entire wheel and biting its tail on one side.

"That snake is an *uroboros,*" Armand said. "It's a symbol whose meaning I cannot fully exhaust, other than to say that it represents the cyclic pattern of the cosmos itself. But I can tell you about the nature of the stone. It is a hole!" Armand put several fingers through it, and Gene wanted to laugh out loud at his uncle's pious regard for a hole.

"You think this is funny because you don't understand the nature of holes at all," his uncle said. "This hole here is filled with air, but holes aren't necessarily empty. Besides, what does 'empty' mean? All that we can really say is that whatever a hole is filled with, it must not be the same as the substance in which it is embedded.

"Ah, well if that is so, then aren't all 'empty' spaces holes in reference to some framework? What about gaps in thoughts? Are the conceptual concepts of all holes the same?

"You now might begin to see that each person's universe, both physical and conceptual, is entirely permeated by holes. There are holes all around and through us. We are living in a world of holes. As a matter of fact, holes cover more space than anything else. It seems strange, then, that all of the words we have for holes refer to a break in the continuity of a substance, such as aperture, bore, cave, cavern, cavity, cleft, crater, enclave, excavation, fissure, gap, grotto, hole, hollow, orifice, puncture, pit, pocket, slit, tunnel, and tube. All of these words come from Indo-European rootwords which refer to a hole as something created, and not as a separate entity, like *beu, bher, ghei, kel, keu, peue, wer,* meaning to cover, to open, to poke or push something into, to punch, to bend.

"Apparently, this configuration in space, like the concept of zero, is relatively recent. But what do people truly feel about holes? Why did artists put holes in Luristan bronzes three thousand years ago? It is because various configurations of a hole and of holes focus energies and can tell secrets. Holes are the language used by entities beyond causality. By this magic we may arise and speak with spirits without knowing ourselves. For, to men with a knowledge of corners and holes, nothing is ever empty."

"And this particular hole is ... important?" Gene ventured, indicated the ancient stone.

"Of course. But holes can  mean nothing significant until you understand that man is merely a flash in the pan compared to what older entities dwelt here first. Those Old Ones, you may learn, still have much influence on this planet though now they are not in the spaces we know but between them. Holes can lead to them. The nature of their names and characters would be meaningless to you, except perhaps for that Entity to Whom this specific hole is sacred. And that is *Yog-Sothoth*, the All-In-One and the One-In-All, the Guardian and Master of all passageways, of all holes. Truly, though, He is nameless, beginningless, endless. How the Dead are drawn after Him! Oh, and how terrible the fate of the living who lucklessly are found in His presence and sail without shadow toward the pyres of His sun."

Gene again grew nervous, feeling uncertain about what was happening.

"Listen, young man, you are not yet ready to understand these matters. I have called you here to do me a favor, and that is, quite simply, to deliver this hole to London. Here is the address."

The crisp, labored hand of his uncle read, *Marc Souvate, 43 Caton St., Lansbury, London.*

"He is an adept in these matters," Armand went on, "and if you are at all curious when you meet with him, he may tell you more about this stone. But now you must leave, even though you have just arrived. This is a place of much power, and if you are found here by night, I would have little hopes for your continued well-being."

This was the opportunity that Gene was looking for, and he grabbed it. As quickly as he could without seeming too impolite, he took the stone and mounted his horse. His uncle pointed out a shorter way back to Maroc, advising Gene to avoid the well on his property as it was also a hole sacred to Yog-Sothoth and therefore a danger to him with the sacred stone. Gene took his uncle's advice and rode swiftly along the narrow trail into the forest, glad in his heart to be returning to a natural world.

He tried to kick the gun under the oak table, but he couldn't find his foot. There was blood on the Minoan prayer rug, and the stone rubrics had been scattered when the body collapsed.

He moved to the window to wait for someone to come. It was night, and there was nothing to do.

The decanter of whiskey was still on the table where he had left it. He wanted a drink, but his hand was not there. It was dangling from the table. He went over and looked at the mess that had been a head. It disturbed him, and already he wanted to go back. Was there any way to go back? It was so messy, he doubted anyone could ever find all of the pieces.

He looked up at the painting by Manet. That woman there, locked on that balcony—her fate was as terrible as his.

He stood for a long time at the window, looking out at the darkness. There was nothing at all to do.

Abruptly, a loud and raucous noise began from behind the knoll. It was the sound of the rusted pulley that drew the rope from the well.

They were coming now.

He felt anxious. It wasn't supposed to turn out this way. It was supposed to be over now. The gun should have done the trick. How could he have suspected otherwise? How could he have known?

The creaking of the pulley became more persistent, and he stared hard into the night. What was going to happen when They came? What would They do?

He backed from the window slowly, though he knew there was no escape.

## The Adept

Dr. Marc Souvate, for all that Gene Mirandola could tell, was of indeterminate age. Though his hair, which was absolutely straight and was combed back flat on his head, was jet black and his posture and gait were remarkably loose and agile for a man as tall as he was, Gene could not help but think of the doctor as being quite old. His skin was olive dark and tight to the skull, and his eyes, green like shattered glass, were netted in wrinkles that told of much physical strain. The thin lips, too, were creased deeply. But other than those few signs of age, the man, for all appearances in his eloquent dress and firm resonant voice, could have been thirty.

"Did your uncle tell you anything about the nature of this stone?" Souvate asked. He was sitting on the edge of his baroque desk, his hands lying idly at the sides of the icon and his eyes fixed on it, as if he were not speaking to Gene at all.

"Yes, he did tell me something about its antiquity and, uh, something about older beings."

"The Old Ones."

"Yes, that was it."

"It's a shame he didn't come with you. There's much I have to talk with him about."

"That's too bad," Gene said, lowering his voice. "I just got word this morning—he's dead."

"Oh?" Souvate turned to face Gene. "What happened? Do you know?"

"The notice, quite bluntly, said that he put himself away with a pistol."

Souvate returned his gaze to the stone, as if to ponder Armand's death.

A long period of silence ensued, and Gene, feeling uncomfortable but not willing to depart without more information that might help him to understand his uncle, asked, "What can you tell me about this stone?"

"Nothing that would make any sense to you, I'm afraid."

"Tell me anyway. I must know more."

Souvate remained silent for a moment and then, without looking at Gene said, "This is a talisman. It was given to men by the Great Lord of the Abyss, Nodens, to protect us from our witless creators. It is one of several that we have to insulate us from the prepotent elemental deities. The only other one that I can speak of is the Elder Sign that guards the dream of the water deity. This here is even more powerful, for it holds sway over Time and the Beast therein: the All-In-One and the One-In-All, *Yog-Sothoth*."

Gene made a perplexed move and sat back further into his chair.

"I told you, these words would mean nothing to you," Marc Souvate said. "You are not an initiate, so at most, if I were fain to speak more, these things would be a mythology to you."

"But are these things relative to man? I mean, are these things you and my uncle have talked about as real?"

Souvate put a finger to the side of his nose and grinned slightly. "How can I tell you about reality? You are a businessman, and I am a sorcerer. For you, volume of sales for some book is real. For me, whatever does not need me is real."

"I want to learn more," Gene said, he thought too eagerly.

Souvate smiled broadly, a hint of fang at the corners. "You would have to make a real commitment. I think, perhaps, you are too well into your own conception of the world to have another one opened to you."

As it would be, that was the last that the two men had to do with each other for over a year. Gene left Souvate with the mysterious stone in his roomy but foreboding house near the river and returned to his flat and his job. But, as these things go, his exposure to his uncle and to the recondite Dr. Souvate had a lasting and pressing influence on Gene. Because he had had one glimpse of other, previously unsuspected, horizons, his appreciation of the world no longer fulfilled him, and he found that his work was not gratifying. He knew now in his heart what he had only suspected and rationalized away in his mind, that the universe was more vast and more accessible than any man in his social circles suspected. He realized, too, that he could not live out the rest of his life without at least trying to grasp more of that whole.

And, naturally, after more than a year of compromising with the world of business and his own impulsive curiosity, Gene Mirandola returned to the roomy and foreboding house by the river and called, once again, on Dr. Souvate. And there, in the drawing room among antiquated furniture, unusual animals, and relics from disparate and largely unknown cultures, Gene and the dark doctor settled the arrangements for the young man's apprenticeship.

The details of Mirandola's training are part of another story; those that are familiar with sorcery know those details intimately, and those who are merely curious would fail to appreciate the slow and awkward process by which Gene learned first to forget time, numbers, and the alphabet, going on to forgetting the elements, starting with water, proceeding to earth, rising to fire, forgetting fire until everything was continuous again. And only then did his apprenticeship truly begin, with his discovering as if by himself (for such is the way of a true teacher) the nature and heuristic use of henbane, betel, oeanthol, opium, blisterfly, and tannis leaf; discovering next how to alter the field of force around the human body in such a way that nerve centers are influenced and valuable visions are generated; and discovering, finally, the secret of holes and the language they speak.

So it came about that Gene Mirandola, instructed by Dr. Souvate, was ready to begin a marvelous quest for knowledge. They met on a prearranged night in the immense caverns that lay partly under the sorcerer's foreboding house by the river. There, in the dark gloom lighted only by a single cool-burning taper, they came upon three large holes, the perimeters of which were marked with worn futhorc inscriptions.

Gene, of course, knew by then that the entire world, indeed the universe, is an intricate manifold of interconnecting holes, some of them blatantly obvious and constant like these three, others invisible and incessantly shifting. All initiates knew of these holes, but only an adept could use them properly. Determining which hole to use necessitated a foreknowledge of where it would take you, and that knowledge precluded logic and was, therefore, available only to an adept. Holes could communicate through space-time, and there were numerous accounts of luckless voyagers who entered into worlds or situations that were biologically disadvantageous or who plummeted through intergalactic voids so vast as to be considered, by all practical values, infinite.

"Now that you have had some glimpse into the nature of things," Souvate told Gene as they stood at the edge of one of the abysses, "you can appreciate what I am going to tell you about myself. Like a good apprentice, you have come here not knowing what task I shall assign you, perfectly willing to fulfill my commands without explanation. Well, because you have been an exceptional pupil, I am going to tell you something few other men know."

Souvate held the taper closer to his face, illuminating his stark, green eyes. "I am a vehicle for the first worshipers of the Great Lord Nodens Whose Presence was last on this planet long before any semblance of man emerged from the Pre-Cambrian slime and Who will return many billions of years from now. Those entities that first worshiped Him, before this earth was even recognizable as a planet, desire nothing more than to be united in His Presence. When He departed and the Old Ones, the entropic deities, emerged, the worshipers began their dread migration through time, utilizing their knowledge of holes to jump large stretches of time, moving constantly toward that future point when Nodens shall return. Some one and a half million years ago, the worshipers took my body as a host. I am their vehicle, and they direct me on this odyssey through history. From them I have acquired complete mastery of my physical form. I am ageless, capable of regenerating whole segments of my body. But I realize that I am only a tool—a willing servant of Nodens.

"I met your Uncle Armand when I first entered this time period, some fifty-three years previous. In return for his help in establishing me in this historical niche, I gave him knowledge of the Old Ones so that his life would lack nothing. However, instead of merely using that knowledge for his corporeal good, he sought to compound his understanding, and he began to study the nature of holes, that is space-time, the domain of the terrible Yog-Sothoth.

"That was sad, because he who seeks the All-In-One will find the One-In-All. But then there is no escape, not even in physical death. Hence, Armand most certainly was taken by Yog-Sothoth to serve that Ancient One for eternity in some hideous manner.

"Now, as the stars are right for me to make another leap through time, I am prepared to leave all that I have here behind, but I do not forget that Armand Saadi befriended me. So, I have trained you, and soon you will have the opportunity to both repay me and save your uncle's soul from its unremitting horror.

"This hole that we will enter is going to deliver us to Laguna Cays, a small archipelago south of Chile. On that speck of land is the oldest temple of Yog-Sothoth still extant. From there I will depart for the future and my destiny. And also there you will find your uncle's soul and have your chance to redeem it. If you succeed, my actions will go unnoticed, and I shall make good my escape, your uncle's soul will be freed, and you shall return here safely."

Souvate opened the burlap sack he had with him and withdrew the serpent stone that Gene had delivered so long ago. "This, as I have told you, is a talisman against Yog-Sothoth. Take it, and do not let it go until you have returned here. It is the only thing which will afford you any protection at all."

Countless questions surged to Gene Mirandola's tongue, but there was time not even for one. Dr. Souvate, chanting and holding Gene's arm, stepped out into the emptiness.

The adept and his disciple found themselves looking down a black, volcanic beach: old horseshoe crabs, broken skates, sand dollars, sea horses, endless numbers of primeval creatures quivering in the sea mud. The waves lapped ice cold at their ankles, and they could see, far out at the horizon, the majestic white cliffs of the Antarctic icebergs as they caught the sunlight. The sky was dark indigo at the zenith, lighter, almost green on the horizons. And though the wind was blowing over the dunes as they crept, there was no sound but the sea.

Gene turned to ask Souvate a question, but the thin man motioned him to silence and led him off along the black sand. The island they were on was tiny, and in half an hour they had circled it. The place was completely desolate; there was nothing but sand. Souvate continued to walk around the island, indicating that they must move spirally toward the center before they would find the temple.

After they had thrice moved about the isle, they saw half-buried in a dune a human skeleton green with growths. "That is a warning," Souvate hissed. By their fifth turn, closing in on the center, the light changed, and the previously unusual atmospheric darkness became darker still. And though the sun, a small, wan disc, was still high, the sky was dark enough to see the brighter stars.

On their seventh turn they reached the center. Nothing seemed to change abruptly, and Gene allowed his tense muscles to loosen. Souvate pointed at his feet. There an urn jutted from the sand. Gene bent low over it and heard, or thought he heard, soft, uncontrollable sobbing, or perhaps a sucking sound.

"That is your uncle," Souvate informed him. "His fate is too hideous to comprehend while you occupy your body. Take the vessel, but do not tip it over. To escape, there is only one way. You must retrace the spiral, and you must be absolutely silent. When you arrive at the place where we began, you will return to London. But you will have to hurry."

Souvate pointed out to sea. There, at the horizon, was what Gene took at first to be another island, large and flat, rising gradually above the sea. "It's a tidal wave," the adept said. "You'd better get out before it hits. And mind you now, if you break the spiral pattern, there can be no escape."

Gene began immediately to follow the spiral backwards, but no sooner had he begun than an old woman, at first existing only as smoke, appeared ahead of him. After she became more solid, he recognized her: It was Ocarina, the newspaper crone. She waited to follow behind Gene, holding a little lamp in one hand that glowed like an icy fan of the sun.

He wanted to ask her who she really was, but the silence in the air was dreadful. He stepped up his pace, glancing nervously out to sea, trying to gauge the progress of that wave (which curiously did not seem to be moving at all), throwing a glance to his back, too, watching the crone who slogged just far enough behind that the wind ripples in the sand covered his footsteps before she reached them. And all the while there was that ominous dark in the sky by which now the southern constellations could be seen, so that Souvate, who was watching from the center and who knew just who that crone was, had reason to fear the worst. Nevertheless, he did not forget his purpose and set about beginning the silent chant and hand sigils that would open the hole he sought.

After Gene's fifth turn, the silence that had been the desolate silence of isolated places became unearthly, and even the waves stopped and were mute, as if they were all drawing back to feed that one mighty surge. Gene heard his breath loud and raucous in the still air. His heart was like a dervish drum, and the odd, unwholesome sucking sound grew louder and more offensive in the urn; and Gene called from his heart for a natural noise from a bird or the sea, but nothing stirred; even Souvate was still. And then and there, before he had even witnessed the horror, Mirandola decided, as he should have done long ago, to forget his interest in sorcery and to return, as quickly as he could, to the quiet, usual life of a chief clerk at a small publishing firm. Then he looked over his shoulder to face Souvate, but the adept was gone, having already decided it was far wiser to slip sidewise into time than to remain any longer in the growing presence of Yog-Sothoth. And Gene Mirandola felt the fear that had been a weight in his throat crush down into his heart as the crone widened the slit of her lamp and let the unnatural, cold light from it illuminate the sand around her. Wherever the light shone, the empty beach vanished and another landscape became visible—a more sinister, less reasonable landscape. The thin air was like a veil burned away by the eerie lamplight, and the absurd shapes and forms that were abruptly emerging edged Gene closer and closer to panic. After one sweep of the crone's lamp, the island was transformed into a staggering arena of monoliths whose very size caused Gene's fear to cascade down into a delirious horror. In his shock at the unfamiliar stars that now crowded the sky and the great insect thing that began to appear around unpredictable corners and edges with mad, swiveling mandibles, Gene dropped both the urn and the stone. And then screaming faster and faster until his cries were incoherent, he fled towards the sea, where Yog-Sothoth's blasphemous half-brother was already rearing his tentacled head.

## Zone of Death

When they reached K'oto Basin, where the lime-colored geodesic domes of the research complex stand out like a mold on the sea cliffs, Cordon Malebolgean swung the hover controls over to his aide, Leroi Nichol. In his black command fatigue, Cordon seemed to fill the tiny cabin. There was a falcon quality about him: the beetling eyebrows, the gaunt lines of his face, the piercing steadiness of his gaze. He sat back in his sling and began gnawing the tip of his decoder. "What's the name of this place again?"

"It's the Blackwolf Project, Colonel," Leroi responded as he lifted the fliteKraft onto the cool thermal current that they would follow down. "Can't understand why they called us here," the aide continued. "They've never done military research before. They're strictly a pure research group."

"Yeah, yeah. Well, they better have some practical menace for us after we've taken this risk. If the ginks come under the wire while we're away, it could cost the whole northeast strategy." Cordon pulled out the personnel review from his flight satchel, asked, "What's the commander's name on this project?"

"No one commander *per se*," Leroi responded. "This is a privately funded project. Della Marduk is the acting administrator."

"Della Marduk," Cordon repeated to himself as he glanced down the review agenda to find her. "Ah, quite impressive scrip on her. She's had plenty of military experience: Cobalt omega and Húhere—the two major laser/maser development projects last decade. They've been most responsible for the favorable turnaround of the war." The attached hologram showed a lean black woman, straight and aloof, her hair meticulously rowed, her eyes sullen.

When the fliteKraft was docked and the two men dropped out of their slings onto the receiving platform, they sifted through the knots of workers looking for Della Marduk. Instead, a short, bearded man in an orange flight jacket with command insignia greeted them. "Hello, hello. Thank God you've come. I'm Dr. Hafiz."

Cordon shifted his eyes inquisitively to his aide. Leroi leaned toward him, said, "V. Hafiz—he's chief engineering director of Blackwolf and the major source of their independent funding."

Hafiz seemed to assimilate Cordon's bewilderment, and as he led them out of the landing area, he added, "I know my name wasn't included in the request transcript—I wanted to remain anonymous because some of the personnel here would find a military presence annoying. I didn't want to draw their fire. Perhaps you were expecting Della. Well, quite frankly, she isn't expecting you."

Before Cordon could respond, Hafiz led them off the receiving platform and along an open catwalk that wound through the numbing roar of hover engines. When next they could talk, the bearded engineer had ushered them into a spacious, circular office the center of which was dominated by a large round desk covered with geometric models. The curved wall was bound with rows of numerically labeled pipes and valves. After Hafiz cleared the room of workers who were cluttered around the incessantly active computer terminal, he seated the two men, said, "This is the ideal conference room. It's sealed and pressurized to keep out the engine noise from the docking port—also, I'm kept completely aware of all operations through that." He pointed his chin at the computer which hummed almost noiselessly in its berth of printout copiers. "Please don't be intimidated by the fact that this looks like a factory control room. All those pipes just feed out superheated steam from the docking port and the main nuclear reactor which supplies all our power."

Cordon shifted restlessly in his chair. "Tell me, Doctor," he began, "why am I here?"

Hafiz smiled unnoticeably behind his beard at the Colonel's directness. "Because Blackwolf has literally stumbled upon the most effective military weapon and the most elusive scientific enigma of all time."

Leroi Nichol had his thin decoder unit out and began to prepare it for record. He looked interrogatively toward Hafiz.

"Four weeks ago," the engineer continued, "our widescan detectors picked up a spontaneous atmospheric disturbance several kilometers north of K'oto Basin. It was a sudden and sustained rift in the radio curtain. The only thing we figured could cause that would be a strong magnetic source on the order of several hundred gauss. But what that magnetic source could be, how it could have merely popped out of thin air, we had no idea. So we dispatched several hovers, strohlKraft, equipped with detectors in all ranges of the electromagnetic spectrum and with laser communicating systems. When they reached the site, the initial disturbance had abated totally, but the strohlKrafts were able to detect residual radiation, most of it high in the red regions of the spectrum. That residual heat described the brief trajectory of the magnetic source before it vanished. It was very close to the ground. When they tracked it, the residual path led them, surprisingly, to an unconscious man. He was lying in one of the fallow fields about a kilometer south of Tsai P'an Plateau. He was unusually dressed—appearing to be in a late Victorian style—and he had with him a large stone disc, singly perforated in the center and circumscribed by an unrecognizable script."

"How big was that disc?" Cordon asked.

"Pretty near a fifty centimeter diameter," Hafiz replied. "After he was admitted to Blackwolf we ran every conceivable test on him and the stone. But I've asked you here to see what we've discovered about that stone. Careful cobalt dating indicates that it was originally carved, as ridiculous as this sounds, over a billion years ago. The material of the stone itself appears to be older than our expectations of the age of the universe. And though that in itself is remarkable, what I have to show you now is even more stunning."

Hafiz rose and led the men on a brief walk through a tangle of corridors to a warehouse-sized room with an immensely high ceiling lost in steel rafters and catwalks. The activity in the room was focused around endless banks of computer components. Just off the center of the chamber was a clear platform, like a glass scaffold, with the pierced stone visible inside it and an unusual metallic sculpture perched on top. It was unusual because it appeared to be constructed of only three sheets of blue gunmetal. But the respective angles and the contiguous points of the sheets seemed to defy the logic of gravity and perspective so that from one position there appeared to be a dozen facets clumped together like a beehive balanced on a pinhead, and from a different standpoint the whole structure had the appearance of a single metallic slab tottering perilously on one corner.

"After it became clear how old the stone was," Hafiz said, "we were anxious to decode the inscription that's on it. It took our entire computer complex over two hundred hours to break it down, which is a remarkably brief time considering the complexity of the code. What it came out with is a mathematical model—not a linguistic phrase, but a numerical expression. Two days ago we completed this geometric projection of that expression. We haven't even begun to determine all the properties of the space that it displaces. But we have good reason now to believe that its nature may undermine our longest accepted notions of causality and interconnectedness."

"Is this the weapon you called us here to see?" Cordon asked.

Hafiz nodded. "We know next to nothing about it, but its most disturbing attribute may well recommend it for military use." The engineer signaled one of the workers over to him and gave him brief instructions. "Somehow, and we have no idea how," he went on after the worker ran off, "the peculiar angles of these planes create a small but significant singularity. That is, there is one point in that maze of angles where there is no reflection, no vibration echo, just a thin black slice through which signals propagate in only one direction—inward. Whatever enters does not return. Look—"

Hafiz pointed at a long metal girder that was being crane-swiveled into position alongside the clear scaffold. The crane moved forward and the thin girder swung toward the sculpture looking as if it would topple it over. Instead the girder began to disappear as if it were entering a hole. Leroi Nichol took several steps forward to see just where the rod was vanishing. It was merely entering the space between the angles of the metal sheets and disappearing. Hafiz signaled the crane; it moved back, and the men could see that only a third of the girder's length remained.

"Its military implications, I think, are obvious," the engineer said.

Cordon slowly circled the structure, drew up close to examine it, asked, "Do you really believe this would be practical in a tactical engagement?"

"Well, there certainly are questions of mobility and application that have to be resolved, but the defensive practicality of it is without question. It would provide an impenetrable shield against detection devices, radar and laser, and offensive systems, projectile or phase."

"But, damn it, Hafiz," Cordon barked as he turned from the scaffold, "where do those things go when they enter?"

Hafiz stared blankly at him, somewhat taken aback that a military man would be concerned about theory. "Uh, we don't know yet."


Cordon Malebolgean had asked his aide to interview Della Marduk. Leroi found her on one of the terrace porticos that overlook the sea. Already the western hills, visible to their left, troughed the light of the day. The wind from the sea was steady and high, ruffling the papers that Della held in her lap. She turned to face him when he introduced himself. Her skin looked almost purple in the twilight, and her eyes, though large and bright, seemed very tired. However, when she learned that Hafiz had called in military advisers, her gaze darkened with anger. At first she refused to talk with him, but he was very cordial, and there was something sincere in his broad, flat face that invited confidence.

Eventually, she told him, "Blackwolf has been in financial trouble for over a year now. Hafiz will do anything to get the necessary funds to keep our research going."

"Why doesn't he invite government help?"

"That would mean he would no longer be running the show. He's certainly egomaniacal. I think that if he didn't see a possibility of selling the warp-structure to the military for a fortune, he'd sell Marc to a carny."

"Who's Marc?"

"The person they picked up with the stone."

"How does he check out?"

"He doesn't. He's more strange than the warp-structure. He was unconscious for over two weeks. During that whole time his body literally refused medication and sustenance. It passed right through his system while he maintained his own biochemical integrity. Lord knows how. We tested his clothes, and they turned out to be genuine 1882 accoutrements. Same with his credentials—Marc Souvate, London, England. But what is stranger still, when we graphed his brain pattern—well, there was more than one directive source."

"How do you mean?"

"More than one mind in his brain is what I'm saying. In fact, there are thousands of minds in his brain."

"That *is* impossible, isn't it?"

"So is the fact that tissue, blood, and bone analysis reveal that his physiology has been out of style for over a million years. We just can't figure it out."

"What happened when he came to?"

"He was in a carefully monitored isolation chamber. We were able to project holographic images of us into the room, but somehow he knew they were unreal and looked directly at our hidden cameras, shocking the wits out of us."

"Have you talked with him?"

"Oh, yes. He's quite vocal, rather pleasant, Continental accent and all. But it's just small talk. He's very interested in getting his stone back, though he won't tell us a thing about it."

"Where is he kept?"

"He isn't. He can open any lock. We just let him roam at will. We keep the stone in the base of the warp-structure. It seems that's the only place he refuses to go. That stone registers off our dating scale. The inscription alone is over a billion years old. We don't want him vanishing with it."

After talking with Della Marduk, Leroi Nichol spent a sleepless night wondering about Marc Souvate. Cordon Malebolgean was not at all interested in the possibility of talking to a man over a million years old. He and Hafiz worked all night discussing the practical ramifications of the warp-structure.

The next morning Leroi went looking for Marc Souvate. He found him squatting in the shadows near the long body of the swamp. He was naked, and his thighs were mud-streaked. Mushrooms, bracken fiddle necks, and bamboo shoots that he had gathered glistened on a small piece of canvas at his side.

He was amiable and appeared to be amused that Leroi had taken so much trouble to find him. He pointed out the limp fish sleeping in the weeds, half hidden by scattered peach petals. Then they walked together for a little bit, and Souvate remarked about the quail's breast sky and smoky hills, and the slopes of Mt. Hiei veiled in haze for the last day of Spring. All of this made Leroi restless. On the other side of the mountain, somewhere in the Himalayas, men were surely dying. He found it unpleasant to be walking in the country, so far from his duty as a soldier.

"Forgive me if I'm boring you," Souvate said, "but it's not often that I find myself in life as in a strange garment. I am always surprised at the earth."

This was as much of an invitation as Leroi felt he was going to get to ask the questions he had wanted to ask all morning. "Who are you? How did you come here, and why do you stay?"

"Why do you ask?"

"I must know, silly as it may sound. I've been a soldier all my life—life and death have been clear cut, until now. I can't believe some of the things they've told me about you."

"I don't know that I can answer you. Soon I'll be gone. That's all I really know. The tall spirit who lodged here has left already. Whatever I have to do has not yet begun."

"I don't understand you."

"Whatever I would tell you is not meant to be understood. I move through time the way you move through space. How can you possibly understand that? I'm following the spoor of a timeless geist, spirit, call it what you will. What follows me is what follows all of us. The laughing ax, only it's different for me. You furiously eat your meals of fire, the silence of animals, so that you may live a little longer, the blood dragging always at your heels. I have no definite time in which to live or die. What follows me is worse for though it too comes from the void it has no substance in this world other than through chance."

"Is what follows you death?"

"It is outside of death. It is the opposite of the spirit I follow. I have names for these things which make discussing them easier. I am tracking what I call Nodens through time. What follows me is entropy, *Yog-Sothoth*. Truly, there was no beginning to this, there'll be no end."

"If it's that irrational then it seems to promise a new order on a supersensible level."

"That's hunger for the sake of hunger. There is nothing rational about this. It simply is."

"But you've been talking about time. That's causality. There's reason there."

"When Yog-Sothoth arrives it will use time as a glove to swat us like insects. Just as when I first arrived, the power of Nodens was strong and there were a string of fortunate coincidences that allowed the computers to crack the inscription of the pierced stone on its first try and eventually to construct a hole in time on the first try. All chance. Soon it'll be working the other way. Unfortunate coincidence will begin to destroy everything."

"If that's true, then what can be done about it?

"I must have the pierced stone back. it's my only means of moving towards Nodens and dragging Yog-Sothoth behind me."

"Why don't you just take it?"

"I don't dare approach that hole. Yog-Sothoth is the Lord of holes, and he would surely destroy me."

"Have you explained this to the others?"

"The others have already been used to build the hole. They can't help me. They belong to Yog-Sothoth now. You can, though. Or your commander. He could help, too. But if we wait too much longer then Yog-Sothoth will hold back no more. We must hurry."


"Well, is it true?" Leroi Nichol asked, leaning across the formica table to face Della Marduk.

"It's true that the stone disc code is complicated enough to have taken our computer system several months to crack. We were lucky, though."

"Luck! But that's what he's saying, Della!"

"Listen, Leroi, I can't just hand over the oldest known artifact in the world because this man has threatened us with a streak of bad luck. Why hasn't he told me about it? You don't have any authority, I don't see why he told you."

Hafiz was sitting to the side resting his head in his hands. "Captain Nichol, you've got to understand that we've only begun to examine that stone. It holds the answers to a lot of mysteries, perhaps about the origin, perhaps even the source. Leave these matters to us, please. And confine yourself to assisting your superior."

Leroi felt a clump of frustration forming in his throat, but before he could speak the intercom on Della's desk squawked out several numbers. Della and Hafiz were both on their feet immediately.

"What's happening?" Leroi demanded.

"There's been an explosion in the microlab," Hafiz snapped. "They think a selenium gas canister has gone off. Come on! Your colonel's working in that area!"

"Everybody's got to be evacuated," Della added. "Selenium gas is odorless and colorless—but it's a lethal nerve poison. We've got to hurry!"


Cordon Malebolgean was alone in the second floor library reading over construction specifications for the warp-structure when the fire alarm rang. He looked up from his work with an annoyed grunt and peered out the window. There was no smoke. He continued his reading, thought better of it, and went to the door. There was no one in the corridor, and there was no smoke. He decided to finish sizing up the construction reports and kept his eyes peeled for the fire. He was only two floors up.

He returned to his desk. When he looked up, two men in glowbrite orange airtight suits with wide plastic reflector head-masks were lumbering toward him.

He stood up. "Is there a fire?" he asked, feeling the first delirious movements of terror in his bowels.

One of the men grabbed him and began leading him quickly out of the room. The other fitted a respirator to his mouth and told him not to get excited.

Cordon tried to turn his head toward one of the men. "Is there a fire?" he asked.

"He died within ten minutes after we got him out," Hafiz explained. "It was a freak explosion. It shouldn't have happened."

Leroi Nichol sat quite still in the small anteroom, looking ahead blankly. Behind Hafiz, he could see Marc Souvate approaching.

Hafiz thrust forward a sheet of crumpled paper. "This is what he was writing when the canister burst."

Leroi glanced at it. It was merely a memo to Strategy specifying the warp-structure. Cordon had heavily doodled on the portion of it containing the Strategy chief's last name.

Souvate took the paper from Leroi, looked at it quizzically. "Why did he underline and mark this person's last name?" he asked pointing at the chief's name, Winston P. Mirandola.

Leroi shook his head. "Mirandola? I don't know. I doubt that he was thinking."

Souvate looked intensely at Leroi. "It's begun, you know."

After Souvate left, Hafiz bent close, said, "I guess you'll be getting back to your command now."

Leroi gave him an angry nod. "Yeah. Right."


Leroi found Della on the portico overlooking the sea again. The tide was out, and the bay was sodden as the bed of an ancient lake. They greeted each other in silence. Leroi made no comment at first. Finally he said, "For a long time I thought death was friendly. It seemed logical, the only way out of the absurd duality that mocks us from birth with paradox. Yeah, well, finally death seeped up from the tiniest capillaries of my toes and made me a soldier. I was a good soldier, too, but now I remember the look I saw on Cordon's face when they carried him out of that room and he knew he'd be dead in less than five minutes. I beat my body now. I shout at myself. I see what I've betrayed. So I've been a good warrior. Who has it helped? Della, I'm ashamed standing here beside you."

Della faced him, put both of her hands to the side of his face. "What do you want to do?"

"I'm not sure. But I can't leave here until I find out about Cordon's death."

"But what is there to find out?"

"How he died. Is Souvate right? Are we the pawns of powers, forces, spirits free of space-time? Right now I'm ready to believe him. I even feel as if there's another being living inside me. He's looking out of my eyes. I can hear him in the wind coming off the sea."

"I know what you mean. I move continually with the conscious-ness of that other, totally alien, nonhuman other, humming inside like a taut drum, carefully trying to avoid any direct thought of it, trying to be attentive to the real world of flesh and stone."

"Della, I want that disc. I want to give it back to Souvate. I think it might end this madness."

Della reached out and touched Leroi's shoulder. "I understand, Leroi. It's frightening, isn't it, being this close to the irrational? I guess I shouldn't have been so stubborn before—but ... I have an overwhelming hatred for the military. I've worked too long for them and seen their evil too close. I was hardened by Cobalt omega and Húhere—building death machines without a thought of what death really is. It took Cordon's death for me to accept the unreality of everything that happened this past month, to be able to put it into a humane context. It seems like a dream. It all happened too fast. How could we have believed that we had any control over any of this? It's too unreal. I believe now in those autonomous, uncon-scious powers. Okay, Leroi. We'll give the stone to Souvate first thing tomorrow."

"But we can't let Hafiz know. He'd never allow it."

"He won't know."


A siren wail woke Leroi Nichol. He threw on a shirt and burst into the corridor where several workers in fire garb were rushing past. One of them told him the trouble was near the landing deck, and he ran at full stride.

Hafiz was standing in the corridor with several workers, all wrapped in asbestos cloth, when Leroi arrived. "What happened?" he asked.

Hafiz's face was dark with blood. "There was nothing we could do. One of the pipes in my circle-office burst. The room's airtight, you know." Hafiz stuttered for a moment, then, "We were helpless. The place filled up instantly with super-heated steam. There was nothing to do. It was over as soon as it began. The room ... hell, the room became a pressure cooker. Della was caught in there alone. She was cooked through. We found her sitting just as she was, as if she were alive. There was nothing ... nothing we could do. It was such a freak."

Leroi met Souvate by the swamp. Five days heat and nothing moved on the water. The air was still, and clouds of insects could be seen hanging motionless over the mud.

"I believe you now," Leroi said by way of greeting. "But I'm confused. I'm so confused."

Souvate gazed thoughtfully at Leroi. The young man's face had a boyish quality but also a hint of ghetto violence. "Look, Leroi, if you believe me, you will help me. If you help me, then you will die."

Leroi's cheeks were sunk slightly, his lips partly open, and on his face there was an ominous and fixed expression—an absorbed, contemplating expression of the unconscious who are ready to die. The two men sat looking at each other for a long time in silence.

"Okay, you will die," Souvate presently said. "You are already swollen by the silent sound of death. You are truly a soldier. I can speak to you and show you things I have not been able to do for centuries. You are one with your death. You are a living man."

A gust of wind struck Leroi's neck, and in the next moment he felt it streaming about his wet ankles. He sensed then that he had fought in so many battles and killed so many men not out of idealism, not for loyalty, as everyone had thought, but that he had won and lost for the same reason, his overwhelming pride. And now that pride was reduced in him to nothing by the sheer certainty of his death. There was nothing he feared now. Nothing he aspired toward. Nothing was all he expected. Only nothing.

Souvate leaned over the still waters of the swamp and cleared the algae from the surface so that the water was black and crystal. He motioned Leroi to look. Floating on the mirror surface, Leroi saw mistings of civilizations, towers, gardens, battles. The water stirred in the breeze, and he saw clouded skyscrapers, webs of cities. And these rippled away to reveal the spread of swamp ferns fronded in a rising mist, and more civilizations, more settlements, more wars, and then the tangled jungle again, and beasts and beasts, and then there came the luminescent dancers, the burning gulfs, the hanging gardens. It was endless.

"You are nothing in all of this," Souvate said. "But you can grow wise, so terrible, sucking death's moldy tits. If you help me, I will run with you like the horizon, and you will leave behind this inscrutable, alien life and return to the familiar, longed-for nothing. Death is silence and silence our native tongue. It's an absence that runs through our whole lives like thread through a needle. Everything we do is stitched with its color. If you help me, you must expect nothing, for that is all there is outside of action."

Leroi sat back on his heels. He realized that this had happened too often before, men consciously giving away their lives to emptiness, to become the void. And it was going to happen too often in the future. It happened too easily. Blood was too much like water. Cries were too much like silence. And shooting somebody in the head was too much like striking a match.

They were silent for a long time. Leroi closed his eyes. He was beginning to feel slightly feverish. He knew that this fever would remain, without there ever being the relief of weariness, until he did what now he felt was his fate. He was quite familiar with the fever. It always came on him before he would have to kill. Perhaps, he thought, it was his defense against fear.

When Leroi left Souvate, he still felt the fever. It was with him all the way back to Blackwolf and with him as he washed his face in his room. It was burning up his fear and with his fear his ambitions, his desires. All his aspirations were like a dream fading, like the sink draining, a transparent rose swallowed by its stem.

He gritted his teeth like a cliff as he broke out his Magnex .52 and loaded it. He stuffed his pockets with extra cartridges. The heat of his fever seemed to be streaming through the tiny holes of his eyes, through the seams of his face, pulsing in the strings of his lips, streaming out through his atoms, streaming out into the black, into the ringing nothing, through the bones of his gritted teeth.

Only once did the fever begin to ebb, when he thought for a moment that what he was doing he was doing for Souvate. But who ... *what* was Souvate? A voice. He was very little more than a voice. They had never done anything together. Nothing shared, nothing mutually discovered or lost. He was only a voice, and the memory of the voice itself lingered around Leroi, impalpable, like a fading echo of some cry, atrocious, savage, without any kind of sense.

And thinking that, Leroi felt a little wind like a cold finger between his shoulders. He felt the fatigue of his spirit shudder through his body. A lonely desolation overcame him as if he had been robbed of a belief or had missed his destiny in life. But then, almost with a cry, he forced himself to stop thinking, and he felt the cardboard of his body begin to warm again.

He wrapped the bulky Magnex in a towel, walked out into the corridor, and headed toward where they kept the warp-structure. Slowly he was beginning to get the feel of his identity. As he passed office after office and rows of laboratories, hearing the muffled voices of researchers, he began to feel like some vengeful demon set out by all that is unmeasurable in the cosmos. He thought of all these men and women making silence in bell jars, refrigerating emptiness, unpicking numbers, tweezing out the gluey hearts of inaudibly squeaking cells. And he felt his heart beginning to pound harder and harder until he had to force himself to calm down.

When he reached the warehouse-sized laboratory where they housed the warp-structure he walked in nonchalantly. Surprisingly, there was no one around. This disturbed him, and he suspected for an instant that something might be wrong.

Then, hearing the scratch of claws on the smooth floor, he turned to face the warp-structure and balked for one long moment in terror. A humanoid with a face flat as a snail, like the underface of a shark, was approaching him. Frantically, he ripped away the towel and discharged two shots into its face. Then in one burst of fear-smooth movement, as the roar of the gun swelled through the chamber, he sprinted to the warp-structure. Two more blasts from the Magnex splintered the clear plastic base, and he scooped out the pierced stone by putting his forearm through the hole. He'd done it, he thought to himself. It had happened so fast, he couldn't believe it. That creature, it must have come from the warp-structure—one of Yog-Sothoth's demons, he told himself. He took careful aim and blew the three metal plates apart. The sound of the metal being ripped sent him wheeling backwards.

Something grabbed his arm, and he spun about to face a bird-head, bald, lizard-eyed, the size of a basketball on two staggering insect legs. He blasted the eggshell object to a blood rag and flung himself past it to the door where another shark-face was opening its fangs. He emptied the Magnex into it, and as he spun past the bubbling mess slammed in another cartridge clip. Yog-Sothoth was everywhere, he thought. He was inescapable. Could he possibly get away with the stone before one of these abominations stopped him?

At the far end of the corridor returning to his room he heard excited voices approaching. Instead he loped the other way, toward the hover port. He scrambled along the catwalks until he reached the landing platform where another creature waited, a belly-ball of hair, with crab-legs, eyeless. Its belly opened, an oven of fangs, and Leroi cut a path through it with the Magnex.

He threw the pierced stone into a fliteKraft and leaped after it. In an instant he had the hover vehicle off the platform, and he was rising, dumbfaced, from the port leaving behind several engineers and workers lying in their blood.

Hafiz and a cadre of others had scrambled after him. They couldn't believe he was cutting down unarmed workers so frantically. Hafiz, in fact, had swung out a high-intensity X-ray projector and had rolled it furiously down the halls after Leroi, barking orders not to shoot lest they blast the pierced stone to dust. When the generator had warmed, Hafiz had moved the bulky projector onto one of the catwalks, and as the fliteKraft rose out of its dock, he opened the beryllium end-window and bathed the hover vehicle in a curtain of maximum-roentgen X-rays. In an hour or two, Hafiz figured, Leroi would be dead.

Six strohlKraft pursued Leroi. They found his hover vehicle half-embedded in a swamp. Hafiz was the first to reach it. Leroi was hunched over the controls. He had blown out his own bowels, and Hafiz had to hold his breath as he searched the cabin for the stone. It, of course, was gone. And they would spend weeks searching the swamp for it even though they had found bare footprints in the mud that led along the water ending abruptly, vanishing a dozen meters away from any tree or rock, disappearing into nothing.

# Dope War of the Black Tong

by Robert M. Price

E erie mists drifted through the place, as though someone had opened the windows and let in the hazy fog that always wandered up from the rotting wharfs and sought entry at every River Street keyhole. But it was a different sort of mist tonight, one that bore the bitter tang of opium, and yet even this was not quite right. The low-ceilinged room was almost as dark as the street outside, lit only by the sputtering flames from tapers bracketed to the damp walls. The faint illumination revealed only the supine forms of the usual gang of River Street dope addicts. They shuffled from one hop joint to another, though in recent days several had entered this particular dive never to be seen again.

The narcotic Nirvana served up a counterfeit peace, one with a heavy price, but even heavier than usual tonight. The tableau held for a moment; then the heavy oak door burst inward as if suffering the impact of a medieval siege engine. Of course not even this disturbance could retrieve the attention of the far-gone dope victims in the place, but the sudden noise, like an explosion, galvanized several of the men who must have been feigning their drugged stupor. Throwing off concealing blankets and shawls, a handful of powerful, armed Orientals, their nationalities obscure in this rich gloom, sprang like Siberian tigers to meet the challenge of whatever army it was who had invaded their secret privacy. And it *was* an army: an army named Steve Harrison.

The one-man posse of River Street set his feet squarely, while the blue steel of twin automatics leaped into his fists and began to discharge a hail of white man's justice into the knot of Oriental thugs. When his guns were empty he cast them aside and reached for the Gurkha knife he had concealed in his belt Eastern style. It descended with the force of a guillotine, cleaving the skull of the first of the assassins to elude the rain of bullets and reach him. Himalayan blood spattered Harrison as he pulled the blade free of the sundered wreck of a head and managed to dodge a sword thrust aimed at himself. Catching the still-plunging arm between his own elbow and side, Harrison trapped the man long enough to bring his own blade into play again. He hacked the man nearly in two, pulling his momentum only enough to avoid completely severing him and catching the edge of the emerging knife himself.

Chance alone saved the detective from the next of his assailants, as he momentarily lost his footing on the freely flowing gore now puddling underfoot. Tripping awkwardly on a severed limb beneath him, he dropped out of the path of the blackjack aimed at his skull. His black locks whipped like lashes with the sweat of exertion, and below them his blue eyes glowed with hatred and determination. Letting go his blade, he launched a good old fashioned punch at his single standing foe—who did not remain erect for long. The ham-like fist connected with the bearded jaw, making a loud snapping sound like that of a rotten tree branch.

Harrison stood alone, soaked now with his own profuse sweat and others' blood. His keen eyes swept the dim expanse of the den to check for the possible approach of more attackers—defenders actually. None came. The place seemed to be littered with corpses, until Harrison realized most were the dreamily tossing carcasses of the clientele. With one exception. Sudden screaming sent chills down the spine of the big detective. Scanning the room again, now sure that the weird shriek must announce the presence of some devil from the Eleven Scarlet Hells of Oriental legend, he crouched in anticipation. A few moments more and he found the unexpected source of the unhallowed noise. It was one of the reclining heaps of doped-up flesh.

Narcotic lassitude had abruptly given way to maniacal lurching and writhing as if the man were bubbling on the griddles of Hell. Harrison had seen his share of bad dope fits but nothing like this. He approached the shaking cot and its terrible burden with a sense of superstitious fear which the earlier fight had not been able to awaken in him. Was the poor wretch demon-possessed? Fighting down the age-old dread of his Celtic barbarian ancestors, Steve reached forward and took the shaking form in his iron grip. Even Harrison had trouble holding him steady for long enough to see the face, and even then all he felt was a sense of dim recognition, as if it were a face he had not seen for many years. Something told him to take the poor devil to safety.

Harrison realized he had only moments to act. More of the Asiatics would surely be swarming in on him any moment. So he gave the struggling skeleton in his arms a quick shot to the jaw. This seemed to sedate him, all right, and the burly lawman hoisted the man over his broad shoulders like a sack of potatoes with no trouble. Quickly he sought egress by the same path he had entered. He knew the slant-eyed devils would never dare follow him out into the open in any real numbers. Even on River Street that would be too bold a move for anyone with a lot to hide. Harrison's flesh, already mottled with the goose bumps of the uncanny atmosphere of the dope den, thrilled to the wholesome evening cool of the street. Even the clammy embrace of the river mists was a welcome relief.

Dumping his burden into the back seat of a waiting car, Harrison barked an order to the driver and assumed the shotgun position beside him, careful to keep an eye on the still-inert form behind him. As the roadster sped to St. Agnes Hospital on the edge of the Oriental Quarter, Harrison reached over and cupped the unconscious face in his huge hand.

"By Judas!" he exploded, startling the driver, an off-duty cop willing to cooperate with Harrison's unorthodox brand of justice. Almost unseated by the other man's outburst, the driver sent the car veering.

"I thought they'd discovered and killed him before I got there," Harrison puzzled loudly. "But it's *him!*"

"*Who*, Steve, who is it?" spat the nonplussed driver over his shoulder as he gripped the great steering wheel and tried to right the direction of the hurtling automobile.

"Jong-tso, the little rat of an informer who got me into this damn mess. I got a phone call from him in my office one night. Just happened to be there late. I pick up and it's Jong-tso. I ask if he's got a tip for me on that smuggling racket, but no, he says, it's somethin' else, somethin' big. Something about a secret Oriental gang called the Black Tong. He says they're peddling some dangerous dope."

Pulling into a vacant spot near the emergency entrance, Bill Waterman, the driver, turned around with a look of incredulity in his eyes. "*Him?* Jong-tso's about as likely to be upset by a run of bad dope as a Holy Roller is about a poisonous snake, Steve, and you and I both know it."

The two men pulled the sleeping figure of Jong-tso from the car, one taking his sandaled feet, the other his armpits. Steve replied, "Yeah, but to tell you the truth, that's why I was so interested. I figured it must be something out of the ordinary. So I agreed to meet with him. Found him in one of the waterfront saloons and heard the whole story—or at least more of it. It's still largely a mystery. Even more so now. Jong-tso said he was worried because he had relatives, friends, disappear after visits to certain joints, like the one we just patronized. Others came back but soon died. They knew something was wrong, but they didn't dare go for medical help because, scum like them, they couldn't be seen in public. Jong-tso and I agreed he'd take a turn, try to switch the dope at the last minute, see if he could sneak some idea of what's going on in there."

The conversation continued after the little Chinaman was admitted. The detective and the policeman waited in the room outside. "But Steve, there's doctors in River Street who make their living off wharf rats like him when they need somebody to lick their wounds. Why didn't the chinks go to *them?*"

"Some did. Mostly the doctors wouldn't help them. Oh, they did at first, but then they clammed up, as if they recognized what was wrong but were somehow afraid to get involved. That's why I brought Jong-tso here, to a white doctor. He might not be able to decide what's wrong, but if he can, I'm betting he'll at least tell us."

At this both men lapsed into silence. Bill gave in to sleep. He had joined his friend after an already long day on the job. Harrison scarcely noticed the snoring as he unfolded a pocketed copy of a girly mag he'd picked up at the newsstand outside. But the charms of the wenches in its pages were not enough to distract Steve's racing mind. He could think of nothing now save the looming peril which hovered over River Street, a menace all the more ominous since its outlines were not yet visible. How can you prepare to fight what you don't know? Steve had never shirked a good fight, but he had to know what he was up against.

Where lust couldn't overcome Steve, weariness finally did. He joined his partner in Morpheus' grasp until he felt himself rudely shaken awake by the hands of a doctor who was saying something in urgent tones.

"Where did you get this man? And, more important, where did he get this ... this ... poison that's in him?"

Straightening his stained slouch hat and his crumpled necktie, Harrison blinked and stammered, "Why, Doc, I'm not sure I can tell you that until you tell me just what's ailing the little ..., er, what's ailing my friend. Sort of police business, you see." So Steve spoke as he took out his Private Investigator's license, soon paired by the addition of Bill's hastily produced police badge. Now, if anything, the physician looked even more scared.

"I might have known! Officers, come with me, please." At this, the three men entered the swinging door and found themselves in a hospital corridor. The reek of disinfectant assailed their nostrils almost as foully as the opium had only a couple of hours before. They lingered here only a moment as the doctor whispered some instructions to a nurse, then rejoined them. "Let me introduce myself. I'm Doctor Randall Bennet. This way, gentlemen."

Another door opened into an oak-paneled office, the walls of which were thickly covered with certificates and diplomas from various institutes of medical learning. More than a few of these were apparently not American, if the language were any indicator. Steve, a man with minimal education, glanced at them with admiration. He figured he had learned what he needed to know in the professional school of the streets, but he respected any man who took his trade this seriously. As his eyes turned to the fine mahogany desk where the doctor was now easing his spry frame into a well stuffed leather chair, Steve noticed the older man had taken a huge and odd looking volume from a shelf and had it marked in a particular place.

"At first, I thought I must be mistaken in my diagnosis, but even a second test produced nothing that fit the usual possibilities. It was only on a whim that I took a look at this old thing. We doctors don't like to admit we're beat, you know, and sometimes we'll go to pretty nearly any lengths to avoid having to. So I saw this as my last resort."

"What is it, Doc?" Harrison grunted. "Some kind of a Bible?"

"In a manner of speaking, yes, Mr. Harrison." The doctor paused to wipe his glasses, as if seeking a moment to decide how much of a secret matter he could risk divulging to two strangers.

"I'm not sure I should even be telling you this. But, you say your friend isn't the only one? If this is spreading, I guess we've got to try to put a stop to it."

Harrison leaned forward in his chair, impatient with the doctor's soliloquy. "A stop to *what*, Doc? I've got to know!"

"Very well. First I'd better tell you about the book. Otherwise, the rest isn't going to make much sense." He indicated the worn spine of the massive book. "Do you read German?"

"Nope, just English. It's good enough for me. Suppose you tell me what it says."

"*Unaussprechlichen Kulten.* That's the title. It means something like 'Unspeakable', or 'Nameless', 'Cults.' It's a kind of encyclopedia of madness and nightmare, compiled many years ago by an old German savant named von Junzt. The man was possessed of a thirst for strange knowledge. His contemporaries compared him to the legendary Doctor Faustus."

"Are you saying this von Junzt sold his soul for what's in that book?" quoth Harrison, skeptical and yet trying to fight down a returning sense of uncanny fear.

"Sold his soul? Why, yes, I suppose he must have. The book contains accounts of his travels to strange forgotten places, some of which reputable scholars still swear are pure myth. In one chapter he claims that Hell is a literal place somewhere on this earth, and that he was there. I won't tell you what he claimed to have learned there. I don't think you'd sleep any better than I do."

Harrison's brow knitted in interest and in fear. "How'd you come by this thing, Doc? I can't imagine it could be printed legally."

"You're right. It isn't. And I agree: It shouldn't be. What I've got is the Bridewall edition. Rare enough, though there are supposed to be even rarer versions with more text. I can only guess what horrors lurk in their pages. I came by this one not too far from here, in a hovel in your own River Street. I was called there on a medical emergency. Street violence, too late when I got there. A man shot down in front of a book store, actually a front for darker dealings in the back room. Apparently somebody had dumped a load of old books robbed from a mansion outside of town. Putting two and two together, I later decided they must have belonged to old John Grimlan. You've heard the name?"

Harrison was paying rapt attention. He had indeed heard the name—plus plenty of stories that still made his nape hairs prickle. He just nodded.

"The way I figure it, thieves broke into the house after his death and took the books for valuable antiques. They thought they'd be able to fence them easily but found no one wanted anything to do with them. On River Street people seem to know of things like this. They must have finally sold them off for pennies just to get rid of them. I happened to spy the title that day and bought the book for a ridiculously small sum. Certainly small compared to the price I've since paid for reading it.

"You see, the book had been the subject of rumor in medical circles for some years because of certain herbs and drugs von Junzt was said to have catalogued, poisons mostly, worthy of a Borgia, but often the same substances can be used for medicines, too, in different doses. Even for anesthesia. I had never paid much attention. It seemed moot, since the very existence of the book was dubious. But once I saw it, I had to know. The rumors turned out to be true enough. I found the information in a chapter on assassin cults. You wouldn't believe some of the ways human beings have devised to kill each other. Many deaths today are dismissed as freak accidents because doctors don't know what von Junzt somehow found out."

"Doc, are you saying Jong-tso in there has been given one of those drugs? Will he survive it?"

He shook his head. "No, I am afraid the Chinaman is already dead. And it's good for him that he is. Believe me, he would be much worse off if he lived. But of course you are right. It was one of the drugs von Junzt listed, something called the Black Lotus. And if somebody is spreading it around, there's a lot more at stake here than some local drug ring. And it's not even the drug, as terrible as it is, that's the real danger. It's the Powers who cultivate the drug and what they use it for. It wasn't designed for anything as mundane as opium dens, Mr. Harrison."

Steve rose to his feet, sensing the interview was at its end. "Well, what *was* it designed for, then?" The doctor was looking down at his desk blotter.

"The details aren't clear, I'm afraid. I told you my copy is one of an abridged edition. I've my suspicions, but they're much too vague to be of any real use to you. I don't have an answer. I'm just giving you a look at the puzzle you brought me when you brought in your dead friend."

"Thanks, Doc," Harrison grunted. As he turned to leave, Bill following him, more puzzled than ever, Steve said, "I think I know somebody who may have the answer or at least know how to get it."

Steve Harrison knew he was out of his depth on this one, far out. He didn't explain much to Bill, dropped him off home to a relieved wife, and continued back into the Oriental Quarter. It was late now, but Harrison couldn't afford to wait until a more civil hour. He guided the borrowed roadster down the more brightly lit streets of the Quarter, his headlights banishing slinking furtive shapes who feared to be transfixed in the beams. Parking by a local Buddhist temple, the safest place he could think of, he covered the rest of his

route on foot. Here the layout of the Quarter bore the look of an
ancient Eastern city, becoming a maze of aimless alleys and convoluted back streets and cul-de-sacs. No map would be of any help,
and the cobbled pathways would never accommodate a car.

He had never had occasion to seek the address he now approached.
He knew the man by reputation only, and he had always hoped it
would stay that way. Still, when dealing with the mysteries of the
East one had to resort to the ways of the East. Ofttimes those ways
were inscrutable. Some secrets a white man could never learn, and
then one had to seek allies. But the prospect was not a welcome one
when the only possible ally was as fearsome as the enemy one
sought to fight.

Harrison came to the corner of Levant Street where the dark
mouth of an alley gaped like the maw of Jonah's whale. There was
no sign, probably never had been, but he knew it for China Alley.
His goal was number 13 along that shaft of darkness. Taking a deep
breath, he plunged in. As it happened, the dark was not absolute.
A dim naked bulb cast its wan radiance over a small bronze name
plate affixed to the grimy brick at eye level only a couple of yards
down the alley. The plaque was corroded almost past recognition,
but the outlines of the numbers just above it told him he had arrived
at his destination. Just to be sure, he tried rubbing the name plate
with the edge of his threadbare coat. Some of the grime reluctantly
came away, and he could see enough of the name to fill in the rest
like a crossword: ZARNAK. With a sense of resignation, Harrison
pressed the buzzer.

Almost at once, as if his arrival had been expected, the door swung
open. The well lit interior blinded him momentarily, but in a second
he could make out the silhouette of a figure fully as massive as
himself. A moment more and Steve could see that the man before
him was a Sikh, a member of one of the mightiest warrior races of
Asia. He had had occasion to fight both against and alongside such
men in his lifetime, both in River Street and in the exploits of earlier
years when he had traveled East.

The tall man's proud head was surmounted by a twisting turban,
his set jaw embellished by a full, jet-black beard. Between these
perched a hawk-like nose and the fierce sharp eyes of a mountain
eagle. The statue spoke: "Mr. Steve Harrison, no? By Nam, we had
expected you ere now." He motioned the baffled detective on into
the foyer. Harrison obliged, taking his hat in his hand as he did so.

"So you know me. That I can figure. I'm well enough known in these parts. But you say you knew I'd be here, Dr. Zarnak?"

At this the swarthy giant's deep chest reverberated with the sound of distant thunder. Harrison supposed it was meant as laughter. "Ah, *sahib* Harrison, I am not that estimable person. It is my honor to serve him. He awaits you within. Will you accompany me?"

As he followed the factotum, Harrison could not help gawking at the exotic furnishings about him. The exterior of the building, a small two-story structure abutted on either side by taller, rotting tenements, gave no hint at all of the interior which looked more like a museum, or maybe the palace of an Oriental monarch, than anything else. The floors were thickly laid with Persian and Chinese carpets. The walls were similarly hidden by silken brocade tapestries depicting scenes from some mad opium dream. Chandeliers and candelabra bore intricate scrollwork and etchings which seemed reminiscent of unknown varieties of marine monsters and mermen. Bookcases everywhere overflowed with volumes bound in unusual materials with titles in who knew what heathen tongue. The great Sikh seemed to move more slowly than one might expect, and Harrison wondered if he did so in order to allow him to take in as much of the place as he could.

As Harrison found himself wondering just how far the narrow building must extend backward to accommodate such an interior, his guide was indicating a heavy teakwood door bordered in bronze. Zarnak, he said with a note of reverence, could be found within. And with that he vanished down another hallway. When Steve looked back at the door, he was surprised to see it standing open, where a moment ago it had been firmly closed.

His eyes swept the interior before he stepped in. Again his eyes had to adjust, as the room was but vaguely lit by two low-burning braziers flanking a great cluttered desk. Behind this desk sat a lone figure, head and shoulders slightly hunched. No feature of this occupant was yet distinguishable. As Harrison took the first step into the room, his feet silent not only from his instinctive cat-like tread but also from the thick lushness of the Bokhara rug, the figure at once rose to his feet.

"Mr. Steve Harrison, is it not so?" said a clear, firm voice of unusual timbre. "Let us have a better look at one another, shall we?" At this, the flames in the two braziers rose higher, as if controlled by an unseen agency. *Some trick*, thought Harrison. He had seen better.

In the brighter light he could see Dr. Anton Zarnak extending a
hand to him. Harrison hesitated but a moment, and yet in that
moment every detail of the other man's exotic appearance was
imprinted upon his memory. He was of no more than average
height, trim of build, serenely proud in posture. His form was
draped in the folds of a deep violet silk jacket, lapels and broad cuffs
encircled with rich quiltwork. A black ascot covered the distance
to his neck, which was crowned with an unreadable face of Eurasian
features. Above the slightly slanting eyes, which had the illusion of
being mostly pupil, delicate brows arched. A high, intellectual
forehead topped these like some mighty mountain fortress. His hair
was fine and black, with the oddity of a single jagged tuft of gray
and white blazing up from the widow's peak. His extended hand,
like its mate, bore several rings, each engraved with a peculiar sigil.
The one Harrison could make out best bore the device of a rooster-
headed figure with curling snakes for legs.

Harrison took the outstretched hand, hoping to learn something
from the man's handshake. It was surprisingly firm, fully as much
as his own. Steve was confused at his inability to judge the man's
age, even approximately. Zarnak motioned him to take a seat across
the desk from him. As he did so, Steve noticed the chair was
comfortably close to the suddenly blazing fireplace. The workmanship of the mantel was fabulous, but what drew his attention was
the collection of remarkable objects atop it. There were statuettes
of various Asian deities, most of which Harrison had often seen
throughout the Oriental Quarter, but many of them seemed slightly
different in some queer way. There was the cross-legged, bloated
figure of Ganesha, but his flap-ears looked to have tentacles trailing
from them. Others were less readily identified. Here and there were
inscribed clay tablets whose language Harrison could not guess.

Above all this, like a great sun shining down on the smaller
objects, was hung a large wooden face painted in garish red. There
were three bulging eyes below a brow surmounted by a crown of
tines bedecked with human skulls. Golden fumes or flames scrolled
from its wide nostrils or drooled from the corners of the tusked
mouth. Puffed cheeks might have denoted the depicted monster's
satiation with human flesh.

"I've seen that before," Harrison ventured. "Yama, the Tibetan
King of the Dead, right?"

"Very good, Mr. Harrison," Zarnak replied with a subtle hint of
a smile. "But in truth it is an older avatar of that entity, known in

elder Lemuria as Yamath, Lord of Flame. The center of his cult was
the metropolis of Patanga. Perhaps you have read of it in Dost-
mann's classic *Remnants of Lost Empires*. Here." The strange savant
hefted a large Victorian-era book.

"No sir, I'm afraid that's a new one on me. I'm not so well read
as you. No time for it. Justice is my business, and River Street keeps
me pretty busy at it."

Zarnak dropped the book on a pile of similar tomes at one corner
of his desk, raising a small mist of dust. "But then I see we are in
the same business, Mr. Harrison. I do not read for leisure, you see.
I am in the same business as you, and these are the tools of my trade."

Involuntarily Steve looked at the spines of the nearest stack of
books. Like those he had spied in the hall, their enigmatic words
meant nothing to him: *The Secret Book of Dzyan*, *The Ponape Scripture*,
*Dhol Chants*.

"Please, Mr. Harrison, do not imagine I mean to belittle you. You
employ your chosen weapons well, as I do mine. And I believe that
it will require both our skills to deal with the menace we both face."

Harrison quickened. Talk was not his line of work, action was,
and now they were coming to the point. "You mean the bad dope?
I don't know how you know about my involvement, but I guess you
probably have your informants." Another cryptic smile from Zarnak. Steve continued, "I had a hunch you'd know the score if
anybody did. Fill me in on what you know, and then we'll work out
a plan. I think I can bring in police reinforcements if we need them."

"I fear their participation would be ill-advised," quoth Zarnak.
He seemed to be taking his time as if explaining a complex matter
as best he could to a well meaning child. "First allow me to tell you
what is at stake here. It will sound fantastic to you, but you have
already seen much, perhaps enough to lend credence to my tale. We
shall begin by sharing what each knows." Harrison, on the edge of
the comfortable chair, settled back to listen.

"What can you tell me of your Chinese friend? What did he tell
you, and what has become of him?"

"Dead, dead of the dope, the Black Lotus. That's what the doctor
at the hospital diagnosed. Do you know of it?"

"I am surprised a Western medical man knows of it. But in River
Street the mists whisper many things from far away to attentive
ears. It may be that we are dealing with the Black Lotus, or we may
not be."

"Doctor Zarnak, all I know from what I saw in that dope dive is that the poor wretches who are fed the stuff all of a sudden pass from a stupor to a state of wild agitation. Jong-tso was raving, saying all kinds of stuff in a language I couldn't understand, though I don't think it was Chinese."

"Presumably you know of the recent killing sprees in the Quarter?"

"There's always stabbings, garrotings, poisonings, mostly Tong wars and personal vendettas. That's standard stuff, though."

"These, then, are killings kept secret from white ears. Terrible butcherings, mutilations, the work of fiends possessed of berserk fury. These, too, are the result of the Black Lotus. Some who take it do not die, but kill. Thus far I have been unable to examine any of the bodies of those whom the drug itself slays. If I could, I would know what I need to know. Can you take me to have a look at the late Jong-tso?"

"'Fraid not, Doc. He had no known relatives. I think he's been incinerated by now. I won't tell you what they do with the ashes."

"I see. I am not surprised. Were you alone when you rescued the Chinaman from the opium den?"

"No, my pal Bill Waterman was waiting outside in the car. What's he got to do with it?"

"I should like to question him, that's all. May we go and see him? I realize it is late. My man Akbar Singh will drive us." Both men rose.

Harrison countered the other man's offer: "No, if you don't mind a few minutes' walk, I've got Bill's car parked not far from here. Might as well drive it back to him." So they departed.

The car was unmolested, to Steve's relief. They got in, Steve driving. Along the way, he sat in silence, partly in the grip of a queer sense of foreboding, partly ill at ease in awe of the strange man beside him. The trip did not take long. As the roadster approached its familiar curb, Harrison's eyes widened to see police officers cordoning off the house and turning away curious, agitated neighbors. The car door flew open and Steve launched himself up the sidewalk. Zarnak followed with a more dignified gait.

By the time the erudite occultist had reached his gruff partner, Harrison was embroiled in a profane dispute with the police lieutenant, whom he seemed to know if not to like. "Damn it, Phil, you've *got* to let me see him! I know enough not to disturb the crime scene, for Pete's sake! At least tell me how Bill died! Was it a burglar? A revenge job?"

The policeman's eyes widened. "Look, Steve, you've got it wrong! Bill's *alive!* He's not the one who was murdered. It was Flora, his wife. We're trying to get Bill under control now."

Harrison grunted, eyes downcast, about the tenderest expression of emotion he was capable of. "Judas, but that's tough! Let me talk to him, Phil."

"You still don't get me," the cop protested. "*He killed her!* Poor devil must have snapped, killed her in her sleep. He's hopelessly insane. It took five of our burliest men to hold him down once they got the call from a neighbor. When they got there, he was *eating* her." Here the lieutenant went pale, not for the first time that night.

Zarnak moved to the fore. He transfixed the eyes of the policeman as Steve watched, intrigued despite his shock over the news he'd just received. The savant spoke soothingly: "Lieutenant, I assure you that it is a matter of the highest urgency that we be allowed to see and, if possible, to question the poor madman. I can guarantee it will aid you in solving the case." Blank-eyed, the compliant cop said nothing but waved the two men through the police cordon.

Harrison dreaded the sight within. He was no stranger to spilt blood. He hadn't a weak stomach, but this was different, a stroke too close to home. Forensic specialists were already at work at the gruesome task of gathering up the savagely sundered pieces of meat that had until recently been Flora Waterman. Others struggled to get the flailing arms of a maniac with a slight resemblance to Steve's old comrade into a straightjacket. He was chewing at the gag. Zarnak at once insisted they remove it. He ignored their wide-eyed protests and began to reach for it himself. Harrison waved away their blue-coated arms.

"Do what he says, boys! If anybody can make sense out of what's happened here, it's Doctor Zarnak!" With an appreciative nod, the occultist stood silently, awaiting whatever shrieked syllables might issue forth from the tongue of the madman. He had not long to wait, as the ranter began to explode into sobbing cries of, "*Iä! Iä! Lloigor fhtagn! Zhar!* The swimmer in the Lake of Hali! Please, oh please! Ahhhhhh—!" The strange words gave out as Zarnak made eye contact with the poor wretch, seeming to fix him in a hypnotic lock. The suddenly limp form slumped over, giving the baffled blue-coats some relief but even more puzzlement.

Turning to the impassive Harrison, Zarnak whispered, "I have heard quite enough. It is even as I feared. Let us now return to my dwelling. I will explain everything." Eager to learn exactly what he had stumbled into, Harrison followed the older man out the front door with only an inexpressive grunt to the lieutenant who was now as reluctant to see the detective leave as he had been a few minutes earlier to let him in. Profanity followed him to the waiting car. "Doesn't look like poor Bill will be needing it," Steve muttered as they pulled away from the curb.

"I guess somebody must've tailed the car to Bill's house, somehow snuck in and administered the Black Lotus. In his sleep or not, I don't know. We both dozed in the hospital, but it couldn't have been then, or I'd have been fed the dope too."

"That would be my guess as well, Mr. Harrison. It is not unlikely that the same men traced the car to my neighborhood, too, but knowing of my near presence they felt ill-inclined to pursue you."

"Judas!" the great detective swore, suddenly swerving to pull the car over to a curb. "For all we know the yellow devils booby-trapped the damn thing!"

The bejewelled hand of his enigmatic companion rested like an alighting bird on his massive shoulder. "A wise precaution, my impulsive friend, but fear not. I would have detected such a crude stratagem when we first approached the vehicle. I assure you, there is no danger—not of that sort, anyway."

Underway again, the unlikely partners filled the short ride back to China Alley with what information they knew. Harrison had little to contribute. Zarnak, on the other hand, continued to explain as they re-entered his study.

"You have now seen for yourself a specimen of the Black Lotus's true power."

"More than I wanted to see, Doc. But tell me this: Why the hell would anyone, even a dope ring, want to smuggle this stuff to its customers? Where's the pay-off? I can see assassins using it, but who'd want to kill off the River Street scum?"

"I venture to say that those poor unfortunates could not evade their karma. But, as you surmise, no mortal agency willed them dead. It is evident that the local smugglers have intercepted a stock meant for someone else. The Black Lotus has a very specific use, and should it be employed otherwise, the results will be as we have seen tonight."

Harrison shifted in his leather chair uncomfortably. He was accustomed neither to such exquisite surroundings nor to such a thick pall of deadly evil as that which now seemed to surround him. "But what legitimate purpose could this infernal stuff possibly have?"

"That will take some explaining, Mr. Harrison, and even then I question whether you will be inclined to understand." Rising from his teakwood desk, the gaunt form drifted to one of the book-lined walls and extracted a peculiar-looking volume. It was quite large, reminiscent of that which Dr. Bennet had earlier shown Steve and his lamented friend at the hospital. But this one seemed not even to be printed in the familiar characters of the Roman alphabet.

"The text is rendered in Egyptian hieroglyphs. It is called *The Black Rituals of Koth-Serapis*. I doubt you have heard of it. It is little known in the West. Even the learned Professor Wallis-Budge makes no mention of it. It contains knowledge of many secret matters, including that of the Black Lotus. It seems the plant was first cultivated long ages ago during the black eons of prehistory, or shall I rather say, of history which has understandably been suppressed. Those who bred and used it were the sorcerer-priests of ancient Stygia, who discovered how it might enhance the worship offered to their secret gods, such as Set-Typhon and Gol-Goroth."

Steve's eyes narrowed with puzzled skepticism, but he continued to listen silently. He'd heard strange stories before that turned out to be all too real. This might be one of them. And the truth would have to be pretty strange to account for what he had seen this night already.

"The ages passed, and the blasphemies of Stygia were at length swept away by the flood-tide of younger peoples with scant patience for the decadent cults of primal magic. And yet the secret of the Black Lotus by no means died with Stygia. By unguessed routes and circuitous stealth the drug was carried East where the hierophants of Leng and Sung in the heart of Asia rediscovered its ritual value. At length it proved too terrible in its danger, too potent in its allure to those who dared pilfer small quantities of the substance for their own use. You have seen the results, and yet so great is the ecstasy that many counted even such a price as worth paying for a few scant moments of bliss.

"The khans of forgotten empires ordered the Black Lotus to be extirpated, but it lingered in use among the little-known Tcho-Tcho people of Burma. There it was successfully restricted to the orders of adepts who alone knew its proper use, those who still understood the prescriptions of *The Black Rituals of Koth-Serapis*. And as it had been meant to do, the Black Lotus opened the minds of the Tcho-Tcho epopts to behold their gods, Lloigor and Zhar. Some of them it sends into an insane killing rage. Such a priest, possessed of the deity, will turn on the bound sacrificial victim, whether beast or man, and rend it to pieces as you have seen this very night. The others present join the visionary in the cannibalistic orgy."

Harrison interrupted. "You're right, Doc. It doesn't make much sense to me—or at least not much of it did till now. I remember poor Bill screaming out those two names, if you can call them that! And the Tcho-Tchos! Every cop in the area knows them only too well: the latest wave of Oriental immigrants to clutter the docks. Damn near every single one of them connected with the criminal underground in one way or another. There are only a few, but even at that, there's too damn many of them if you ask me!"

"Yes, they have earned quite a dark reputation for themselves, both here and in their homeland. Few know of them; all who do both hate and fear them. They were certainly those for whom the stock of the Black Lotus was intended. By now I am sure they have exacted a terrible vengeance upon those who deprived them of the drug."

"Guess I gave them a head start back at the dope den. Then those Asians must have been the middlemen, really dupes who stumbled into a death trap. Must have been the Tcho-Tchos who caught up with Bill. But tell me, Doc, is all you've told me contained in that book? Most of your story takes place in the Far East, not Egypt."

"Very observant, detective. I see you do not miss many clues. No, my information comes by a rather different channel. You see, I *myself* once served in the remote Plateau of Sung as the high priest of the cult of Zhar and Lloigor. In fact, that is the meaning of the characters that make up my name: Zhar-Nak, the mouthpiece of Zhar."

Harrison's mouth fell open. "Naw, that can't be! You're not one of those squat little devils!" At least Steve hoped the man was lying. The chill of superstition returned and leaped down his vertebrae like a blue arc across electrical poles.

"I have not said that I was, Mr. Harrison. You should be aware that these dwarf-like figures belong to a warrior caste specially bred. Not all the Tcho-Tchos are like them, nor have I expressly claimed to be of their nation. My origins shall remain my secret. They are not relevant to our purpose.

"But I did hold sway over the sect until a crafty priestling called E-poh, a devil of a man addicted to the Lotus in small enough doses to stave off dissolution, stole the priestly tiara away from me by promising access to the drug to all who would join him. I have told you of the potent temptation of the drug to those who know of its powers. Thus degraded, the sect turned from me, and the Tcho-Tchos became the malevolent creatures you see today.

"It were a vain hope to regain my pontificate. What use to preside over such degenerates? And yet I must do what I can to prevent the sublime worship of the divine Lloigor and Zhar from being further profaned. You and I, between us, possess the means, I believe, to stop the blight of the Black Tong of the Tcho-Tchos from spreading its stain into the New World.

"Well, Detective Harrison, I have told you what I know. It is for you to decide whether you will fight by my side."

Steve remained silent for a few moments. He wanted very much to dismiss what the bizarre figure before him had recounted. It sounded like a drug-induced fantasy itself! And yet he could not deny it was the sort of shadow that tended to fall on River Street where the deepest darkness of the Elder World always seemed to collect. And if even half of what Zarnak had said were true it provided the only clue he had to ending an awful plague of crime and doom. And there were Bill and Flora Waterman to think about. He couldn't afford to turn down even the slimmest reed of a chance to avenge them. He rose and extended his hand.

"Doctor Zarnak, I'm with you. Lead the way. Somehow I think my usual methods aren't going to count for much in this case."

"Excellent, my young friend! But you are quite wrong about one thing: Your abilities will prove useful indeed. While it is true we are ranged against more than human Powers, they are served by flesh and blood since it is the world of flesh and blood they would conquer. There are forces of dark sorcery at work here, yes, but I believe there is every chance at evening up the odds, as I believe you would say. Come with me."

He led the puzzled detective through the door and down the carpeted hall to a finely inlaid curio cabinet. It was a tall, glass-fronted display case, offering scrutiny of a set of rare Mediterranean antiquities. But Zarnak reached around the back, seeking for some hidden catch. A panel sprang open, revealing a peculiar staff bolted to a quilted recess. The thing was about three feet in length, some sort of stave. One end was sharpened, issuing in a deadly looking spike. The other was delicately carved with the head of one of the great jungle cats. Zarnak quickly released the fastenings and passed the object to Steve. The latter was surprised at the weight and apparent hardness of the thing.

"It is a powerful talisman, once owned by an ancestor of yours. I believe you will find it as useful as he did."

Steve *did* feel a strange sense of familiarity, as if he had trained with the staff, as if it were somehow as natural to him as one of his own limbs. He looked forward to using it with terrible effect in the battle to come.

The day arrived for what had unofficially come to be known as the Mardi Gras of River Street, that day when several major and minor religious festivals of the many different sects represented in the Oriental Quarter spilled into the crowded avenues celebrating their favorite totems. It seemed as if time had rolled back and Steve Harrison, Anton Zarnak, and the latter's manservant Akbar Singh strode the convoluted alleys of ancient Tyre. Here four strong sets of swarthy arms bore up the tabernacle of an obscure Moslem *weli*, or saint, surrounded by a crazed throng of Muhammadans frothing at the mouth and lashing themselves as they recited Arabic verses from the Koran. There a band of equally god-intoxicated Siva devotees shambled in a trance state as they ran spikes and pins through their own seemingly bloodless flesh. Two Chinese paper dragons flowed gracefully through the crowds, borne up by hidden puppeteers. Steve knew that the festival was largely a cover for an open hunting season on tourists and the innocent. Oh yes, the cutpurses were out in full numbers, worshiping the only god they knew: Mammon.

Harrison, Zarnak, and Akbar Singh strolled through the crowds as inconspicuously as they might, swathed in concealing costumes. To any casual passerby, they must have appeared as a wealthy Easterner flanked by two burly bodyguards, not an uncommon sight. Akbar Singh wore only facial disguise to supplement his usual apparel, but his master had affected the fine silks of a merchant of the Old World. A veil masked his features, too, though few even in River Street would have been able to put a face to the well known but mysterious name of Anton Zarnak. Steve Harrison in his own way was fully as notorious, only his white face and dress were unmistakable in such surroundings. Thus on this day he appeared almost as the double of Akbar Singh, most of his mighty frame concealed in detail if not in outline. And it was Steve who first noted something curious in the scene.

"Hey Doc," he whispered, "will ya get a load of *that!* You ever seen a Chinese dragon like that before?" His gloved finger indicated a puzzling conglomeration of paper mache and brightly hued limbs twisting into view out of one of the side alleys. It looked more like it was supposed to be an octopus or a squid than anything else.

"Strange indeed. It represents the totem of no familiar sect or cult. Yet it would be quite out of character for the servants of the Old Gods so to show their hand. I wonder if it is not perhaps intended as a—"

"*Diversion!*" finished Steve, throwing the bulkier portions of his disguise aside. For out of the mouth of an opposite alleyway, dark as midnight even in the light of noonday, there now poured a stream of miniature juggernauts, the stunted but powerful forms of the dreaded Tcho-Tcho thugs. Harrison and Akbar Singh lost no time in unsheathing their weapons to meet the drawn daggers and guns of their squat opponents. A tidal wave of alarm swept through the crowd which promptly melted away, receding like a morning mist in all directions. Some sought the cover of storefronts, others manholes. And though neither Steve nor his Sikh companion had leisure to note the fact just then, Zarnak had disappeared, too. Whether he had succumbed to the surprise attack in its first moments or decided that a diversion might be turned back upon its authors was impossible to judge.

The Tcho-Tchos were all over the two giants like hunting dogs on a lion. Terrible odds, but at least, Steve thought, the tactic made it impossible for any more to join the fray for the moment. The initial cluster of attackers functioned as a kind of barrier against others. Steve laid about him viciously with both Gurkha knife and staff. In the last few days of waiting, he had fine-tuned his performance with the strange weapon, and now it circled and thrusted with merciless precision. Though he did manage a deep gash or gouge here and there, it seemed as if the lightest touch with the cat-headed stave was enough to disable many of the Tcho-Tchos. Zarnak had anticipated that the gang members, whenever they revealed themselves, would have sought to fortify themselves by means of black sorcery, the same as that used to no avail a generation earlier in the Boxer Rebellion. Then British victory had been narrowly achieved with the secret employment of the same juju staff Steve used so devastatingly now. It seemed that the magical reinforcement of the Tcho-Tchos, like the Boxers before them, had actually made them more vulnerable to the counter-magic of the wand of Solomon.

Not daring to draw his pistols at such close quarters, Steve nonetheless rapidly evened the odds, cutting the forms of the malevolent dwarfs from him as if knocking the fruit from a tree trunk. His knife and his stave sought and found sheathing in non-Aryan flesh again and again. Their furious efforts stymied by the very denseness of their assault, the Tcho-Tchos wounded more of their own number than their intended victims. Though streaked with blood from a dozen minor cuts and grazes, neither of the giant combatants had yet taken a serious blow, though each had by now inflicted many. As he split one domed, bald Tcho-Tcho skull to the greenish teeth, Akbar Singh cried, "Such is the fight when cowardly assassins face warriors in the open air!"

But Steve had a different theory. It suddenly occurred to him that with this many well trained killers arrayed against them, the two, no matter how valiantly they fought, must surely have met their doom ere now—unless their attackers had been ordered *not* to kill them at all! Suppose their orders were instead to *capture* ...

He reached the conclusion of his thought with a blackjack punctuating his sentence for him. He didn't even know it when he went down beneath the swarm of gloating Tcho-Tchos. Nor could Steve see Akbar Singh following him only moments later.

A blank eternity later Steve Harrison felt the scene of his nightmare shift. Now he seemed to be lying prone and bound in a dungeon with only a dim hint of illumination. He tried to turn his body over and found he couldn't. He seemed to be tied to something that prevented him. He quickly realized that he was awake, that his feverish dreams had come to an end. Had they drugged him to keep him under after the effect of the blackjack wore off? His eyes began to adjust. Shapes were creeping inch by inch into focus. And so were smells. At once he realized he had been roped face to face with a corpse, and not a fresh one. Was it the sadistic joke of the Tcho-Tcho devils to let him die this way, the unwilling companion of one who had already been on ahead into Death's grim kingdom?

Harrison knew with the pragmatism of his barbarian ancestors that he dared not let himself be overcome with the horror of his situation. The only thing to do was to treat it as one more trap and begin looking for a way out of it. Then he could afford to think up a little sadism of his own. So he began to assess his position. Abortive attempts to flex his muscles quickly revealed that he was tied not at the wrists, as he had half-expected, but rather just behind the elbow. His forearms, and those that dangled listlessly from the stiff in front of him, were free. The same with his legs: They were lashed to the putrefying members of the other just above the knee. It might be possible, if he dragged the dead form to one of the walls, to hoist himself and his burden up to a standing position. Then, if he could keep his balance with this sack of rotten potatoes hanging from his front, possibly he could get to the cell door and see how secure it was. Maybe less than his captors thought.

Grunting, sweat pouring from him even in the musty cool of the cell, Steve had about half accomplished his objective when a new blow took the wind out of his sails. For when he was able to rise up into a fugitive gray beam of light coming through a vent in the oak door, he was aghast to see that he knew the face, or the twisted caricature of a face, of the man opposite him—it was Bill, poor Bill Waterman!

So the Tcho-Tcho Tong had gotten to him, gotten around the police surveillance (no problem, Steve himself was used to doing the same) and finished their business with their victim. This Steve realized as he slid to the ground once more, dragged by the bulk of his dead comrade. But as he braced himself for another attempt, he was startled again, and this was the worst of all. He could feel the corpse beneath him begin to stir with blasphemous animation. His nape hairs prickled with unnatural dread and chills swept over him. Here was the power of the lowest hell, the zombie-conjure. Suddenly he felt that he himself was the burden, that his form must seem but an annoying impediment to the superhuman strength of the fiend who had come to possess the inert husk of his friend. The thing beneath him began to shiver, to shudder, then to buck with an almost serpentine litheness, to be rid of the mortal atop him. Steve could not drive from his mind the grotesque image of a rodeo ride astride the devil's charger! Could he somehow win the contest and save his soul?

Instinctively the detective knew that he must not let his opponent gain freedom of movement. The iron-limbed revenant had already broken one of the leg-bands and was working on one of the arm ropes. Steve knew he must try to keep him down and off balance. If he let the demon win free, he should never be able to survive its ripping talons. So he summoned his knowledge of the wrestling ring, learned many years before in the amateur contests on board ship as he rode a merchantman from one South Seas backwater to another. He used the massive bulk of his body as a blunt instrument, shifting his weight to throw his macabre opponent off balance and onto the hard floor. He dared not reach with his unfettered hands for the throat of the thing that had been Bill, lest it seize the same chance and bring a more powerful demoniac grip to bear on Steve's own windpipe.

It was on his adventures in the South Seas and East Asia that he first learned of the antique evils he later felt obliged to fight in River Street. Among them was the dread rite of the *rolang*, the corpse who dances. In it, or so whispered secret rumor, the mystic adept voluntarily undertook the same contest in which he now found himself engaged. If he could hold onto his sanity long enough, he stood to gain great occult power through the ordeal. But what was the secret of finally disabling the necromantic ogre before it was too late? It had been long ago, and Steve, then young and in the grip of the naive rationalism of youth, had not paid much attention. If only he could *remember!*

Now the dead eyes of the *rolang* had come open, their lost pupils swimming back into view. They gazed at Steve with an utterly unhuman intelligence, straight from the Pit. The crumbling mouth began to open, and Steve knew not which was worse, the charnel stench or the cacodaemoniacal chortling. He felt madness and death were not far away from him now, and he was not far from welcoming their embrace. If only he could recall! And then came a voice, from some distance, and Steve took it for the voice of his antagonist, calling from the far reaches of Tartarus.

"The *tongue, sahib* Steve! Sever the tongue!"

But no, Steve realized through his superstitious panic, that was the voice of a living man! It had to be Akbar Singh! Somehow he had managed to free himself, and now he was trying to rescue Steve as well. What had he said? The tongue? That hardly made any sense. Maybe madness had come for him. But something bade him try the repellent suggestion. Gagging, Harrison opened his own clenched teeth and brought his involuntarily sneering mouth into an un-speakable kiss with his hellish counterpart. The depth of wretchedness came when he fished about in the cesspool cavity with his own tongue, seeking the shriveled stump of the dead man's. But he found it and seized it between protesting jaws, gnawing hard till at last it gave. He had it, spat it to the invisible floor beneath him, and felt the ghoulish form go limp, its sudden weight dragging him down with it.

But now the door sprang open, and the giant silhouette of Akbar Singh filled the doorframe. Stooping, he produced Steve's own knife to cut the remaining bonds. Bracing up Steve's unsteady form, he helped him from the tiny room and out into the hall. In the stronger light of the corridor Steve could see its length was littered with the savaged carcasses of Tcho-Tcho guards. The great Sikh's booted foot found an unattached Tcho-Tcho head and sent it smacking like a rotten fruit against the stone of the wall.

"There are greater numbers of the fiends than any of us had surmised, *sahib* Steve. But most of them are gathered elsewhere, where we are headed now." In answer to his companion's query, Akbar Singh explained, "They put too few of their comrades in charge of me. I led them to think I remained unconscious until I was able to take them by surprise. They had ingenious tortures prepared for me indeed, but Nam be praised, I was able to forestall them. Now the devils will taste of their own terrors many times over in the hells to which I have sent them."

Harrison was now fully able to trot alongside the Sikh down twisting halls surprisingly empty of any prowler but themselves. "I'm sure lucky you showed up when you did, pal! But what of Zarnak? Did they take him, too? Do you know where they're keeping him?"

"I have done a bit of searching, but the whereabouts of my master I do not know, unworthy slave that I am. And yet I did find *something*." Withal, he produced from the folds of his tattered silk greatcoat a familiar-looking carved staff, handing it to Steve. He took it with gratitude.

"One thing I don't get, though, Akbar Singh. With this you could have made short work of that zombie yourself, no?"

"I think not. Not even Zarnak himself would dare employ the power of the stave. It may be awakened and controlled only by its destined wielder. And should I have interposed physically, I fear for my immortal soul, just as you feared for yours. The power of the *rolang* is great, and the means of stopping it are few."

The two figures had slowed their momentum, and Harrison followed the other's example in crouching to continue their progress on their knees. As they made their way through what seemed like an inactive drainage tunnel, Harrison whispered, "So where are we? I can usually get my bearings pretty much anywhere in the Quarter, but I can't place this joint."

"I will not swear to it, my friend, but I imagine we find ourselves in a set of tunnels leading from a warehouse to the waterfront. It seems likely that the Tcho-Tcho devils stumbled upon it and found new uses for the remnants of an old smuggling operation. If I am correct, we have now returned from an area of holding cells, probably designed for the white slave trade, and are very near the warehouse itself. No doubt we have retraced the path by which they led us to our intended doom. Do you hear the chanting just beyond? Let us venture closer."

In a moment the two welcomed the chance to rise to their full height, though they did not decrease their stealth. As they eased open a wall panel in what appeared to be an old accounts office, they could hear more distinctly the sounds the acute ears of the Sikh had detected a moment before. Harrison envied the other man his wilderness-honed senses. It did sound like chanting, repetitive, antiphonal. Someone was leading, many other voices following. So there was a leader. Who might be masterminding the operation? Steve wondered, because whoever it was, he was a dead man as far as Steve was concerned.

The swelling chorus of guttural voices gave Steve a hint of his earlier dread. Deep down he knew that his Celtic forbears had driven the reptilian kindred of these dusky trolls away from the open spaces of human habitation. His knife thirsted for their stinking blood. He seemed to know that his statuesque companion shared his own primal hate for the Little People. Akbar Singh's ancestral mythology would know them as the Asuras, eternal enemies of the Aryan gods.

As both men inched toward a better vantage point, still well concealed, they hoped, they gained a better view of the single figure who stood behind an onyx altar stone placed atop a draped dais at one end of the two-story-high chamber. His arms were extended, occasionally upraised as in supplication. At first Harrison thought they were still too far away to make out the words he was saying, but soon he realized that the chant was in no language he knew, probably the same barbarous patois he had heard from Bill Waterman's raving mouth a few days before. Yes, there were the same words: "*Iä! Iä! Lloigor! Zhar fhtagn! Cfyak vulgtlm vultlagn!*" He felt vaguely nauseated at hearing the arcane vocables. They had a queer resonance, as if they struck a chord on some deeper, forgotten level than mere hearing.

Akbar Singh abruptly shook the giant shoulders next to him, startling Harrison out of the hypnotic torpor beginning to seduce him. "It is even as I feared, *sahib* Steve! He has opened the Gate, and *Something* has deigned to answer the summons!"

The sound of the chanting had subtly changed, taking on a subdued quality, as of waiting and expectancy. The quality of the

light had changed, too. It had something of the look of the pall
announcing an impending tornado. And from this disturbed atmosphere there began to congeal a Form, hard for the mind of the
observer to comprehend, but recalling in some vague way that paper
squid shape during the River Street festival. There seemed to be a
tangle of criss-crossing arms or feelers or tentacles obscuring whatever central body they stemmed from. There was a great splashing
sound, though no water was visible. And the Shape was expanding,
as when a cloud of smoke begins to dissipate. Only it did not
dissipate; as it expanded it only grew more distinct. Its feelers now
waved over the cowering dwarfs whose worship had summoned it.
Of these, some trembled, overcome with religious awe, while others
seemed ready to flee in terror, hesitating perhaps only for fear that
flight might be the more dangerous course, not the less.

The scene held thus for a moment more before fully two thirds
of the Tcho-Tchos bolted for the doors. The two eavesdroppers rose
from concealment, their visibility now irrelevant, and made for the
platform. For the shadowed hood of the mysterious celebrant on the
dais had fallen away, revealing the sweat-streaked visage of *Anton
Zarnak!* He had now lapsed into Mandarin, a tongue Steve had a
working knowledge of. "O most Holy Zhar, destroy these profaners
of thy Mysteries, as once thou didst smite the men of Leng! Iäo
Thamungazoth, for thy name's sake!"

That was all Steve could make out, as the litany of Zarnak was
drowned by the screams of the fleeing Tcho-Tchos. For all their
seeming clumsiness, the gigantic appendages of the glowing apparition struck swiftly and with deadly effect. The panicked goblins
disappeared, one by one, enveloped in the smoky embrace of their
indefatigable pursuer. The mouthpiece of Zhar had spoken, and his
word had not been in vain. Steve and Akbar Singh had arrested their
reckless advance and now returned to their concealment, little
knowing whether it would protect them from the questing tentacles
of this Thing. When they dared look up again, after the shrieks had
died away, the billowing death-cloud still hovered.

"I believe it is what my master called the Tulku of Zhar, the
projected image of the god who sleeps in fitful repose in a grotto
deep beneath the Plateau of Sung. But behold the master himself!
I fear he is lost to us!" Zarnak stood erect, hands aloft, and with eyes
wide. He no longer spoke. And the cloudy Entity continued to
expand. Its quarry now accounted for, it began to extend itself in
the direction in which the doomed Tcho-Tchos had made to flee.

Was it going to round up a few of them that it had missed? But Steve would have sworn none of them could have made it that far. And that meant ... He looked at the paling face of Akbar Singh.

"He can't send it back! Its hunger has been awakened, and it's going to head for River Street!"

"I fear you are correct, *sahib*. But what can we do? It were death to charge the thing, by Nam!" But Harrison did not hear him. He was again listening to the echo of what his ancestors once knew. The cat-headed stave in his whitening fist grew strangely warm. He knew that there was one thing he could try.

Standing erect, he whispered, "I'm sorry, Akbar Singh. Forgive me, Doc!" And with that he sent the sharpened staff sailing through the weirdly charged gloom like a javelin—*straight for the unprotected breast of Anton Zarnak!*

The great Sikh groaned in lament as the missile went home and Zarnak crumpled in a heap. But all at once, the spectral visitant from the shunned heart of Asia was gone, as if the sun had risen, cutting through the heavy morning sea mist. Confident they were now safe, the two men hastened to the dais. There was a body all right, but it was that of a bound Tcho-Tcho, no doubt the priest who had intended to preside over a very different ceremony. Zarnak must somehow have dispatched him before the crowd assembled. Harrison ripped asunder several yards of the fallen canopy which now draped the wreckage of the altar, on the chance that Zarnak's falling body might have become entwined in the stuff, but this, too, proved a disappointment. Nor was there any sign of the stave. Akbar Singh was content to let Harrison pursue his frenzied search by himself. He seemed resigned to the strange circumstance.

"May it not be that Zarnak returned with the avatar of his god to his adytum in Asia? I should suppose so. We will not find him, though I would not prevent you from searching further, my friend."

"What do you mean?" asked the nonplused detective, feeling that, after what he had seen, even the wildest theory of the Sikh might well be true. "Dead or alive?"

"I know as little as you. Indeed, it is not my business to know whether Doctor Zarnak himself was ever physically present among us. He himself may have been a *tulku*. I know not. I will simply return to his dwelling and wait. One day he may have use for my services again, and perhaps, who can say?, he may require your own as well. Go in peace, my brother."

Without a word, Steve Harrison turned about and found the door. The Sikh had been right about one thing: The place was a warehouse, one of the oldest and outwardly most dilapidated on the waterfront. In a few minutes, silhouetted against the wholesome light of the breaking dawn, Harrison trudged the length of River Street, hardly noticing the strange looks from the few early risers whose honest affairs compelled them to be up at such an hour. As he walked on through the Oriental Quarter, his huge frame stooped by exhaustion, he felt for the first time, despite the exotic otherworldliness of the place, that on its ancient streets he had re-entered the real world.

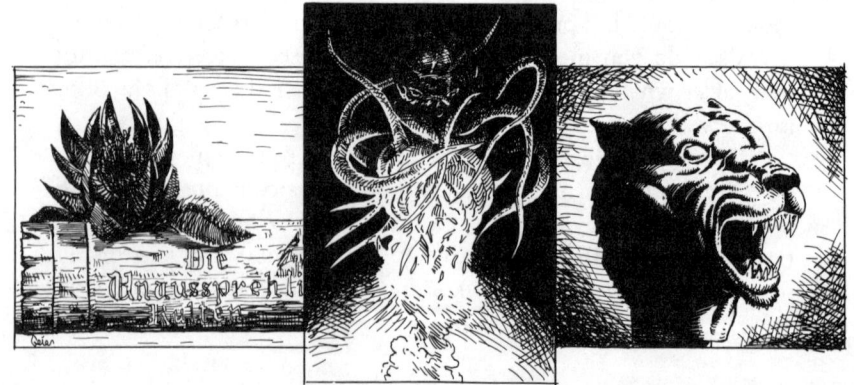

# Darkness, My Name Is

by Eddy C. Bertin

*Irgendwo, auf einem einsamen Platz*
*Wo Sie niemals bleiben wollten*
*Irgendwann, in diesen leeren Raum*
*Werden Sie einen Weg finden*
*Das Pfad im Dunkeln.*

—from the rewritten version of *Von denen Verdammten, oder: Eine Ver-hand-lung über die unheimlichen Kulten der Alten* by Edith Brendall, 1907, based on the original and suppressed, untitled book by Kazaj Heinz Vogel.

## Prologue: Liyuhh

Please be so kind to forgive my boldness; I know it's very unusual to walk up to a nice-looking young woman and simply start talking to her, without any kind of introduction. There's no need to be frightened, of course, nothing could happen to you here in this crowded little restaurant in the heart of Hamburg. I won't tell you my name yet, because that hardly matters, and there's no need to tell me your name because that doesn't matter either at the moment. But I'm glad you accepted my invitation for a drink, even if that was only the result of feminine curiosity. Be assured that I will satisfy your curiosity. You see, I asked you here to show you a book and some pictures. Oh no, please stay! It isn't what you think, it really isn't! Do I look like an exhibitionist trying to sell obscene photographs, or like someone trying to interest you in a world's encyclopedia? So please remain, *bitte sehr, Fräulein*, and take these five photographs. They're only pictures of five statuettes.

You recognize them, I see. Maybe you don't understand yet why or how, because you probably have never seen them in reality, maybe even have never heard of them, and yet you know you *know* them. *Das stimmt, nicht wahr?* These five images are called the Vaeyen. They appear also in this book here. It is only a xerox copy, an almost unknown old German translation titled *Liyuhh,* and in it are sketches of five statuettes, there called Feiaden, and no doubt you'll agree that they are identical. You know *what* they are, my dear, there's no need to hide it now, and you also know what they are used for. Be assured, I'm no enemy, but I had to be sure that you were indeed what I thought you were. I felt the affinity between us as soon as I spotted you in that warehouse, and walked up to you. You must have known too then, else you wouldn't have followed me. Now please listen to the story I must tell you first, so that you may understand everything. Do not interrupt me; I am sure that the story will answer all questions you may have in your mind. So listen ...

# I. Cyäegha

Where the dark is blacker than black and a color of its own, where nothing is something, and the dark is yet clearer than light, It was. It had always been there; It thought at those times when It was able to think at all, those short periods of consciousness between eternally seeming periods of what could only be sleep or nonexistence, and maybe It died each time and was reborn, if It could die at all, which It didn't know either. Then It tried to think of Itself, and It knew that It had a name, which was Cyäegha, which told It nothing about Itself except that It did exist. It just was, it couldn't be touched in Its somewhere place which was nowhere, but neither could It touch other things.

It could be called evil, if evil would have had a rational meaning to Its existence, which it hadn't. Rather Cyäegha was something beyond the man-made laws of good and evil, a natural force, or a natural happening like a wood-fire or a tornado, or a storm, or just plain death, something to which no artificial laws apply.

Sometimes during those scarce moments when It was allowed to think, or maybe allowed Itself to think, because It didn't know if the sleep-death periods were or weren't created by Itself, It tried to remember more than Its name. Then there came sights of millennia of blue ice and then of fire-spitting volcanoes, warts on the face of the Earth, and it all seemed so utterly stupid and unimportant to Cyäegha that it revolted It, so It went back to death and slumber. Time had no real meaning either, it was just something which went by unnoticed, utterly unimportant to something such as Cyäegha, trapped in Its maybe self-made prison and only by Its mind in contact with the outer reality. And at those times when It was awake, fully awake, It hated, as only something can hate which is beyond good or evil. Its whole consciousness became that hate, because that was the only thing It could do. It saw with eyes that were not eyes, and It heard with ears that were not ears, and It thought with Its whole being because It didn't possess such primitive organs as brains either. Silently It hated.

Through the aeons some of Its alien dreams touched men and drove them gibbering mad. Some were more strongly protected and just felt the outer touches of Its dreams, and tried to interpret them consciously in essays, or used them unconsciously in weird stories. Some authors wrote them down as stories, knowing that the world would never accept such an utterly alien reality. Of course they too were considered as insane, as those who really had been driven mad by Its dreams. None had the knowledge and the possibilities to search for other clues. Because Its name had already been written down long ago, or other names which they thought were Its, carved on limestone tablets; and Its shape had been painted on the walls of subterranean caves, still waiting to be opened. But Its shape was not real and constantly changed, and later they wrote about It with trembling fingers on ancient scrolls, and still later on parchments, and all were burned when they were discovered. And when some dared to print Its name, the writers and printers were burned together with their books. But some always survived, some always stayed sane or at least partly, and interpreted Its dreams. Some prayed to It, offering It still warm, beating hearts torn out of the bleeding chests of sacrificial victims, and still others cursed It in many languages, but It couldn't care less. It didn't hate them more or less for what they did. It hated them *all* with Its whole being.

And sometimes Cyäegha dreamed too, dreamed of the others, just like Itself, and yet so different, as ancient as Itself and as hidden as Itself, by aeons of nameless terror. And It wondered where *they* were.

In hiding, or chained, as Itself? Waiting ... always waiting.

Hating ... always hating.

## II. Freihausgarten

Herbert Ramon watched the train leave. Slowly moving, it crept snail-like along its rust-eaten rails, groaning as an old tired animal. The locomotive seemed as ancient as the small station where he had stepped from the train. There was a last sniffling note, a tired cough, before the wheels finally disappeared from Herbert's sight, the last sign of whatever passed for civilization in this place in the *Frankische* Jura Mountains.

A pity, he thought, that the train couldn't transport him straight into Freihausgarten, the village which was his final destination. But Freihausgarten lay at the end of a small valley, encircled by mountains that opened only at the place where the station was, and when they had put the railway here it had been more practical to let the rails continue past the valley. The village wasn't that remote; nothing was really undiscovered in this era of airplanes and international tourism. Freihausgarten could be found on some of the more detailed maps of this part of Germany, but it hadn't really been touched by civilization because it was just too unimportant to bother with, and too difficult to reach to make it "an undiscovered sunny spot for your holidays" in the advertisements of the travel agencies.

Herbert stood alone on the platform, covered with dust and sweating under the hot, burning sun. Slowly he fished a handkerchief out of his pocket, and wiped the sweat out of his eyes and from his neck. He looked in vain for a porter, and finally bent down cursing, picking up his two heavy traveling bags himself. He carried them outside the station. There was no gate at the end of the platform, and no one asked for his ticket. There was an old man, probably the station chief, sitting on a rocking chair that had known better times.

"*Guten Tag,*" Herbert said, but the man didn't answer his greeting. He continued to move slowly backward and forward like an eternally swinging pendulum, pretending not to notice Herbert, though his eyes followed him. Outside the station there were no taxis. Well, yes, there was *one*, though Herbert had his doubts if this *thing* could still qualify for the title of "taxi."

The car possessed the same characteristic as the station: old age. There was no glass in the windows, and dust was driven straight into Herbert's face during the fortunately short drive to Freihausgarten. The dust seemed to be everywhere, on his clothes and face, in his eyes and mouth and nostrils. The car was shaking uncomfortably and irregularly, and Herbert didn't know if it were due to the car's condition or to the bad road, or probably to a combination of both; and words weren't invented yet to describe the sounds the engine made. After only about twenty minutes, however, Herbert was delivered, still in one piece, on the doorsteps of the only hotel Freihausgarten seemed to possess. The village was nothing to fall in love with at first sight: a seemingly completely irrational conglomeration of old houses, disturbed in their growth by one long, stoneless street.

Saying that he disliked the hotel was another understatement. The place was shabby and ancient, completely in order with the general appearance of the village. Part of the hotel's roof was slightly tilted forward toward the entrance, giving the impression that the whole roof was ready to come down and bury the unfortunate visitor. Looking up, Herbert noticed that there was only one other story, and two of its windows were broken. They had been covered with old weather-stained newspapers, mostly flapping loose now.

He had a short, unsettling impression of *déjà vu*, as if he had already seen all this before, or else had expected it to be this way. He shrugged the uncomfortable feeling off.

The wood of the walls was dry, and crumbled as he touched it, leaving a dark stain on his fingers. The whole building spoke of age and careless decay, but there was no other choice.

*Well, so much for the tourist attraction of Freihausgarten*, Herbert thought, *but then, I didn't come here on vacation.*

He paid the driver and went inside, carrying his two bags. There was no one at the registration desk, which was as old and covered with dust as the rest of the shabby room. The keys on the wall behind told him immediately that he would be the only guest. There was no bell to ring for attention either. Herbert put down his bags and banged his fist on the desk.

"*Bien, bien,* I'm coming, all right!" a voice barked from somewhere above. "Be with you in a moment!" Shortly afterward the hotel keeper came down the staircase. He was not so very big but rather bulky with a tendency to obesity. His face was red and wrinkled, and his short-cut hair was already thinning. He wrinkled his nose with seeming distaste, taking in Herbert's typical "city" appearance and his luggage. "I was upstairs," he grumbled; "no need to make a noise fit to raise the dead, *nicht wahr?* With what can I help you?"

"Sorry if I disturbed you at your work," Herbert said with calculated sarcasm, "but I'd like a room."

"You didn't disturb me," the man said, seemingly unmindful of the sarcasm; "was just cleaning up a few things. Rooms enough, no one here at the moment in this bloody nest, no one comes, no one goes. How long will you be staying?"

"I don't know yet," Herbert said. "Maybe a few days, maybe a couple of weeks. It depends."

"Hmph. What you're going to do in this nest for so long? Well, sorry, I didn't mean to pry, it's none of my business, *parbleu.* Come along, I'll show you the room."

He bent and picked up Herbert's bags, carrying them up the staircase as if they weighed nothing. There were four rooms upstairs, and the hotel keeper kicked open the first door with his foot, and carried the bags inside.

"Suits you?" the keeper asked. "*Ça va?*"

Herbert looked around. The room had a window opening on the side of the hotel. He went over to it, and pushed away the curtains. The harsh sun fell straight inside, spitting in his eyes. The burning sun rays made a light show out of a million dust particles sluggishly moving in the static air.

The room held an old table, an armoire of unknown origin, a few chairs, and a bed without a mattress or sheets.

"I'll bring up the bed stuff in a minute," the keeper said. "Be back immediately." Without waiting for an answer he went down, and soon reappeared. He started making up the bed, finishing his work by putting a typical German down blanket on it which Herbert was sure he would not need in this climate. "Sorry for the appearance," the keeper said, "but I almost never get guests here."

"The room suits me as it is," Herbert said. "I don't need much, I'll be mostly outside anyway. Just need a place to sleep and to store my things." Looking out of the window again, he pointed and said, "Isn't that the Dark Hill, over there?"

The keeper snorted. "Yes, that's *Dunkelhügel,* the Dark Hill. You've been here before?"

"No, I haven't," Herbert said, but didn't bother to explain his knowledge.

"You like the free nature stuff." The keeper made another try. "Real city man, aren't you, *oui?*"

Herbert smiled, but without mirth. "In a way, yes," he said. "I'm a writer. Got lots of trouble, stomach, nerves, and things like that. The doctor said I work too hard, and advised me to get some change of air. So I decided to retire for some time, to some forgotten small town, and take a well earned rest. I'll probably do some work in the evenings when it is cooler, but mostly I'll just take long walks and loaf. My time is my own anyway."

"Forgotten town, quite well chosen," the keeper said. "Hot as hell here in summer, and cold as the South Pole in winter. Nothing ever changes in Freihausgarten; you couldn't have picked a better spot to do nothing. You're not German, are you?"

"No," Herbert replied. "I've been living in Germany for some years now, but I'm an American."

"Thought so; you can't hide that accent, no matter how fluently you speak German."

"That makes two of us, then. You're French, aren't you?"

"*Moi? Oui*, and proud of it. I came here on impulse, bought this stupid place without having seen it except in some pictures. Thought I could make a nice living here, and now I'm stuck here for at least another couple of years before I can sell this damn place and move out. Well, I manage to keep myself alive, but that's about it."

"Where are all the people of the village? I didn't see anyone."

"They're all on the fields, or inside. Much too hot now; they'll come out in the evening when it's cooler."

"How are they? The villagers, I mean."

"Boring. I don't mingle much with them, and they leave me alone too. Bloody *parvenus*, arrogant stock. Think they're better than anyone not German. They say hello and good night, and that about wraps up my usual conversation. There's a café a bit farther up the street, and if you care to meet some of them, you can go there in the evening hours. You'll find them almost all there, sipping their *Bier und Schnaps*—I still wonder how they can drink it together, beer and brandy. You're a writer ... well, you'll get your share of local color. And don't let it bother you when they look at you as if you were something *apporté par le chat*—sorry, how do you say it? Like something the cat has brought in from the wet, yes?"

"Strange that there's no real business in this village. One would think that an unspoiled piece of nature like this would draw the tourists and travel agencies."

"Nothing here to do business with. No minerals, nothing worth exporting. Even the fields give only enough to keep them alive. And tourists, you say? You'll understand after you've talked with some of them. Don't expect to find the eager-to-please, warmhearted beer-drinking jolly type of friendly German here. Ice blocks, that's what they are, all of them, devoid of human warmth, human feelings. They don't want any contact with the outside world; they've probably been living like this for centuries and will be only too pleased to keep it that way. They work, eat, drink, and sleep, and I suppose they make love to their wives now and then, as some children *are* born here, but not many, just enough to keep the status quo with the old and dying. I wouldn't be surprised if they still made love like in the sixteenth century, wearing a long nightshirt with a hole cut at the fitting place. Bloody ignorant farmers, and I'm stuck here for another few years. *Mon dieu!* I would like to start screaming every time I think of it."

The keeper took a deep breath, as if the long monologue had tired him. "But I'm telling you only how I think about it; you may very well like Freihausgarten if you want peace and quiet. Maybe we can go down and you can sign the register now?"

"Sure." Herbert followed the man down, and wrote his name in the guest book. The man looked over his shoulder, rubbing his hands at his sides. "Herbert Ramon," he read. "Which reminds me that I haven't even introduced myself. Julien's the name, Julien-Charles Pandira."

They shook hands. "*Enchanté*, Julien," Herbert said, and the keeper's face split in a wide grin.

"*Parbleu*, you are the first who seems to be able to pronounce my name correctly. That calls for something." His hands dived behind the registration desk and came up with two cognac glasses, which he filled from a dusty bottle out of the same hiding place. He pushed one of the glasses into Herbert's hand, and lifted his own. "*A votre santé*; cheers," he said.

"To your health," Herbert said, and tasted his drink carefully. He had to admit that it was good stuff.

"Should be good," Julien said, "the real Napoléon, and not the vitriolic acid they call 'brandy' here. Real French cognac, my only weakness. Once every four months I drive back to France and get my supply. But it is worth it."

Herbert agreed, while emptying his glass slowly, appreciating the soft yet burning aftertaste of the cognac. "Well, thanks, Julien," he said, "but I guess I'll go up now and start unpacking some of my things. By the way, is there a place here where I can eat?"

"Sorry, there's no restaurant," Julien said. "As I said, they discourage tourists. I told you this nest is a ghost town, populated by the mummified spirits of the past, who only *think* they're still alive. You can buy all you need from some farmer, and make your own dinner. Or else, if you like garlic and onion, and French spices, you can join me every day. It's not extra trouble cooking for two instead of for myself alone, and it will be a pleasant change not having to eat alone. I won't charge you much, only the cost of the extra stuff I have to buy."

"It's a deal, then. I never was a good cook, so unless your very first dinner poisons me, I'll be joining you with pleasure. See you later."


## III. Von denen Verdammten


Herbert went into his room and locked the door behind him. The dust clung to everything, but that didn't bother him. It was the kind of atmosphere he was used to in his research. He carelessly threw his cloak on the bed, and put his fingers through his hair. The mirror on the wall was broken, and reflected five times his own image: a somewhat older-looking man in his late thirties, with a sharply lined face and cold gray eyes.

The small room was indeed all he needed. On top of the armoire there was room enough to stack his books, and the table was big enough to work on. He started unpacking his two bags, carelessly throwing his clothes, underwear, and similar things on a chair. He unpacked his working materials with much more care. A portable typewriter, other writing materials, stacks of paper, some geometrical instruments, a microscope, digging tools, small chisels, flashlights, batteries. Then came the books, most of them loosely bound Xerox copies, or handwritten copies in his own small, almost illegible handwriting.

Some of the things contained in these copied books were as old as human knowledge ... and as old as human fear. Their titles would have sounded very strange to Julien, and to most other men, and their contents would have sounded even weirder. A few of the intact books had been collector's items for years, some even for centuries. Others were only to be found in the restricted departments of special libraries and private collections, and Herbert had needed all his influence to get a look at some of them, even then with the explicit prohibition not to copy them. But a very expensive and very effective miniature camera, which could be hidden in the palm of one's hand, could indeed work miracles. He had been able to photograph those parts he needed, even while a guard was watching him from the other end of the reading room, to see that he didn't take notes or tear pages out of the precious manuscripts or parchments. It had been child's play to rewrite the needed parts from blown-up photographs. And here he had them now, those fragments from the *R'lyeh Text*, and the original notes by Ludvig Prinn for his *De Vermis Mysteriis*. Prinn was burned at the stake in Brussels, but before he had been living first in Bruges, and then in Ghent, where he had finished his book. Discovering his handwritten notes in the private collection had been sheer luck, especially since the owner hadn't the slightest idea about their real contents and kept them only because they were old and thus valuable. There was *Liyuhh*, the almost unknown German translation, or rather adaption and analysis, of the *R'lyeh Text*; and a badly damaged copy of François-Honoré Balfour, le Comte d'Erlette's *Cultes des Goules*, rather disappointing because its author had possessed more fantasy than knowledge about the hideous things he was writing about. There were other titles as well, even more alien that these, and he often cursed, thinking that the one he really needed was not there. If only he could have obtained a copy of the *Necronomicon*! He had tried in vain, and then had tried to get the book through someone with even more influence than he had himself, but neither one had even been allowed to *see* the book.

Here were books of power, books *about power* greater than anything else on Earth, and books about *knowledge*. Knowledge about things older than man, books whose authors had been tortured and murdered because of what they wrote. Books which tried in vain to tell man that he was indeed far from alone in the universe!

He went to the window and looked out at the valley, still sweating under the sun. Luck had indeed been with him when Julien chose the first room. Herbert Ramon looked at the hill at the end of the valley, and it was as if unseen eyes reached out for him from that hill, locking with his own in an unholy union. *I am here*, he thought. Déjà vu. *Yes, I have never been here before and yet I recognize it, and I know I have felt this before. Is it my imagination, or are the growths really darker on that hill? It very well could be!*

His hands gripped the window. *I am here*, he thought. *Whatever you are, I am here, and I* know *you are there!*

He didn't have to take his copy of *Von denen Verdammten, oder: Eine Verhandlung über die unheimlichen Kulten der Alten*—"Of the Damned, or: A Treatise about the Hideous Cults of the Old." Even his Xerox copy was not made from the original, which dated back at least two centuries. The author, Kazaj Heinz Vogel, had been a German immigrant, who had returned from America to write his blasphemous text in his native country, Germany. No one knew what had become of him; maybe he had died in some state prison, or else had simply been liquidated by the church's servants. His *Von denen Verdammten* had been an untitled book, published and immediately forbidden. Copies must have survived somewhere, but only two were known to be kept hidden in the locked parts of German libraries. Sometimes, if one knew someone with enough influence, it was possible to leaf through the book. That was what a young German student, Edith Brendall, had done in 1907. The girl had an astounding photographic memory, and she had rewritten the book. Unfortunately she had also published it, at her own expense since no publisher would touch it. Shortly afterward all copies in bookshops had sold out, and then the copies in public libraries started disappearing. Edith Brendall moved from Hamburg-Altona, her native city, to Berlin, and then to Bonn. No use—she disappeared on March 27, 1910, and her body was found floating in the Rhine eight days later.

Herbert Ramon didn't need *Von denen Verdammten* to recall the verses with which Brendall introduced her revision. He knew them by heart by now:

> *Irgendwo, auf einem einsamen Platz*
> *Wo Sie niemals bleiben wollten*
> *Irgendwann, in diesen leeren Raum*
> *Werden Sie einen Weg finden*
> *Das Pfad im Dunkeln*
> *Und Dunkeln, ist mein Name.*

[Somewhere, in a lonely place
Where you would never want to stay
Somewhen, in that hollow space
There you will find a way
A way into darkness,
And Darkness, my name is.]

"Yes," Herbert whispered, "and I will find that way. Because I know *where to find it*. Maybe *Von denen Verdammten* wouldn't have been enough, but *Liyuhh* gives me the missing elements."

He turned away from the window and took his copy of *Liyuhh*. On the fifth page was the fading sketch of a map. The lines were hazy, but they were all he had. The map showed a valley, but only the strong lines had remained clearly visible. On one side of the valley was an opening; the rest was encircled by hills. A few strange symbols had been marked on the place where the valley continued into flatland, but these were unrecognizable. At the other end of the valley a figure was shown, resembling a creature with the aspects of a vulture and a bat.

Herbert placed his copy of *Von denen Verdammten* beside it. The book contained only two maps, but the one he was comparing *Liyuhh* with now was very sharply drawn. The creature guarding the opening of the valley had slightly different body proportions, but was essentially the same. The second map also showed much more. On top of the greatest hill, the most distant from the beginning of the valley, strangely asymmetrical buildings were shown, built from great chunks of stone. There were several smaller structures, or whatever they represented, placed in a circle around a higher building. This looked somewhat like a pyramid with one extremely projecting side. Seven obelisks formed a line toward the entrance of the pyramidical structure, which was partly opened up so one could see what was inside. With incredible precision the artist had designed a long hall, with a stone altar (?) at its end.

Herbert often wondered who that artist had been, and what had become of him. Certainly the drawings in *Von denen Verdammten* were not the work of Edith Brendall herself, though she must have given the artist all the details from her photographic memory. Still, considering that fact, it was even weirder that the drawing of the being above the altar resembled so much the creature guarding the entrance of the valley in *Liyuhh*. Man had always had a bizarre vision of his self-created gods, but this artist had surpassed himself and his contemporaries. This drawing here was much more than just a being with aspects of a vulture and a bat: The thing was partly human or seemed so at first sight, but no longer when one looked closely at its details. The eyes were cold and fishy, all four of them, and placed sidewise of the head. The body itself had scales; the five arms were long and spidery, covered with hair or thorns. The hands, each possessing a different number of fingers, were clumps of veined flesh, the fingers nailless and looking more like small twisting tentacles. The lower part of the body had explicit male and female sexual organs, but obscenely oversized ones. It stood on two feet, ending in bird-like claws. The creature held two of its "arms" in front of it. In one it held the nude and seemingly unconscious body of a woman, from whose back bat wings sprouted. In the other outstretched tentacle-arm it had a toad-like being with oversized bulging eyes and two forked tongues.

Herbert closed the two books. Fifteen years, he thought, fifteen years spent in libraries and with private collectors of rare books on demonology and the occult, hunting for those scarce clues to find that valley, that hill. And now he had found it, or at least he was reasonably sure that he had found it. This had to be that valley, and there, on that hill, the remains of that temple.

A temple built for a god so frightening that they didn't even mention his name in the books. *Liyuhh* spoke about "the thing that waits in darkness" but gave no further details. *Von denen Verdammten* was more explicit on every aspect except about the nature of "*das wartende Dunkel*": "the waiting dark." Still it was strange that no one seemed to know about the existence of that temple. If it really had been as big as the drawings showed, he should be able to see the remains from here. But there was nothing on top of the hill.

*Power and knowledge,* he thought, *they are still there, on top or maybe even inside that hill, and I will find them. And your memory too lies there, alien god who once was worshiped by man. You are gone, long gone now, but the artifacts, the stones, maybe even manuscripts, they still should be there. And I will find them.*

But before that he had to find out if the people here knew something, and how much. The temple could have been brought down, stone by stone; they could have stripped the hill bare of its treasures. And if they had, he would find out what they had done with them.

He closed his room, and went down to see if Julien had fixed something to eat.

## IV. Dunkelhügel

After a sober but very enjoyable dinner, Herbert decided that it was too late to do anything else today, so he took Julien's advice and went to the café for a drink. The inn had only one big room, which was completely crowded. Maybe Freihausgarten's citizens didn't care much for socializing, but they certainly wanted their drinks. All places around the small, circular tables were taken. The smell of pipe tobacco mingled with the smells of beer and human sweat. A few card games were going on, but there was not much real talking. Most of the customers were middle-aged; there were almost no young people except for a few sullen-looking youngsters. Most seemed satisfied just standing at the bar with their oversized pints of beer. The heat was smothering in the room, and Herbert felt the sweat running down his ears and back after only a few minutes inside. He ordered a brandy, and tasted it suspiciously. Compared with Julien's brandy it was cheap stuff, but it was drinkable. It took him over an hour before he succeeded in mingling in the conversation. The topics were typical: the weather, the heat and the danger it represented to the crops of this season, some buildings that needed much fixing, some talk about housewives, a dog which had run away from its owner and hadn't been found yet—all typical small-town talk. He subtly tried to lead the conversation to things that interested him more, without mentioning them directly. However, he soon noticed that a few hostile glances were being thrown at him, and the townspeople simply continued to talk about their own interests. He tried it another way, bringing up the pastoral aspects of the valley, its geographical position and natural beauty, and all went well until he mentioned the hill. There was a short moment of total silence, and then immediately everybody began chatting about entirely different things. The hint was too obvious to ignore.

He spent another two hours at the inn, paying for a few drinks to wash away the ill feeling he somehow had conveyed, and talked with them about the weather and the differences between country life and life in the big cities. He stuck to his tale of being a writer on vacation, and carefully kept away from the subject of the hill.

He got up very early the next morning with a slight headache
from the poor brandy. The sun was just rising, and outside it was
still fresh and cool. He dressed in jeans and a light sweater, and took
his first long walk. He had nothing specific in mind; what he
wanted to have first of all was a general firsthand knowledge about
the geography of the valley and the hill. The valley was enclosed
between two hills. The first one was far to the left of the valley's
entrance, a low and unimportant hill taking in about one sixth of
the incomplete circle. The second hill locked with the first one and
completed the circle, except where the valley flooded into the
lowlands. There was also the station whose trains passed but never
entered the valley. The village itself was situated at the opposite end
of the valley, leaning against Dunkelhügel, the Dark Hill, where it
reached its highest point. He walked aimlessly through the valley,
and then made for the Dark Hill. In full daylight it didn't seem
more menacing or strange than any other hill. He wondered about
the strange dark appearance of the hill when seen from a distance.
Maybe it was due to some trick of the light after all? The vegetation
seemed completely normal anyway.

He took a few readings with his instruments, and took a few
soil samples with him. There proved to be nothing abnormal in
them either.

The next day he covered the hill completely, and this time his
trip left him completely baffled, and doubting the information
given him by *Liyuhh* and *Von denen Verdammten*. There was nothing
on the hill, absolutely *nothing!*

Which was plainly impossible. This *had* to be the valley mentioned in his books; it all fitted too closely. Still, a temple as shown
in the drawings couldn't just disappear, though if he looked at it
realistically, the only place where it could be would be *inside* the
hill. Which was impossible. It had taken this hill countless centuries to form, erode under the seasons' influences, take on vegetation
as wild as here. Nothing had touched this hill for centuries, he was
absolutely certain of that, so the notion that maybe a landslide had
covered the temple proved as ridiculous as all the rest. Besides, the
books were very clear: The temple had been on top of the hill. There
were a few reasonably bald spaces there, but none big enough on
which to construct a temple of that size, and even then, there would
be traces left.

Brendall had done some research of her own when rewriting *Von
denen Verdammten*, and had added her own notes to the book. The

temple was not mentioned any longer after 1850, but she wrote about old and hideous ceremonies which were conducted "at a dark and hidden place where they speak of The Waiting Dark." That "dark and hidden place" could be nowhere else but inside that temple. Or was it possible that the temple was a symbol? That this was nothing else but the folkloristic tradition of some conventional witches' coven, maybe meeting in some hidden cave? But no, *Liyuhh* too mentioned the temple, so maybe the members of the coven (if *that* was what it was) could have brought the remains of the temple into their hidden meeting place.

Still, would Kazaj Heinz Vogel then have written so much about it? A witches' coven was not so very frightening or blasphemous in present times, when there was even an official Church of Satan. Did that coven still exist? After more than two centuries this was doubtful, but possible. The tradition could have been passed down through generations, and it would explain the villagers' negative reaction to his inquiries, no matter how discreet they had been. Or maybe the existence of this mythical coven was not generally known? Even in a small community like this it could pass unnoticed if its members were careful enough.

He continued his search along the hill, but found no traces anywhere. The vegetation was growing completely unchecked here, and made the going difficult. With his armpits stinging with sweat, and the sun now burning down on him from the cloudless sky, he felt as if he were returning through time to a landscape straight out of prehistoric times, when dinosaurs still walked the earth and mankind was nothing more than the far-off dream of some unimaginable deity.

Arriving at his room in the hotel, he immediately saw that someone had been inside. Nothing was missing, but some things had been slightly displaced. Fortunately his books and notes were in the traveling bag which was always locked, and they, whoever they had been, hadn't dared pick the lock. He confronted Julien with his evidence, but the hotel keeper raised his eyebrows.

"Sorry, but no," he said. "Only I was in your room, to open the window and let in some fresh air. I made up the bed, but I didn't touch anything, *mais non!*"

"Have you been at the hotel the whole day through?"

"Well ... no," Julien said. "I went out two or three times, once to the café for a pint of cold beer, and then I had to do some shopping. And I must admit I slept part of the afternoon too; nothing else to do. I hope nothing is missing."

"No, not as far as I noticed," Herbert said. "But I'll double-lock the door in the future. And maybe you'd better take your spare key with you in the future when you leave."

The happening disturbed him. He believed Julien. Anybody could have walked in during his absence, using the spare key from the board to get inside, and maybe it had just been an ordinary thief looking for something of value. But he didn't really believe that.

## V. Vaeyen

The next three days passed uneventfully. During the day he took long walks, not always straight in the direction of the hill so as not to make his interest too obvious, but he always managed to end up there in the later hours. During the evenings he worked on his notes, and sometimes went to the pub. He didn't succeed in getting himself accepted by the locals, however. They answered his greetings, and made some small talk, but their looks spoke of distrust and suspicion.

He found the thing on the sixth day, literally stumbling over it by pure coincidence. He was descending the hill along a narrow path when his foot caught in something. He stumbled and went down, managing to break his fall with his arms. He then started looking for what had tripped him. It didn't take long to dig it out of the earth, once he had seen that it was not a tree root. As he wiped the clods of dirt and earth from it and stood up, he almost couldn't believe his luck.

It was not so very big, about twelve centimeters, but it was heavier than it looked. The small statue had probably once been painted, but time had taken care of that and left only its naked, petrified form. Small fragments were broken off, but it was still recognizable. The statuette was a crude image of the vulture-bat thing which was shown on the map in *Liyuhh*. It stood upright here, its wings folded on its back. Now that he had it so close, he easily saw that he had been mistaken. The vulture-bat being from *Liyuhh* was not the same as the statue inside the temple as shown in *Von denen Verdammten*. He had been wondering about that: why a deity worshiped inside the temple in one book should be shown so far away from that temple in the other.

He grinned. This was what he had been looking for, finally a material proof for the real existence of the temple. He had been right in coming here. No matter how impossible it seemed, it was the only answer, and this statue proved that somehow there had to be a way to get inside the temple.

He put the statuette in his bag, and while returning slowly to the village, he noted something he should have observed long before.

He had never encountered *anyone* near the hill.

Arriving back at the village, he went straight to Julien. He had grown to like and trust the bulky Frenchman, and wanted to know what he thought of the thing he had found.

Julien looked up from his newspaper. He was sitting, or rather lying, in one of his chairs, and smoking one of his eternal stinking cigars.

"Hi," he said. "Had a nice walk?"

"Sure, and I even brought something interesting and unusual with me," Herbert said, taking the statuette from his bag and putting it on the table in front of Julien.

He had expected a mild reaction of curiosity and interest, but not this. Julien jumped up, throwing his chair backward, and turning white as chalk. He even dropped his cigar.

"A Vaeyen," he said hoarsely. "Take that thing away!"

"A what?" Herbert said, surprised. "It's only a statue I've found."

"Sure it's only a statuette, but take that bloody thing away before any of them sees it," Julien said. "You've been poking around on the Dark Hill, that's where you've found it, and that's where you'd better put it back."

Slowly Herbert put the statuette back in his bag. "I tripped over it," he said. "It was almost completely under the earth; only the head stood out. I would never have seen it—what did you call it?"

Julien bent down and recovered his cigar. Now that the statuette was out of his sight, he seemed to calm down too.

"I didn't call it anything," he said, "and if I said anything, forget it. I'll forget that I ever saw that thing in your hands, but please take care that no one from the village ever sees it or learns that it is in your possession. I would rather that you put it back where you found it."

"Don't play games with me, Julien. You called it by a name, and if you don't answer my question I can go and ask elsewhere."

"I wouldn't do that, not if I wanted to avoid trouble," Julien said. "Believe me, I know what I'm talking about, though it isn't much."

"Then tell me *what* you know."

"That ... thing is called a Vaeyen. It's the image of an old kind of demon, if you like. It's a guardian, a watcher of the Dark Hill. There are several of them, but I have never seen them. I have heard about them, though."

"From whom, Julien?"

But Julien didn't answer. He was standing in the doorway now, and pointed. "Look: There it is, in the full sunlight. Yet it looks dark, unnatural, a thing of evil. No one from the village goes there now, and neither should you."

"Why do you say 'no one goes there *now?*' Is there another time *when* someone goes there, Julien? Who, and for what purpose? Come on, you're a rational modern man, don't tell me that you're frightened of a stone statuette of some old demon?"

"You're not in the big city here. You're in Freihausgarten, which is an old island in the sea of what calls itself civilization. The people here don't speak and don't think like us. That's why I want to get away from here as soon as I can manage it financially. I don't belong here; no one who wasn't born in Freihausgarten *belongs*. I am only tolerated here. No, I'm not superstitious, but I don't want anyone to find out that you have found one of their precious Vaeyens. But if you want to know more, why don't you go and see *der Pfarrer* tomorrow? The vicar wasn't born here either, but he has been here over twenty-five years now, and he is accepted by the community because he minds his own business. That's what I want to do too."

And with those words ended their conversation of the evening.

Herbert went up to his room, and there completely cleaned the statuette. It was very old, no doubt of that, and he couldn't place it in a specific period. The weight still surprised him. He tried to scratch it with his tools to find out if maybe it contained some heavy metal, but it was useless.

He returned to his notes, searching for a clue to his discovery. One paragraph in *Liyuhh* caught his eye:

"*... und Seine Welt is eine Welt die schwarzer ist als das Schwarze und dunkler als das absolute Dunkel zwischen den Sternen.*"

"... and his world is a world blacker than black," he translated roughly, "and darker than the absolute darkness between the stars." Strange that *Liyuhh* carried so many references to darkness. Somewhere among those lines was a solution to be found for the strange optical illusion of the Dark Hill? The phenomenon was strange, but then, when these notes had been made, there was a temple up there, and not only a bloody hill!

He switched to *Von denen Verdammten*, and did find a part of the text which could have some specific meaning:

*Und Das Dunkel Dasz Wartet hat fünf Diener, fünf Wächter des Tempels, und fünf Wächter des Dunkels, genannt die Feiaden: das schwarze Licht, das weisse Feuer das schwarzer ist als die Nacht, das weisse Dunkel das roter ist als das Feuer, das geflügelte Weib, und der grüne Mond, die Ihm halten und dienen in Seine Dunkelheit.*

*Damn*, Herbert thought, *why don't they give "Him" a name?* Why again has it to be "the Dark That Waits?" So "It" has five servants, five waiters—no, wait, *Wächter* means watchers or guardians. Five who guard the temple and the Dark, and they are called *Feiaden*. That could fit; taking into account German pronunciation, *Feiaden* could have become *Vaeyen*. Five of them: the Black Light, the White Fire which is Blacker than Night, the White Dark which is more red than the Fire, the Winged Woman, and the Green Moon. They all "keep and guard Him in His Darkness." It fitted with the drawing: five guardian demons, to guard the temple and serve the deity. The drawing in *Von denen Verdammten* showed the deity with a "winged woman" in its one hand, and a toad-like thing in the other. That one could be any of the remaining four, and so could be this statue. If only he knew what color it had been originally, that would have been a clue to its identity. And then, these titles could be symbolical too. "The Black Light": an allusion to night, when the ceremonies were held? "The White Fire": a fire constantly kept alive inside the temple? "The Green Moon": the moon shining over a green valley, a green hill? But then what about the "White Dark?"

It was no use trying to draw conclusions at this point of his research; he already knew too much, but not yet enough.

## VI. The Temple on the Dark Hill

He went to see the vicar first thing the next morning. *Der Pfarrer*, the "soulkeeper", was a man in his late forties. His face had a tendency to make him look fat, which he wasn't really. He had the strong body structure and the raw hands of a man who is used to other things as well as saying grace in church on Sunday mornings. His greeting was cordial but reserved.

Herbert had decided that the only way to learn something here would be to play with open cards right from the start. So after the usual exchange of formalities and polite remarks, he took the statuette out of his pocket and placed it on the table.

"I have been told that this is called a Vaeyen," he said, "supposed to be some kind of evil spirit. I have also been told to keep it out of sight of the villagers and to ask *you* if I wanted to learn more about it."

The vicar didn't answer right away, and neither did he show the frightened reaction of Julien. He took up the Vaeyen, and whistled softly when he noticed its weight. He looked it over carefully, then put it down again.

"Lucky to find it," he said. "I suppose you have an idea of the value of this statuette? I know it dates back at least five centuries, but I suppose that it is much, much older ... maybe as old as mankind. Since you know that much, it is indeed a Vaeyen, even the first one, *das schwarze Licht*, the Black Light."

"But *what* is it? Why was I told to keep it hidden?"

The vicar looked at him intensely, rubbing his double chins.

"Suppose, Mr. Ramon, you tell me first who *you* are, and what your specific interest is in this statuette? I have heard that you are a writer, supposedly here to rest, which isn't exactly an explanation for your very long and very tiring walks ... which strangely enough are always in the neighborhood of *Dunkelhügel*, the Dark Hill. Are you a writer of fiction? Maybe you are looking for material here for a novel or something?"

How much could he tell this man? Herbert asked himself. Not everything certainly; maybe just enough to satisfy his curiosity. But then the vicar was no fool. He chose his words carefully.

"I write fact," he said, "science-fact as well as biographical material. At the moment I'm working on a study of the works of an American writer, who died in 1937. Howard Phillips Lovecraft. You may have heard of him, as many of his stories have been published in German translations, and even some of his letters and critical work. He wrote mainly what we would call 'supernatural fiction.' Most of his longer work deals with alien 'deities', beings who were on Earth long before mankind and originated many bizarre cults. He had a very peculiar way of mixing reality with his fiction, especially when it came to those cults and to ancient books on witchcraft. As a result, in a recent article in a well known periodical, it has been said that some of those cults very well might exist in *reality*, and that this author knew about it but disguised his knowledge as fiction. For my biographical work, I'm trying to separate truth from his own fiction. So I took up studying old and forgotten cultures, getting admittance to study certain old books dealing with mankind's belief in the occult, magic, superstition, and its varied religions. Some of those books contained maps, and information which formed strange parallels with cults that existed even at the start of this century in America. So I'm trying to find the possible cultural and religious connections to link those American cult beliefs with those I'm informed existed in the eighteenth and even nineteenth century in Europe, and in Germany. I want to find out if these pagan beliefs in strange deities already existed in those separate countries—and if so, where they all originated—or if they were imported in one of them."

The vicar nodded. "At least you're not from some nut cult, then," he said, and then laughed. "Sorry about those words; I've had only two of those during the last twenty-four years I've been here, but they were enough to last a lifetime." His joking manner suddenly vanished as unexpectedly as it had come. "What else do you know?"

Herbert hesitated now. What more should he tell? Well, a bit more could do no harm, even if it might set them on the wrong track.

"I am particularly interested in the temple which should be on top of your Dark Hill, and which isn't there. That's why I really came here, to find out what is true and what is just fiction."

The vicar nodded, and sat down in his chair. He took a long sip of his brandy, then looked again at Herbert.

"There was," he said. "And it still *is there*."

"Where?"

The vicar spread his arms. "That's what I hoped *you* could tell me, Mr. Ramon. You have been very frank with me, and now I'll be the same. Because I think that you and I can be of great help to each other. You're a good liar, but not good enough. Certainly, I have heard of that author you mentioned, Lovecraft. You see, I read very much; there's not much else for me to do here. I get many literary magazines, and when I read in a book review of what Lovecraft wrote about, I ordered all his books from Insel Verlag, the German publisher. Of course he wrote fiction—those deities and all the powers he gave them, who would believe that to be *fact?* But there are other things ... some seemingly universal beliefs and cults, and those are *not* fiction. They do, indeed, exist—even now. And don't ask *me* where they came from, I don't know. I only know that they *exist*, in Europe as well as in England and in the States. So now I will tell you what I know. Of course, you'll understand that this is not an official conversation. What I will tell you will remain between us. You have seen my church: It's small, simple, but sufficient for my needs and those of my people. I have been living here now for twenty-four years with them; they are all present at the services on Sunday. I know them all, my people, and yet ... yet I don't. Tell me—do you believe in the power of the mind?"

"I don't quite understand what you mean by that."

"Not the occult, not the supernatural. I'm talking about telepathy, teleportation, telekinesis ... auto-suggestion, mass-hypnosis, and all the other powers the mind is supposed to harbor. Would you believe me if I told you that this village—or its inhabitants—hasn't changed for three hundred years? Oh, I don't mean that they don't die, I mean the general ... oh, it's so difficult to put a name on it. Their way of living, their way of thinking, their whole mentality. What I know about it comes from the papers left by my predecessors. Have you ever heard about ... Cyäegha?"

"Yes, I have, though only the name. It is mentioned in some of the books I've studied. It is supposed to be some kind of god of the earth, or caves, or something like that."

"Cyäegha ... The Waiting Dark, the Lord of the Caves, indeed. It is the name of a very old deity, a kind of earth elemental. This ... god, if you wish, was worshiped here from the seventeenth century on. Probably earlier, but there are no records before that time. This deity was supposed to live inside the Dark Hill, and its worshipers even brought it ... sacrifices, though it could not reach them. That deity was served by five Vaeyens—five servant demons—who at the same time had a kind of guardian duty. To guard the deity and its valley from unwelcome visitors. Now what I tell you may seem strange, and unbelievable. But since those times, there has been a barrier around this valley ... a psychological barrier, warding off all change, creating a kind of static mentality, unable to change! And the center of this barrier was that accursed temple. I don't know when it was built, or even who built it—I never saw it myself. Maybe it was no more than a sacrificial altar, on top of that hill. But its power still exists."

"You said the Vaeyens had a double function?"

"Yes. The worshipers feared this ... deity. Maybe *they* made those Vaeyens, because the Vaeyens kept the valley and the hill as they were, but also restrained the deity."

"What happened?"

"The worship became too big; rumors leaked out about ... human sacrifices. The rumors spread, and about 1860 a young priest came here, a young dedicated man, with the necessary knowledge. He put an end to the whole affair, or so my papers tell me. But how much can one believe of those old scripts? They say also that he tore the temple down with his bare hands and the use of sacred words. He also spoke words over the five Vaeyens, and placed them to guard the hill forever. He died on that hill."

"But you said the cult still exists."

"Yes, I *know* it does. As I told you, they come to me with all their usual problems; they come every Sunday. Yet each full moon night, the city is dead, and I *know* they are up there, on the hill. Don't ask me why, or what they do there. No sacrifices as such; maybe it is no more than a tradition, kept through generations and centuries. But why do they keep an old ceremony alive?"

"Why don't you ask them?"

The vicar hesitated, took a deep breath, and continued. "That is why I think that you and I can help each other, why I asked you if you believed in the power of the mind. Because I *have* asked them ... and *they don't know!* When I speak to them about what they do on full moon nights, they don't act like people who are trying to hide something ... they are people who don't know anything about it! They just look blank as if they don't know what I'm talking about. *They don't remember!*"

"That is impossible!"

"You think so? But it is, nevertheless. You must have noticed that they fear the hill; they never go there. Yet I know that once every month, they are all up there ... for what?"

"There is one way to learn."

"Of course there is. Don't you think I haven't tried going up that hill myself on one of those nights? Do you know what happened? I woke up here, in my house. The last thing I remembered was setting out for the hill; I even remember starting to climb that narrow path leading upward, and seeing lights burning on top of the hill. And then ... nothing! Absolutely nothing, except that suddenly I find myself back here, where I started. Now do you think I'm mad?"

"No, I don't. With the knowledge I have, I don't think you're insane. But neither can I offer you an explanation."

"And that's where we can help each other. You have knowledge in other fields than mine, and I don't know what you really *want*. But it comes to the same thing for both of us: knowledge. Because with knowledge, I can free my people of that curse which has reigned over them from the Dark Hill for centuries. I can ask for no official help; I can't ask for an exorcist without being considered completely insane. How can I explain to my superiors that I believe that a malignant influence still lives on that hill, that it manages to take my people from me one night every month? If we work together, maybe you'll find what you came to find here, and I can free my people of those paganistic superstitions and rituals."

"I don't know. You have told me very much, and I am very grateful for that. I only wish I could tell you as much, but I can't. I don't know enough."

"You'll have to find out, then ..."

After his visit to the vicar, Herbert noticed that the looks and attitudes of the villagers were even more openly hostile. Not that he cared much; they must have noticed his many walks to the Dark Hill, as they had told the vicar about them. He had managed to make peace with Julien, however, by telling him that he had left the Vaeyen at the vicar's house.

He tried in vain to make reasonable sense out of it. He had suspected that they upheld an ancient tradition here, but the vicar's tale threw doubts on his theory. He couldn't find out from the villagers if they didn't know anything, but that made no sense. He needed time. Which was the only thing he didn't have. Because that night the dream attacked him.


## VII. Nagaäe


There was no other word he could find for the phenomenon but "attack", because he usually never dreamed, and if he did and could remember the dream, it had been about rational things.

He had been studying the Vaeyen that evening, after a long but fruitless search of the Dark Hill. He had made several sketches of the statuette, and fell asleep with its mental picture still foremost in his mind, which was probably what started the dream in the first place. If it was a dream ...

He thought that he awoke, and found himself standing at the beginning of a long valley which was surrounded on all sides by black mountains with ragged edges, almost as if he were standing inside a lunar crater. The earth under his feet was black-purple, a dark grinning purple, and full of clefts that seemed to reach down into the stomach of the Earth, as if the Earth itself were sick and these were the pores from which it tried to rid itself of its inner corruption and evil.

In his dream, Herbert slowly took his eyes from the tortured earth and looked down into the valley. At its end, so very far and yet seemingly within his arms' reach, a building stood. It had been built from titanic pieces of roughly cut stone, rudely constructed into a pyramid. A rank of slender obelisks stood on one side, covered with alien signs and symbols rudely cut into the stone. He could see the strange signs very clearly, though they were so far away from him. The top of the pyramid was flattened, and there a sacrificial fire was burning, with a strange white fire which yet was darker than the surrounding night. Far above the building and the fire an enormous pale green moon was staring down from a starless, uniformly black sky.

Nothing seemed illogical or absurd in that dream. It all seemed perfectly normal to his drifting yet waking mind. He knew that he was waiting for something to arrive, for something to happen, yet hadn't the slightest idea what this was supposed to be. There were no feelings of curiosity or fear; it was as if an invisible parasite had sucked all emotions out of his mind and put a dark block instead. He was a watcher, a sentinel, a puppet hanging loosely on its strings, waiting for the puppet master to make it move.

Then something moved in the shadows and came crawling at him. He watched the being, yet was unable to feel any emotion at its sight. The toad-like body was transparent, the pulsating innards covered only by a thin layer of leathery skin. It had the hind legs of a frog, and the forelegs of a man. It moved crab-like, crawling on its lumpy belly and pushing with the force of its hind legs, giving itself direction by muscular movements of its belly. The forelegs were raised mantis-like as in prayer, all four of them. The face, if such it could be called, consisted mainly of bulging eyes and an oversized mouth with two forked tongues. The thing left a deep trail in the earth by its movement.

Herbert was unable to feel fear or revulsion. Although he knew that the thing was there, he also knew it wasn't what he was kept here waiting for.

He didn't have to wait for long.

The moon split. He realized then that the sky was not a sky, and that the illuminated green thing was not the moon, but the eye of an enormous dark shadow which spread as a dark blot between Earth and the real sky. The eye looked down at him with horrible contempt, and for a short moment he obtained a realization of the enormity of the being which hung watching above him.

He looked up at the thing in his dream, and then spoke the words he knew, though he had never consciously realized that he did know them. They came unbidden to his lips, as swimmers out of the dark seas of his racial consciousness, words out of a time when man still spoke with a tongue not fit to utter civilized words. He spoke them because the moon-eyed shadow wanted him to, and because he knew he *had* to speak them.

The shadow in the sky changed, and then there was something which was blacker than black, darker than dark, and an enormous claw came down and reached for him.

He screamed. And fell.

The earth was coarse under his hands. Staggering, he rose and looked up. The moon was a partly hidden shadow in the sky, now covered by black clouds. He was standing on top of the Dark Hill, holding the Vaeyen in his hands.

*This was not a dream anymore!*

He was fully dressed, and the night wind felt cold on his warm face. He felt something close, very close, something so cold and dark that his waking mind was unable to comprehend it, to absorb and understand more than the faintest touch of Its Being. Something which was watching, and waiting.

He looked up at the moon. The big, green moon.

Herbert screamed and ran. As he ran down the hill with great jumps, uncaring whether he tore his clothes or not, he noticed a few deep trails drawn in the earth, as if something big and crawling had passed here, possessing more legs than it should have.

*The Nagaäe,* his mind screamed at him, *the Nagaäe!*

It seemed as if something were laughing behind his back, but he didn't turn around to find out. Twice he stumbled and fell, severely hurting himself, but he rose and continued running till he reached the hotel.

A piece of paper was nailed on the door, and he tore it down. There were strange signs on it, and he didn't have to look closely to know that he had seen them before. In *Von denen Verdammten.*

Breathing coarsely, he entered the hotel.

A single light bulb was still burning above the reception desk. Julien was still up. In fact, he was up a bit way above the ground. He had been nailed feet up to the wall. It wouldn't be fitting to say "head down," because the head was gone.

Even most of the blood had already disappeared between the cracks in the floor.

Herbert fell back against the outside door, closing it with his back, just before he was violently sick. When he partially regained consciousness he was sitting on his knees, and his stomach was still heaving. He brought his hands to his lips to wipe away the last remains and their dirty taste, and then noticed the dry, dark red spots on his hands. Wiping them on his pants as he stood up, he saw that he was still about two meters away from the place where the blood had dripped down on the floor. A big kitchen knife, its blade dark red, was lying beside the nailed-up corpse. Julien was pinned to the wall like some hideously bloated spider, and Herbert didn't have to reason very long to know whose fingerprints would be found on the kitchen knife. It all fitted together too closely.

His mind rebelled. *This is insane*, he thought. *This can't be happening, not to me, not to Julien.* Unfortunately, it was. To Julien. And to *him.*

Julien had no answers, of course. His head had been severed rather crudely, almost sawed off the body with the knife, and then torn loose, once the spine had been severed, with brute force. Shreds of flesh and muscles were hanging loose from the throat.

*They must be mad*, Herbert thought. *They must be wholly, completely mad! But they are all asleep, the whole village, and only I, I am awake. Or am I?*

Full realization started sinking in. Where had he been these last hours? Dreaming? While his body was up there on the Dark Hill? There was no time to think further. It didn't matter right now who had done this horrible thing, and he preferred not to think about the blood on his own hands right now. It was all a bloody setup (indeed, it was literally) to trap him, to stop his research. A fake to nail him down (as they had nailed Julien up). He had to get out; that was all that counted now. He went upstairs, carefully avoiding another close look at the blood-drained corpse on the wall, and started collecting the things he would need most of all now, putting them in one of his bags. No time now to take his books and his instruments. He had other things with him, which he needed more now, because tomorrow was the night of the full moon. He had thought he had lots of time to learn more, but there was no time left now.

He left the hotel silently through the back door, leaving the single light burning, and went back to the hill.

The moon was normal now, cold and unemotional.

His mind, however, was shrouded in the fog. He knew that he wasn't reasoning logically, that he shouldn't react like this, but still he obeyed the ways of his body and its primitive urge to get away.

Herbert paused at the bottom of the hill, starting to recollect his thoughts. He could still go to the vicar, if he would believe him. Maybe he would, and then maybe not; he couldn't take the risk anyway. Not now that they had even killed just to stop him. Not now, now that things had gone this far.

It would be better now to find a good hiding place here and spend the night. Tomorrow he could see what had to be done.

He made himself as comfortable as was possible under the circumstances and tried to sleep immediately, trying to keep all rational thoughts out of his mind. Especially all thoughts about Julien, and what they had done to him.

When he finally slumbered away, however, sleep brought no refreshment, because as soon as his rational thoughts drifted away, he entered the alien world below the green moon. Again the alien toad-like being, which he now knew to be a Nagaäe, crept up to him, and this time he could smell its sharp, musky reptilian odor, a dirty smell like one he had experienced before in the reptile house at the zoo. The thing was so close he could touch it, but it crawled past him, ignoring him, though he knew it was watching him, watching all the time.

In his dream he re-entered the temple, and as he was walking him, though he knew it was watching him, watching all the end, it seemed as if there were no temple roof above him but only the empty sky. That sky was slowly being torn apart, and from it descended a darkness darker than dark, flowing down the temple's walls like an amoeba with long searching tendrils, before the mass of its body came down to drown him, filling the temple with its hideous substance, filling his own body and mind.

He tried to turn, but couldn't. He tried to scream but there were no sounds left. The darkness took it all, absorbed it, became everything, a purposeful, *knowing* black cloud of evil.

He awoke, with the unvoiced scream still strangling in his throat. It took some time to clear his thoughts, as he instinctively felt for the blankets and the warmth and secure softness of the bed, and only met the hard, dry earth under him and some twigs above his face. Then he realized, becoming fully awake, that he was on the Dark Hill, and that it was morning.

## VIII. The Thing That Waits in Darkness

He spent the day alternately in preparing the ingredients he would need to survive the next night, and at the same time keeping a watchful eye on the village through his binoculars. He carefully kept all thoughts of Julien out of his mind. What had happened could not be undone. Maybe he could not forget, but he could ignore it for the time being.

As the evening drew closer, so grew the feeling of *déjà vu* which he had already experienced so often since his arrival. The feeling got stronger during the day. In a strange way, he felt as if he were doing preordained things, following orders given to him aeons before. It was as if he were only reliving an ever-returning dream which was now becoming a reality, a dream which he had always forgotten but kept just below the threshold of his knowing and conscious mind, and which he was now remembering while he turned the dream into reality.

When the first shadows started to fall, he watched them leaving their houses, not in groups, but one by one, stealthily. He watched them approaching the hill, meeting each other on their way, not talking, making no gestures of recognition. So this was true too; they were keeping their monthly appointment on the Dark Hill. To what ends, he would soon find out.

He rose from his hidden position and, taking his prepared things with him, went higher up the hill now, till he was close to the place where he had found the Vaeyen. There he searched for a good hiding place, and finally found the ideal spot behind some bushes covering a gap between two rocks. Here he could sit completely unobserved, and at the same time this gave him a good view over the greatest part of the hill, and especially on that part which seemed the best suited for nocturnal ceremonies. Not far from here, right under his eyes, was the place where the mythical temple should have been.

He put the Vaeyen in front of him, and then took a paper bag filled with crushed colored chalk. Very slowly and carefully he began to spread the chalk powder in the figure of a pentagram around the Vaeyen, then imprisoned this pentagram in a greater star in which he himself also sat. With chalk of another color, he made three red circles around himself, then set up the small tripod he had fabricated out of some cut branches during the day. On this he placed an asbestos plate, and deposited a mixture of chemicals and herbs of a very specific nature.

When the real darkness came, only a few scarce windows lit up in the village. They were almost all up on the hill by now, and when the first visitors stopped only about a hundred meters from his hiding place, he acknowledged his luck. There was an open space there, with only a few isolated rocks, so whatever was going to happen—though he had his own ideas already fixed—could be watched easily.

The villagers had all dressed in flowing, long dark robes, without any decorations; only an older man and a young woman each wore a heavy silver necklace from which hung a small metal sculpture. From this distance, he couldn't make out if these were images of a Vaeyen. He recognized the woman as the daughter of a farmer, and he had seen the man in the village too. It was the local butcher. As they were standing apart from the others, it was not hard to guess that they were going to take the parts of the high priest and the living altar of the cult. Through his binoculars he watched as more and more people arrived, and Herbert recognized most of them from his meetings at the café, though it became harder to see now that night was almost complete. None spoke; they just all took a place in the accumulating crowd, and patiently waited.

After about an hour, he saw that three men from the group were placing the loose rocks in certain positions in the middle of the open place, so that the stones formed a rude triangle...or the horizontal image of a pyramid. Now they went to the ends of the open place, and began digging in the earth with their bare hands. They didn't fumble and search, but acted as if they knew perfectly well where to find what they wanted. Then there was an agitated moment and Herbert understood why when they went to the high priest. They carried four statuettes, which they placed around their rock triangle. Four of the five Vaeyens ... they had discovered that one was *missing*. For a moment Herbert feared that they would put a stop to their ceremony right there, but after a heated discussion, their leader made a sign in the air. The others bent their heads, and then went and ignited three fires, situated at the tips of the triangle.

So they would go on with it. He wondered how much they really *knew* about what they were doing. He had known very early in his research that he would encounter opposition from religious maniacs, though he had never expected that they would go to such ends as the sadistic murder of Julien. And no doubt a similar or worse fate was reserved for him, if they found out that he had their precious missing statuette. The vicar had his ideas about their ceremony, but he was wrong, very wrong. No innocent man is murdered and mutilated in cold blood to protect a folkloristic tradition, and very probably they had expected to get him too that evening. Maybe Julien had just got in their way, or had surprised them. And, as he had said, he was a foreigner too after all, not one from the village's blood. Maybe they really didn't know what they were doing .... He would soon know.

He fished a small bag out of his pocket, and shed the grayish powder in it on the Vaeyen, murmuring: "I conjure you now, Great Adonai, by Johavam, Agla, Tagla, Almouzin, Arios, Membrot, Aqua, Etituamus, Zariatnatmik. ..."

*Rather in the classic tradition*, he thought, satisfied. He threw the rest of the powder on the mixture in the tripod, and placed the upper part of a skull on top of it. The skull was very big, and the eye sockets were strangely shaped. A strong odor assaulted his nostrils as the mixture of the chemicals took fire, burning with a sizzling light, hidden inside the skull. Only small shreds of thin bluish smoke drifted out of the eye holes, as if the skull were breathing.

"Aglon, Tetagram, Yaycheon, Stimulatamathon Erohares ... Ratragsmahon Clyorian Icion. ... Hear me, Hastur and Zhar, Ithaqua and Lloigor; listen to my voice, Great Nyarlathotep, Tsathoggua, Shub-Niggurath and Yog-Sothoth, Nyogtha and The Hidden Watchers. ..."

The fires around the crowd lit up brightly now, and Herbert stopped his own silently spoken incantations to watch. Their fires threw red gloomy shadows at the darkness surrounding them. The high priest and the woman were now standing in the middle of the triangle of stones. The man spread his arms in a mocking simulation of crucification, as his voice thundered against the hill.

"Hear my humble voice, Thou, Lord of the Dark Hill, Thou Who Waits in Darkness, Great Lord of the Caves, Great Cyäegha, hear my voice and accept my tribute, and the tribute of my people, of Your people, so that Thou may rest in Your Darkness, Sleep in Your Mountain of Darkness. ..."

He continued in this vein for some time, the crowd repeating his very words after each sentence. Then he made a sign, and two men stepped out of the group, and took the silver chain and the robe of the girl. Completely nude now, she stepped forward, turned and kneeled before the high priest. She touched his feet before going to the last stone of the triangle, and there spread herself upon it, lying down on her back. The living altar was formed. The two men who had taken her robe now kneeled, one at her feet and one at her head, their faces almost down in the earth. The priest turned toward the group, and made an $X$ cross in the air.

"*Benedicat vos omnipotens*," he said, and then turned back to the altar. Herbert noticed the stiffness of the girl's body. She was drugged, he thought, or even more likely in a state of self-hypnosis or auto-suggestion.

"*Dominus vobiscum*," the priest said, and the crowd answered, "*Et cum spiritu tuo*."

*Indeed, the Lord be with you*, Herbert thought, *but not the Lord for whom those words originally were intended.* The high priest now took a bowl from below his robe, and through his binoculars Herbert saw the curled-up mountain snake lying inside it, probably dead.

"*Ece Agnus Dei, ecce, qui tollit peccàta mundi. ...*" He lifted the bowl, and then gently deposited the snake's body on the abdomen of the girl. "*Hic est énim Calix Sanguinis mei, novi et aetérni testaménti; mystérium fidei: qui pro vobis et pro multis effundétur in reminissiónen peccatórum.*" He bent down, kissing the breasts and the belly of the girl. "*Hoc est enim Corpus meum ...*"

With a melodramatic gesture, he rose, touching the eyes, nose, ears, mouth, and nipples of the girl, and then throwing his arms wide open. "Great Lord Cyäegha, The One Who Waits in His Eternal Darkness, The One Who Slumbers through aeons of unnamed time. Dweller in the Dark Hill, Master of Time, Master of Life, Master of Death, hear me speak in the name of my people, of Thy people, accept our offer, our humble unworthy offer, accept our prayers, our humble unworthy prayers, absorb them into Your

Darkness, and forgive us The Signs, forgive us The Vaeyens for You know that we need them. Forgive us because we cannot share in Your Darkness, forgive us our ignorance of Your Ways because we are only human and cannot be like You, cannot share with You. ..."

*Ignorant peasant*, Herbert thought, *stupid fools!* An unsuspected aura of self-confidence had come over him as he listened to their words, which were no more than a variant of the Black Mass. Did these idiots really think that they could offer prayers to Cyäegha? They feared him, and they didn't know very much. They thought they could keep him inside the hill because of the power of their Vaeyens, and the words they had retained from the priest who had imprisoned The Waiting Dark. But that priest was long dead, killed by the very power he had used, and what they had retained of his words was useless, because now they lacked one of their precious Vaeyens.

Herbert spread his fingers, and touched the now hot skull bone. It burned his fingertips, but he didn't take them away.

"Onera Erasyn Moyn Meffias Soter ... Emmanual Saboth Adonai, Your Names are Turned, Your Image has been changed but It is, It was, It always will be! The Time is Now, the Time is This, the Time is Past, the Time is Future, and *All* are You! *Iä, Iä*, Cyäegha! The Snake has eaten its Tail, and formed the circle of Bones! The Star has been broken, the Elder Sign has lost its tip!"

There was a short flash of rationalism and he thought, *This is madness. I'm no more sane than they, I too am speaking words without meaning, words fit only for the insane. Then why do I continue?* And he knew the answer: *Because I have to. Because the time is* now, *and I have been through this before, though I don't know when or where, and I will have to go through this again and again. The time is past, and the time is future, and the Circle of Bones has opened into* now.

"*Mn'gwayii, Cbyorgä!* Open to me now, oh Lord of the Dark, oh Lord of the Waiting Dark, oh Lord of the Patient Waiting Dark! *Ph'ngläyä ft'gglhnayn! N'cryastaepecioggl'n bggn'th flwaägor!*"

He had never suspected to be able to memorize the words from the old manuscripts, far less pronounce them, yet now they rolled from his tongue, torturing his mouth and ears, almost as if someone else spoke the alien words in his place, using his voice.

"So here you are, murderer!" a voice said behind him. His back froze, as he slowly turned his head around without moving his body. The vicar was a dark blurred shape behind him, yet the gun he pointed at Herbert's back glittered in the soft light his protected fire threw around him.

"So you've finally managed to climb the hill, Vicar," Herbert said, "but of course, the protection is incomplete now that they're missing one of the Vaeyens. There was nothing to stop you from coming now."

"You ... beast! Why? I don't understand it. I see what you're doing here, yet why are you not with them over there? Why did you have to ... murder Julien? Why?"

"You really think I killed him, Vicar?" Herbert's voice tittered. "You should know better. Perhaps you recognize this ritual, the Vach-Viraj Ritual and its incantations, and the looped cross drawn on the skull. Of course I'm not using it as it was intended; every ritual can be turned backward, every exorcising ritual can be reversed. And of course I'm not with them; you should know by now that I'm not one of them. If you don't believe me, keep pointing that gun at me, but take my binoculars and have a good look at what *they* are doing. Go on. You and I want the same thing: to stop them. So take a good look ..."

Slowly, without making a suspicious movement, he offered his binoculars to the vicar. Hesitatingly the vicar accepted them and looked, but the muzzle of the gun remained pointed at Herbert. Then the vicar made a gasping sound; he dropped the gun and the binoculars, turned away, and vomited.

Herbert took up the field glasses and looked himself. He had known in advance what he would see. The high priest took the severed head of Julien from below his robe, holding it above the rigid body of the girl, before he split the skull with a stroke of his sacrificial knife! The brains dripped down on the living but unmoving altar.

"*Ph'nglui mglw'afhn Cthulhu R'lyehhgand gah'ln fhtgagn.* ... Yr et *Dho-Hna Ephrai Nmagl'n nagoghnath, Iä! Shub-Niggura'pwai Feyadia gnl!* Accept our offer, Great Old One, Ancient Slumberer in the Caves of Darkness, Nameless One from Beyond the Wall of Sleep, Stalker between timeless stars and the dark spaces between the stars, Dreamer of the second night, *Rgth'll R'Liyuhai tec djivvai!* By the Names of Tyr-Fharle and The Thing with Three Faces, accept our humble gift and sleep, oh Thou Great One, slumber in the Hill of Darkness and let us be, protected by the five Vaeyens from Your wrath, hear us, Waiting Dark, and let us be, by the Black Light and the White Fire, by the White Dark which is blacker than night, and the Green Moon and the Winged Woman!"

The vicar's face was very close now, his eyes glowing pinpoints. "They're mad," he whimpered, "they're mad!" He wasn't paying any attention to Herbert anymore, but suddenly stood up and crashed through the protecting wall of bushes. "Murderers!" he yelled. "You bunch of dirty heathen assassins!"

There was a moment of petrified silence, then the crowd moved as the vicar ran at them, brandishing his gun.

Herbert stood up now and took the skull off the plate. The flames of the burning chemicals rose, emitting a sharp, stinging smoke.

"Open to me now, oh Lord," he screamed with a voice which no longer seemed his own. "*Phlegethor k'yarnak, Cyäegha kn'aa stell'hsna, nilgh're kadishtu na Ya!*"

He reached down and took the Vaeyen, lifting it with both hands above his head. His hands too no longer were his own; an unimaginable power seemed to run through his veins and muscles, burning his brain with the coldness of space. He broke the statuette in two, then crumbled the pieces into dust between his fingers.

A sudden gust of wind whirled around him, and suddenly the bushes were full of sound and movement, as if many small things hurried away in all directions. The part of him which still thought as Herbert was a frightened frozen entity somewhere in the depths of his brain, a madly shrieking being which tried to hold on to its own knowledge, its own reality.

"Open to me, oh Great Cyäegha, oh Father!" his voice shrieked.

## IX. No-Time

The darkness became a rigid reality, slipping into his body, freezing it and taking his mind with it. His careless feet disturbed the pentagram, broke through the protecting three circles. During a shard of a second he fell through reality and was part of the vacuum, the space between reality and time. During an abominable second he was part of the Thing which slept in its submerged city below the Pacific Ocean, he was one with the unnamed being which walked the African jungle, hiding in those caves no man had yet set foot into, and part of the hideous shape which stalked the Himalayas.

The valley was changing. A green mist was clouding the moon, and the earth of the hill was turning a purple-black, filled with deep clefts. And through the hill, where the hill had been, the temple stood, hideous in its alien architecture. The entrance was black, a waiting dark mouth. On top of the building an alien fire was burning, sending small streamers of flame upward to the green moon.

He went forward, no more seeing the frozen crowd of worshipers, passing through them as if they were immaterial ghosts of a dead past. He went into the temple, where his feet threw no echoes, passing along the aisle with its abominable statues and inscriptions till he stood in front of the image. He didn't lift his head and look It in Its face, but his hands reached out and took the book which was lying opened at the clawed feet of the image. His whole being rebelled at the touch of the book, yet his fingers caressed it as he turned the pages. His eyes stared down at formulas and words which he knew his tongue wasn't meant to utter, yet his mouth moved and he began speaking.

"*Tec djivvaiga nicoigh'lnaäaëyi ... micaroï gghln'häe. ...*"

*Throw it away*, his mind screamed at his body. *Drop it and run!* But his mind was a prisoner inside his own skull, his body no longer obeyed the commands of his brain; and suddenly he realized that in fact his body had seemingly been acting on its own for some time. He tried to close his eyes, but in vain. His lips continued their forming of alien words, speaking them loudly, and the most horrible thing was that he also *understood them* and *knew* what he was doing.

"*Ggh'lghà djëcai Cyäegha pfh'gai d'whoggl, micaroï tec ....*"

His hands closed the book and he spread his arms, for the first time looking up at the hideous face of the titanic statue.

"*Tec Cyäegha djivvaigh! Tec Cyäegha fht'hgain!*" he screamed, and the walls of the temple took his words and repeated them in an endlessly continuing alien gibbering.

The walls shuddered, and then the earth below his feet moved sluggishly as if an enormous fat worm were trying to get out. Outside there was confused screaming, but then there came a scream so loud that it seemed to tear his eardrums, and a maniacal mindless cackle whose pitch rose higher and higher, a horrible wordless sound of triumph and hate. Cracks appeared in the walls of the temple, and small but growing streams of dust began to fall down. The statues collapsed and broke as they crashed on the ground. Above his head, great cracks spiderwebbed with lightning's speed across the ceiling; great chunks of stone came loose and fell down, but turned into the dust before they reached the ground. Herbert fell down on his knees, burying his face in the dirt, and frantically held his hands over his ears trying in vain to stop the sound.

Then suddenly the sounds diminished, and an alien silence fell on the hill. Slowly he looked up. The temple was gone, and he was sitting on top of the Dark Hill. All around him, people were lying on the ground in varied positions. Some were still squirming, their fingers eating into the sides of their heads, their faces distorted, painful masks of agony. Others too were rising, their staring eyes frightened orbits in their faces, redly lit by the still burning fires. They looked up at the moon, the great green moon above the valley and the hill.

Then there came a faint but quickly accelerating sound of howling laughter, a high-pitched shrieking and gasping sound as no human throat could produce. The air began moving around the moon, as if the moon were the center of a great black cloud, just before membranous veils lifted from the moon and they saw that it was a gigantic eye staring down at them. Around the eye, the sky split; deep clefts opened through which darkness began to ooze, a darkness blacker than the night, which crawled down as a set of slimy tentacles, taking on more form, more definite shape.

Then finally something was standing, outlined against the black sky, something which had tentacles of darkness and a green-glowing eye, something which just laughed at them, an insane laughter.

Herbert turned and ran, and so did the others. The Thing didn't follow them; it didn't need to. Its shadow was everywhere over the valley.

*Through Its own layers of reality, Cyäegha looked down on the miniature valley, and at the same time It looked upward through the hill from below and inside, where parts of Its gigantic body were lying, buried in subterranean depths. Yet it did not matter now what body was which, because finally the barrier was crumbling, the realities were shifting and flowing together into one Being which was Cyäegha. And It hated with the power and strength of aeons of cultivating that hatred. It had no eyes as such, but It tasted reality with all the feelers of Its multiple body, and so It also watched the crumbling of the temple where these idiot beings had been worshiping for centuries an image which didn't look like Cyäegha at all, because Its shape changed as Its own reality. These idiot beings had maintained Its imprisonment by keeping the guardians, but now the five-pointed star had lost one of its points; the Elder Sign was gone. It did not matter that the idiot beings had done this all through stupidity; even the revenge It had been waiting for was devoid of any real emotion, except hatred. Revenge demands a reason, and It had no need for a reason. It was only hatred.*

Herbert realized all this as he was stumbling and falling down the Dark Hill, fighting his way through the darkness. His feet slipped as the earth trembled again under him. Falling, he turned around and saw the hill move, as if something big were worming its way out of the earth, a colossal molehill, spitting earth, rocks, and vegetation in all directions. Then the top of the hill split wide open, and from inside the hill they came, crawling awkwardly on their clawed legs, shifting their bloated leathery bodies: the Nagaäe, beings like those he had seen in his all too real nightmares. A continuing stream of the toad-like monstrosities rose from the depths of the hill, pale and eyeless, adapted to the hideous life in tunnels and subterranean caves of darkness. And after them, something else came, a shape throwing its gelatin tentacles upward where they met the dark essence of the moon-eyed shadow, and they fused, flowed together and became one hideous abomination, an affront to all laws of Earthly nature.

Whimpering and screaming men and women hurried past Herbert, pushing each other in their hurry to get away. Some fell and remained on the ground, trying to bury their faces into the earth to escape the glances of the green eye.

*This must be madness*, a small part whimpered in Herbert's brain. *Surely this can't be really happening. It's all rubbish after all, a crazy experiment in pseudo-science, just some old formulas and incantations. I'm having a nightmare, and I must wake up. God, I must awake, I must awake before I go mad too!*

His skull imploded, bones seeming to wring their shards into his brain, and then he knew that it *was real*. Something wriggled itself out of the deep caverns of his mind, something very cold and slimy, and very frightening because it was known yet unknown to his waking mind. As he slowly stood up, he felt his body going numb, the blood becoming thicker in his veins and then stopping to run altogether. There was a brief white flash in the back of his head as his heart stopped. He brought up his hands and saw dark spots beginning to appear on their backs, as the body tissues quickly degenerated below the skin. The soft skin layers, flesh, muscles, and sinews became fluid, an amoeba-like mass. His curled-up tongue dried in his mouth, a piece of hard leather pushing against his teeth, before it crumbled into dust choking his throat. His body was swaying as he felt his mind changing, trying to save itself while the body died with him still inside it. There was a fleeting sense of movement, of well defined searching for something which his mind knew to be there, a meeting point somewhere in the senseless void through which he drifted aimlessly, and then he ...

Was staring down at the valley. He was watching the many running small figures, and not so very far away the scarce microscopic pinpointed lights of the lit windows in the village of Freihausgarten. He was somewhere and nowhere yet; somewhere in him stars were burning that were a part of him, yet they seemed distant, not so much in space as in reality—as if several layers of reality intermingled, as glass plates stacked upon each other, so that he could observe several at the same time yet not all very clearly. He felt as if he were spinning a cocoon around the valley, closing his own body into a web in which time was suspended. An unimaginable vitality coursed through his body as he stretched it, changing and adapting all the time. There lurked a faint memory of a No-Place, a dreamlike, unreal memory of waiting, endless and sleepless waiting, and a knowledge of things so hideously alien that Herbert's normal brain would never have been able to stand it. Yet now he felt as if he had always known them; he recognized these memories as part of his own. And he hated, hated with a ferocity beyond all his human understanding, beyond all his human reason. A small shard of him tried to keep his frail shell of humanity intact, but it all came too quickly; it was impossible to absorb it with human intelligence. The hatred flowed over and into his new being, and with a final shock of horror he realized that the hatred came out of *him too*, that it had always been a part of him, that he himself was part of the being he belonged to now. His mortal body had been only a messenger, one of the many fragments Cyäegha had used, a small shard of essential *being*, a demon seed sent out through the centuries, a combination of cells, a genetic structure engraved in the DNA chains of the amino acids in his brain cells, which one day would find the way, the necessary gate into darkness where its parent body was waiting, dreaming ... and hating.

It howled with Its body cells unfit to utter any human sounds. It howled with the essence of sound, a raw vicious cry of triumph. Then it bent and scooped up some of the small figures amid a lot of rubble. It brought them up to what passed for Its face, and then closed Its claw, afterward dropping the mess of crushed bones, bloody tissue, and dirt to the ground far below. It didn't have to move; the whole of Its body was a cloak of alien darkness around and over the valley, completely enclosing the world It now had for Its own pleasure. Cyäegha's servants, the Nagaäe, were hungry too; they were slow hunters, but very certain of their promised prey. Many of those were unconscious or just in shock, waiting to be taken and eaten, but the Nagaäe had their own idea of fun and hunted the running ones first.

It watched the woman who had served as altar running, her nude body a clearly illuminated target, lit by the black light of Its own darkness, as she tried to avoid the Nagaäe's greedy claws. There was no way out, they were everywhere now, and there came always more out of the black hell-pits of the Dark Hill's innards. They encircled the girl, watching her turn in panic before they reached her, and very slowly dismembered her, eating each part they took off first before helping themselves to another piece from the insanely shrieking and squirming body. They had all the time, and she took all her time dying.

It bent another time, now scooping up a random running human and bringing him up to Its own height. It was the vicar. Devoid of any emotions except the hatred, It squeezed the human being till he opened his mouth in agony, his body squirming as the ribs broke and speared stomach and lungs. Then It formed a long hooked nail and went down through mouth and throat, ripping the human open from his insides, and dropping the messy pieces It found.

*I am mad*, Herbert was screaming soundlessly. *Please let me die, please let me go mad so I don't have to watch. Please, please!*

It turned Its attention to the waiting village now, and from Its outer body a rain of dark shivering tentacles went down to the houses, crushing them and those still inside them, ripping open the roofs and walls, exposing the houses' innards as It even went down into the cellars, hunting for the huddling survivors. Its tentacles found them, as It cracked the houses open like eggshells, and absorbed them, and Herbert tasted their small essences in his own extensions, parts of the tentacles of darkness. It melted their bones and fed on the remaining shapeless mess, leaving only wet slimy skins behind.

## X. All-Time

Herbert Ramon clawed down into himself, his entity now close to a mindlessly shrieking shiver, a spark of being, a shard of the total entity which knew Itself as Cyäegha, The Thing That Waits in Darkness. As Cyäegha grew, so Herbert felt himself expanding, and the rational part of him which still existed realized how strong the father/mother body was. This was not a lesser earth elemental as Its brother Nyogtha! Herbert was somewhere, and yet nowhere, in a no-space, no-time plane of existence. The valley, the sky, the Earth itself all seemed unreal, as toys of his imagination, so fragile and unimportant. His spiritual body was expanding into no-space/no-time which was all-space/all-time in the same eternity. Stars were glowing cinders in Its/his body, gradually growing smaller as he grew outside the Earth and absorbed them, yet at the same instant he had the unreal impression that It/he was growing smaller, shrinking all the time instead of expanding, because all around It/him he now felt the presence of others, who were still greater than It/he, and still more frightening in their existence. He felt the icy fingers of the dreaming entity in R'lyeh and with hideous clarity saw and understood where R'lyeh *really* was, and he shrank away from the hostile fire-spitting thing which was Cthugha, which filled him with a feeling of utter hatred and revulsion. He crawled with Tsathoggua, the Toad Thing, and for a petrified moment of madness danced in the center of Chaos, twisting his microscopic/gigantic body before the Blind Idiot God, Azathoth, to the sounds of insane pipers. He absorbed lonely stars, then whole galaxies, yet didn't really touch them, but tasted their reality and took it all inside him as he grew, feeling triumph and fear as he came closer to the All. *Ubbo*, his mind screamed, *Ubbo-Sathla, The Unbegotten Source, help me now! Great Abhoth, Yog-Sothoth, Shub-Niggurath, break the bounds! Help me now that I'm free, wreck the barriers, I'm free, the Elder Star is broken and I'm free! Come now and help me, and help yourself. Shatter the stars, they are old and weak. Help me and you will be free too!*

Yet there was a strange fear in his plea for help, a fear that was accumulating as he expanded and touched the All, as he was *taken into the All, where no-time and no-space were all-time and all-space.* He gibbered and screamed, spitting out the sounds as gulps of hideous black vomit which left the All and came back to It. His expanded body was absorbed into the All, and became part of It, part of the eternal torture and *being the all, the distorted, torn One Existence.* Alien powers ripped at him, and he felt and recognized and understood them and shrieked in mindless, eternal alien agony. Old Ones and Elder Gods, the Beginning and the End of All Creation, black and white, night and day, the start of life and its final telophasis, they all were the torn shreds of a continuing never-beginning, never-ending circle, a shattered puzzle of a mindless composite Being which was *all-time/all-space*. He felt himself splitting, his being torn apart by powers coming from himself, yet each one of the separate powers was greater and mightier than he, an implosion of utter terror, and it all was in balance. He had found the way into alien darkness, and the Total Darkness was a composite of all colors, not in the black holes between stars, and not in the alternate worlds of primitive black and white magic, but *inside, inside the All* and inside each one of the innumerable things, and beings who had created the *All* and kept it in existence by being.

The screaming part which once had been Herbert Ramon then realized that there was no help to be had from the others, because they were all fighting themselves; they were all only fragments, isolated shards of the All, reflecting Its eternal duality in themselves, their own prisoners, their own guardians, battling their own inner minds, and he was as much part of them all as he was part of the All, and they all with him. There were no emotions, no thoughts, only the balance. Cyäegha screamed.

It/he kept on screaming, the scream becoming an essential part of Its reality, a scream of utter despair in the realization that all was lost because it never could have been gained, because the winner, the loser, and the stake were all the same one continuity. It started contracting, imploding in Itself, Its gibbering scream sending convulsive nova shudders through Its innards. It spread across an eternally dying and reborn cosmos of utter unimportance, Its eyes blazing supernovas, Its claws far star-clouds still unborn in the abyss of all-time. Dying, It began to fall into the pit of Its own self-recognition, and part of It felt every microsecond of life in every amoeba and in every insect on the microscopic planet called Earth by the idiot beings who formed its leading race. The part of It that was still essentially Herbert Ramon felt the duality of life/death in each life-form on that planet, and strengthened one part of the balance. Something started its own cancerous growth inside It, and It was unable to fight the newcomer. It fed on the new thing, which kept on growing as Cyäegha died, and on Earth insects died and animals ran crazily, and men ran amok and slaughtered without a reason, or simply went quietly mad through the centuries. A drinking and suicidal poet by the name of Edgar Allen Poe, who had seemingly found his way back to reason, was found delirious in the gutter, and died in a hospital uttering words in a gibbering language. An unimportant outdated story writer named Howard Phillips Lovecraft threw insightful flashes of abysmal horror into his stories, masquerading his second sight as fiction. A European author of weird tales, at the start of a promising career, had such horrible visions and nightmares that he started drinking and finally threw himself out of the window of his flat on the sixth floor.

And all the time, the part of Cyäegha which once had been called Herbert Ramon grew, while other parts of It died and were absorbed by the needs of the balance of the All. That balance was changing, adapting, as it was doing all the time, without the need of conscious thought or intelligence, and the Dark of Cyäegha was shrinking until it met the balance. Stars streamed out of Its body, and It kept on screaming mindlessly when they reached the barrier of the dark gateway. It was still screaming as the Gate of Darkness closed in on It, as no-time spread like a cancer through Its body, changing It as the reversal went more quickly than Its growth had been, and as time was shrinking, and then reversing to reinstall the precious balance of the All. One day ... two days ... a week. ... The something which once had been Herbert Ramon came back into its body, somewhere on a small unimportant planet, where once had stood a hideous Dark Hill, and below that hill with its ultra-dimensional temple was an enormous crypt, sealed by a dark gate, where once something had been sleeping and waiting for centuries, and now was waiting again.

And just as Herbert Ramon had returned to his mother/father body, so now his own body was adapting to this new condition as it returned through time, to the Dark Hill where once Cyäegha had risen, but this had been no more in no-time, and what once had been had become a could-have-been in the Now.

The balance had been restored as it had always been and always would be in the All, self-destructive and self-procreating, Old Ones and Elder Ones, good and evil, angels and demons, something less than all these and something more than all these, and each was a small shard of the entity which was Cyäegha and Herbert Ramon, the Prisoner and the Guardian, the Prison and the Gate, the Past and the Present and the Unborn and Never To Be Future. And none of them were really dead or really alive, or had ever been completely alive in the reality which was being reborn to a past present.

## Epilogue: Guardian

There is a small railway station in that isolated valley, so you can go there by train, but not inside the valley, which you can reach only by car. And maybe, when you find that valley and stay there long enough, meet the gentle but backward people and get them to talk in the evening hours at the local café, they will tell you a strange tale. The pub is kept by a Frenchman, named Julien-Charles, but now he's been living there so long, after he took over the café, that they just call him Johann. He's also the owner of the only hotel the village Freihausgarten boasts, and maybe if you speak to him in French he won't understand you. He has a weird scar around his neck, and if you ask him whatever caused that he will smile and you will notice a strangely absent look in his eyes, as if he tries to remember something which he knows he shouldn't forget but can't remember. He will then make a joke about it, that someone once tried to cut his throat but failed, and they will all laugh about it and forget it. He, or they, will not tell you that he doesn't remember how he got that scar. Neither will repeated questions furnish any answer as to some very strange happenings which in fact never happened. Has something which no one remembers ever really happened? The houses are all intact in Freihausgarten, and so is the Dark Hill, *Dunkelhügel.* You can discover all this for yourself, if you search for the valley, and get through its barrier, which is only a barrier of the mind.

Oh yes, if you ask them, they will tell you gladly about the day the stranger came, because they *do* remember that day. That man stepped from the train on a very hot summer afternoon. He stayed there and watched the train leave. Then he took his handkerchief and wiped his face, then bent down to pick up his two traveling bags. Maybe, if you can get one of the villagers drunk enough, he will tell you what they all know but can't put into words, the strangest dizzy feeling they ever had, all of them at the same moment, which they later compared by their watches: a feeling, a stoppage of movement, a feeling of petrification, as if one second had been standing still in time. Some felt sick immediately afterward, but no one of them can tell you how it feels when something of your own mind and body suddenly turns alien.

Anyway, the feeling lasted but one second or less, and they all blame it on the heat. But the man who had arrived at the station didn't pick up his bags. He froze, then remained standing there for more than half an hour without making any movement. Then the porter went to that man, and he said that it was strange: It looked as if the stranger's clothes didn't fit him; they were too large for him. Then the porter saw the man's face, and began screaming, as the stranger fell to the ground. The porter never told anyone what the stranger's face looked like; he went straight to fetch the doctor, and together they drove the stranger's body to the vicar. It seems that the stranger regained consciousness there, but no one knows what was said there behind closed doors. The stranger, who was named Herbert Ramon, died that same evening, and they buried him at the vicar's request on the Dark Hill. The personal effects of the stranger mysteriously disappeared, but two nights later there was a fire in the vicar's garden and he burned some things which carried strange smells into the village. But no one asked any questions. Two weeks later, the vicar hung himself.

Maybe you will also meet the local butcher, a great bulky man, who is now kept alive by the village's charity. You'll never see his hands, as he always wears gloves. He can utter only the most simple sounds now. Maybe if you drop a remark about a girl who was once a local beauty, the daughter of an older farmer, you'll get no response. She never shows her face in public now, and is completely paralyzed ... and completely insane. Some memories cannot die, not even when turned backward.

Of course, they will not tell you about the annual ceremony on top of the Dark Hill, which was not held the year the stranger came to die there, and which has not been kept since then. Even if you ask them they will not tell you that they once opened the grave of the stranger, but immediately covered it and never went there again. But ask the children, and maybe they will tell you about the Guardian of the Vaeyens: the strange old man whom they have never met face to face, but who they know is there, the Dead Man who lives on the Dark Hill, whose hair is as long and gray as the fog. But if you are not quick enough to ask the right questions, the mothers will come and take their children inside, and you will hear no more.

Maybe, if you dare go up the Dark Hill, you will catch a glimpse of him, of his petrified white face, which is dark yet transparent, as bottomless as the starless deeps of the universe's seas. And if you have the chance to look into his eyes, you will see that they are not eyes but fathomless dark pits, tunnels into darkness, and if you dare look into them very closely, you might see yourself in there, very small, the prisoner of dark eternity ...

There's no need to tell more, I think. You don't have to ask me how I know all this, because now you know too. There's an affinity between us, which I recognized immediately, or else I would never have spoken to you. The seed of Cyäegha is widespread. Herbert Ramon was not a fool, but he didn't know enough; in fact he didn't know anything at all, in reality. When he realized what he was, it was already too late. But *you* know, and I know. Herbert Ramon was alone, searching, and frightened by what he thought he discovered. We aren't, you and I. Not any longer. Don't try to push it; let the realization sink in, absorb it slowly with your whole being, dive down into the darkness which you now know is inside you. Memory will come, is coming—I see it—but you must give it time to be absorbed and understood by the whole of your being, the whole of your mind, so that we may not fail as Herbert Ramon failed. Remember, he was all alone: We aren't.

Yes, I know where Dunkelhügel is.

# The Terror from the Depths

## by Fritz Leiber

Remember thee!
Ay, thou poor ghost, while memory holds a seat
In this distracted globe.

— Hamlet

The following manuscript was found in a curiously embossed copper and German silver casket of highly individual modern workmanship which was purchased at an auction of unclaimed property that had been held in police custody for the prescribed number of years in Los Angeles County, California. In the casket with the manuscript were two slim volumes of verse: *Azathoth and Other Horrors* by Edward Pickman Derby, Onyx Sphinx Press, Arkham, Massachusetts, and *The Tunneler Below* by Georg Reuter Fischer, Ptolemy Press, Hollywood, California. The manuscript was penned by the second of these poets, except for the two letters and the telegram interleafed into it. The casket and its contents had passed into police custody on March 16, 1937, upon the discovery of Fischer's mutilated body by his collapsed brick dwelling in Vultures Roost under circumstances of considerable horror.

Today one will search street maps of the Hollywood Hills area in vain for the unincorporated community of Vultures Roost. Shortly after the events narrated in these pages its name (already long criticized) was changed upon the urging of prudent real estate dealers to Paradise Crest, which was in turn absorbed by the City of Los Angeles—an event not without parallel in that general neighborhood, as, when after certain scandals best forgotten, the name of Runnymede was changed to Tarzana after the chief literary creation of its most illustrious and blameless inhabitant.

The magneto-optical method of detection referred to herein, "which has already discovered two new elements", is neither fraud nor fancy, but a technique highly regarded in the 1930's (though since discredited), as may be confirmed by consulting any table of elements from that period or the entries "alabamine" and "virginium" in *Webster's New International Dictionary*, second edition, unabridged. (They are not, of course, in today's tables.) While the "unknown master builder Simon Rodia" with whom Fischer's father conferred is the widely revered folk architect (now deceased) who created the matchlessly beautiful Watts Towers.

\*   \*   \*

It is only with considerable effort that I can restrain myself from plunging into the very midst of a description of those unequivocally monstrous hints that have determined me to take—within the next eighteen hours and no later—a desperate and initially destructive step. There is much to write and only too little time in which to write it.

I myself need no written argument to bolster my beliefs. It is all more real to me than everyday experience. I have only to close my eyes to see Albert Wilmarth's horror-whitened long-jawed face and migraine-tormented brow. There may be something of clairvoyance in this, for I imagine his expression has not changed greatly since I last saw him. And I need not make the slightest effort to hear those hideously luring voices, like the susurrus of infernal bees and glorious wasps, which impinge upon an inner ear which I now can never and would never close. Indeed, as I listen to them, I wonder if there is anything to be gained from penning this necessarily outré document. It will be found—if it is found—in a locality where serious people do not attach any importance to strange revelations and where charlatanry is only too common. Perhaps that is well and perhaps I should make doubly sure by tearing up this sheet, for there is in my mind no doubt of the results that would follow a systematic, scientific effort to investigate those forces which have ambushed and shall soon claim (and perhaps welcome?) me.

I shall write, however, if only to satisfy a peculiar personal whim. Ever since I can remember I have been drawn to literary creation, but until this very day certain elusive circumstances and crepuscular forces have prevented my satisfactorily completing anything more than a number of poems, mostly short, and tiny prose sketches. It would interest me to discover if my new knowledge has freed me to some extent from those inhibitions. Time enough when I have completed this statement to consider the advisability of its destruction (before I perpetrate the greater and crucial destruction). Truth to tell, I am not especially moved by what may or may not happen to my fellow men; there have been *profound* influences (yes, from the depths indeed!) exerted upon my emotional growth and upon the ultimate direction of my loyalties—as will become clear to the reader in due course.

I might begin this narrative with a bald recital of the implications of the recorded findings of Professors Atwood and Pabodie's portable magneto-optic geo-scanner, or with Albert Wilmarth's horrendous revelations of the mind-shattering, planet-wide researches made during the past decade by a secret coterie of faculty members of far-off Miskatonic University in witch-haunted, shadow-beset Arkham and a few lonely colleagues in Boston and Providence, Rhode Island, or with the shivery clues that with nefarious innocence have found their way even into the poetry I have written during the past few years. If I did that, you would be immediately convinced that I was psychotic. The *reasons* that led me, step by step, to my present awesome convictions would appear as progressive *symptoms*, and the monstrous horror behind it all would seem a shuddersome paranoid fantasy. Indeed, that will probably be your final judgment in any case, but I will nevertheless tell you what happened just as it happened to me. Then you will have the same opportunity as I had to discern, if you can, just where reality left off and imagination took up and where imagination stopped and psychosis supervened.

Perhaps within the next seventeen hours something will happen or be revealed that will in part substantiate what I shall write. I do not think so, for there is yet untold cunning in the decadent cosmic order which has entrapped me. Perhaps they will not let me finish this narrative; perhaps they will anticipate my own resolve. I am almost sure they have only held off thus far because they are sure I will do their work for them. No matter.

The sun is just now rising, red and raw, over the treacherous and crumbling hills of Griffith Park (Wilderness would be a better designation). The sea fog still wraps the sprawling suburbs below, its last vestiges are sliding out of high, dry Laurel Canyon, but far off to the south I can begin to discern the black congeries of scaffolded oil wells near Culver City, like stiff-legged robots massing for the attack. And if I were at the bedroom window that opens to the northwest, I would see night's shadows still lingering in the precipitous wilds of Hollywoodland above the faint, twisting, weed-encroached, serpent-haunted trails I have limped along daily for most of my natural life, tracing and retracing them ever more compulsively.

I can turn off the electric light now; my study is already pierced by shafts of low, red sunlight. I am at my table, ready to write the day through. Everything around me has the appearance of eminent normality and security. There are no signs remaining of Albert Wilmarth's frantic midnight departure with the magneto-optic apparatus he brought from the East, yet as if by clairvoyance I can see his long-jawed, horror-sucked face as he clings automatically to the steering wheel of his little Austin scuttling across the desert like a frightened beetle, the geo-scanner lying on the seat beside him. This day's sun has reached him before me as he flees back toward his deeply beloved, impossibly distant New England. That sun's smoky red blaze must be in his fear-wide eyes, for I know that no power can turn him back toward the land that slips uncouth into the titan Pacific. I bear him no resentment—I have no reason to. His nerves were shattered by the terrors he bravely insisted on helping to investigate for ten long years against his steadier comrades' advice. And at the very end, I am certain, he saw horrors beyond imagining. Yet he waited to ask me to go with him and only I know how much that must have cost him. He gave me my opportunity to escape; if I had wanted to, I could have made the attempt.

But I believe my fate was decided many years ago.

My name is Georg Reuter Fischer. I was born in 1912 of Swiss parents in the city of Louisville, Kentucky, with an inwardly twisted right foot which might have been corrected by brace, except that my father did not believe in interfering with the workings of Nature, his deity. He was a mason and stone cutter of great physical strength, vast energy, remarkable intuitive gifts (a dowser for water, oil, and metals), great natural artistry, unschooled but profoundly self-educated. A little after the Civil War, when he was a young boy, he had immigrated to this country with his father, also a mason, and upon the death of the latter, inherited a small but profitable business. Late in life he married my mother, Marie Reuter, daughter of a farmer for whom he had dowsed not only a well but a deposit of granite worth quarrying. I was the child of their age and their only child, coddled by my mother and the object of my father's more thoughtful devotion. I have few memories of our life in Louisville, but those few are eminently wholesome ones: visions of an ordered, cheerful household, of many cousins and friends, of visitings and laughter, and two great Christmas celebrations; also memories of fascinatedly watching my father at his stone cutting, bringing a profusion of flowers and leaves to life from death-pale granite.

And I will say here, because it is important to my story, that I afterwards learned that our Fischer and Reuter relatives considered me exceptionally intelligent for my tender age. My father and mother always believed this, but one must allow for parental bias.

In 1917 my father profitably sold his business and brought his tiny family west to build with his own hands a last home in this land of sunlight, crumbling sandstones, and sea-spawned hills, Southern California. This was in part because doctors had advised it as essential for the sake of my mother's failing health, slow victim of the dread tubercular scourge, but my father had always had a strong yearning for clear skies, year-round heat, and the primeval sea, a deep conviction that his destiny somehow lay west and was involved with the earth's hugest ocean, from which perhaps the moon was torn.

My father's deep-seated longing for this outwardly wholesome and bright, inwardly sinister and eaten-away landscape, where Nature herself presents the naïve face of youth masking the corruptions of age, has given me much food for thought, though it is in no way a remarkable longing. Many people migrate here, healthy as well as sick, drawn by the sun, the promise of perpetual summer, and broad if arid fields. The only unusual circumstance worthy of note is that there is a larger sprinkling than might be expected of persons of professed mystical and utopian bent. The Brothers of the Rose, the Theosophists, the Foursquare Gospelers, the Christian Scientists, Unity, the Brotherhood of the Grail, the spiritualists, the astrologers—all are here and many more besides. Believers in the need of return to primitive states and primitive wisdoms, practitioners of pseudo-disciplines dictated by pseudo-sciences—yes, even a few overly sociable hermits—one finds them everywhere, and the large majority awaken only my pity and distaste, so lacking in logic and avid for publicity are they. At no time—and let me emphasize this—have I been at all interested in their doings and in their ignorantly parroted principles, except possibly from the viewpoint of comparative psychology.

And they were brought here by that excessive love of sunlight which characterizes most faddists of any sort and that urge to find an unsettled, unorganized land in which utopias might take root and burgeon, untroubled by urbane ridicule and tradition-bred opposition—the same urge that led the Mormons to desert-guarded Salt Lake City, their paradise of Deseret. This seems an adequate explanation, even without bringing in the fact that Los Angeles, a city of retired farmers and small merchants, a city made hectic by the presence of the uncouth motion-picture industry, would naturally attract charlatans of all varieties. Yes, that explanation is still sufficient to me, and I am rather pleased, for even now I should hate to think that those hideously alluring voices a-mutter with secrets from beyond the rim of the cosmos *necessarily* have some dim, continent-wide *range*.

("The carven rim," they are saying now here in my study. "The proto-shoggoths, the diagrammed corridor, the elder Pharos, the dreams of Cutlu ...")

Settling my mother and myself at a comfortable Hollywood boarding house, where the activities of the infant film industry provided us with colorful distraction, my father tramped the hills in search of a suitable property, bringing to bear his formidable talent for locating underground water and desirable rock formations. During this period, it occurs to me how, he almost certainly pioneered those trails which it is my own invariable and ever more compulsive wont to walk. Within three months he had found and purchased the property he sought near a predominantly Alsatian and French settlement (a scatter of bungalows, no more) bearing the perhaps exaggeratedly picturesque name Vultures Roost, redolent of the Old West.

Clearing and excavation of the property revealed an upthrust stratum of fine-grained solid metamorphic rock, while a little boring provided an excellent well, to the incredulous astonishment of his initially hostile neighbors. My father kept his counsel and began, mostly with his own hands alone, to erect a brick structure of moderate size that by its layout and plans promised a dwelling of surpassing beauty. This occasioned more head-shaking and lectures on the unwisdom of building brick structures in a region where earthquakes were not unknown. They called it Fischer's Folly, I learned later. Little did they realize my father's skill and the tenacity of his masonry!

He bought a small truck and scoured the area as far south as Laguna Beach and as far north as Malibu, searching for the kilns that would provide him with bricks and tiles of requisite quality. In the end he sheathed the roof partly with copper, which has turned a beautiful green with the years. During these searches he became closely acquainted with the visionary and remarkably progressive Abbott Kinney, who was building the resort of Venice on the coast ten miles away, and with the swarthy, bright-eyed, unknown master builder Simon Rodia, self-educated like himself. All three men shared a rich vein of the poetry of stone, ceramics, and metals.

There must have been prodigious reserves of strength in the old man (for my father was that now, his hair whitely grizzled) to enable him to accomplish so much hard labor, for within two years my mother and I were able to move into our new home at Vultures Roost and take up our lives there.

I was delighted with my new surroundings and to be rejoined with my father, and only resentful of the time I must spend at school, to which my father drove me and from which he fetched me each day. I especially enjoyed rambling, occasionally with my father but chiefly by myself, through the wild, dry, rock-crowned hills, spry despite my twisted foot. My mother was fearful for me, especially because of the hairy brown and black tarantulas one sometimes encountered and the snakes, including venomous rattlers, but I was not to be restrained.

My father was happy, but also like a man in a dream as he worked unceasingly at the innumerable tasks, chiefly artistic, involved in finishing our home. It was a structure of rich beauty, though our neighbors continued to shake their heads and cluck dubiously at its hexagonal shape, partly rounded roof, thick walls of tightly mortared (though unreinforced) brick, and the area of brightly colored tile and floridly engraved stone. "Fischer's Folly," they'd whisper, and chuckle. But swarthy Simon Rodia nodded approvingly when he visited and once Abbott Kinney came to admire, driven in an expensive car by a black chauffeur with whom he seemed on terms of easy friendship.

My father's stone engravings were indeed quite fanciful and even a little disconcerting in their subject matter and location. One was in the basement's floor of natural rock, which he had smoothed. From time to time I'd watch him work on it. Desert plants and serpents seemed to be its subject matter, but as one studied it one became aware that there was much marine stuff too: serrated looping seaweeds, coiling eels, fishes that trailed tentacles, suckered octopus arms, and two giant squid eyes peering from a coral-crusted castle. And in its midst he boldly hewed in a flowery stone script, "The Gate of Dreams." My childish imagination was fired, but I was a little frightened too.

It was about this time—1921 or thereabouts—that my sleep-walking began, or at any rate showed signs of becoming disturbingly persistent. Several times my father found me at vary-ing distances from the house along one of the paths I favored in my limping rambles and carried me tenderly back, chilled and shiver-ing, for unlike Kentucky in the summer, Southern California nights are surprisingly cold. And more than once I was found huddled and still asleep in our cellar alongside the grotesquely floor-set "Gate of Dreams" bas-relief—to which, incidentally, my mother had taken a dislike which she tried to conceal from my father.

At that time too my sleeping habits began to show other abnor-malities, some of them contradictory. Although an active and apparently healthy boy of ten, I was still sleeping infancy's twelve hours or more a night. Yet despite this unusual length of slumber coupled with the restlessness my sleepwalking would seem to have indicated, I never dreamed or at any rate remembered dreams upon awakening. And with one notable exception this has been true for my entire life.

The exception occurred a little later on, when I was eleven or twelve—in 1923 or thereabouts. I remember those few dreams (there were no more than eight or nine of them) with matchless vividness. How else?—since they were my life's only ones and since ... but I must not anticipate. At the time I was secretive about them, telling neither my father nor my mother, as if for fear my parents might worry or (children are odd!) disapprove, until one final night.

In my dream I would find myself making my way through low passages and tunnels, all crudely cut or perhaps *gnawed* from solid rock. Often I felt I was at a great distance under the earth, though why I thought this in my dream I cannot say, except that there was often a sensation of heat and an indescribable feeling of pressure from above. This last sensation was diminished almost to nothing at times, though. And sometimes I felt there were vast amounts of water far above me, though why I suspected this I cannot say, for the strange tunnels were always very dry. Yet in my dreams I came to assume that the burrows extended limitlessly under the Pacific.

There was no obvious source of illumination in the passages. My dream explanation of how I then managed to see them was fantastic, though rather ingenious. The floor of the tunnels was colored a strange purplish green. This I explained in my dream as being the reflection of cosmic rays (which were much in the newspapers then, firing my boyish imagination) that came down through the thick rock above from distantmost outer space. The rounded ceiling of the tunnels, on the other hand, had a weird orange-blue glow. This, I seemed to know, was caused by the reflection of certain rays unknown to science that came up through the solid rock from the earth's incandescent, constricted core.

The eerie mixed light revealed to me the strange engravings or ridgy pictures everywhere covering the tunnels' walls. They had a strong suggestion of the marine to them and also of the monstrous, yet they were strangely *generalized*, as if they were the mathematical diagrams of oceans and their denizens and of whole universes of alien life. If *the dreams* of a monster of supernatural mentality could be given visual shape, then they would be like those endless forms I saw on the tunnels' walls. Or if *the dreams* of such a monster were half materialized and able to move through such tunnels, *they would shape the walls in such fashion.*

At first in my dreams I was not conscious of having a body. I seemed to be a viewpoint floating along the tunnels at a definitely *rhythmic* rate, now faster, now slower.

And at first I never saw anything in those tormenting tunnels, though I was continually conscious of a fear that I might—a fear mixed with desire. This was a most disturbing and exhausting feeling, which I could hardly have concealed upon awakening save that (with one exception) I never woke until my dream had played itself out, as it were, and my feelings were temporarily exhausted.

And then in my next dream I did begin to see things—creatures—in the tunnels, floating through them in the same general rhythmic fashion as I (or my viewpoint) progressed. They were worms about as long as a man and as thick as a man's thigh, cylindrical and untapering. From end to end, as many as a centipede's legs, were pairs of tiny wings, translucent like a fly's, which vibrated unceasingly, producing an unforgettably sinister low-pitched *hum*. They had no eyes—their heads were one circular mouth lined with rows of triangular teeth like a shark's. Although blind, they seemed able to sense each other at short distances and their sudden lurching swerves then to avoid colliding with each other held a particular horror for me. (It was a little like my lurching limp.)

In my very next dream I became aware of my own dream body. In brief, I was myself one of those same winged worms. The horror I felt was extreme, yet once more the dream lasted until its intensity was damped out and I could awaken with only the memory of terror, still able (I thought) to keep my dreams a secret.

The next time I had my dream it was to see three of the winged worms writhing in a wider section of tunnel where the sensation of pressure from above was minimal. I was still observer rather than participant, floating in my worm body in a narrower side passageway. How I was able to see while in one of the blind worm bodies, my dream logic did not explain.

They were worrying a rather small human victim. Their three snouts converged upon and covered his face. Their sinister buzzing had a hungry note and there were sucking sounds.

Blond hair, white pyjamas, and (projecting from the right leg of those) a foot slightly shrunken and *twisted sharply inward* told me the victim was myself.

At that instant I was shaken violently, the scene swam, and through it my mother's huge terrorized face peered down at me with my father's anxious visage close behind.

I went into convulsions of terror, flailing my limbs, and I screamed and screamed. It was hours literally before I could be quieted down, and days before my father let me tell them my nightmare.

Thereafter he made a strict rule: that no one ever try to shake me awake, no matter how bad a nightmare I seemed to be having. Later I learned he'd watch me at such times with knitted brow, suppressing the impulse to rouse me and seeing to it that no one else tried to do so.

For several nights thereafter I fought sleep, but when my nightmare was never repeated and once more I could never remember having dreamed at all when I wakened, I quieted down and my life, both sleeping and waking, became very tranquil again. In fact, even my sleepwalking became less frequent, although I continued to sleep for abnormally long hours, a practice now encouraged by my father's injunction that I never be wakened unnaturally.

But I have since come to wonder whether this apparent diminishment of my unconscious night-wandering were not because I, or some fraction of me, had become more cunningly deceitful. *Habits* have in any case a way of slipping slowly from the serious notice of those around.

At times, though, I would catch my father looking at me speculatively, as though he would have dearly liked to talk with me of various deep matters, but in the end he would always restrain this impulse (if I had divined it rightly) and content himself with encouraging me in my school studies and rambling exercise despite the latter's dangers: There *were* more rattlesnakes about my favorite paths, perhaps because opossums and raccoons were being exterminated; he made me wear high laced shoes of stout leather.

And once or twice I got the impression that he and Simon Rodia were talking secretly about me when the latter visited.

On the whole my life was a lonely one and has remained so to this day. We had no neighbors who were friends, no friends who were neighbors. At first this was because of the relative isolation of our residence and the suspicion that Germanic names uniformly called forth in the years following the World War. But it continued even after we began to have more neighbors, tolerant newcomers. Perhaps things would have been different if my father had lived longer. (His health was good save for a touch of eyestrain—dancing colors he'd see briefly).

But that was not to be. On that fatal Sunday in 1925 he had joined me on one of my customary walks and we had just reached one of my favorite spots when the ground gave way under his feet and he vanished from beside me, his startled exclamation dropping in pitch as he fell rapidly. For once his instinct for underground conditions had deserted him. There was a little scraping rumble as a few rocks and some gravel landslided, then silence. I approached the weed-fringed black hole on my belly and peered down fearfully.

From very far below (it sounded) I heard my father call faintly, "Georg! Get help!" His voice now had a strained, higher pitched sound, as if his chest were being constricted.

"Father! I'm coming down," I cried, cupping my hands about my mouth, and I had thrust my twisted foot into the hole searching for support, when his frantic yet clearly enunciated words came up, his voice still higher pitched and even more strained, as if he had to make a great effort to get sufficient breath for them: "Do *not* come down, Georg—you'll start an avalanche. Get help ... a rope!"

After a moment's hesitation I withdrew my leg and set off for home at a hobbling gallop. My horror was heightened (or perhaps a little relieved) by a sense of the dramatic—early that year we had listened for weeks on the little crystal set I'd built to the radioed reports of the long, protracted, exciting efforts (ultimately unsuccessful) to rescue Floyd Collins from where he'd gotten himself trapped in Sand Cave near Sand City, Kentucky. I suppose I anticipated some such drama for my father.

Most fortunately a young doctor was making a call in our neighborhood and he was foremost in the party of men I soon guided back to where my father had disappeared. No sounds at all came from the black hole although we called and called, and I remember that a couple of the men had begun to look at me dubiously, as if I'd invented the whole thing, when the courageous young doctor insisted against the advice of most on being lowered into the hole—they'd brought a strong rope *and* an electric flashlight.

He was a long time going down, descending about fifty feet in all while calls went back and forth, and almost as long being drawn up. When he emerged all smeared with sandy dirt—great orange smudges—it was to tell us (he made a point of laying his hand on my shoulder; I could see my mother hurrying up between two other women) that my father was inextricably wedged in down there with little more than his head exposed and that he was, to an absolute certainty, dead.

At that moment there was another grating rumble and the black hole collapsed upon itself. One of the men standing on its edge was barely jerked to safety. My mother shrieked, threw herself down on the shaking brown weeds, and was drawn back too.

In the subsequent weeks it was decided that my father's body could not be recovered. Some bags of concrete and sand were dumped into what was left of the hole to seal it. My mother was forbidden to erect a monument at the spot, but in some sort of compensation—I didn't understand the logic of it—Los Angeles County presented her with a cemetery plot elsewhere. (It now holds her own body.) An unofficial funeral service conducted by a Latin-American priest was eventually held at the spot and Simon Rodia, defying the injunction, put up a small, nonsectarian ovoid monument of his own matchlessly tough white concrete bearing my father's name and beautifully inset with a vaguely aquatic or naval design in fragmented blue and green glass. It is still there.

After my father's death I became more withdrawn and brooding than ever and my mother, a shy consumptive woman full of hysterical fears, hardly encouraged me to become sociable. In fact, almost as long as I can remember and certainly ever since Anton Fischer's

tragic and abrupt demise, nothing has ever bulked large with me
save my own brooding and this brick house set in the hills with its
strange, queerly set stone carvings and the hills themselves, those
sandy, spongy, salt-soaked, sun-baked hills. There has been altogether too much of them in my background; I have limped too long
about their crumbling rims, under their cracked and treacherous
overhanging sandstones, and through the months-dry streams that
thread their separating canyons. I have thought a great deal about
the old days when, some Indians are said to have believed, the
Strangers came down from the stars with the great meteor shower
and the lizard men perished in the course of their frantic digging
for water and the scaly sea men came tunneling in from their
encampments beneath the vast Pacific which constituted a whole
world to the west, extensive as that of the stars. I early developed
too great a love for such savage fancies. Too much of my physical
landscape has become the core of my mental landscape. And during
the nights of my long, long sleepings, I hobbled through them both,
I am somehow sure. While by day I had horrible fugitive visions of
my father, underground, dead-alive, companied by the winged
worms of my nightmare. Moreover, I developed the notion or
fantasy that there was a network of *tunnels* underlying the paths I
limped along and corresponding to them exactly, but at varying
depths and coming closest to the surface at my "favorite spots."

("The legend of Yig," the voices are droning. "The violet wisps,
the globular nebulae, Canis Tindalos and their foul essence, the
nature of the Doels, the tinted chaos, great Cutlu's minions ..." I
have made breakfast but I cannot eat. I thirstily gulp hot coffee.)

I would hardly keep harping on my sleepwalking and on the
unnaturally long hours I spent so deeply asleep that my mother
would vow that my mind was elsewhere, were it not associated with
a lapse in the intellectual promise I was said to have shown in earlier
years. True, I got along well enough in the semi-rural grade school
I trudged to and later in the suburban high school to which a bus
took me; true too that I early showed interest in many subjects and
flashes of excellent logic and imaginative reasoning. The trouble
was that I did not seem ever able to pursue any of those flashes and
make a steady and persistent effort. There would be times when my
teachers would worry my mother with reports of my unpreparedness
and my disregard of assignments, though when examination time
came I almost invariably managed to make a creditable showing.
My interests in more personal directions, too, seemed to peter out

very quickly. I was certainly peculiarly deficient in the power of attention. I remember often sitting down with a favorite book or text and then finding myself, minutes or hours later, turning over pages far ahead of anything I could remember reading. Sometimes only the memory of my father's injunctions to study, to study *deeply*, would keep me plodding on.

You may not think this matter worth mentioning. There is nothing strange in a lonely sheltered child failing to show great willpower and mental energy. There is nothing strange in such a child becoming slothful, weak, and indecisive. Nothing strange— only much to pity and reproach. The powers that be know I reproached myself often enough, for as my father had encouraged me to, I felt a power and a capability somewhere in myself, but somehow inhibited. But there are only too many people with power they cannot loose. It is only *later* events that have made me see something significant in my lapsings.

My mother followed to the letter my fathers' directions for my higher education, which I only learned of now. Upon my graduation from high school I was sent to a venerable eastern institution of learning not as well known as those of the Ivy League, but of equally high standing—Miskatonic University, which lies on the serpentine river of that name within the antique town of Arkham with its gambrel roofs and elm-shaded avenues quiet as the footsteps of a witch's familiar. My father had first heard of the school from an eastern employer of his talents, a Harley Warren for whom he had done some unusual dowsing in a cemetery within a swamp of cypresses, and that man's high praise of Miskatonic had imprinted itself indelibly upon his memory. My previous school record did not permit of this (I lacked certain prerequisites) but I just barely managed—much to the surprise of all my previous teachers—to pass a stiff entrance examination which required, like that of Dartmouth, some knowledge of Greek as well as Latin. Only I knew how much furious, imagination-invoking guessing that took. I could not bear to fall utterly short of my father's hopes for me.

Unfortunately, my efforts were in vain. Before the first term ended I was back in Southern California, physically and mentally depleted by a series of attacks of nervousness, homesickness, actual ailment (anemia), an increase in the hours I devoted to sleep, and an almost incredible recurrence of my sleepwalking, which more than once carried me deep into the wild hills west of Arkham. I tried for what seemed to me a long time to stick it out, but was advised by the college doctors to give it up after some particularly bad attacks. I believe that they thought I was not cut out to be even a moderately strong individual and that they pitied me more than they sympathized with me. It is not a good thing to see a youth racked by sentiments and longings proper to a fearful child.

And they appeared to be right in this (although I know now that they were wrong), for my malady turned out (*apparently*) to be simple homesickness and nothing more. It was with a feeling of immense relief that I returned to my mother and our brick home in the hills, and with each room I re-entered I gained more assurance—even, or perhaps especially, the cellar with its well swept floor of solid rock, my father's tools and chemicals (acids, etc.), and the marinely decorated, floor-set rock inscription "The Gate of Dreams." It was as though all the time I had been at Miskatonic there had been an invisible leash dragging me back, and only now had its pressure slackened completely.

(Those voices *are* continent-wide, of course: "The essential salts, the fane of Dagon, the gray twisted brittle monstrosity, the flute-tormented pandemonium, the coral-encrusted towers of Rulay ...")

And the hills helped me as much as my home. For a month I roamed them daily and walked the old familiar paths between the parched and browning undergrowth, my mind full of old tales and scraps of childhood brooding. I think it was only then, only with my returning, that I first came fully to realize how much (and a little of *what*) those hills meant to me. From Mount Waterman and steep Mount Wilson with its great observatory and hundred-inch reflector down through cavernous Tujunga Canyon with its many sinuous offshoots to the flat lands and then across the squat Verdugo Hills and the closer ones with Griffith Observatory and its lesser 'scopes, to sinister, almost inaccessible Potrero and great twisting Topanga Canyons that open with the abruptness of catastrophe upon the monstrous, primeval Pacific—all of them (the hills) with a few exceptions sandy, cracked, and treacherous, the earth like rock and the rock like dried earth, rotten, crumbling, and porous: All this had such a hold on me (the limper, the fearful listener) as to be obsessive. And indeed there were more and more symptoms of obsession now: I favored certain paths over others for ill-defined reasons and there were places I could not pass without stopping for a little. My fantasy or notion became stronger than ever that there were *tunnels* under the paths, traveled by beings which attracted the venomous snakes of the outer world because they were akin to them.

Could some eerie reality have underlaid my childhood night-mare?—I shied away from that thought.

All this, as I say, I realized during the month after my defeated return from the East. And at the end of that month I resolved to conquer my obsession and my revolting homesickness and all the subtle weaknesses and inner hindrances that kept me from being the man my father had dreamed of. I had found that a complete break such as my father had planned for me (Miskatonic) would not work; so I determined to work out my troubles without running away: I would take courses at nearby UCLA (the University of California at Los Angeles). I would study and exercise, build up both body and mind. I remember that my determination was intense. There is something very ironic about that, for my plan, logical as it seemed, was the one sure course to further psychological entrapment.

For quite some time, however, I seemed to be getting on success-fully. With systematic exercise and better controlled diet and rest (still my twelve hours a night), I became healthier than I ever had been before. All the troubles that had beset me in the East vanished completely away. No longer did I wake shuddering from my dreamless sleepwalking; in fact, as far as I could determine at the time, that habit had gone for good. And at college, from which I returned home nightly, I made steady progress. It was then that I first began to write those imaginative and pessimistic poems tinged with metaphysical speculation that have won me some little atten-tion from a small circle of readers. Oddly, they were sparked by the one significant item I had brought back with me from shadow-beset Arkham, a little book of verse I'd bought at a dusty secondhand store there, *Azathoth and Other Horrors* by Edward Pickman Derby, a local poet.

Now I know that my spurt of new effort during my college years was largely deceptive. Because I had decided upon a new course of life that brought me into a few new situations (though keeping me at home) I thought I was progressing vastly. I managed to keep on believing that for all my college years. That I could never study any subject profoundly, that I could never create anything that took a protracted effort, I explained by telling myself that what I was doing was "preparation" and "intellectual orientation" for some great future effort. For several years I managed to conceal from myself the fact that I could only call a tithe of my energy my own, while the residuum was being shunted down only the powers that be know what inner channels.

(I thought I knew what books I was studying, but the voices now are telling me, "The runes of Nug-Soth, the clavicle of Nyar-lathotep, the litanies of Lomar, the secular meditations of Pierre-Louis Montagny, the *Necronomicon*, the chants of Crom-Ya, the overviews of Yiang-Li ..."

(It is midday or later outside but the house is cool. I have managed to eat a little and made more coffee. I have been down to the basement, checking my father's tools and things, his sledge, carboys of acid, et cetera, and looking at "The Gate of Dreams" and treading softly. The voices are strongest there.)

Suffice it that during my six college and "poetic" years (I couldn't carry a full load of courses) I lived not as a man, but as a fraction of a man. I had gradually given up all grand ambitions and become content to lead a life in miniature. I spent my time going to easy classes, writing fragments of prose and an occasional poem, caring for my mother (who except for her worries about me was undemand-ing) and for my father's house (so well built it needed hardly any care), rambling almost absent-mindedly in the hills, and sleeping prodigiously. I had no friends. In fact, we had no friends. Abbott Kinney had died and Los Angeles had stolen his Venice. Simon Rodia gave up his visits, for he was now totally preoccupied with his great single-handed building project. Once on my mother's urging I went to Watts, a settlement of flower-decked humble bungalows dwarfed by his fabulous backyard towers that were rising like a blue-green Persian dream. He had trouble recalling who I was and then he watched me strangely as he worked. The money my father had left (in silver dollars) was ample for my mother and myself. In short, I had become, not unpleasantly, *resigned*.

This was all the easier for me because of my growing absorption in the doctrines of such men as Oswald Spengler who believe that culture and civilization go by cycles and that our own Faustian western world, with all its grandiose dream of scientific progress, is headed toward a barbarism that will engulf it as surely as the Goths, Vandals, Scythians, and Huns engulfed mighty Rome and her longer-lived sister, dwindling Byzantium. As I looked from my hilltops down on bustling Los Angeles always a-building, I placidly thought of the future days when little bands of blustering, ill-kempt barbarians will walk the streets of humped and pitted asphalt and look on each of its ruined, many-purposed buildings as just another "hut"; when high-set Griffith Park Planetarium, romantically rock-built, high-walled, and firmly bastioned, will be the stronghold of some petty dictator; when industry and science will be gone and all their machines and instruments rusted and broken and their use forgotten ... and *all* our works forgotten as completely as those of the sunken civilization of Mu in the Pacific, of the fragments of whose cities only remain Nan Matol and Rapa Nui, or Easter Island.

But *whence* did these thoughts really come? Not entirely or even principally from Spengler, I'll be bound. No, they had a *deeper* source, I greatly fear.

Yet thus I thought, thus I believed, and thus I was wooed away from the pursuits and tempting goal of our commercial world. I saw everything in terms of transiency, decadence, and decline—as if the times were as rotten and crumbling as the hills which obsessed me.

It was that I was *convinced*, not that I was morbid. No, my health was better than ever and I was neither bored nor dissatisfied. Oh, I occasionally berated myself for failure to manifest the promise my father had seen in me, but on the whole I was strangely content. I had a weird sense of power and self-satisfaction, as if I were a man in the midst of some engrossing pursuit. You know the pleasant relief and bone-deep satisfaction that comes after a day of successful hard work? Well, *that was the way I felt almost all the time, day in and day out.* And I took my happiness as a gift of the gods. It did not occur to me to ask, "*Which* gods? Are they from heaven ... or from *the underworld?*"

Even my mother was happier, her disease arrested, her son devoted to her and leading a busy life (on a very small scale) and doing nothing to worry her beyond his occasional rambles in the snake-infested hills.

Fortune smiled on us. Our brick dwelling rode out the severe Long Beach earthquake of March 10, 1933 without sustaining the least damage. Those who still called it Fischer's Folly were nonplused.

Last year (1936) I duly received from UCLA my bachelor's diploma in English literature, with a minor in history, my mother proudly attending the ceremony. And a month or so later she seemed as childishly delighted as I at the arrival of the first bound copies of my little book of verse, *The Tunneler Below*, printed at my own expense. In my hubristic mood of auctorial conceit I not only sent out several copies for review but also donated two to the UCLA library and two more to that at Miskatonic. In my covering letter to the erudite Dr. Henry Armitage, librarian at the latter institution, I mentioned not only my brief attendance there, but also my inspiration by an Arkham poet. I also told him a little about the circumstances of my composition of the poems.

I joked deprecatingly to my mother about this last expansive gesture of mine, but she knew how deeply I had been hurt by my failure at Miskatonic and how strongly I desired to repair my reputation there, so when only a few weeks later a letter came addressed to me and bearing the Arkham postmark, she hurried out into the hills quite against her usual wont, to bring it to me, I having just gone out on one of my rambles.

From where I was, I barely heard, yet also recognized, her mortal screams. I rushed back at my most desperate limping speed. At the very spot where my father had perished, I found her writhing on the hard, dry ground and screaming still—and near to her and whipping about, the large young rattlesnake that had bitten her on the calf, which was already swelling.

I killed the horrid thing with the stick I carry, then slashed the bite with my sharp pocketknife and sucked it out and injected antivenom from the kit I have always with me on my walks.

All to no avail. She died two days later in the hospital. Once more there was not only shock and depression, but also the dismal business of a funeral to get through (at least we already owned a grave lot), this time a more conventional ceremony, but this time I was wholly alone.

It was a week before I could bring myself to look at the letter she'd been bringing me. After all, it had been the cause of her death. I almost tore it up unread. But after I had gotten to it, I became more and more interested and then incredulously amazed ... and frightened. Here it is, in its entirety:

> 118 Saltonstall St.,
> Arkham, Mass.,
> Aug. 12, 1936

Georg Reuter Fischer, Esq.,
Vultures Roost,
Hollywood, Calif.


My Dear Sir:—

Dr. Henry Armitage took the liberty of letting me peruse your *The Tunneler Below* before it was placed on general circulation in the university library. May one who serves only in the outer court of the muses' temple, and particularly outside Polyhymnia's and Erato's shrines, be permitted to express his deep appreciation of your creative achievement? And to tender respectfully the like admirations of Professor Wingate Peaslee of our psychology department and of Dr. Francis Morgan of medicine and comparative anatomy, who shares my especial interests, and of Dr. Armitage himself? "The Green Deeps" is in particular a remarkably well sustained and deeply moving lyric poem.

I am an assistant professor of literature at Miskatonic and an enthusiastic amateur student of New England and other folklore. If memory serves, you were in my freshman English section six years ago. I was sorry then that the state of your health forced you to curtail your studies, and I am happy now to have before me conclusive evidence that you have completely surmounted all such difficulties. Congratulations!

And now will you allow me to pass on to another and very different matter, which is nonetheless peripherally related to your poetic work? Miskatonic is currently engaged in a broad interdepartmental research in the general area of folklore, language, and dreams, an investigation of the vocabulary of the collective unconscious, particularly as it expresses itself in poetry. The three scholars I have alluded to are among those active in this work, along with persons in Brown University, Providence, Rhode Island, who are carrying on the pioneering work of the late Professor George Gammell Angell, and from time to time I am honored to render them assistance. They have empowered me to ask you for your own help in this matter, which could be of signal importance. It is a matter of answering a few questions only, relating to the accidents of your writing and in no way impinging on its essence, and should not cut seriously into your time. Naturally any information you choose to supply will be treated as strictly confidential.

I call your attention to the following two lines in "The Green Deeps":

> Intelligence doth grow itself within
> The coral-palled, squat towers of Rulay.

Did you in composing this poem ever consider a more eccentric spelling of the last (and presumably invented?) word? "R'lyeh", say. And going back three lines, did you consider spelling "Nath" (invented?) with an initial "p"—i.e., "Pnath"?

Also in the same poem:

> The rampant dragon dreams in far Cathay
> While snake-limbed Cutlu sleeps in deep Rulay.

The name "Cutlu" (once more, invented?) is of considerable interest to us. Did you have phonetic difficulty in choosing the letters to represent the sound you had in mind? Did you perhaps simplify in the interests of poetic clarity? At any time did "Cthulhu" ever occur to you?

(As you can see, we are discovering that the language of the collective unconscious is almost unpleasantly guttural and sibilant! All hawking and spitting, like German.)

Also, there is this quatrain in your impressive lyric, "Sea Tombs":

> Their spires underlie our deepest graves;
>
> Lit are they by a light that man has seen.
>
> Only the wingless worm can go between
>
> Our daylight and their vault beneath the waves.

Were there some proofreading errors here?—or the equivalent. Specifically, in the second line should "that" be "no"? (And was the light you had in mind what you might call orange-blue or purple-green, or both?) And, in the next line, how does "winged" rather than "wingless" strike you?

Finally, in regard to "Sea Tombs" and also the title poem of your book, Professor Peaslee has a question which he calls a "long shot" about the subterranean and submarine tunnels which you evoke. Did you ever have fantasies of such tunnels really existing in the area where you composed the poem?—the Hollywood Hills and Santa Monica Mountains, presumably, the Pacific Ocean being nearby. Did you perhaps try actually to trace the paths overlying these fancied tunnels? And did you happen to notice (excuse the strangeness of this question) an unusual number of venomous serpents along such routes?—rattlers, I would presume (in our area it would be copperheads, and in the south water moccasins and coral snakes). If so, do take care!

If such tunnels should by some strange coincidence actually exist, it would be scientifically possible to confirm the fact without any digging or drilling (or by discovering an existent opening), it may interest you to know. Even vacuity—i.e., nothing—leaves its traces, it appears! Two Miskatonic science professors, who are part of the interdepartmental program I mentioned, have devised a highly portable apparatus for the purpose, which they call a magneto-optic geo-scanner. (That last hybrid word must sound a most clumsy and barbarous coinage to a poet, I'm sure, but you know scientists!) It is strange, is it not, to think of an investigation of dreams having geological repercussions? The clever though infelicitously named instrument is a simplified adaptation of one which has already discovered two new elements.

I shall be making a trip west early next year, to confer with a man in San Diego who happens to be the son of the scholarly recluse whose researches led to our interdepartmental program—Henry Wentworth Akeley. (The local poet—alas, deceased—to whom you pay such generous tribute, was another such pioneer, it happens oddly.) I shall be driving my own British sports car, a diminutive Austin. I am something of an automobile maniac, I must confess, even a speed demon!—however inappropriate that may be for an assistant English professor. I would be very pleased to make your further acquaintance at that time, if entirely agreeable to you. I might even bring along a geo-scanner and we could check out those hypothetical tunnels!

But I perhaps anticipate and presume too far. Pardon me. I will be very grateful for any attention you are able to give this letter and its necessarily impertinent questions.

Once more, congratulations on *The Tunneler!*

> Yrs. very truly,
> Albert N. Wilmarth

It is quite impossible to describe all at once my state of mind when I finished reading this letter. I can only do so by stages. To begin with, I was flattered and gratified, even acutely embarrassed, by his apparently sincere praise of my verses—as what young poet wouldn't be? And that a psychologist and an old librarian (even an anatomist!) should admire them too—it was almost too much.

As soon as the man mentioned freshman English I realized that I had a vivid memory of him. Although I'd forgotten his name in the course of years, it came back to me like a shot when I glanced ahead at the end of the letter and saw it. He had been only an instructor then, a tall young man, cadaverously thin, always moving about with nervous rapidity, his shoulders hunched. He'd had a long jaw and a pale complexion, with dark-circled eyes which gave him a haunted look, as if he were constantly under some great strain to which he never alluded. He had the habit of jerking out a little notebook and making jottings without ceasing for a moment to discourse fluently, even brilliantly. He'd seemed incredibly well read and had had a lot to do with stimulating and deepening my interest in poetry. I even remembered his car—the other students used to joke about it with an undercurrent of envy. It had been a Model T Ford then, which he'd always driven at a brisk clip around the fringes of the Miskatonic campus, taking turns very sharply.

The program of interdepartmental research he described sounded very impressive, even exciting, but eminently plausible—I was just discovering Jung then and also semantics. And to be invited to graciously to take part in it—once again I was flattered. If I hadn't been alone while I read it, I might have blushed.

One notion I got then did stop me briefly and for a moment almost turned me angrily against the whole thing—the sudden suspicion that the purpose of the program might not be the avowed one, that (the presence in it of a psychologist and a medical doctor influenced me in this) it was some sort of investigation of the delusions of crankish, imaginative people—not so much the incidental insights as the psychopathology of poets.

But he was so very gracious and reasonable—no, I was being paranoid, I told myself. Besides, as soon as I got a ways into his detailed questions it was an altogether different reaction that filled me—one of utter amazement ... and *fear.*

For starters, he was so incredibly accurate in his guesses (for what else could they possibly be? I asked myself uneasily) about those invented names, that he had me gasping. I *had* first thought of spelling them "R'lyeh" and "Pnath"—exactly those letters, though of course memory can be tricky about such things.

And then that *Cthulhu*—seeing it spelled that way actually made me shiver, it so precisely conveyed the deep-pitched, harsh, inhuman cry or chant I'd imagined coming up from profound black abysses, and only finally rendered as "Cutlu" rather dubiously but fearing anything more complex would seem affectation. (And, really, you can't fit the inner rhythms of a sound like "Cthulhu" into English poetry.)

And then to find that he'd spotted those two proofreaders' errors, for they'd been just that. The first I'd missed. The second ("wingless" for "winged") I'd caught, but then rather spinelessly let stand, feeling all of a sudden that I'd perpetuated something overly fantastic when I'd put a figure from my life's one nightmare (a worm with wings) into a poem.

And topping even that, how in the name of all that's wonderful could he have described unearthly colors I'd only dreamed of and never put into my poems at all? Using exactly the same color words I'd used! I began to think that Miskatonic's interdepartmental research project must have made some epochal discoveries about dreams and dreaming and the human imagination in general, enough to turn their scholars into wizards and dumbfound Adler, Freud, and even Jung.

At that point in my reading of the letter I thought he'd hit me with everything he possibly could, but the next section managed to mine a still deeper source of horror and one most disturbingly close to everyday reality. That he should know, somehow deduce, all about my paths in the hills and my odd daydreams about them and about the tunnels I'd fancied underlying them—that was truly staggering. And that he should ask *and even warn me* about venomous snakes, so that the very letter my mother was carrying unopened when she got her death sting contained a vital reference to it—really, for a moment and more then, I did wonder if I were going insane.

And finally when despite all his jaunty "fancied's" and "long shot's" and "hypothetical's" and English-professor witticisms, he began to talk as if he assumed my imaginary tunnels were real and to refer lightly to a scientific instrument that would prove it ... well, by the time I'd finished his letter, I fully expected him to turn up the next minute—turn in sharply at our drive with a flourish of wheels and brakes in his Model T (no, Austin) and draw up in a cloud of dust at our door, the geo-scanner sitting on the front seat beside him like a fat black telescope directed downward!

And yet he'd been so damnably *breezy* about it all! I simply didn't know what to think.

(I've been down in the basement again, checking things out. This writing stirs me up and makes me frightfully restless. I went out front and there was a rattlesnake crossing the path in the hot slanting sunlight from the west. More evidence, if any were needed, that what I fear is true. Or do I hope for it? At all events, I killed the brute. The voices vibrate with, "The half-born worlds, the alien orbs, the stirrings in blackness, the hooded forms, the nighted depths, the shimmering vortices, the purple haze ...")

When I'd calmed down somewhat next day, I wrote Wilmarth a long letter, confirming all his hints, confessing my utter astonishment at them, and begging him to explain how he'd made them. I volunteered to assist the interdepartmental project in any way I could and invited him to be my guest when he came west. I gave him a brief history of my life and my sleep anomalies, mentioning my mother's death. I had a strange feeling of unreality as I posted the letter and waited with mixed feelings of impatience and lingering (and also regathering) incredulity for his reply.

When it came, quite a fat one, it rekindled all my first excitement, though without satisfying all my curiosity by any means.
Wilmarth was still inclined to write off his and his colleagues'
deductions about my word choices, dreams, and fantasies as lucky
guesses, though he told me enough about the project to keep my
curiosity in a fever—especially about its discoveries of obscure
linkages between the life of the imagination and archeological
discoveries in far-off places. He seemed particularly interested in
the fact that I generally never dreamed and that I slept for very long
hours. He overflowed with thanks for my cooperation and my
invitation, promising to include me on his itinerary when he drove
west. And he had a lot more questions for me.

The next months were strange ones. I lived my normal life if it
can be called that, keeping up my reading and studies and library
visits, even writing a little new poetry from time to time. I
continued my hill-ramblings, though with a new wariness. Sometimes during them I'd stop and stare at the dry earth beneath my
feet, as if expecting to trace the outlines of a trap door in it. And
sometimes I'd be consumed by sudden, wildly passionate feelings
of grief and guilt at the thought of my father locked down there
and at my mother's horrible death too; I'd feel I must somehow go
to them at all costs.

And yet at the same time I was living only for Wilmarth's letters
and the moods of wonder, fantastic speculation, and panic yet
almost delicious terror they evoked in me. He'd write about all sorts
of things besides the project—my poetry and new readings and my
ideas (he'd play the professorial mentor here from time to time),
world events, the weather, astronomy, submarines, his pet cats,
faculty politics at Miskatonic, town meetings at Arkham, his
lectures and the local trips he'd make. He made it all extremely
interesting. Clearly he was an inveterate letter-writer and under his
influence I became one too.

But most of all, of course, I was fascinated by what he'd write
from time to time about the project. He told me some very
interesting things about the Miskatonic Antarctic expedition of
1930-31, with its five great Dornier airplanes, and last year's
somewhat abortive Australian one in which the psychologist Peaslee
and his father, a one-time economist, had been involved. I remembered having read about them both in the newspapers, though the
reports there had been curiously fragmentary and unsatisfying,
almost as if the press were prejudiced against Miskatonic.

I got the strong impression that Wilmarth would have liked very much to have accompanied both expeditions and was very much put out at not having been able (or allowed) to, though most of the time bravely concealing his disappointment. More than once he referred to his "unfortunate nervousness", sensitivity to cold, fierce migraine attacks, and "bouts of ill health" which would put him to bed for a few days. And sometimes he'd speak with wistful admiration of the prodigious energy and stalwart constitutions of several of his colleagues, such as Professors Atwood and Pabodie, the geo-scanner's inventors, Dr. Morgan, who was a big-game hunter, and even the octogenarian Armitage.

There were occasional delays in his replies, which always filled me with anxiety and restlessness, sometimes because of these attacks of his and sometimes because he'd been away longer than he'd expected on some visit. One of the latter was to Providence to confer with colleagues and help investigate the death under mysterious circumstances involving a lightning bolt of Robert Blake, a poet like myself, short-story writer, and painter whose work had provided much material for the project.

It was just after his visit to Providence that with a curious sort of guardedness and reluctance he mentioned visiting another colleague of sorts there (who was in poor health), a Howard Phillips Lovecraft, who had fictionalized (but quite sensationally, Wilmarth warned me) some Arkham scandals and some of Miskatonic's researches and project activities. These stories had been published (when at all) in cheap pulp magazines, especially in a lurid journal called *Weird Tales* (you'll want to tear the cover off, if ever you should dare to buy a copy, he assured me). I recalled having seen the magazine on downtown newsstands in Hollywood and Westwood. I hadn't found the covers offensive. Most of their nude female figures, by some sentimental woman artist, were decorously sleek pastels and their activities only playfully perverse. Others, by one Senf, were a rather florid folk art quite reminiscent of my father's floral chiselings.

But after that, of course, I haunted secondhand bookstores, hunting down copies of *Weird Tales* (mostly) with Lovecraft stories in them, until I'd found a few and read them—one, "The Call of Cthulhu", no less. It cost me the strangest shudders, let me tell you, to see *that* name again, spelled out in cheapest print, under such very outlandish circumstances. Truly, my sense of reality was set all askew and if the tale that Lovecraft told with a strange dignity and

power were anything like the truth, then Cthulhu was *real*, an
other-dimensional extraterrestrial monster dreaming in an insane,
Pacific-sunken metropolis which sent out mental messages (and—
who knows?—tunnels) to the world at large. In another tale, "The
Whisperer in Darkness", *Albert N. Wilmarth* was a leading character,
and that Akeley too he'd mentioned.

It was all fearfully unsettling and confounding. If I hadn't
attended Miskatonic myself and lived in Arkham, I'd have thought
surely they were a writer's projections.

As you can imagine, I continued to haunt the dusty bookstores
and I *bombarded* Wilmarth with frantic questions. His replies were
of a most pacifying and temporizing sort. Yes, he'd been afraid of
my getting too excited, but hadn't been able to resist telling me
about the stories. Lovecraft often laid things *very* thickly indeed. I'd
understand everything much better when we could really talk
together and he could explain in person. Really, Lovecraft had an
extremely powerful imagination and sometimes it got out of hand.
No, Miskatonic had never tried to suppress the stories or take legal
action, for fear of even less desirable publicity—and because the
project members thought the stories might be a good preparation
for the world if some of their more frightening hypotheses were
verified. Really, Lovecraft was a very charming and well-intentioned
person, but sometimes he went too far. And so on and so on.

Really, I don't think I could have contained myself except that,
it now being 1937, Wilmarth sent me word that he was at last driving
west. The Austin had been given a thorough overhaul and was
"packed to the gills" with the geo-scanner, endless books and papers,
and other instruments and materials, including a drug Morgan had
just refined, "which induces dreaming and may, conceivably, he
says, facilitate clairvoyance and clairaudience. It might make even
you dream—should you consent to ingest an experimental dose."

While he was gone from 118 Saltonstall his rooms would be
occupied and his cats, including his beloved Blackfellow, cared for
by a close friend named Danforth, who'd spent the last five years in
a mental hospital recovering from his ghastly Antarctic experience
at the Mountains of Madness.

Wilmarth hated to leave at this time, he wrote. In particular he
was worried about Lovecraft's failing health, but nevertheless he was
on his way!

The next weeks (which dragged out to two months) were a time
of particular tension, anxiety, and anticipatory excitement for me.

Wilmarth had many more people and places to visit and investigations to make (including readings with the geo-scanner) than I'd ever imagined. Now he sent mostly postcards, some of them scenic, but they came thick and fast (except for a couple of worrisome hiatuses) and with his minuscule handwriting he got so much on them (even the scenic ones) that at times I almost felt I was with him on his trip, worrying about the innards of his Austin, which he called the Tin Hind after Sir Francis Drake's golden one. I on my part had only a few addresses he'd listed for me where I could write him in advance—Baltimore; Winchester, Virginia; Bowling Green, Kentucky; Memphis; Carlsbad, New Mexico; Tucson; and San Diego.

First he had to stop in Hunterdon County, New Jersey, with its quaintly backward farm communities, to investigate some possibly precolonial ruins and hunt for a rumored cave, using the geo-scanner. Next, after Baltimore, there were extensive limestone caverns to check out in both Virginias. He crossed the Appalachians from Winchester to Clarksburg, a stretch with enough sharp turns to satisfy even him. Approaching Louisville, the Tin Hind was almost swallowed up in the Great Ohio Flood (which preoccupied the radio news for days; I hung over my superheterodyne set) and he was unable to visit a new correspondent of Lovecraft's there. Then there was more work for the geo-scanner near Mammoth Cave. In fact, caves seemed to dominate his journey, for after a side trip to New Orleans to confer with some occult scholar of French extraction, there were the Carlsbad Caverns and nearby but less well known subterranean vacuities. I wondered more and more about my tunnels.

The Tin Hind held up very well, except she blew out a piston head crossing Texas ("I held her at high speed a little too long") and he lost three days getting her mended.

Meanwhile, I was finding and reading new Lovecraft stories. One, which turned up in a secondhand but quite recent science-fiction pulp, fictionalized the Australian expedition most impressively—especially the dreams old Peaslee had that led to it. In them, he'd exchanged personalities with a cone-shaped monster and was forever wandering through long stone passageways haunted by invisible whistlers. It reminded me so much of my nightmares in which I'd done the same thing with a winged worm that buzzed, that I airmailed a rather desperate letter to Tucson, telling Wilmarth all about it. I got a reply from San Diego, full of reassurances and more temporizings, and referring to old Akeley's son and some sea caverns they were looking into, and (at last!) setting a date (it would be soon!) for his arrival.

The day before that last, I made a rare find in my favorite Hollywood hunting ground. It was a little, strikingly illustrated book by Lovecraft called *The Shadow over Innsmouth* and issued by Visionary Press, whoever they were. I was up half the night reading it. The narrator found some sinister, scaly human beings living in a deep submarine city off New England, realized he was himself turning into one of them, and at the end had decided (for better or worse) to dive down and join them. It made me think of crazy fantasies I'd had of somehow going down into the earth beneath the Hollywood Hills and rescuing or joining my dead father.

Meanwhile mail addressed to Wilmarth care of me had begun to arrive. He'd asked my permission to include my address on the itinerary he'd sent other correspondents. There were letters and cards from (by their postmarks) Arkham and places along his route, some from abroad (mostly England and Europe, but one from Argentina), and a small package from New Orleans. The return address on most of them was his own—118 Saltonstall, so he'd eventually get them even if he missed them along his route. (He'd asked me to do the same with my own notes.) The effect was odd, as though Wilmarth were the author of everything—it almost re-aroused my first suspicions of him and the project. (One letter, though, among the last to come, a thick one bearing extravagantly a six-cent airmail stamp and a ten-cent special delivery, had been addressed to George Goodenough Akeley, 176 Pleasant St., San Diego, Cal., and then forwarded care of my own address in the upper left-hand corner.)

Late the next afternoon (Sunday, April 14—the eve of my twenty-fifth birthday, as it happened) Wilmarth arrived very much as I'd imagined it occurring when I'd finished reading his first letter, except the Tin Hind was even smaller than I'd pictured—and enameled a bright blue, though now most dusty. There *was* an odd black case on the seat beside him, though there were a lot of other things on it too—maps, mostly.

He greeted me very warmly and began to talk a blue streak almost at once, with many a jest and frequent little laughs.

The thing that really shocked me was that although I knew he was only in his thirties, his hair was white and the haunted (or hunted) look I'd remembered was monstrously intensified. And he was extremely nervous—at first he couldn't stay still a moment. It wasn't long before I became certain of something I'd never once suspected before—that his breeziness and jauntiness, his jokes and laughs, were a mask for fear, no, for sheer terror, that otherwise might have mastered him entirely.

His actual first words were, "Mr. Fischer, I presume? So glad to meet you in the flesh!—and share your most salubrious sunlight. I look as if I need it, do I not?—a horrid sight! This landscape hath a distinctly cavish, tunnely aspect—I'm getting to be an old hand at making such geological judgments. Danforth writes that Black-fellow has quite recovered from his indisposition. But Lovecraft is in hospital—I do not like it. Did you observe last night's brilliant conjunction?—I *like* your clear, clear skies. No, I will carry the geo-scanner (yes, it *is* that), it's somewhat crankish. But you might take the small valise. Really, so very glad!"

He did not comment on or even seem to notice my twisted right foot (something I hadn't mentioned in my letters, though he may have recalled it from six years back) or imply its or my limp's existence in any way, as by insisting on carrying the valise also. That warmed me toward him.

And before going into the house with me, he paused to praise its unusual architecture (another thing I hadn't told him about) and seemed genuinely impressed when I admitted that my father had built it by himself. (I'd feared he'd find it overly eccentric and also question whether someone could work with his hands and be a gentleman.) He also commented favorably on my father's stone carvings wherever they turned up and insisted on pausing to study them, whipping out his notebook to make some quick jottings. Nothing would do, but I must take him on a full tour of the house before he'd consent to rest or take refreshment. I left his valise in the bedroom I'd assigned him (my parents', of course) but he kept lugging the black geo-scanner around with him. It was an odd case, taller than it was wide or long, and it had three adjustable stubby legs, so that it could be set up vertically anywhere.

Emboldened by his approval of my father's carvings, I told him about Simon Rodia and the strangely beautiful towers he was building in Watts, whereupon the notebook came out again and there were more jottings. He seemed particularly impressed by the *marine* quality I found in Rodia's work.

Down in the basement (he had to go there too) he was very much struck by my father's floor-set "Gate of Dreams" stone carving and studied it longer than any of the others. (I'd been feeling embarrassed about its bold motto and odd placement.) Finally he indicated the octopus eyes staring over the castle and observed, "Cutlu, perchance?"

It was the first reference of any sort to the research project that either of us had made since our meeting and it shook me strangely, but he appeared not to notice and continued with, "You know, Mr. Fischer, I'm tempted to get a reading with Atwood and Pabodie's infernal black box right here. Would you object?"

I told him certainly not and to go right ahead, but warned him that there was only solid rock under the house (I had told him about my father's dowsing and even had mentioned Harley Warren, whom it turned out Wilmarth had heard of through a Randolph Carter).

He nodded, but said, "I'll take a shot at it nonetheless. We must start somewhere, you know," and he proceeded to set up the geo-scanner carefully so it was standing vertically on its three stubby legs right in the middle of the carving. He took off his shoes first so as not to risk damaging the rather fine stone work.

Then he opened the top of the geo-scanner. I glimpsed two dials and a large eyepiece. He knelt and applied his eye to it, drawing out a black hood and draping it over his head, very much like an old-fashioned photographer focusing for a picture. "Pardon me, but the indications I must look for are difficult to see," he said muffledly. "Hello, what's this?"

There was a longish pause during which nothing happened except his shoulders shifted a bit and there were a few faint clicks. Then he emerged from under the hood, tucked it back in the black box, closed the latter, and began to put on and relace his shoes.

"The scanner's gone crankish," he explained in answer to my inquiry, "and is seeing ghost vacuities. But not to worry—it only needs new warm-up cells, I fancy, which I have with me, and will be right as rain for tomorrow's expedition! That is, if—?" He rolled his eyes up at me in smiling inquiry.

"Of course I'll be able to show you my pet trails in the hills," I assured him. "In fact, I'm bursting to."

"Capital!" he said heartily.

But as we left the basement, its rock floor rang out a bit hollowly, it sounded to me, under his high-laced leather-soled and -heeled shoes (I was wearing sneakers).

It was getting dark, so I started dinner after giving him some iced tea, which he took with lots of lemon and sugar. I cooked eggs and small beefsteaks, figuring from his haggard looks he needed the most restorative sort of food. I also built a fire in the big fireplace against the almost invariable chill of evening.

As we ate by its dancing, crackling flames, he regaled me with brief impressions of his trip west—the cold, primeval pine woods of southern New Jersey with their somberly clad inhabitants speaking an almost Elizabethan English, the very narrow dark roads of West Virginia, the freezing waters of the Ohio flooding unruffled, silent, battleship gray, and ineffably menacing under lowering skies, the profound silence of Mammoth Cave, the southern Midwest with its Depression-spawned, but already legendary, bank robbers, the nervous Creole charms of New Orleans's restored French Quarter, the lonely, incredibly long stretches of road in Texas and Arizona that made one believe one was *seeing* infinity, the great, long, blue, mystery-freighted Pacific rollers ("so different from the Atlantic's choppier, shorter-spaced waves") which he'd watched with George Goodenough Akeley, who'd turned out to be a very solid chap and knowing more about his father's frightening Vermont researches than Wilmarth had expected.

When I mentioned finding *The Shadow Over Innsmouth* he nodded and murmured, "The original of its youthful hero has disappeared *and* his cousin from the Canton asylum. Down to Y'ha-nthlei? Who knows?" But when I remembered his accumulated mail he merely nodded his thanks, wincing a little, as though reluctant to face it. He really did look shockingly tired.

When we'd finished dinner, however, and he'd taken his black coffee (also with lots of sugar) and the fire was dancing flickeringly, both yellow and blue now, he turned to me with a little, venturesomely friendly smile and a big, wonderingly wide lifting of his eyebrows, and he said quietly, "And now you'll quite rightly be expecting me to tell you, my dear Fischer, all the things about the project that I've been hesitant to write, the answers I've been reluctant to give to your cogent questions, the revelations I've been putting off making until we should meet in person. Really, you have been very patient, and I thank you."

Then he shook his head thoughtfully, his eyes growing distant, as he slowly and rather sinuously and somehow unwillingly shrugged his shoulders, which paradoxically were both frail and wide, and grimaced slightly, as if tasting something strangely bitter, and said even more quietly, "If only I had more to tell you that's been *definitely proved*. Somehow we always stop just short of that. Oh, the artifacts are real enough and certain—the Innsmouth jewelry, the Antarctic soapstones, Blake's Shining Trapezohedron, though that's lost in Narragansett Bay, the spiky baluster knob Walter Gilman brought back from his witchy dreamland (or the non-temporal fourth dimension, if you prefer), even the unknown elements, meteoric and otherwise, which defy all analysis, even the new magneto-optic probe which has given us virginium and ala-bamine. And it's almost equally certain that all, or almost all those weird extraterrestrial and extra-cosmic creatures *have* existed—that's why I wanted you to read the Lovecraft stories, despite their lurid extravagances, so you'd have some picture of the entities that I'd be talking to you about. Except that they and the evidence for them *do* have a maddening way of vanishing upon extinction and from all records—Wilbur Whateley's mangled remains, his brother's vast invisible cadaver, the Plutonian old Akeley killed *and couldn't photograph*, the June 1882 meteor itself which struck Nahum Gardner's farm and which set old Armitage (young then) studying the *Necronomicon* (the start of everything at Miskatonic) and which Atwood's father saw with his own eyes and tried to analyze, or what Danforth saw down in Antarctica when he looked back at the horrible higher mountains beyond the Mountains of Madness—he's got amnesia for that now that he has regained his sanity … all, all gone!

"But whether any of those creatures exist *today*—there, there's the rub! The overwhelming question we can't answer, though always on the edge of doing so. The thing is," he went on with gathering urgency, "that *if they do exist*, they are so unimaginably powerful and resourceful, they might be—", and he looked around sharply, "anywhere at any moment!

"Take *Cthulhu*," he began.

I couldn't help starting as I heard that word pronounced for the first time in my life. The harsh, dark, abysmal *monosyllabic* growl it came to was so very like the sound that had originally come to me from my imagination, or my subconscious, or my otherwise unre-membered dreams, or …

He continued, "If Cthulhu exists, then he (or she, or it) can go anywhere he wants through space, or air, or sea, or earth itself. We know from Johansen's account (it turned his hair white) that Cthulhu can exist as a gas, be torn to atoms, and then recombine. He wouldn't need tunnels to go through solid rock, he could *seep* through it—'not in the spaces we know, but between them.' And yet in his inscrutability he might choose tunnels—there's that to be reckoned with. Or—still another possibility—perhaps he neither exists nor does not exist but is in some half state—'waits dreaming', as Angell's old chant has it. Perhaps his dreams, incarnated as your winged worms, Fischer, dig tunnels.

"It is those monstrous underground cavern-and-tunnel worlds, not all from Cthulhu by any means, that I have been assigned to investigate with the geo-scanner, partly because I was the first to hear of them from old Akeley and also—Merciful Creator!—from the Plutonian who masked as him—'great worlds of unknown life down there: blue-litten K'n-yan, red-litten Yoth, and black, light-less N'kai', which was Tsathoggua's home, and even stranger inner spaces litten by colors from space and from earth's nighted core. That's how I guessed the colors in your childhood dreams or nightmares (or personality exchanges), my dear Fischer. I've glimpsed them also in the geo-scanner, where they are, however, most fugitive and difficult to discern. ..."

His voice trailed off tiredly, just as my own concern became most feverishly intense with his mention of "personality exchanges."

He really did look shockingly fatigued. Nevertheless I felt impelled to nerve myself to say, "Perhaps those dreams can be repeated, if I take Doctor Morgan's drug. Why not tonight?"

"Out of the question," he replied, shaking his head slowly. "In the first place, I wrote too hopefully there. At the last minute Morgan was unable to supply me with the drug. He promised to send it along by mail, but hasn't yet. In the second place, I'm inclined to think now that it would be much too dangerous an experiment."

"But at least you'll be able to check those dream colors *and* the tunnels with your geo-scanner?" I pressed on, somewhat crestfallen.

"If I can repair it ...," he said, his head nodding and slumping to one side. The dying flames were all blue now as he whispered mumblingly, "... If I am *permitted* to repair it ..."

I had to help him to bed and then retire to my own, shaken and unsatisfied, my mind a whirl. Wilmarth's alternating moods of breezy optimism and a seemingly *frightened* dejection were hard to adjust to. But now I realized that I was very tired myself—after all, I'd been up most of the previous night reading *Innsmouth*—and soon I slumbered.

(The voices stridently groan, "The pit of primal life, the Yellow Sign, Azathoth, the Magnum Innominandum, the shimmering violet and emerald wings, the cerulean and vermilion claws, Great Cthulhu's Wasps ..." Night has fallen. I have limpingly paced the house from the low attic with its circular portholes to the basement,

where I touched my Father's sledge and eyed "The Gate of Dreams."
The moment draws nigh. I must write rapidly.)

I awoke to bright sunlight, feeling totally refreshed by my
customary twelve hours of sleep. I found Wilmarth busily writing
at the table that faced the north window of his bedroom. His smiling
face looked positively youthful in the cool light, despite its neatly
brushed thatch of white hair—I hardly recognized him. All his
accumulated mail except for one item lay open and face downward
on the far left-hand corner of the table, while on the far right-hand
corner was an impressive pile of newly written and addressed
postcards, each with its neatly affixed, fresh, one-cent stamp.

"Good morrow, Georg," he greeted me (properly pronouncing it
GAY-org), "if I may so address you. And good news!—the scanner
is recharged and behaving perfectly, ready for the day's downward
surveying, whilst that letter George Goodenough forwarded is from
Francis Morgan and contains a supply of the drug against tonight's
inward researches! Two dosages exactly—Georg, I'll dream with
you!" He waved a small paper packet.

"That's wonderful, Albert," I told him, meaning it utterly. "By
the way, it's my birthday," I added.

"Congratulations!" he said joyfully. "We'll celebrate it tonight
with our drafts of Morgan's drug."

And our expedition did turn out to be a glorious one, at least
until almost its very end. The Hollywood Hills put on their most
youthfully winning face; even the underlying crumbling, worm-
eaten corruptions seemed fresh. The sun was hot, the sky bright
blue, but there was a steady cool breeze from the west and occasional
great, high, white clouds casting enormous shadows. Amazingly,
Albert seemed to know the territory almost as well as I did—he'd
studied his maps prodigiously and brought them along, including
the penciled ones I'd sent him. And he instantly named correctly
the manzanita, sumac, scrub oak, and other encroaching vegetation
through which we wended our way.

Every so often and especially at my favorite pausing places, he
would take readings with the geo-scanner, which he carried handily,
while I had two canteens and a small back pack. While his head was
under the black hood, I would stand guard, my stick ready. Once I
surprised a dark and pinkly pale, fat, large serpent, which went
slithering into the underbrush. Before I could tell him, he said
correctly, "A king snake, foe of the crotaloids—a good omen."

And ... on every reading, Albert's black box showed vacuities of some sort—tunnels or caves—immediately below us, at depths varying from a few to a few score meters. Somehow this did not trouble us by bright outdoor day. I think it was what we'd both been expecting. Coming out from under the hood, he'd merely nod and say, "Fifteen meters" (or the like) and note it down in his little book, and we'd tramp on. Once he let me try my luck under the hood, but all I could see through the eyepiece was what seemed like an intensification of the dancing points of colored light one sees in the dark with the eyes closed. He told me it took considerable training to learn to recognize the significant indications.

High in the Santa Monicas we lunched on beef sandwiches and the tea-flavored lemonade with which I'd filled both canteens. Sun and breeze bathed us. Hills were all around and beyond them to the west the blue Pacific. We talked of Sir Francis Drake and Magellan and of Captain Cook and his great circumpolar voyagings, and of the fabulous lands they'd all heard legends of—and of how the tunnels we were tracing were really no more strange. We spoke of Lovecraft's stories almost as if they were no more than that. Daytime viewpoints can be strangely unworrying and unconcerned.

Halfway back or so, Albert began looking very haggard once more—frighteningly so. I got him to let me carry the black box. To do that I had to abandon my flat back pack and empty canteens—he didn't seem to notice.

Almost home, we paused at my father's memorial. The sun had westered most of his way and there were dark shadows and also shafts of ruddy light almost parallel to the ground. Albert, very weary now, was fumbling for phrases to praise Rodia's work, when there swiftly glided out of the undergrowth behind him what I first took to be a large rattlesnake. But as I lunged lurchingly toward it, lashing at it with my stick, and as it slid back into thick cover with preternatural rapidity, and as Albert whirled around, the sinuous, vanishing thing looked for an instant to me as if it were all shimmering violet-green above with beating wings and bluish scarlet below with claws while its minatory rattle was more a skirling hum.

We raced home, not speaking of it at all, each of us concerned only that his comrade not fall behind. Somewhere mine found the strength.

His postcards had been collected from the box by the road and there were a half-dozen new letters for him—and a notification of a registered package for me.

Nothing must do then but Albert must drive me down to Hollywood to pick up the package before the post office closed. His face was fearfully haggard, but he seemed suddenly flooded with a fantastic nervous energy and (when I protested that it could hardly be anything of great importance) a tremendous willpower that would brook no opposition.

He drove like a veritable demon and as though the fate of worlds depended on his speed—Hollywood must have thought it was Wallace Reid come back from the dead for another of his transcontinental racing pictures. The Tin Hind fled like a frightened one indeed, as he worked the gear lever smartly, shifting up and down. The wonders were that we weren't arrested and didn't crash. But I got to the proper window just before it closed and I signed for the package—a stoutly wrapped, tightly sealed, and heavily corded parcel from (it really startled me) Simon Rodia.

Then back again, just as fast despite my protests, the Tin Hind screeching on the corners and curves, my companion's face an implacable, watchful death's-mask, up into the crumbling and desiccated hills as the last streaks of the day faded to violet in the west and the first stars came out.

I forced Albert to rest then and drink hot black coffee freighted with sugar while I got dinner—when he'd stepped out of the car into the chilly night he'd almost fainted. I grilled steaks again—if he'd needed restorative food last night he needed it doubly now after our exhausting hike and our Dance of Death along the dry, twisting roads, I told him roughly. ("Or Grim Reaper's Tarantella, eh, Georg?" he responded with a feeble but unvanquishable little grin.)

Soon he was prowling around again—he wouldn't stay still—and peering out the windows and then lugging the geo-scanner down into the basement, "to round out our readings," he informed me. I had just finished building and lighting a big fire in the fireplace when he came hurrying back up. Its first white flare of flame as the kindling caught showed me his ashen face and white circled, blue eyes. He was shaking all over, literally.

"I'm sorry, Georg, to be such a troublesome and seemingly ungrateful guest," he said, forcing himself with a great effort to speak coherently and calmly (though most imperatively), "but really you and I must get out of here at once. There's no place safe for us this side of Arkham—which is not safe either, but there at least we'll have the counsel and support of salted veterans of the Miskatonic project whose nerves are steadier than mine. Last night I got (and concealed from you—I was sure it had to be wrong) a reading of fifteen down there under the carving—*centimeters*, Georg, not meters. Tonight I have confirmed that reading beyond any question of a doubt, only it's shrunk to *five* under the carving. The floor there is the merest shell—it rings as hollow as a crypt in New Orleans's St. Louis One or Two—*they* have been eating at it from below and are feasting still. No, no arguments! You have time to pack one small bag—limit yourself to necessities, but bring that registered parcel from Rodia, I'm curious about it."

And with that he strode to his bedroom, whence he emerged in a short while with his packed valise and carried it and the black box out to the car.

Meanwhile I'd nerved myself to go down in the basement. The floor did ring much more hollowly that it had last night—it made me hesitate to tread upon it—but otherwise nothing appeared changed. Nevertheless it gave me a curious feeling of unreality, as if there were no real objects left in the world, only flimsy scenery, a few stage properties including a balsa sledgehammer, a registered parcel with nothing in it, a cyclorama of nighted hills, and two actors.

I hurried back upstairs, took the steaks off the grill and set them on the table in front of the softly roaring fire (for they were done) and headed after Albert.

But he anticipated me, stepping back inside the door, looking at me sharply—his eyes were still wide and staring—and demanding, "Why aren't you packed?"

I said to him steadily, "Now look here, Albert, I thought last night the cellar floor sounded hollow, so that is not entirely a surprise. And any way you look at it, we can't drive to Arkham on nervous energy. In fact, we can't get even decently started driving east without some food inside us. You say yourself it's dangerous everywhere, even at Miskatonic, and from what we (or at least I) saw at my father's grave there may be at least one of the things loose already. So let's eat dinner—I have a hunch terror hasn't taken away your appetite entirely—and have a look inside Rodia's package, and then leave if we must."

There was a rather long pause. Then his expression relaxed into a somewhat wan smile and he said, "Very well, Georg, that does make sense. I'm frightened all right, make no mistake of that, in fact I've walked in terror for the past ten years. But in this case, to speak as honestly as I'm able, I have been even more concerned for you—it suddenly seemed such a pity, such a disservice, that I should have dragged you into this dreadful business. But as you say, one must bow to necessity, bodily and otherwise ... and try to show a little style about it," he added with a rather doleful chuckle.

So we sat down before the dancing, golden fire and ate our steaks and fixings (I had some burgundy, he stayed with his sweet, black coffee) and talked of this and that—chiefly of Hollywood, as it turned out. He'd glimpsed a bookstore on our headlong drive and now he asked about it and that led to other things.

Our dinner done, I refilled his cup and my glass, then cleared a space and opened Rodia's parcel, using the carving knife to cut its cords and slit its seals. It contained, carefully packed in excelsior, the casket of embossed copper and German silver which sits before me now. I recognized my father's handiwork at once, which reproduced quite closely in beaten metal his stone carving in the basement, though without the "Gate of Dreams" inscription. Albert's finger indicated the Cutlu eyes, though he did not speak the name. I opened the casket. It contained several sheets of heavy bond paper. This time it was my father's handwriting I recognized. Standing side by side, Albert and I read the document, which I append here:

15 Mar 1925

My Dear Son:

Today you are 13 but I write to you and wish you well when you are 25. Why I do so you will learn as you read this. The box is yours—*Leb'wohl!* I leave it with a friend to send to you if I should go in the 12 years between—Nature has given me signs that that may be: jagged flashes of rare earth colors in my eyes from time to time. Now read with care, for I am telling secrets.

When I was a boy in Louisville I had dreams by day and could not remember them. They were black times in my mind that were minutes long, the longest half an hour. Sometimes I came to in another place and doing something different, but never harmful. I thought my black daydreams were a weakness or a judgment, but Nature was wise. I was not strong and did not know enough to bear them yet. Under my father's rule I learned my craft and made my body strong and always studied when and as I could.

When I was 25 I was deep in love—this was before your mother—with a beautiful girl who died of consumption. Pining upon her grave I had a daydream, but this time by the strength of my desire I kept my mind white. I swam down through the loam and I was joined with her in full bodily union. She said this coupling must be our last but that I now would have the power to move at will under and through the earth from time to time. We kissed farewell forever, *Lorchen* and I, and I swam down and on, her knight of dreams, exulting in my strength like some old kobold breasting the rock. It is not black down there, my son, as one would think. There are glorious colors. Water is blue, metals bright red and yellow, rocks green and brown, *undsoweiter.* After a time I swam back and up into my body, standing on the new-made grave. I was no longer pining but profoundly grateful.

So I learned how to divine, my son, to be a fish of earth when there is need and Nature wills, to dive into the Hall of the Mountain King dancing with light. Always the finest colors and the strangest hues lay west. Rare earths they are named by scientists, who are wise though blind. That's why I brought us here. Under the greatest of oceans, earth is a rainbow web and Nature is a spider spinning and walking it.

And now you have shown you have my power, *mein Sohn*, but in a greater form. You have black night dreams. I know, for I have sat by you as you slept and heard you talk and seen your terror, which would soon destroy you if you could recall it, as one night showed. But Nature in her wisdom blindfolds you until you have the needed strength and learning. As you know by now, I have provided for your education at a good eastern school praised by Harley Warren, the finest employer that I ever had, who knew a lot about the nether realms.

And now you're strong enough, *mein Sohn*, to act—and wise, I hope, as Nature's acolyte. You've studied deep and made your body strong. You have the power and the hour has come. The triton blows his horn. Rise up, *mein lieber Georg*, and follow me. Now is the time. Build upon what I've built, but build more greatly. Yours is the wider and the greater realm. Make your mind white. With or without some lovely woman's help, now burst the gate of dreams!

Your loving Father

At any other time that document would have moved and shaken me profoundly. Truth to tell, it did so move and shake me, but I had been already so moved and shaken by today's climactic events that my first thought was of how the letter applied to them.

I echoed from the letter, "Now burst the gate of dreams," and then added, suppressing another interpretation, "That means I should take Morgan's drug tonight. Let's do it, Albert, as you proposed this morning."

"Your father's last command," he said heavily, clearly much impressed by that aspect of the letter. Then, "Georg, this is a most fantastic, shattering missive! That sign he got—it sounds like migraine. And his references to the rare-earth elements—that could be crucial. And colors in the earth perceived perhaps by extrasensory perception!—the Miskatonic project should have started investigating dowsing years ago. We've been blind—" He broke off. "You're right, Georg, and I am strongly tempted. But the danger! How to choose? On the one hand a supreme parental injunction and our raging curiosities—for mine's a-boil. On the other hand Great Cthulhu and his minions. Oh, for an indication of how to decide!"

There was a sharp knocking at the door. We both started. After a moment's pause I moved rapidly, Albert following. With my hand on the latch I paused again. I had not heard a car stop outside. Through the stout oak came the cry, "Telegram!" I opened it.

There was revealed a skinny, somewhat jaunty-looking youth of pale complexion scattered with big freckles and with carrot-red hair under his visored cap. His trousers were wrapped tightly around his legs by bicycle clips.

"Either of you Albert N. Wilmarth?" he inquired coolly.

"I am he," Albert said, stepping forward.

"Then sign for this, please."

Albert did so and tipped him, substituting a dime for a nickel at the last instant.

The youth grinned widely, said, "G'night," and sauntered off. I closed the door and turned quickly back.

Albert had torn open the flimsy envelope and drawn out and spread the missive. He was pale already, but as his eyes flashed across it, he grew paler still. It was as if he were two-thirds of a ghost already and its message had made him a full one. He held the yellow sheet out to me wordlessly:

LOVECRAFT IS DEAD STOP THE WHIPPOORWILLS DID
NOT SING STOP TAKE COURAGE STOP DANFORTH

I looked up. Albert's face was still as ghostly white, but its expression had changed from uncertainty and dread to decision and challenge.

"That tips the balance," he said. "What have I more to lose? By George, Georg, we'll have a look down into the abyss on whose edge we totter. Are you game?"

"I proposed it," I said. "Shall I fetch your valise from the car?"

"No need," he said, whipping from his inside breast pocket the small paper packet from Dr. Morgan he'd shown me that morning. "I had the hunch that we were going to use it, until that apparition at your father's tomb shattered my nerves."

I fetched small glasses. He split evenly between them the small supply of white powder, which dissolved readily in the water I added under his direction. Then he looked at me quizzically, holding his glass as if for a toast.

"No question of to whom we drink this," I said, indicating the telegram he was still holding in his other hand.

He winced slightly. "No, don't speak his name. Let's rather drink to *all* our brave comrades who have perished or suffered greatly in the Miskatonic project."

That "our" really warmed me. We touched glasses and drained them. The draft was faintly bitter.

"Morgan writes that the effects are quite rapid," he said. "First drowsiness, then sleep, and then hopefully dreams. He's tried it twice himself with Rice and doughty old Armitage, who laid the Dunwich Horror with him. The first time they visited in dream Gilman's Walpurgis hyperspace; the second, the inner city at the two magnetic poles—an area topologically unique."

Meanwhile I'd hurriedly poured a little more wine and lukewarm coffee and we'd settled ourselves comfortably in our easy chairs before the fire, the dancing flames of which became both a little blurred and a little dazzling as the drug began to take effect.

"Really, that was a most amazing missive from your father," he chatted on rapidly. "Spinning a rainbow web under the Pacific, the lines those weirdly litten tunnels—truly most vivid. Would Cthulhu be the spider? No, by Gad, I'd liefer your father's goddess Nature any day. She's kindlier at least."

"Albert," I said somewhat drowsily, thinking of personality exchanges, "could those creatures possibly be benign, or at least less malevolent than we infer?—as my father's subterranean visionings might indicate. My winged worms, even?"

"Most of our comrades did not find them so," he replied judiciously, "though of course there's our *Innsmouth* hero. What has he really found in Y'ha-nthlei? Wonder and glory? Who knows? Who can say he knows? Or old Akeley out in the stars—is his brain suffering the tortures of the damned in its shining metal cylinder? Or is it perpetually exalted by ever-changing true visions of infinity? And what did poor shoggoth-stampeded Danforth really think he saw beyond the two horrific mountain chains down there before he got amnesia? And is that last a blessing or a curse? Gad, he and I are suited to each other ... the mind-smitten helping the nerve-shattered ... fit nurses for felines. ..."

"That was surely heavy news he sent you," I observed with a little yawn, indicating the telegram about Lovecraft, which he still held tightly between finger and thumb. "You know, before that wire came, I had the craziest idea—that somehow you and he were the same person. I don't mean Danforth but—"

"Don't say it!" he said sharply. Then his voice went immediately drowsy as he continued, "But the roster of the perished is longer far ... poor Lake and poor, poor Gedney and all those others under their Southern Cross and Magellanic shroud ... the mathematical genius Walter Gilman who lost heart most terribly ... the nonagenarian street-slain Angell and lightning-frozen Blake in Providence ... Edward Pickman Derby, Arkham's plump Shelley deliquescing in his witch-wife's corpse. ... Gad, this is hardly the cheerfulest topic. ... You know, Georg, down in San Diego young Akeley (G.G.) showed me a hidden sea cave bluer than Capri and on its black beach of magnetite the webbed footprint of a merman ... one of the Gnorri? ... and then ... oh yes, of course ... there's Wilbur Whateley, who was almost nine feet tall ... though he hardly counts as a Miskatonic researcher ... but the whippoorwills didn't get him either ... or his big brother. ..."

I was still looking at the fire, and the dancing points of light in and around it had become the stars, thick as the Pleiades and Hyades, through which old Akeley journeyed eternally, when unconsciousness closed on me too, black as the wind-stirred, infinite gulf of darkness which Robert Blake saw in the Shining Trapezohedron, black as N'kai.

I awoke stiff and chilled. The fire at which I'd been staring was white ashes only. I felt a sharp pang of disappointment that I had not dreamed at all. Then I became aware of the low, irregular, inflected humming or buzzing that filled my ears.

I stood up with difficulty. My companion slumbered still, but his shut-eyed, death-pale face had a hideously tormented look and he writhed slowly and agonizedly from time to time as if in the grip of foulest nightmare. The yellow telegram had fallen from his fingers and lay on the floor. As I approached him I realized that the sound filling my ears was coming from between his lips, which were unceasingly atwitch, and as I leaned my head close to them, the horridly articular droning became recognizable words and phrases:

"The pulpy, tentacled head," I heard in horror, "*Cthulhu fhtagn,* the *wrong* geometry, the polarizing miasma, the prismatic distortion, *Cthulhu R'lyeh,* the positive blackness, the living nothingness ..."

I could not bear to watch his dreadful agony or listen to those poisonous, *twangy* words an instant longer, so I seized him by the shoulders and shook him violently, though even as I did so there sprang into my mind my father's stern injunction never to do so.

His eyes came open wide in his white face and his mouth clamped shut as he came up with a powerful shove of his bent arms against the chair's arms which his hands had been clutching. It was as if it were happening in slow motion though paradoxically it also seemed to be happening quite swiftly. He gave me a last mute look of utter horror and then he turned and ran, taking fantastically long strides, out through the door, which his outstretched hand threw wide ahead of him, and disappeared into the night.

I hobbled after him as swiftly as I could. I heard the motor catch at the starter's second prod. I screamed, "Wait, Albert, wait!" As I neared the Tin Hind, its lights flashed on and its motor roared and I was engulfed in acrid exhaust fumes as it screeched out the drive with a spattering of gravel and down the first curve.

I waited there then in the cold until all sight and sound of it had vanished in the night, which was already paling a little with the dawn.

And then I realized that I was still hearing those malignant, gloating, evilly resonant voices.

"*Cthulhu fhtagn,*" they were saying (and have been saying and are saying now and will forever), "the spider tunnels, the black infinities, the colors in pitch darkness, the tiered towers of Yuggoth, the glittering centipedes, the winged worms ..."

Somewhere not far off I heard a low, half-articulate, whirring sound.

I went back into the house and wrote this manuscript.

And now I shall place the last with its interleaved communications and also the two books of poetry that led to all this in the copper and German silver casket, and I shall carry that with me down into the basement, where I shall take up my father's sledge (wondering in which body I shall survive, if at all) and literally carry out his last letter's last injunction.

*   *   *

Very early on the morning of Tuesday, March 16, 1937, the house-holders of Paradise Crest (then Vultures Roost) were disturbed by a clashing rumble and a sharp earth shock which they attributed to an earthquake, and indeed very small tremors were registered at Griffith Observatory, UCLA, and USC, though on no other seismo-graphs. Daylight revealed that the brick house locally known as Fischer's Folly had fallen in so completely that not one brick remained joined to another. Moreover, there appeared to be fewer bricks in view than the house would have accounted for, as if half of them had been trucked away during the night, or else fallen into some great space beneath the basement. In fact, the appearance of the ruin was of a gigantic ant lion's pit, lined with bricks instead of sand grains. The place was deemed, and actually was, dangerous, and was shortly filled in and in part cemented over, and apparently not long afterwards rebuilt upon.

The body of the owner, a quietly spoken, crippled young man named Georg Reuter Fischer, was discovered flat on its face in the edge of the rubble with hands thrown out (the metal casket by one of them) as though he had been trying to flee outdoors when caught by the collapse. His death, however, was attributed to a slightly earlier accident or insane act of self-destruction involving acid, of which his eccentric father was once known to have kept a supply. It was well that easy identification was made possible by his conspicuously twisted right foot, for when the body was turned over it was discovered that something had eaten away the entire front of his face and also those portions of his skull and jaw and the entire forebrain.